I0565754

Amazon Hammer

A Novel by
Gloria G. Brame

Moons Grove Press
British Columbia, Canada

Amazon Hammer

Copyright ©2021 by Gloria G. Brame
ISBN-13 978-1-77143-492-8
First Edition

Library and Archives Canada Cataloguing in Publication
Title: Amazon hammer / a novel by Gloria G. Brame.
Names: Brame, Gloria G., 1955-, author.
Identifiers: Canadiana (print) 20210238542 | Canadiana (ebook) 20210238658
| ISBN 9781771434928 (softcover) | ISBN 9781771434935 (PDF)
Classification: LCC PS3602.R36 A73 2021 | DDC 813/.6—dc23

Artwork credit: Front cover artwork © Julian Murphy
Julian Murphy's contact info:
Facebook: https://www.facebook.com/julianmurphyart

Moons Grove Press is an imprint
of CCB Publishing: www.ccbpublishing.com

Moons Grove Press
British Columbia, Canada
www.moonsgrovepress.com

Dedicated to all people who live their truths,

quietly or out loud.

⇒ Contents ⇐

❧ Preface ☙

FOREPLAY

From a distance, a stranger might see a tall, full-bodied woman hesitating on the curb as if afraid to cross the wide avenue. But Jax was deliberately standing still. She tilted her chin up and let the moonlight wash her cheeks. Her feet were planted firmly, her body erect but at rest. It was her favorite pose: standing completely still and consolidating herself inside as her own little universe. The clouds had parted, revealing clear silver mists through which the moon beamed brighter than ever before. Stars spilled out across the black sky above as if sprung from a net.

She contained lives within lives within lives, like a tree. From her central core, she'd grown rings around herself. Each ring contained a different story, a different phase of her life. If you cut her open, you'd see the variegated textures and tints, the scorched rings of her bad years, the cracks of misfortune, but also golden rings and perfect formations and a thick bark to contain it all.

She breathed in the cool air of streets freshly washed by

snow and rain, filling herself up with icy contentment. Every night was the most beautiful night because the next night might never come. Mortality was always at the back of her mind, a silent fear that anyone could die at any time for any reason. She had accepted the wisdom of her grandfather Paul's philosophy: Be happy now. Be as happy as you can be now.

She walked the last block to her building. It was a nondescript factory building on the outside, but past a locked door, the foyer was marble and brass. She checked her mailbox and smiled to see the letter she'd been expecting. She slipped it into her purse and walked up the steep staircase to her home. Each landing reminded her of the people who lived there and her histories with them. She loved the building's familiarity, even though the climb up four flights of stairs was getting tiresome for her and challenging for Paul.

Once inside the apartment, Jax removed her shoes and tiptoed across the living room to the kitchen in case Paul was asleep. Her mind was racing too hard after her long weird adventure driving their taxicab. Breakfast would calm her down, make her drowsy. At least, it would wash down the last of the jalapeno that had lit her throat on fire. She turned on the light over the sink, washed up and opened the fridge. She grabbed some cheese and six eggs.

It had been the longest, strangest night she had since she lived in California. First, she had driven a couple of swingers to a mansion on Long Island, and they tried to convince her to come inside and join the party. She finally agreed when they said she could just watch and decide for herself if she wanted to join in. She got a diet Coke at the bar and sat against one wall, watching the couples, throuples, quadruples and other assorted clusters swim naked on beds and couches and even up against walls. At one point, activity was so rampant, it seemed like a sea of bodies. All the shades of humanity softly swarmed in its waves. Aesthetically, she liked it, but sexually, she decided to leave.

When she got back to the city, a tuxedo-clad man in his mid-30s lurched out of a swanky bar and staggered into the back seat of her cab. He was a talkie drunk. Within 10 minutes he had told her how his rich-bitch girlfriend dumped him for another man because he had a bigger dick. After that, he seemed to have a religious experience and said God had picked Jax to find him at the club because she was meant to be his wife. She hit the accelerator and raced to his Sutton Place building. He refused to get out, grew frustrated, and started throwing bills at her. She collected them silently and put them in her moneybox.

He threw a tantrum. "I knew it! Money! That's all you ever wanted from me," he shouted, "all you women are the same!"

The doorman spotted the scene and ran out to open his door. Dickie locked the button in defiance so she lowered the window. The doorman plucked the button up. Dickie locked it again. Jax almost laughed out loud as the men kept struggling for door-button dominance. The doorman finally caught him off guard, yanked open the door, and pulled him onto the sidewalk. Dickie fell to the ground and curled into a fetal position. Jax didn't stick around to watch the rest of the drama.

She drove downtown. She was starving and a juicy taco at her favorite late-night stand would hit the spot. She put on her hat to hide her hair, turned up her collar and hoped that would keep further suitors off her ass.

She barely had time to unwrap her taco when Booker contacted her out of the deep complicated past. She'd spoken with him on and off over the years, they had run into each other a couple of awkward times at parades and political events, but this conversation would live on in her memory.

After apologizing for being out of touch, and affirming she was still driving her grandfather's cab, Booker begged her to fetch his boyfriend, who was having a panic attack at a BDSM club.

"You're the only one I can trust for this," Booker said. "Please do me this favor."

"Ok, Booker," she said dubiously. She despised the club he mentioned because it had a reputation for letting prodoms work secretly on premise and letting them rip off their clients. She didn't think it was fair to have unsuspecting subs discover only after they played that the woman expected money or gifts in return. That was never her world. But she agreed to look for him and bring him back to the Ansonia Hotel where Booker still lived.

She was a little pissed that Booker, the boy who broke her heart, now wanted her to fetch his boy toy. She reasoned that she owed him. He once did her the biggest favor when she needed it most. She still cared for him. When he reminisced about their best times together, she softened up. When he paid her by credit card and added an outrageously huge tip, she felt oddly humbled by his generosity. She was ripe for the picking when he proposed that she move in with them and become the femdom-in-residence so she could do his wonderful boyfriend on demand. "Wouldn't that be fun?" he kept repeating.

The more he repeated it the less fun it sounded to her. Though she liked the boy she drove home, Booker trying to buy her back into his life pissed her off. She regretted accepting his ridiculous tip.

"I'm a tree, Booker," she said aloud to herself when she cracked the eggs into a bowl. "Ha ha ha, fucker, you are all balls," she said as she whisked the fragile yellow blobs into a froth, giggling. She stopped regretting the tip. She deserved to get paid for indulging his egotistical fantasy for a few hours.

The kitten-footed clan was assembling, mewling and rubbing against her.

"Yes, yes, yes, yes," she said as she poured kibble into their bowls, "I got you covered, no worries, little ones."

Pitty-Pat, the spooky tabby, jumped out of the dark, always the first to attack dry food. Meeper, the black Persian, circled the bowls indifferently, then sat and began grooming her paws. She was waiting for Jax to open a pouch of wet food. Don Juan casually walked in as if he was the only cat, tail high, eyes averted from the other cats. He paused beside her to stretch and head-butt her to remind her that he was her first cat, her oldest cat, her best cat.

She bent down to rub his ears. "Yes, you are," she murmured, "you will always be my goodest boy."

The kitchen light came on and Paul stiffly walked in on creaky legs.

"I thought I heard you talking to yourself again. Did you just get home?"

"You heard me? Shit, I'm sorry. I was trying to be quiet. I got a private hire for the night and the money was too good to turn down. Why are you up so late?"

"Mehhh," he shrugged. "The art didn't go well. I was trying all vaginas for a change."

"That would be a change," she said. "Do you want some eggs?"

"No, no, I ate."

"Ate what?" He didn't answer so she pushed. "What did you eat?"

He dropped carefully into a chair, sighing. "The bitterness of old age."

"Uh-huh. So how's your arthritis today?" At 75, Grandpa's body was deteriorating one piece at a time. Last year, it was a shoulder replacement and corneal transplant. Now the doctors were talking about replacing his kneecaps. At least others parts still worked, to judge by all the condoms that traveled through their medicine cabinet.

As if he knew what she was thinking, he volunteered, "I have a few more bar crawls in me. Today was just a shitty day." He shrugged. "It happens."

"Tell me about it," she said before she shoveled the warm eggs into her mouth.

"Oh? Was your day shitty too?" He leaned over the table wearing his concerned look: his bushy gray eyebrows knit, his eyes searching her face.

Her fork lingered in mid-air. "It was... more like an accidental learning experience." She locked gray eyes with him. "Meh," she shrugged.

Paul looked at her plate longingly.

"Your half is in the pan." She went to the stove and scooped the remaining ham and eggs onto a plate for him. "I kept it warm just in case."

"You know me too well."

"There is no such thing as knowing you too well, Grandpa. You are constantly evolving and changing."

"I try," he said modestly. "That's why I think we should sell the cab," he said. "I'm ready for more change. Aren't you?"

"You mean we're turning into a boring old married couple together?" she teased.

"Ewww." He made a face. "Don't ever say that to your

grandfather. I mean we could use the money to travel. We've never traveled together. Wouldn't that be fun?"

He was right, of course. Prices for taxi medallions were at an all-time high. She just wasn't ready to give it up. It gave her a different life every day. Some nights, it meant driving hours north to a mansion in Chappaqua to bring a sex worker back to the city after a long night of sucking dick. Sometimes fares took her out to Sheepshead Bay or City Island for seafood dinners. After she dropped them off, she'd make her way to the water's edge to watch the glimmering waves. But she also enjoyed the short fares that sent her pinballing at right angles around Manhattan, spinning around corners and skirting disasters. Her favorite rides were with people who treated the backseat like a confessional booth, telling her things about their lives they'd never told anyone else before.

Driving a cab made her feel like she was part of the big game of city life, a constantly moving player in the vast Metropolis. The cab gave her worlds of social engagement without social obligations. It was a far cry from her life as a professional dominatrix. She didn't have to talk to passengers. She didn't have to be in a good mood. She had time to think, time to stop and look closely at things, time for everything a thinking woman needs time to do.

She changed the subject. "Books hired me tonight to drive his boyfriend around."

"Books! Really?" Paul's eyes misted. "We all used to be so close. He and Steve were like two peas in a pod. You should invite him over sometime."

"OK," she said.

"You mean no?"

Jax shrugged at him.

"So, was Booker your accidental learning experience?"

"He was."

"What did you learn?"

"I learned that you can't put your foot in the same river twice," she said. "Whoever he is today, he is not the guy I fell in love with when I was 18."

"And you're not the same woman."

"Most definitely not."

Paul nodded in agreement. "So I guess we will cross him off our extensive guest list."

She took his hand across the table and squeezed it. She knew how much he missed seeing old friends. Hook-ups with fuck buddies couldn't make up for deep conversation and genuine caring.

"I hope you don't think I'm disappointed with this." He patted her hand. "I'm so proud of us and the relationship we've built." She froze. He was about to launch into his affirmation routine. "I want you to know how proud I am of you. I never dreamed I'd have a grandchild as wonderful as you," Paul said.

As much as they paralyzed her with embarrassment, they were words she somehow always needed to hear, no matter how old she got. She dashed the dishes to the sink, quickly wiped her tears, and came back to hug Paul when suddenly a dark force clawed her leg.

"Get the fuck off me, demon!" she cried. Don Juan had attacked her pant leg and was trying to climb her. Paul laughed and pried the cat's claws off her thigh.

"He's jealous," the old man said, "he wants in on the hug!"

"Fucking cats," she grumbled. She put her arms around Paul's neck. "Thank you for loving me so much, Grandpa."

"Well, I wouldn't go that far," he said.

"I love you to the moon, Paul," she kissed the top of his gray head. He threw his arm back and pulled her forward so he could kiss her cheek. "My beautiful granddaughter," he said. "I love you to the moon and back."

"So tell me about the vaginas," she said.

"I wanted to do a grouping, but I can't get them to work, I don't know why."

"You got one to work in real life, I'm sure you'll conquer an army of them on canvas."

"Ha ha, very funny. I wish I shared your faith in me," he said.

"My faith in you is well-founded," she said. "You are the best man I've ever met."

"Well, that's just tragic." He winked at her. "You need to get out more."

❧ Chapter 1 ❧

THE CASSANDRA COMPLEX

The first time Jax met Paul she was 18. It was the worst year of her life, but also the best year. If she hadn't been in so much pain, she wouldn't have sought him out, and if she'd never found Paul, she didn't know how she would have ended up. Not good, though. Maybe a suicidal alcoholic like her father, Barry. Maybe a money whore like her mother, Lucille. Maybe, who knows, a suicidal alcoholic money whore!

That year, everything had come to a head. Her turbulent inner worlds and dysfunctional outer worlds collided in a cosmic superstorm of angst. She had been struggling throughout adolescence with, as she remembered it, literally fucking EVERYTHING. She was forced to wear clothes her mother bought her and to get the haircuts her mother wanted her to have and to eat the food her mother ordered for her at restaurants. Her grades were mediocre. She was bad at sports. She wasn't cute or perky enough to get the attention of her peers, even though inside she thought she deserved to at least get invited to other kids' birthday parties. Her whole existence, she thought, was about being ignored or wounded by a malicious system of cruel judgments and hurtful injustices. Her mother's point of view was different. Her mother thought she was the Antichrist.

When Jax tried to talk to Barry about her woes, he defended Lucille. "She's your mother and Mother is always right."

She took that to mean that he too believed everything was her fault. She was the reason her parents were so unhappy. She was a problem child, a crazy dreamer with weird obsessions that psychologists couldn't explain. Her hobbies drove her mother to rage.

One year, she collected troll dolls, and arranged them obsessively in rows, conferring the title of Queen to the one with lavender hair. The next year she moved on to magnifying glasses and used them everywhere she went, as if searching for clues to a murder. Jax soon replaced the magnifiers with baby turtles she got at a local pet shop and stole bowls from the breakfront to repurpose them as turtle habitats, using dirt and leaves she gathered in Central Park. She loved watching them awkwardly move around inside their shells. She identified with them.

"What is wrong with you!" Lucille cried when she spotted her elegant serving bowls filled with reptiles and debris. "They're shitting in my Waterford!"

"It's very tiny shit," Jax said. "You want to see? It's so cute."

"You're insane, Jacquinta! This is the stupidest thing you've ever done."

When Jax got home from school the next day, the turtles were gone and the bowls were in the dishwasher. The theft of the turtles and their possible horrible deaths haunted her nightmares for months. She never brought a live animal home after that.

In puberty, Jax developed a fascination with metal buckles. She got shoes with buckles, bags with extraneous buckles, pants with buckled legs, even a metal buckle barrette in her hair. She'd stand in front of the mirror for hours, admiring how they glinted and clanked when she moved. Lucille caught her at it one day.

"That's it. Something's wrong with you mentally," she snarled, "you look like a walking hardware store. I'm on my last nerve with you!"

Lucille sent her to a psychiatrist who listened disinterestedly while Jax unloaded her young heart, then wrote her a prescription for Adderall. When that didn't work, the psychiatrist put her on Ritalin, and then on Valium, and then on Prozac. After two years of taking drugs that left her exhausted and empty, almost numb inside, Jax revolted and started throwing them away.

When Lucille found an antidepressant floating in the toilet, her infamous last nerve blew. She sent Jax to a child psychologist, Dr. Frank, on the Upper East Side. Jax liked Dr. Frank because he was very gentle. She looked forward to the tray of cookies his wife baked every day for his young clients. He never thought she was stupid or crazy. He seemed to pity her. She liked that.

The therapy was going well, right until Lucille requested to speak with Dr. Frank privately to get an update on how her daughter was doing. That's when he told her that Jax was not the real problem in their household, and that Barry and Lucille needed marriage counseling. Lucille fired him on the spot and stormed out of his office, crying, "Fraud! Quack!" She dragged her bewildered daughter out of the waiting room and told her that therapy was over. Dr. Frank couldn't fix her.

Her next move to erase Jax's quirks was to yank her from her posh liberal girl's school and enroll her in a Catholic school. Jax knew they bribed the school to take her in because they weren't even Catholic! Creepy nuns walked the halls and classes were dull and the students were unfriendly. The uniform really annoyed her. The green plaid jumper made her feel like she should be marching in a St. Patty's Day parade.

It didn't take long for Jax to get reprimanded for hiking her uniform skirt up above the "skirt length" limit. She got detention for cursing in sewing class and was sent to the principal's office for punching a boy who tried to snap her bra strap in the schoolyard. When a teacher caught her smoking a joint in the girls' bathroom, she was promptly expelled. Even Lucille's money couldn't buy her back in.

Jax was triumphant. She hated that school and its ugly jumpers. But her new public reputation as a troublemaker and drug user got her blacklisted at the snotty private schools Lucille tried to get her into. Even her old school wouldn't take her back now that she was Baddy McBadFace. Lucille paid the Rich Bitch social price for Jax bringing shame on the family and called Jax a degenerate who was ruining the family name.

But her time with Dr. Frank had emboldened and nourished her. Her fall from grace on the Upper East Side was an opportunity to seize a crumb of freedom on the other side of Central Park. She harangued Lucille about attending a Montessori school on the Upper West Side, showing her a pamphlet she sent away for. Jax had been out of school for a month, and everyone was in a panic about where else she could go. Sending Jax to public school, Lucille said, would end her social life. Jax insisted that Montessori was the solution. It was still a private school and plenty of other rich kids went there. It could even make Lucille seem more modern and open-minded than her friends. The next day, Lucille handed Barry the paperwork for Jax to get in.

It was magical to be driven across Central Park every morning, sliding under the stone overpass, getting whiffs of trees, then emerging into a land of towering buildings. The less it resembled her neighborhood, the happier she felt. She loved going to Montessori. The school's neighborhood was more interesting, filled with quirky shops and cheap eateries. The classes were more interesting too, and teachers seemed to admire the very traits that made her a weirdo on the East Side. Now her strange fashion choices were "creative" and her perverse sense of humor was "darkly intelligent." There were people who finally got her jokes and the rest just classified her "the artsy type," which was a badge of coolness at this school. Her grades soared. Soon, she had friends and invitations galore. She still didn't fit in, but she felt accepted as an original, a bohemian, even a thinker.

The ride home was funereal. Sometimes she'd get a migraine on the way back. She always approached the front door with dread, never knowing if Lucille would be happily chatting with friends on the phone or sitting in the darkened living room with a bottle of scotch and a resting bitch face.

With school going so well, escaping Lucille became her prime obsession at home. It was stupid and unfair that her parents even had a child. Now she was trapped in their depressing triangle of unrelenting discord. Daddy came home late or locked himself in his office almost every night, while Lucille lived on the telephone, constantly making arrangements and appointments in a desperate effort to fill her days with every distraction money could buy.

It wasn't nearly as bad when she was a child. As a little kid, Jax got Saturdays all alone with Barry. Lucille would go to the beauty salon and then do lunch with her friends, while Daddy babysat. They'd wait until Lucille left, then he would put her in a jacket and hustle Jax out the door to go on one of their special Daddy/girl "secret adventures." Barry made her swear never to tell Lucille about their outings and she crossed her heart, feeling special and loved by him to be given a sacred duty.

Sometimes, they went to SoHo to visit art galleries. Sometimes, they'd meet up at a pub with Uncle Bob, who Daddy described as his best high school friend. She felt very grown up eating at a table with the two men who didn't treat her like a child, but like a young lady, and let her pick whatever she wanted off the menu, even if it was ice cream for lunch and dessert. She got to meet artists with wild hair and shaggy beards, instead of the buttoned-down conformists her mother befriended.

The secret trips came to a sudden halt when she was about 12. After a particularly vicious fight with Lucille, Barry locked himself in his home office one Friday morning and had dinner served to him there, too. When Jax nervously knocked on the door Saturday morning, dressed for their habitual outing, he shouted at her like a madman.

"Why are you tormenting me? Stop tormenting me! Leave me alone," he called from behind the door.

After that, the outings stopped as if they had never existed in the first place. There was no conversation, no explanation. There was so much that didn't make sense to her over the next few years. Little by little, Daddy seemed to be vanishing in plain sight. He let Lucille have the last word in every argument, seemed distracted when Jax talked to him, and withdrew to his office whenever he was home. The last two years were the worst. Her once funny, light-hearted father turned into a cantankerous recluse who barely emerged from his office. On the rare occasions when he joined them for dinner, he looked gaunt and worried. This version of Barry wasn't her father anymore. Her father was the man who took her on secret trips to exciting places. Her father was the wisest and strongest and kindest man in the world. This Barry looked frightened and broken. She blamed Lucille. Lucille had destroyed him with her constant bickering and blaming. Lucille probably found out about their Saturdays and laid down the law.

One day, when she was 18, she was awakened by her mother screaming. Doors opened and slammed shut and a maid ran in noisy slippers down the hallway. Jax sat up and clutched her chest, terrorized. The next thing she knew, their house was being invaded by men shouting to each other and talking into radios.

Her mother opened her door. Lucille was in a state of shock.

"What's happening?" Jax whispered, terrified.

"The house is full of cops. Stay in your room. I'll come for you when they're gone."

"But..."

"No buts. Stay in your room until I get back!"

Jax listened as more people ran through the apartment's halls, then walked out more slowly, speaking in loud whispers. What happened? Did Daddy have a heart attack? She cried and trembled, not wanting to know the answer. It sounded really bad.

Just as suddenly, the house was so quiet she could hear the big clock in the living room ticking. A few minutes later, she heard her mother's brisk footsteps.

"Daddy killed himself last night," Lucille said, wiping a tear from her eye.

"What? Are you sure??!"

"Of course I'm sure. He was pronounced dead and they zipped him up in a bag."

"Oh my God, no, no."

"I don't know what he was thinking, to do a thing like that to us," Lucille said sadly. "He didn't even have the courtesy to leave us a goodbye note."

"No!" Jax sobbed. "Why?? No!"

Lucille sat down on Jax's bed. "Nobody knows why people kill themselves. They could be sick, they could be sad, we don't know. I would never kill myself, but I don't know, your father had weakness in him."

"No he didn't!" This couldn't be true. None of it could be true. "Why?"

"You don't know," Lucille said. "You can't know. You didn't know him the way I knew him."

"What does that mean?"

"We protected you from all his problems," Lucille said.

"What problems?"

"He was an unhappy man from the day I met him," Lucille said, a few more tears trickling down her face.

Jax's mind was a broken record. "But WHY?"

"I really don't know, Jax. I'm not a psychic. Maybe he couldn't handle being a man. I don't know."

That strange pronouncement hit her hard. What did her mother mean by "being a man?" Was he unable to perform in bed? He was a good earner, he looked like a man and dressed like a man, he paid his bills, he went to work every day and came home every night at the same exact time. What did Lucille mean?

She turned her mother's words over and over. Maybe she meant he never stood up to her enough. Or maybe what really made him unhappy was being married to Lucille. Maybe Lucille was the reason he killed himself. She'd felt like killing herself over her mother. She just couldn't go through with it because she was afraid of hurting her mother.

In the chaos of the weeks that followed, Jax felt disconnected from reality, like an alien among the human race. Lucille became consumed with notifying friends and relatives while making all the funeral arrangements. Furniture movers came and went. Jax meanwhile struggled with simple things while the humans glided through the world effortlessly. She spilled her drinks and fought with the buttons on her shirt. Even though Barry had made little noise in the house, the apartment felt vastly quieter, so devoid of life she could hear her own pulse throb in the dark.

One day, while Lucille was out choosing his coffin, Jax snuck into her father's office. Lucille had declared it off-limits so this was her only opportunity to poke around. Maybe answers to her father's mysterious suicide lurked in the desk drawers or cabinets. She checked the clock: she had at least 2 hours until Lucille would be back.

She walked to the door and nudged it. It creaked open and she went inside. The excavation of Barry from their home was almost complete. Bookshelves stood empty, his credenza was gone, his advertising posters had been removed from the walls and the top of his formerly-crowded desk was bare. She sat behind the desk in her father's swivel chair and put her forehead on his blotter. She stretched her arms to rub the corners of his most prized possession, the ornate mahogany desk with a multitude of drawers and hidden compartments. It was so big, it overpowered the room, but he liked it that way. She remembered him sitting in the swivel chair, surrounded by stacks of important looking correspondence.

She opened his pencil drawer. It still held a few number 2 pencils, a brass letter opener with his name engraved on it, plus miscellaneous rubber bands and paperclips. The top drawer on the right opened to reveal an empty quart bottle of gin and a dozen empty little bottles, the kind you get on airplane fights and in hotel rooms.

The next one revealed a collection of expensive pens, dozens of them, most of them boxed and unused. So, she wasn't the only collector in the family, she mused. The bottom drawer was locked. She used the brass letter opener to jimmy it open. This drawer was filled with correspondence from business contacts that he either deemed important or intended to answer some day. She skimmed through them before noticing that there was a secret compartment at the back of the drawer. It, too, was locked. It took some work to force that lock open, but she finally succeeded.

She reached in and pulled out a neatly rubber-banded stack of envelopes. Except for the last few letters on top of the first bundle, all of them had been opened. She noticed that every one of them came from a "Paul Namora." Her heart stopped. Who was he? Was Daddy having a gay affair?! That would be so strange. Strange thrilling, because it seemed so radical, but also uneasy thrilling for the same reason. Maybe Lucille was right. Maybe she had no idea who her father was.

She analyzed the name in the upper left corner of the envelope. She knew that Barry's dead father's name was Paul. She kept repeating the name and started to rearrange the letters. Namora was an anagram of her own last name, Roaman! That couldn't just be a coincidence. She had to know. She couldn't stop herself. She didn't want to stop herself. She removed one of the letters with shaky hands. There, on the first page, she read, "Dear Son."

She sat back on her heels and dropped the letter to the floor. Lucille's father was dead, so what other man would call him son? Was Grandpa Paul actually alive? She checked the postal stamp. The letter arrived only 6 months earlier.

Her parents were vague about what happened to him. She realized now they never actually said he was dead. Her father said they lost him a long time ago, but he refused to discuss how grandpa died and got upset when Jax pressed him for more information. Lucille finally pulled her aside.

"Stop asking questions. He's gone from us. It's too painful for your father to talk about. Can't you see you're hurting him?"

After that, Jax let it drop, and grandpa became a tragic dead superstar in her mind, a missing link in her bloodline, perhaps the very person who could have fixed the family's problems had he survived. Yet the letter could surely be from no one but Barry's father. It was hard to process that he might actually be alive. If he was alive, she had to find him! If nothing else, she had to unravel the ancestral mystery that haunted her since childhood.

Still, what if she was disrespecting Daddy's wishes? She broke into his office and then pried open his secret compartments. It was so wrong of her. What if he wanted to take his secrets to the grave? He had that right, didn't he? On the other hand, he left it all there. He must have known someone might find them. Wasn't it for the best that she found these letters before Lucille threw them away like trash? Maybe Barry even wanted her to find them on some subconscious level.

An overwhelming need to meet this Paul Namora burned through her. If he was her long-lost grandpa, maybe he could answer all her questions. Who was her father really? And what was her real last name? She couldn't know herself if she didn't even know her real name! If Grandpa Paul was still alive, she had to find him. She had to know why he left and why people lied to her about him.

Jax heard Lucille enter the front door, so she hurriedly tore the address off an envelope, shoved all the letters back in their compartments, and sprinted back to her bedroom to brood. She looked up the street address and found out it was an obscure block in the West Village, close to the Hudson River. She knew Grandpa was only 17 when Barry was born. That would make Paul 57 now. He could definitely be alive. He could be living at that address. The grandfather she'd never met, and was never allowed to ask about, could be the key that unlocked a million urgent life mysteries.

Jax felt redeemed the next day when the desk and all its secrets were hauled away and thrown into a big green truck downstairs. Jax watched the workers from the living room window, struggling to carry his majestic Chippendale mahogany desk to the curb. She cringed at how carelessly they lifted it. The unlocked drawers all wept open, scattering papers, pens and bottles in the gutter. The haulers gestured wildly to one another then disposed of all the bottles and papers in nearby trash cans, and divided the pens among themselves.

Now she regretted not stealing the entire contents of Daddy's desk. No one would have known. Day by day, every trace of his existence had diminished in the house. Colognes and grooming tools cleared out of the bathroom, coats and galoshes removed from the front hall closet, golf clubs donated to their country club. By the end of two weeks, nothing was left to visibly remind Jax that he ever lived there.

"I'm going to Palm Springs for a while, to recuperate from all this," her mother announced after it was over. "Your father left me quite a mess. And dealing with lawyers and morticians, Jesus spare me." Lucille closed her eyes and the back of her wrist flew to her forehead.

Time was still blurred to Jax, who had stayed home from school the week of the funeral and still hadn't gone back. She knew she attended the funeral, but she couldn't swear she was really there. It was more like a slow-paced horror movie than real life.

"I just don't care about anything anymore," Lucille said.

"Not even about me?"

"Why must you always make it about yourself?! This has nothing to do with you. I'm a widow now. Nobody wants a widow. You can't understand, you can't possibly understand how alone I feel."

Jax understood perfectly. Lucille was saying that she was worried she wouldn't be able to find a new husband at the ripe old age of 40.

If Lucille could have had all the things her rich husbands had provided -- the facade of being a successful wife and mother and a sense of economic superiority over all other mortals except the ones with more money -- she might have learned to be happy on her own. But since Lucille believed that men were the necessary tool for women to gain social power, a rich husband was as critical to her public image as her breast implants. Rich suckers 1 and 2 were long gone, married and divorced in under a year, but generous with their divorce settlements. Then came Barry, fat, shy and socially awkward, but already running a successful business. Lucille saw his potential.

The sudden trip to Palm Beach told Jax that Mother was probably already hunting for a new man. Jax wanted to scream at Lucille, but words failed her. What could she say? That her mother was a cold-hearted bitch? That she'd ruined her husband's and her daughter's lives? That her father was the only parent Jax had ever really loved? What was the point? She was trapped alone with her now.

If her own father wasn't strong enough to escape her mother, why did Jax think she could succeed? And yet she had to try. She had to. When her mother left, she would get her best, maybe her only, chance to escape. She could search for a job and a place to live while Lucille was gone. It didn't matter if she had to live poor for a while. She would find a way to earn a living. As long as she felt free, she would find happiness. She was convinced of it.

A few days later, Jax watched from her bedroom window as Lucille and her Vuitton suitcases got into a black limo and drove away.

She sat on the floor and unfolded the corner scrap with Paul's address on it. Paul Namora's house would be the first stop in her crusade to get away from her mother.

This was her chance to find that other life she felt so sure was waiting for her somewhere. Maybe Paul had remarried and had a happy life, with new kids. Maybe -- if indeed Paul Namora was Barry Roaman's real father -- Grandpa Paul would take her in.

"No!" she said out loud. "No, don't even go there."

She couldn't expect anything from him. She was a stranger. Maybe his current family wouldn't appreciate a stranger showing up and claiming to be their relative.

If she found him, she would just act grateful. She wasn't going to ask for anything. This was her journey. It was up to her to find her own way.

Of course, if he offered to help her, that would be amazing but she wouldn't count on it. If he threw her out the minute he found out who she was, at least she'd still know the truth, that her whole life had been a fucking lie, and she didn't know a fucking thing about her own fucking heritage.

She was going. No one could stop her. This was the chance her father didn't have the balls to take. The chance to escape Lucille, to live life the way she wanted to live it, to dress the way she wanted to dress, and pursue her passions without apologies.

She examined her closet and picked a flashy dress Lucille bought her. It fit well and the fabric was woven silk that slid over her like a second skin. It had pockets, which she loved, and it made her butt look nice but it was neon pink, so pink it made her feel like a human sandwich sign for an ice cream boutique. Still, she felt like she should dress up for her first meeting with Grandpa if he was her grandpa, so she tried to put her faith in her mother's opinion that it was chic and trendy, then added black tights, a black belt and a black scarf because wearing black made her feel more like herself.

She grabbed her favorite teddy bear from her bed and threw it in her big school bag for good luck. Then she walked the long blocks to the East 86th Street subway entrance and rode the IRT until the train reached Astor Place. She was unfamiliar with the area, but had a pocket map to guide her along East 8th Street to Sixth Avenue, and then to the smaller named streets beyond.

It always surprised her how one neighborhood could be so different from another in New York. In her parents' neighborhood, traffic on even the widest avenues seemed to move in a purring, dignified way and the side streets were long, straight, logical paths that led from 5th Avenue to the East River where limousines and delivery trucks moved silently. Here, 5th and 6th Avenues endlessly flowed with noisy slow-moving cars and buses.

After that, the streets were a crazy quilt of narrow passages that led to other narrow passages, as if without order or plan. Most of the streets had names she'd never heard before: Morton, Bedford, Barrow, Grove, even a Cherry Lane. And while the long, wide streets uptown were organized into a neat and utilitarian grid, at this end of Manhattan, streets were crooked and truncated. That West 4th Street joined up with West 12th Street really bothered her. "What happened to West 4th Street?" she asked the map. "How can it just disappear in the middle of itself?"

When she reached Christopher Street, something inside her stirred. It was so quaint, like a city in Europe. The maze-like streets enchanted her. The further she explored, the more excited she became. It was like a tiny city within the city, its own little world, filled with gay people and hippies. She felt like she belonged here.

She could see herself inside the boutiques that lined Bleecker, standing behind a counter, modeling shiny little earrings in one place or helping a customer select a hand-blown glass vase in another. She noticed that most of the female store clerks wore all black clothes and low-heeled shoes, and clipped their hair back, and she vowed to dress like that when she applied.

She dawdled and window-shopped, and bought a hand-dipped ice cream cone. It was delicious. She lingered outside a palm-reader's shop to read all the neon signs and gazed up at the witchy lady seated at an ornate table inside, but when the lady beckoned her to come inside, she darted away. Then she stopped at a drugstore and bought a modest clip to pin back her hair, already practicing for the day she'd go job-hunting in the neighborhood.

Finally, she ordered an espresso at the counter of a coffee bar to give her strength and swigged it back, hoping for clarity. Now she was ready. No more dawdling. No more hesitation. She headed with a firm step towards the address in her pocket.

Rounding the corner to the address written in perfect script on the envelope in Dad's desk, she found herself in yet another micro-world. This was the strangest little street of all. It was lined in old cobblestones and crammed with tiny, crooked homes of a type she'd never seen before. They looked like they were built for hobbits. Maybe gay hobbits, because rainbow flags hung in a few windows. She smiled knowingly to herself. She knew the Village was gay and now she was in the gay heart of gayland! It struck her as unbelievably adorable that there was an obscure enclave of gay hobbit houses right in the middle of New York.

In front of one of the tiny buildings, a man diligently swept his stoop. When she got closer, she saw that he had piercings in his lips and ears and eyebrows and even his cheeks. She imagined his whole face jangling when he laughed. He noticed her and smiled, waving hello to her.

"Nice outfit," he called out, smiling.

"Thanks!" she called back, embarrassed. Did a gay man just come onto her or was he just complimenting the dress? Either way, it made her heart race, and she walked faster.

The address turned out to be a small industrial-looking brick building near the end of the street. It was squeezed on three sides by massive new construction that cast a shadow over the building. Paul Namora's building looked sleepy and uninhabited from the outside. The wide front door once used for deliveries was blocked off with plywood, so you had to enter through a narrow side door whose wood frame was painted over so many times, it looked at first as if it had been painted shut. She peeked through the glass and saw a small vestibule with yellowing tiles, gleaming aluminum mail boxes built into one wall, and a cold fluorescent light overhead to illuminate the space.

She leaned on the door with her body and it slowly eased open, the hinges making a small squeal. She wasn't a snob, but the lobby smelled of urine and bleach. It filled her with foreboding. If a mouse popped out of a wall, she wouldn't have been surprised. Holding her bag tight against her body in case she had to run, she scanned the metal boxes and quickly spotted his name. Paul Namora was listed alongside a second name, Steve Carpenter, in Apartment 4A.

She pressed the button and a buzzer instantly responded, as if someone was waiting for her to arrive. If her grandfather was expecting a delivery, he was going to be very disappointed, she smiled ruefully to herself. She pushed the door into the interior lobby and felt a little better. Here the tile was bright white, as if it had been painstakingly bleached. There were even decorative touches, including a brass wall sconce and a surprisingly large ficus that colonized the back wall. It was even nicer on the first floor where someone had put an oriental carpet runner in the corridor, along with a small table and chair, so you could sit down and rest your groceries.

The building was deceptively bigger inside than it appeared on the outside. There were two apartments per floor, A and B, front and back. The apartments were probably a lot nicer than the rat-holes she thought they'd be, at least judging by the furniture in the halls.

She stopped to look at the abstract art on the walls. Nobody dared to decorate the public halls where she lived. Here, people had the freedom to express themselves beyond their apartment. Jax's heart jumped with joy. Maybe this was all a big art commune! Maybe they'd let her live here. She would do chores for them in exchange for room and board if they'd let her.

The second floor was clean and fairly ordinary, though a painting of two naked men dancing hung on the far end, so discrete she wouldn't have noticed it if she hadn't walked right up to it to figure out what it was. When she realized it was naked men, she blushed and laughed. What kind of a place was this? Did her grandfather really live here?

She was so excited, she raced to the top floor. A thick modern rug spanned it wall to wall. Huge pastel paintings hung on the walls and there was a small coffee table flanked by club chairs. She paused at the pastels, then gaped. Her memory flashed to an exhibit she saw with her father when she was 9 or 10. She remembered seeing it or something very much like it. It had to be the same painter. She remembered that Barry told her the art was about "male energy in motion." At the time they looked like long lava blobs, but now she saw them with adult eyes. They were penises! Just penises, penises and more penises.

"Oh my Gawd," she repeated to herself as she gawked at them, stifling her giggles in case someone could hear her. She dropped her bag to the floor and sat down. Her legs felt weak. This was too much. She took a deep breath. She could do it, she could ring the bell, she could go inside, she could get answers. Or could she? How did she know, even now, if this was really her grandfather? It seemed so unlikely.

She had to know. She stood up again and walked to the only door on the floor. "Paul Namora, Artist" was engraved on a brass plaque by the doorbell. She jabbed the button so hard her thumb hurt.

The door swung open and she froze. Before her stood a short, thin man with chopped pink hair that matched her dress. He wore black jeans and a tight pink t-shirt, as if he'd deliberately coordinated his outfit to match hers. He looked like he was in his late 50s, but there was no resemblance whatsoever between him and her father. Her stomach sank.

"Does Paul Namora live here?" she asked meekly.

"Paul," he called into the apartment with nasal sarcasm, "my doppelganger is here and she wants to talk to you. You've got to see this!"

Jax didn't understand what he was saying.

A tall thin man with a short gray beard and round horn-rimmed glasses appeared beyond him. At first sight of him her body seemed to respond on a molecular level. He looked like a sophisticated, calm, and wrinklier version of her father. But his eyes! Why were the eyes she saw in her mirror every day on his face!? Gray, penetrating, strange eyes that everyone noticed. She felt it in her blood, as if her genetic material had its own consciousness and recognized their kinship. They had the same eyes!

"Is something the matter, Steve?" Paul glanced at Jax, puzzled. "Who is that?"

Steve burst out laughing. "OK, who put you up to this, sweetie?" he asked Jax. "Are you an actress? Is this a counter protest to my Silence Equals Death protest?"

Paul protectively put his arm around Steve and peered coldly at Jax. "Did someone hire you, young lady?" He sounded stern and she panicked. He removed his glasses and wiped them clean. "Is this some kind of stupid political prank to mock Silence Equals Death?"

"What?" She was so confused.

"Why are you wearing pink and black?" Steve asked her again, but this time with a softer look on his face.

"It's... it's... a dress my mom bought me?"

Paul and Steve were nonplussed. She was transfixed by Paul. He looked just like her from certain angles. Her heart pounded. He was her grandpa! A little voice inside her screamed, "Yes, yes, yes." And yet, even if he was, she suddenly felt ashamed. She should have tried calling first, breaking the news to him that she wanted to meet him in a polite, civilized way. This was too much of a shock. He might get angry that she was intruding on his life.

Steve suddenly took her hand. "Are you lost, sweetie? Come inside, you look like you need to sit down."

"Thank you," she whispered as he led her to a chair. She was grateful for his hand. It felt safe.

Steve looked like an artist. Or maybe he was gay. Did they live here together or was he just visiting? The way they stood close before letting her in, protective of one another, made her think they were more than friends.

"You have Paul's eyes," he said, not letting go of her hand, "you even have his chin dimple. You can't see it because it's under the beard, but he has one. And he had curly blonde hair when he was young too. Oh my God," he whispered, "you're Jackie! Barry's daughter. Oh my."

She was shocked to be identified by the name Barry always called her.

Steve slid his arm around Paul's back. "Paul, it's Jackie. Jaquinta!"

"Jax," she mumbled, "I go by Jax."

"Jax!" Paul didn't know what else to say. "It's really you. My grandchild, Jax! I never thought this day would come."

Jax couldn't interpret his tone. Was he pleased or horrified?

"Stay here, I'll get us some drinks," Steve said.

"I'll help you," Paul called out, hurrying after him. She heard them whispering furiously in the kitchen.

Jax looked around. The apartment was huge, set up like a loft with a huge open area and a galley kitchen at the southern end. The north and south sides were partitioned off so you couldn't see what was behind them. The sprawling living room/dining room was furnished with expensive antiques. Art covered every wall. Thick rugs were strewn on the floors. Everything felt comfortable and lived in, not like the overstuffed couches and hard chairs that filled her mother's house.

Paul returned first. "So, Jax, you found me. I have to say, I'm a little overwhelmed."

"I'm sorry, I can go."

"No, no, that's not what I meant," he said. "I'm... glad. Really. Stay."

"Oh. Ok." He was just trying to be polite. He was not glad. She looked down at her feet, conscious that he was examining her with his eyes.

"You look like your mother," he finally said.

She shrank inside. His voice sounded cold, analytical. She should never have come. If Paul wanted to see her, surely he would have sought her out by now. It was obvious he simply had no interest in her. What was she to him, really? She was the sperm of one of his sperm. That was billions of faceless sperm ago. He didn't owe her anything.

She felt an urgent need to leave, but when Steve walked in with a tray of drinks, she sat back in her chair, defeated. There were cocktails for the men, and a small pitcher of sparkling water with fresh lemon for her. Steve sat on the couch next to Paul.

Paul must have been gorgeous when he was young. He was thin and buff, and more handsome than Barry, who had lost his hair at 30 and gained 40 pounds after he got married. But beyond his appearance, Paul had a certain other-worldliness about him, as if he lived in a purer atmosphere than other mortals. He was immaculate, precise, crisp, like a military officer. But the beard and his loose clothes and sandals made him look like a Christ-like, free spirit.

"I swear I'm seeing your eyes stare out of her head!" Steve shook his head at Paul. He reached for Jax's hand again and began petting it like it was a small dog. "I love that you found us! You're amazing. Paul, isn't she amazing?" He gazed so fondly into her face that she blushed. "Wait! This makes me your step-grandpa! Oh my Lord, Paul, we're grandparents!"

"You mean I have two grandpas?" she squealed. Steve squealed with her.

So Grandpa was definitely gay.

"Mazel tov," Paul said, pouring himself another drink. He nervously ran his paint-stained fingers through his thick white hair. Jax pulled on her curls. He was gay! Grandpa was gay!

"How did you find us, Jaquinta?" Paul lowered his voice. "Did Barry give you my address?" He looked worried. "What did he tell you about me?"

Jax's heart stood still. Did he not know that his son had died? She had not even considered that! She looked from him to Steve, and panicked at the thought of telling these two sweet old men that Barry had died. How could she tell Paul? It would be cruel. He'd never forgive her. She couldn't tell him that his only son was dead by his own hand. He'd never be able to look at her without thinking about the death of his son. Worse, he might agree with Lucille that Jax helped drive him to an early grave.

But there was no getting out of it. The die was cast. Maybe this was what this whole side-quest was about. Maybe she was the designated messenger. Maybe Daddy was watching and guiding her from Heaven to find his father and to give him the mournful news of his passing. Maybe that was why she felt such a powerful, almost spiritual need to find him. God was telling her to come.

Fuck. She just couldn't break an old gay man's heart. It wasn't fair, she was only 18, it was too much of a burden.

"I have to go." She put down her empty glass.

"No! Not yet. Are you serious?" Steve started.

"What? Really?" Paul said. "Please stay a little longer."

"You can't leave yet," Steve said. "You've come this far, Jax." She locked eyes with him, surprised. "I know how hard it was for you to come here. I don't know all the reasons why it was so hard, or why you came here now, but I know it took guts to do it." He was speaking her language. Like Dr. Frank. "I think you're very brave. Please be brave enough to give us a chance to get to know you."

Paul sat at the edge of the couch, leaning towards her. She needed him to hug her so badly.

"Please stay, Jax, I want to know everything about you. We both do. I know you may find this hard to believe, but we've loved you since the day you were born."

A tiny voice came out of her mouth. "Would you... could you hug me?"

The men jumped to their feet and helped her to the couch, putting her between them, and wrapping their arms all around each other. She wept like a baby, and they patted her hair, and said calming things, and told her not to worry, she was safe with them, she was their granddaughter, they loved her.

Slowly, she told them the whole story, in her own words, through her own anxiety-clouded lens. Her life with her parents. Her expulsion from parochial school. Her psychiatrist, Dr. Frank. The turtles. Everything. And then, finally, her whole body shaking, she told them about Barry's suicide and her agonizing search for answers to why he killed himself one night in his home office.

Hours passed, as the three of them wept and mourned together and fell into dark silences together, too. This was the first time Jax had a place to share her true feelings about Barry, and Lucille, since her visits to Dr. Frank.

Steve held her hand. "You poor child," Paul murmured again and again. "I'm so sorry. I had no idea Lucille was such a narcissist. I thought Barry was happy. I thought you were happy!" He choked. "I thought you were better off without me around. That's how he made it sound in his letters."

"It was Lucille who forced Barry to stop seeing us. Did you know?" Steve asked.

"Well fuck a duck," she blurted. "Fuck a fucking duck." She stomped her foot. "Figures!" Her mother was evil. So, as it turned out, was Barry's mother, who Jax called Mawmaw.

Now Grandpa told her his side of things. How he fought with Mawmaw for years to get custody of Barry and how the courts turned him down time and again for being homosexual. She finally agreed to joint custody, but Paul in turn had to change his last name, move to another part of town, and never appear at their door again. When Barry married Lucille, Mawmaw convinced Lucille that he posed a danger to her child, and said it would be best if Barry and Lucille never mentioned him at all.

Despite the cruel obstacles the women imposed, Paul managed to stay in touch with Barry after Jax was born, through letters and by meeting at art galleries and openings downtown.

"Paul!" Jax cried. "You're explaining my childhood to me!"

Paul smiled. "Do you remember going to galleries with Barry?"

"Of course. I think about it all the time. But I don't remember meeting you."

"Oh, that was off the menu," Paul said matter-of-factly. "Barry was very nervous about introducing us. He was afraid you'd tell your mother and Lucille would divorce him. So we were allowed to see you, but not talk to you."

"He was so paranoid," Steve said. "He'd walk around twitching, always looking to see if someone was watching."

"That's not fair!" Paul said without conviction, like he knew it was technically true, but he didn't want to admit it. "He was doing the best he could under the circumstances."

"Under paranoid homophobic circumstances," Steve said drily. "He didn't have to..." Steve trailed off, glancing at Jax.

Paul shrugged and emptied his drink. "Yeah, well," he said, "old story. Same story."

She absorbed it all quietly, in a mix of despair and delight. So Grandpa always knew about her! He'd even seen her as a child. She felt more connected to him than before.

At the same time, it meant that her entire life had been a lie. All the adults had conspired to deprive her of the nicest, most interesting person in their family. A rising sense of outrage and a thirst for revenge swelled together in her chest. She had always felt they were lying, she knew it all along. She couldn't live in Lucille's house another moment.

"What about Bob?" She suddenly remembered her father's best friend. Now their platonic lunches together took on a different meaning. Was Barry gay too? She never saw anything gay or gayish about his friendship with Bob, except that both of them had to lie to their wives about meeting up on Saturdays.

"Bob? Bob, his high school friend?"

"Yes, we always had lunch with him after going to the art galleries. Did you know him?"

Grandpa looked at Steve. "I knew of him," Paul finally said.

"We only met him one time."

"Was Bob gay?" Was this the big secret buried at the root of her father's unhappiness?

"He never said so," Paul said slowly, "I never had any reason to believe he was..."

"Oh, honey," Steve patted Paul's knee, "Bob put the fruit in fruitcake."

"Like I said," Paul loudly cleared his throat, "Barry never talked about it. They were on the same swim team and did homework together. That's all I know."

She decided not to push it.

"Your father stopped coming downtown about three years ago. Then, he stopped writing to me. I knew something was wrong. There was nothing I could do except send more letters. I guess I didn't want to believe something bad had happened. I didn't let myself think that way."

She didn't want to think of her father as a coward, but she felt sick to her stomach about it. What kind of a family erases a blood relative from their lives for no reason, but because he's gay? Ignorant asshole families! She didn't want to be part of that family.

"So many hurts on so many levels," she cried into her palms. "Life is so unfair. Why?"

Paul suddenly reached for her, nearly lifting her off the couch in a powerful hug. He held her and cradled her, and gave her a kind of fatherly love she couldn't remember experiencing since she was a toddler. She bawled like a baby, snot dripping from her nose.

"It's okay, shhhh, it'll be okay. Things will be okay now." Paul's voice broke. "You are with your grandpa now."

"Can I live with you? Please??" The words leaped out of her.

She regretted them even before she finished speaking them.

"What?" Paul and Steve said simultaneously, looking alarmed. "Oh, no, no, no, what? Oh. We're not sure we're prepared... are you sure? Is that legal?"

"I'm sorry, I'm sorry." She was so stupid. She wanted to crawl into a hole, vanish into thin air, stop living. What was wrong with her? Her desperation was not their problem. Grandpa and Steve were wonderful. They had been so nice to her. Now she was putting them in a ridiculous spot. No old gay couple would want a lost girl of 18 to move in with them. "I'm stupid, I'm so stupid, I'm sorry, I didn't mean it."

Paul leaned his chin into his palm, looking at her. Steve jumped to his feet.

"Girl, you need a glass of wine. Are you old enough to drink wine?"

"Not legally, I'll be 19 next month."

"Well, I'm old enough." He retrieved a bottle from the kitchen and poured himself a generous glass.

"Do you really want to live with us?" Paul asked in a hollow voice.

"Yes, yes, yes, yes. Oh yes!"

"You're emancipated at 18," he said. "So it's legal for you to move out without permission. Are you sure you want to do that?"

"I can't go back now, knowing what I know." She burst into tears again. "I'd rather die than go back. I'm sorry. I shouldn't have come. I know I'm asking for too much." She recited the litany of Lucille's accusations, "I'm selfish and reckless and weird and inconsiderate."

"Here," Steve cut her off and gave her a Hershey's bar, "eat some chocolate, it will calm you down."

She bit into the bar and tried to focus on how good it tasted melting in her dry mouth. Food didn't fix everything, but her tears vanished after a few bites.

"We could fit you in for a while, I guess," Paul said.

"You could?!" She wanted to kiss his feet, she was so happy.

"Steve won't be cleaning up after you, we'll expect you to do your own dishes and keep your room tidy. Right, Steve?"

"I don't mind doing dishes."

"No, I will do my dishes. I will be a perfect houseguest! The most perfect!" She couldn't believe it. Paul was saying YES!

"You have to do your own laundry too. You'll have to graduate high school and find a job to help out."

"I promise all that, I swear. I'm going to start looking for a job right away!"

"What's next?" Steve piped up. "No men in her room after 10 pm?"

"Support me on this, Steve," Paul said.

Paul planted his powerful hands on her shoulders. They were so strong and so steady. The hands of an artist.

"Jax, there's something you need to know."

"Yes, Grandpa?"

"Steve and I are life partners. You'll be living with gay men. It will be a huge change from your old life uptown. We're not rich either. Are you sure this is what you want?"

"I love that you are gay! I love that you love each other."

"You really are a horse of a different color," Steve said admiringly. "You have a big heart. Paul, take back what you said about her looking like Lucille. She looks exactly like you and you know it."

Steve touched her heart. Out of the growing flame of bravery inside her, a voice said what she had never admitted out loud, not even to her best friends.

"I'm not straight either! I'm kinky! Like, I have really kinky thoughts. You know, like tying people up and stuff. I mean, I haven't tried it, yet, but I want to."

Both men's jaws dropped.

"Do you know what BDSM is?" she asked them. "I think that's what I am. I might be bisexual, too, I don't know yet," she said earnestly, "but it's possible because I think women are really hot."

"Jesus on a Cheeseburger!" Steve said. "This is so fucking cute I can't stand it."

"I know," Paul said, "I'm having a cuteness stroke myself." He smiled. "I always wanted a daughter."

"It's true." Steve nodded. "We tried, but I couldn't get pregnant."

They laughed raucously at the joke, a wave of relief washing away the emotional drama that had possessed them only moments ago. Paul kissed the top of her head like millions of grandpas around the world do with their beloved grandchildren and she nearly fainted with joy.

"You've passed every test and then some. I guess you're in," Paul broke the spell, staring deeply into her eyes which looked so much like his eyes that they both shuddered at their self-reflecting eyeballs.

"Group hug!" Steve cried. "Group hug with the granddaughter!" She squirmed with happiness as they wrapped her in affection.

"We'll find a spot for you here. We've got plenty of room," Paul said.

"I don't have much stuff to pack," she said. At 18, she didn't need much. She wanted to live minimally. She would limit herself to one suitcase and fit into whatever accommodations they provided, even if it was the lobby. "I'm going to leave most of my clothes behind. I could move in tomorrow!!"

"TOMORROW?!" Steve looked terrified, as if "tomorrow" was many months faster than he imagined.

Paul said, "Tomorrow is fine."

It was settled. Paul spread his powerful artist arms around Steve and Jax and drew them in until both of them were crushed against his muscled chest.

"We're family now," Grandpa Paul announced. "Nothing will ever tear us apart again."

Jax leaned in hard, her strong young heart racing. Her arms felt like steel, her core surged with electricity, her face flushed hotter than the sun. The only sounds that escaped her lips now were happy sighs and coos. She wanted to say something profound, but all she could do was mewl, "I love you, Grandpa, I always loved you, I'll always love you," over and over and over again, while tears puddled in her dimple before dripping off her chin like fresh dew.

She hadn't just found him. She had found HIM! HIM! The better, kinder, more sensitive father. The stronger one. The prouder one. The defiant one! The handsome, cool, counter-cultural one she'd always dreamed of having. He was like a mythological god to her. Jax had never felt so happy in her entire life. Paul was the original Barry, the better, happier, stronger version of Barry.

Maybe it was fated by God. Or Karma. Or the stars. However you explained it, this was meant to be. She was born to live with Grandpa. The reason everything had happened the way it happened was to force her to find him. She was so grateful to him, she couldn't speak, just stared at him and lightly touched his arm again and again, as if to prove to herself that he was real.

The skies were growing dark. She reached into her purse and pulled out the stuffed bear she brought for good luck. She put the teddy on the chair where she first sat.

"This is Bamboozle. May he stay here until I come back?"

"Like a placeholder?" Paul was amused.

"He looks a little worn and chewed up. He's not a drug addict, right?" Steve asked. "Because we don't allow that here." He and Jax grinned at each other.

"We will treat him like a member of the family," Paul promised.

They kissed goodbye, and hugged goodbye, and then they did a group hug again.

She sprinted on air to the subway. She felt like she could run a marathon. Her new life began tomorrow. In less than 24 hours, she would be living in Greenwich Village with the grandfather who had always loved her.

She threw herself into bed when she got home, her body exhausted, her brain still racing. This was the last night in her mother's house. She exulted. She was the hero of her own story. She had completed her quest. She was Cassandra. She always knew another life waited for her in the shadows of her existence. Now she had found it. She had finally found a world where she was welcome.

Chapter 2
QUEER FAMILY VALUES

Once Jax moved in with Grandpa Paul, she felt she had taken the most important step of her life. She could relax now. Grandpa's place was a temporary harbor where she would find nourishment for her soul. In a few months, she would launch the magnificent ship of her life towards success and romance without Lucille around to fuck it up. The enormity of her new freedom swept over her, making her feel stronger and sexier.

On the morning after she met Paul, she woke up extra early and went to her parents' bedroom, carrying a sheet of paper and a pen with her. She sat at her mother's vanity table, drummed her dimpled chin with the pen for a few minutes, and decided to keep the details vague for now. Lucille didn't need to know exactly where she was staying. Maybe she'd never tell her. Jax wouldn't even have to lie. Lucille was too busy to worry about where her daughter went and never doubted that her daughter would always buzz back to the money hive like a brainwashed bee. Jax could vanish and Lucille would just assume she'd be home when she ran out of funds.

Lucille would be the last to know if she ended up in a hospital or on the side of a road. What if she'd been kidnapped by a biker gang? In her pajamas! How humiliating! She'd be in Oregon by the time Lucille called the police. She imagined men in black leather jackets zooming off with her, diabolically yet comfortably bound to a motorcycle, speeding down unmarked roads. She felt a trembling thrill between her legs and giggled. It was so hot to think about that! She slipped her hand between her legs. She was so moist she was blurping moist, that sound her body made inside when her pussy gushed juice.

There was no real rush to finish the letter. She slid down to the floor and rolled over, squeezing her thighs as she rubbed her lips with her hand. She threw the other arm out and grabbed a leg of the desk to steady herself as the sadistic bikers dancing in her brain carefully unbound her and led her into the club where terrible things would happen. She imagined them examining her, looking her up and down. One of them grabbed her roughly by the neck and stripped off her pajama top. That did it. She groaned as wave after wave of ecstasy washed through her and she fell onto her back, her heart pounding in her ears. She muffled her groans just in case Honey was cleaning nearby, then she sighed with relief and rolled onto her side, clear-headed and calm. She always felt a little weird after coming. The things that got her off in fantasy would be a fucked up nightmare in reality. Still cool, though.

She jumped back in the chair and began writing enthusiastically. She knew exactly how to manipulate her mother. She claimed that Lucille's bravery in moving on from their family tragedy had inspired her. Now it was time for her to follow in her mother's footsteps and seek her own happiness. Then she crossed out "happiness" and replaced it with "fortune," because to Lucille "fortune" meant "riches" and to Jax it meant "I could be joining the Peace Corps, or maybe a biker gang, or getting rich and famous!"

Jax reread the paragraph, admiring her Machiavellian diplomacy. Lucille would be smug that Jax claimed to be walking in her footsteps. That brag would carry currency in her circle of friends. "My daughter is just like me!" was the highest compliment her friends could ever pay to their kids. "Look, I made a clone!" She laughed darkly to herself.

She would never admit to Lucille that she had a short-lived hope her father's death meant Lucille would focus on her and try to have a closer new relationship with her. No, she'd never admit to wanting what other children naturally wanted. She would rather bury it and burn with resentment.

Lucille could have taken Jax to Palm Springs, and spent the time reconnecting and healing with her daughter. She could have made the effort to be a better mother, instead of abandoning Jax and hunting down some schmuck who'd fulfill her selfish needs.

Jax continued the letter. She wrote that she had lined up job interviews so Lucille would think she had been planning her departure carefully, and not just suddenly jumping at the first opportunity, which is exactly what had happened, however she was not going to give Lucille the satisfaction of knowing that. But she did have a perfect plan! She would simply hit all the cool boutiques on Bleecker Street, and by the end of a couple of days she would be employed. She'd never had a job but it sounded like it would be easy: go in, look hip, sound eager, be amiable, get hired. She conveyed all that optimism in the letter, and finished formally: *"I look forward to being in touch when I have good news to report!"*

She signed it, "Your daughter, Jaquinta," as if her mother had any other daughter, and savored her subtle sarcasm. Then she went back, inserted a caret between *Your* and *daughter*, and added the word "only," hoping it would sharpen the sting. If she hadn't been raised better than that, she would have added "P.S. Fuck you!" at the end. She was proud of her own restraint. Then she folded it and printed MOTHER in curly capitals on the blank side, and arranged it on Lucille's pink-on-pink pillow.

Her work done, Jax took a long final look around her parents' bedroom. When she was little, the furniture was all Danish Modern, with bright amber woods and white linens and curtains that brightened the room. Now it was dark as a viper's pit. The massive wood headboard blocked two-thirds of the window. The heavy drapes were pink-on-pink chintz. The bedcover and pillows, the vanity seat cushion, and the overstuffed armchair all matched the curtains. She laid down on the side of the bed Daddy once claimed. How did he feel going to bed every night in Lucille's super-feminine flower hell?

She closed her eyes and remembered creeping in as a toddler to crawl into the warm cozy spot between her parents, her face buried in Daddy's back and her toes nudging her mother's neck. She remembered that they slept back to back, almost at the opposite edges of their opulently carved queen-size bed.

Suddenly, the bed felt cold and lifeless beneath her. She stood up quickly, disconcerted by a sudden image of Lucille bringing a stranger to her marital bed. She imagined Lucille with her legs and arms wrapped around a new sucker. "The spider must be fed!" she whispered. A deep shudder of disgust sent her hurrying from the bedroom.

There wasn't much to pack. There was no way of knowing where they'd put her. She might only get one drawer! She didn't need to be dragged down by materialism. She said goodbye to the ugly clothes and fur jacket her mother had bought her. She opted for a red ski jacket and tops and bottoms in black and denim. Things that were essential even a few days ago, like her action figure collection, her lava lamps, and her Russian Dolls, now looked childish to her. She packed her Gameboy, hesitated, then went to her closet and found an expensive leather bound writing journal someone gave as a birthday gift years ago. She replaced the Gameboy with the journal. She was leaving her youth behind and starting her journey into adulthood with a diary. She would take notes every day about everything she saw and learned. Then she would write a book about it and become famous. Maybe even infamous!

At the last minute, she slid two slinky cocktail dresses off their hangers. One was a blood-red chiffon goddess dress and the other was a silver sequined number that flowed like crystal waters. She held them up and admired them in the mirror. Somehow they felt essential to her future life.

She called out to the maid, Honey, who quickly appeared. If Honey had seen her slip into her mother's bedroom or had questions about the clothes strewn on the floor, she was too well-trained to pry into the family's life.

"Can you bring me the biggest and strongest shopping bags we have saved?" she asked the maid. "Ones with strong handles?"

A few moments later Honey returned, bags from expensive boutiques draped over her arm. Jax examined them, pleased. Honey knew her shopping bags! They had reinforced bottoms and wood handles. They could serve many purposes in her future frugal life. Maybe she could even turn one of them into a lightweight backpack with some nylon cord.

"Do you want dinner tonight, Miss?" Honey asked.

"No. You won't be needed to cook again until Mother comes back." She felt a little sad. She'd miss Honey. Honey had always been nice to her, buying her popular candies her mother didn't allow, like Sour Jacks, Jujyfruits, and her favorite, Pixy Stix.

Honey was always there to help her with school projects and Halloween costumes, and made her hot tea with honey and lemon when she was sick.

"No dinner?" Honey asked. "Mrs. Roaman said I should make dinners for you while she's gone."

"I'm going away too for a bit," Jax said. "I guess Mother forgot to tell you," she added.

"No, Miss. She didn't tell me. Does that mean you won't need me tonight?"

"Take tonight off," Jax said. "Actually, please take off all the nights until Mother returns."

"I don't know when that will be, Miss."

"Neither do I!"

They exchanged a long, meaningful look. Lucille had trained Honey into robotic obedience, but she couldn't hold back.

"That's not right for a mother!" Honey blurted. Apparently, as the mother of six children, the idea of any mother going on holiday and not telling the children when she was coming back was alarming.

"You're so right," Jax said. It was the closest Honey had ever come to criticizing Lucille. Jax felt oddly grateful to her, and another twinge of sadness passed through her. Honey had been her surrogate mother since she was three.

"I'm very sorry, Miss. I didn't mean to question Mrs. Roaman. I'm sure she knows best."

"That's my mother for you, she always does whatever is best for herself without considering the people around her."

"I understand, Miss." For a second Honey seemed to want to say more, but instead she returned to her chores. Jax waited until she closed the door then finished packing and dragged the bags out the front door quietly while Honey vacuumed in another room.

The familiar walk to the elevator felt strange, as if the hallways had shrunk. Her bags bumped the walls. The elevator car felt unusually hot and stifling. When she glanced up at the mirrored ceiling, she saw a squat, sweaty gnome with shopping bags and looked away in horror. By the time the elevator door slid open, she was hyperventilating and felt faint. She plowed past the concierge and the doorman before they could hear her release several loud belches. She stepped into the sunlight and hurried to the subway.

She couldn't believe how easy it was to walk away from the life she felt trapped in. Here she was, running away from home, and no one tried to stop her, not Honey, not the building staff, and most certainly not the absentee Lucille. She smiled at strangers. They didn't know she was a runaway. She grinned as she got on the train. A couple of subway passengers glanced at her and looked away. They didn't know they were seeing her on the first day of her new life as a rebel.

She alone knew she was changing the course of her future. She alone knew why she was carrying her clothes in shopping bags and where she was traveling to. She glanced around to see if anyone else could tell she was different from them, or how much stronger she felt today than yesterday, but they couldn't know, of course they couldn't. It was her precious secret and she gloated that she knew what they could not even perceive – that she was embarking on a heroic journey.

She found a seat and put the shopping bags on the floor between her knees, suddenly tired of their weight. It occurred to her that subways and lines and finding a way to pay for expenses would be her life now. It was a little intimidating, but if other people could do it, she could too.

By the time the train pulled into 34th Street her thoughts cycled back to her conversation with Honey and the long look they exchanged. Maybe Honey knew, after all. Honey knew everything. But what did she feel? Jax never knew if Honey was nice to her because she was paid to be nice to her or whether Honey felt sorry for her. On the other hand, why would she feel sorry for her? Jax was, after all, a privileged princess whose parents could bribe their way through anything, while Honey worked hard just to put food on the table for her children and buy their school supplies.

Now her thoughts turned to Lucille. What duties does a daughter owe a self-centered, cold-hearted mother? None. But her mind kept racing. What did she owe her? What did she owe Lucille for a life she never wanted in the first place?

Still, if Lucille took ill, Jax would feel morally obligated to move back in. She'd never be able to live with herself if she abandoned Lucille when she needed her most. That would make her a horrible person, to scoot off when her mother was sick or, God forbid, dying. Suddenly Jax wondered what would happen if Lucille suddenly died. Like, she returned and found the note Jax left and stroked out on the spot? Jax could visualize that happening, Lucille reading the note, clutching her fake boobs and going down like the Titanic, creating waves that threw Jax's little boat into rocks.

What if Lucille's last words were about Jax, like, "Jax did it." Would the cops come looking for her or name her their chief suspect?? She imagined headlines braying that New York's leading socialite died of heartbreak after her ungrateful bitch of a daughter ran away. What would she do then?

A man seated next to her began to comfortably spread his legs and crowd her thighs. She whirled her head and gave him a death ray with her eyes that said, "Not today, motherfucker." He snapped his knees back together and looked away.

She returned to brooding. What did she owe Lucille morally? She didn't choose to be born. She didn't choose to be raised in a toxic household. Most importantly, she didn't choose Lucille to be her mother. Lucille probably would never choose to have a daughter like her. What if she was just like her mother? It was a terrifying, demoralizing thought. She was a spoiled, entitled bitch, too. She was useless. The only really practical skill she had learned was how to unzip a man's fly with her teeth because she watched a tutorial online and it looked sexy. What a moron!

She wearily carried her bags out of the subway. They felt heavier now, as if someone had thrown iron bars in them. She stopped on every block, bent over from the bags like an old lady. She hated herself even more than she hated her mother. She really was a terrible daughter and here she was, causing trouble again. Hadn't she learned her lesson? She made her father so unhappy he killed himself. Now she was running away, with a few hundred dollars she stole from the jar where her mother kept petty cash for delivery men and tips for maintenance workers. She had abandoned her widowed mother only 2 weeks after her father's death. What was next? How low would she go? Would she destroy Paul and Steve's lives? Would she infect her grandfathers with her family's toxins? Would she turn into Lucille one day?

By the time she reached her grandfather's door, the sleek, self-confident 18-year-old her gay grandpas had seen the day before was nowhere in sight. This Jax had puffy red eyes and a crooked mouth. Her meticulously straightened hair shrank into a frizz from humidity and looked like a clown wig on her head.

They welcomed her in with open arms, then seemed baffled when she grunted, "Hi," and limped past them to the teddy bear, dropped her bags and knocked the teddy to the floor to sit in its place. She stared at the bear. Its shiny eyes looked tearful. Why did she even bring something so childish? She was an idiot. It was so embarrassing to her now. They probably laughed about it all night. They'd be sick of her after a few days. They knew it and she knew it. She bet they were counting on her realizing her mistake and running back home. Maybe she would. She wasn't going to unpack. No point. If they kicked her out tomorrow, she would replace the money she stole so that would be at least one less sin on her fragile conscience.

The men looked at her and then spoke to each other with eye signals and hand gestures. Steve went to the kitchen. Paul sat on the sofa across from her, folded his arms and leaned back, staring at the ceiling, thinking.

"So... you're here," he finally said to the ceiling.

"Yep."

"We're glad you want to stay with us," he said.

"I'm glad you're glad," she said numbly.

"We are." His gray eyes shot left and right. He was unreadable. Like a total stranger. Which he was. The overwhelming love she felt for him yesterday seemed like a dream. He was just an old guy. An old guy with a gay wife, or husband, she wasn't sure. She didn't know how gay people lived. She was nothing to him.

"Are you sure?" she asked.

"Yes, of course we are," Paul said. "Are you?"

"Drink some water, darling." Steve returned with a tall glass of ice water. "You look dehydrated." He lightly patted her frizzy blond hair. "I see you went natural today," he said. "I love the curls. So cute!"

She felt disgusted by the compliment but drank obediently. Steve was suspiciously nice. "Thank you." It did make her feel a little better. Steve sat next to Paul and the two men joined hands. She almost cried to see how sweet they looked, two wrinkly old men holding hands like young lovers. She didn't deserve them. And they certainly did not deserve Lucille's problem child.

"How did it go with Lucille?" Paul asked.

"Fine." She could tell Paul wanted more details. "Well, since she's away, and I don't know when she's coming back, I wrote her a letter to explain everything."

"Everything?" Steve looked dubious.

"Well, not everything everything," she said, "more like, um, everything essential. Like I'm okay, and I'll be in touch." The water had fully revived her now. Her panic was lifting and energy levels were improving. "I went on a school trip two years ago and Lucille forgot I was going. When I got back, she said she'd been wondering why she hadn't seen me for three days. So, yeah, I think a letter's good enough."

Paul slapped his hand over his mouth, but Steve was unflustered.

"Well, sweetie, we're just glad you're here," Steve said.

Paul stood up. "Let's get you settled in your room, then you can wash up and be ready in time for dinner. Steve is making fried chicken and mashed potatoes with a salad. You'll eat that, right?"

"Yes!" That was her favorite dish to order at restaurants. They couldn't have known, but how did they know? "I love chicken and mashed potatoes."

"Good," Paul said. "Ok, grab your bags and follow me!" He pointed to the south end of the loft.

By now her hands were so sore she dreaded lifting the bags again. Before she could reach for them, Steve picked them up with ease in one hand, and grabbed her other hand.

"Come on, little one," he said, though she was at least four inches taller than him. It was so strange and so pleasant to hear him address her that way, like she was one of his little chicks and he was showing her around the roost. His hand felt warm and strong, and finally she began to relax. Steve was so kind.

Paul darted on his long legs to the colorful wall at the south end of the loft and opened an invisible door that had been camouflaged by a huge abstract mural that spanned across it. They entered a narrow hall lined with closed doors, some of them padlocked shut. At the very end of the passageway a door leaked light into the hall.

"That will be your space," Paul said, walking ahead of them. She expected to be disappointed. Her room at Lucille's was big and bright in the early afternoon. She knew this one would be cramped and dark. The living room and kitchen relied on artificial light, so she assumed it would be even darker than that, unfurnished, maybe even dusty. It looked like no one had gone back to this part of the apartment except, perhaps, to store mysteries behind locked doors.

"We hope you like it." Steve stepped ahead of her and placed her bags on the floor.

She followed him in, head bowed. But oh! No! The room was magical! It was beautiful! It had enormous windows on the east and south walls from floor to ceiling, with spectacular views over the streets and buildings. It was like stepping into the sky. Her eyes were dazzled. The sudden overload of sunbeams and rays almost blinded her.

The room was smaller than her room at Lucille's, but the windows made it seem like a glass house with an infinite horizon. She adored the furniture. There was a beautifully painted dark blue dresser, with spirals of stars across it, like in the Van Gogh painting. The nightstand beside the bed was painted to match. On top of the nightstand was an old fashioned digital alarm clock and an even funkier turquoise ceramic lamp with a built-in ashtray and little box attached, like she'd seen in old movies on TV.

"The lamp is a trip!" she said.

"I found it at a flea market!" Steve said excitedly. "You can imagine Cary Grant taking a match from that box, can't you?"

"Oh," she fibbed, "yeah." She was imagining keeping a few rolled joints in it.

"I put a fresh bulb in it for you."

"Thank you so much," she said.

She turned to Paul. "Did you paint this furniture?"

"I did," he said. "Do you like it?"

"I love it! It's gorgeous."

Paul looked happy. "I hoped you would like it."

She realized both men had put thought into how she might feel and her gratitude overflowed. Everything about the room felt right to her, like she had magically stepped into the room she was always supposed to have. It's like they knew her even before they met her.

A double bed was pushed up against the inside wall and a bright Mexican blanket hung from a peg above it, both artsy and practical, for winter nights. The bed was dressed with icy blue sheets, an azure coverlet and a poufy white pillow as soft as a cloud. There was even a thick blue rug next to the bed to keep her feet warm when she got up.

Under the east-facing window, a long, narrow writing table was arranged with a simple chair, perfect for working on her laptop and staring out onto a broad vista. On the south wall, a floor-to-ceiling window had sliding patio doors. Noticing her curiosity, Steve slid the door open.

"This is the main attraction." He beckoned her. "We replaced the old windows when we converted to apartments." He pointed to the fire escape outside. "It's like a balcony. You can put a plant out there, even a hibachi, in the summer."

"You're giving me your balcony," she gasped.

"We're lending you our fire escape," Paul corrected her. "Indefinitely," he added.

"The fire escape has history," Steve winked. "We used to have nude sunbathing parties out there. You can fit 4 or 5 people safely."

"Steve," Paul said in a warning tone. "Not now."

"OMG, really, are you really going to be like this?" Steve said.

"We don't have THOSE parties anymore," Paul said to Jax.

"Oh." She felt a little disappointed. Naked adult men on a fire escape, that was fodder for fantasies. She didn't want them to see her blush, so she stepped out onto the fire escape. But looking down to spaces between iron slats to the streets five stories below made her dizzy. She sat on an iron step and waited for it to pass. She tested the metal railings. They were surprisingly stable.

Steve popped his head out the window. "Don't worry! We had them reinforced when we remodeled. They are guaranteed to last for decades."

She stood up again and walked to the edge of the fire escape. On the right, the Hudson River twinkled with sunlight on every crest. Below, tiny people moved towards unknown destinations. Straight ahead, she could see small buildings gradually build to the tall towers of Wall Street. She checked out the neighboring buildings. Some people had gardens and seating areas on their roofs. It never occurred to her that the rooftops of brownstones could be so festive. On one, she saw an enormous black tent. Was it for private parties or did someone live there?

"It's wonderful," she cried, coming back inside. "I can't believe this. It's... beyond beyondness."

"Beyond beyondness?" Paul echoed. The men laughed.

It was ideal -- an artsy studio, far from Lucille, in a neighborhood her mother would never even visit, with views that belonged in a magazine and grandparents who wanted her. It was as if they had kept it waiting for her all along. At her mother's place, she could only peek out from a few windows. The view was blocked by the tall, boring buildings that faced them. From the fire escape, she could see the whole world!

"We're not sure you have enough storage, though," Paul said. The men started discussing whether to bring in a wardrobe for her clothes, and Steve said he saw one at a store on 14th Street that might work.

"Not necessary," she said and sprinted to the small closet she had noticed next to the door. She was going minimalist, one dresser and one closet were more than enough. She opened the closet. It was basically a broom closet, with a tiny rail that held three wire hangers.

"I'm sorry," Paul said, "I know women like closet space. Maybe we can find a decent standing closet to give you more storage. It could go there, I guess." He pointed to the wall where the writing desk stood. It would be impossible to add a closet without obstructing the view.

"Oh," she said, "I see."

"See that lamp?" Steve pointed to the green banker's lamp on the desk. I only paid 25 bucks for it! Could've saved another 10 bucks if I'd thrown in a blowjob."

"STEVE!" Paul was outraged. Jax almost laughed out loud.

She decided there and then that she loved gay men. They were so fresh, so real.

"Oh grow up, Paul, she's not a virgin."

"I am," Jax said. "Technically."

"You hear that, Steve?"

"She said technically!"

"But she meant functionally!" Paul looked directly at her. "Functionally, right?"

"What does that mean?"

"You haven't done it yet, right?"

"Oh, yeah," she blushed, "right." Despite the embarrassment, she was having the best, most grown-up moment of her life watching them argue over how adults should talk in front of a virgin. It was the funniest thing she'd ever heard.

"The thing is, she is OUR kid, and we're not here to give her a sex education!" Paul said stiffly.

She couldn't help herself. "I was kind of hoping you would!" She smiled nervously. "You could teach me about men."

"No," Paul said immediately. "No, we cannot." Steve grinned. She knew he was the one who'd teach her the ways of the world and bit her lip.

She considered telling him that she was tired of being a virgin but it seemed too complicated and embarrassing now. She had never met anyone she actually wanted to do it with. She had experimented a little, but she wanted to be in love with the first guy she made love to. She wanted the whole LOVE experience, not just a dicking. She could get herself off without a dick. That was easy. What was hard was meeting someone she wanted to kiss and be kissed by, someone who'd take her breath away and then hold her all night.

"You know what, I don't want more furniture! The room is perfect as it is. Look!"

Jax's energy was on high as she swiftly removed her clothes and undies from one bag, and threw them into the capacious dresser's top three drawers, leaving the bottom two drawers empty. She fished out the 2 evening dresses and their matching shoes, and hung them in the closet. Her down jacket had been thumped and stuffed into a small plastic bag. Now she removed it, fluffed it back up to full size, and tried to hang it next to the dresses, but she couldn't get the closet door to close. So she folded it as tight as she could and stuffed into the dresser's bottom drawer. She arranged her sneakers and flats in a small row beside the dresser. Finally, she got out her laptop and notebook, and some cables and other gear, and set them on the writing table.

"That's everything!" she gloated. "I totally fit! Like Cinderella's shoes."

The men watched her with their hands on their faces, alternately surprised and amused by her manic unpacking.

"So you do, Jax," Paul said emotionally. "So you do."

She went to the bed and bounced on it. The mattress felt so cozy she lay all the way down. The pillow was thick and fluffy. It was perfect. Everything was perfect.

Overhead, a penis piñata, but with a bulb inside, hung spryly from the ceiling. She pointed at the fixture, unable to speak.

"Oh, shit, I thought we got rid of that!" Paul cried. "Steve, you said..."

"Oh dear, I forgot the cock lamp. Now I've ruined her virginity."

"Steve! Really?" Paul growled.

"Please let it stay. It's amazing. Really. Please." She pleaded with them both.

"Let it stay, Paul," Steve echoed. "Everyone likes to wake up to a penis."

She couldn't hold back. She howled with laughter. She loved Steve!

"Oh my God you two." Paul wasn't angry, though. His eyes twinkled. "OK, granddaughter, you can keep the penis lamp."

This made her wonder what lay behind the padlocked doors! Were there other penis lamps? Maybe penis chandeliers? What was so obscene that they needed to lock those doors? Sex toys? Porn? She could not imagine her Grandpa and Steve actually doing it together. What did gay men even do together, she wondered? Was one of them the man, or were both of them the man? How did that work?

"Thank you, Grandpa," she said coyly. With the penis lamp in her bedroom, and possible collections of dildos and penis pumps just a few doors away, she felt like her journey into adulthood had finally begun.

Everything she knew about sex was learned from reading or from friends who confided their experiences. At 18, she had not yet taken that all-vital devirginizing step into adulthood. She had been diligently preparing for it. She learned to give good handjobs thanks to a couple of eager Montessori boys and had started working on her oral sex skills using peeled cucumbers. Now she'd get serious sex education on how to please men from the best possible experts. Gay men definitely knew more about what men really wanted than those surveys in Cosmo she memorized.

"One more thing to see," Steve said. He motioned her back to the hall. The door closest to hers was closed, but not locked. He opened it to reveal a clawfoot tub, a sink and a toilet crammed inside the tiniest bathroom she'd ever seen. You could almost jump from the doorway into the tub. But it was perfectly clean and utilitarian.

"Madame's dressing room," Steve bowed with flair.

"Nice!" she said. "I've never had my own private bathroom before."

"Awww. Well, you do now." He patted her shoulder. "OK, I need to finish dinner. The salad won't chop itself."

Paul lingered in the doorway, watching her.

"Are you sure about this, girl?" he asked her somberly. "It's not going to be easy. You're walking away from a lot of things you may never get back. Have you considered that? You're so young. You have to think about this. It's a serious decision. It will change your life forever."

"That's what I want," she said. "I want to change my life."

"This is a radical way to do it," he said. "Believe me, we won't be angry if you change your mind. We'll understand. We'll still want to see you. We hope you'll want to see us, too."

"Do you want to change your mind, Grandpa? About me moving in?" She held her breath. "I know it's a horrible imposition."

"Do you think we would have stayed up all night fixing the room for you if we didn't want you?"

"You did? You stayed up all night fixing it up for me?" She was shocked. "Really?"

"Van Goghs don't paint themselves," he teased. "Which reminds me, the paint might still be a little sticky on the nightstand drawers, so be careful."

Suddenly, Grandpa was at her side and gathered her up in his big artist arms like a tiny kitten. "Oh my God, I've always wanted to meet you, to know you, to be able to hug you."

She leaned into him and he held her close as a baby for a moment. "You're my child!" he said. "The only child of my only child!"

No arms had ever held her so completely. No words had ever touched her so deeply. In his voice she heard the timbre of her own soul, the inner voice that had driven her to find him. She never wanted to leave his arms.

"I love you, Grandpa! I love you." She clung to him.

He gently moved a frizzy curl off her forehead.

"You've given me the best gift," he said. "The best gift of my life."

They locked eyes, unable to break away, puddling up together.

"OK. Phew, no tears," Paul said. "We should be celebrating. I'll see you in the kitchen in 30 minutes on the nose. Wash up and join us at the table." He touched his nose with his index finger. She solemnly touched her nose back.

Thirty minutes later, to the minute, and decked out in her red goddess dress and matching shoes, she danced into the kitchen. The men both burst into applause.

"Well done, Jax!" Paul said. "Wow, we got a fashion show!"

"I wish I had a red carpet for you to walk on," Steve said.

"You look so chic!" said Paul.

"Like a movie star," said Steve.

They made her spin around a few times, complimenting the outfit but most of all, admiring HER. They made her feel like a princess and a queen. She felt seen and validated and appreciated. She wanted to jump to the ceiling and slap it.

THIS. THIS was what she had to run away to find.

Together they sat down to a meal of juicy, crisp chicken. It was the most succulent bird she had ever tasted. The mashed potatoes tasted better than the ones she ordered at her parents' favorite fancy restaurant. Even the simple chopped salad of iceberg lettuce, sliced tomatoes and blue cheese crumbles made her happy. The special ingredient was love. By the time dinner ended, she was exhausted and went right to sleep.

The light woke her up the next morning. Something was different. Then she realized everything was different, and she smiled. She never woke up happy, not even as a little girl, but she did that day, and the smile only got bigger when the aroma of frying bacon drew her to the kitchen, where Steve was cooking breakfast.

"Waffles, Jax?" he asked over his shoulder.

Waffles suddenly struck her as the most beautiful word she'd ever heard.

"Yes, please! Waffles!! Yum!"

"With bacon and eggs or just bacon?"

"Everything, I'll eat everything you put on my plate."

"Everything coming right up!"

Paul greeted her over the newspaper, then put it down when the plates arrived. Eating breakfast with them fed her soul, too. The cheerful chatter, the passing of plates hand to hand instead of waiting for a maid to do it, the two reviewing their daily schedules and then inquiring about hers. She was taken aback. No one had ever asked for details about her day.

"I'm going to school today," she said. "I've been gone two weeks. I have to catch up."

"Good! That's really important," Paul said. "When do you think you'll get back?"

"Probably by 4 or 5 pm at the latest," she said, leaving herself a margin of time to get lost in shops or stop at a cafe.

She waited for someone to complain or tell her to adjust her plans, but the men just nodded.

"Sounds good. Do you need any pocket money?" they asked.

"Oh no," she was too embarrassed to tell them she'd stolen a few hundred dollars from Lucille's jar. "Lucille left money," she said, rationalizing that it was technically true.

They told her dinner was at 7 pm, but they'd expect her by 5 pm. Steve said he'd be home all day, cleaning and catching up on phone calls, so if she was early, he'd let her in. He was going to get another key made for her so she could come and go when she needed to. This was a revelation. She never had a key at Lucille's. She had to depend on adults to let her in and out. She couldn't believe she'd have her very own key to their apartment. It felt so grown-up.

She left first and strolled the empty early morning streets of the Village at a lazy pace. She had plenty of time to get to school. The bacon flavor was still in her mouth, her belly was full of coffee, her head filled with new memories she would cherish forever. She couldn't understand why Paul and Steve were doing so much for her. The leafy trees bent gracefully over the sidewalks and the pristine brownstones crowded shoulder to shoulder, like old friends. Was she in heaven? It felt like heaven.

She resolved that, from now, she would learn to do more for herself so that one day, when they were old and feeble, she would be able to do things for them. Maybe, one day, they could live with her and her future husband in their future home. Maybe it would be in the country. If they had a home in the country, she would build them their own cottage with an art studio for Paul and a garden for Steve.

She got on the subway and stood the whole way uptown, still plotting the kind of house she would one day share with a husband and children and many pets and her gay grandfathers. She would need to have her babies as soon as possible so they could get to know what wonderful people Paul and Steve were.

By the time she reached school that day, she felt she'd aged 10 years in the 2 weeks since Barry died. People approached her in the halls to express their sympathies, her teachers were extra nice to her. Three of her girlfriends even took her out to lunch.

But she felt out of place among them now, as if she had already moved to her next life, one that wouldn't include them. While their conversations were filled with plans for prom and summer vacations, she was preparing to join the workforce and look for her own place. While they all knew where they would be next year and the year after that, she wasn't sure where she would be in a month. When they talked about their mothers and fathers, she remained silent. She couldn't let anyone know where she was living or who she was living with. That could get back to Lucille and ruin everything.

Everyone seemed to have a concrete plan except for her. They already knew whether they wanted to be doctors or teachers or step into waiting jobs with their family businesses. She didn't know what she wanted to do with her life. When she was little, she wanted to be a ballerina, a famous writer and an actress. She still couldn't imagine any one thing she'd like to do for the rest of her life.

She could leave her mother's trap and then volunteer to be trapped in mundanity, following the same well-trod paths her school friends blindly accepted. For them, it was high school, then college, then marriage, then kids, then retirement, grandchildren and finally death. She didn't want that life. She wanted her own, totally original, life.

She wasn't even sure she wanted to go to college anymore. She was afraid she would get stuck studying "The Thing" so she could find a job doing "The Thing" and become so enslaved to "The Thing" that she never got the time to do all the other things she dreamed about. She wanted to travel, but she wanted a cozy nest where she could cook for herself and raise a cat or two. She wanted to work for human rights and be a hippie, but she could also see herself managing a retail empire from behind a mahogany desk, like Barry. And now there were grandfathers to consider!

She had to leave her options open. That meant getting the best grades she could so, if and when she was ready to get a degree, her GPA would be good enough to get her into a decent school when she was ready. Besides, what if she got a job in the fancy antique store she spotted? They surely would recognize her quality. She'd make sure of it. She'd work as hard as she could to get ahead. Maybe in a couple of years, she would be a famous antique dealer in her own right, the kind of person who flew to Paris to buy rare vases for wealthy clients.

Most of these thoughts came to her after she had dinner with her grandfathers, and sat on the fire escape to smoke a joint, dreaming and fantasizing as the black waters of the Hudson River sparkled in the moonlight.

While attendance at school and meaningless conversations dragged on by day, every evening with Paul and Steve gave her new ideas, new information, new food for thought.

About a week into her stay with them, they got out the booze and told her the story of how they came to live in their building. She had naively assumed that since he was an artist who had gallery shows, Paul must be rich. Maybe not as rich as

Barry, but richer than most. Then they told her the full story, chapter by chapter, over the course of the first week. She learned that it was faithful saving and small investments by Steve, who worked for 30 years as a mail carrier, that kept them afloat. Paul's income had always been erratic, depending on whether his work was hot or not that year.

"Some years, we could summer on Fire Island and some years we could not," Paul said.

"More like some years we ate steak and some years we subsisted on beans," Steve said.

They bought the abandoned factory building at a foreclosure sale with five of their closest friends, three gay men and a lesbian couple. Undeterred when they saw that the property was trashed and gutted inside, they assured themselves that, as artists, they would restore the building to its former glory and better. They set to work sanding and polishing floors, rewiring the building, repairing and repainting the interiors, installing kitchens, and adding amenities like bathtubs and showers. Steve and Paul took the fifth floor, Rolf had the fourth floor all for himself, Em and Chaz took the third floor and Carl and Eddie split the second floor. The main floor was turned into three parts: a public art gallery, a private community storage space, and a big storage space they hoped to rent to local artists who lived in cramped apartments.

Finally, they held an opening party for the new gallery and named it Rainbow West. It seemed like every artist and art patron they knew attended, drawing so much attention to their commune it put them on the gay art map.

"We hosted monthly open house days where people came through our private studios. I sold pieces every single time! And then someone wrote a story about us for the newspaper and art critics started to show up, followed by gallery owners. We were sure our collective would become an institution. We all thought we were on the road to wealth and fame and there was no turning back," Paul said ruefully. "Someone called Rainbow West 'The Heart of New York's Gay Art!'"

"That was *The Village Voice*," Steve told Jax proudly.

"People started called me the gay Warhol."

"Wait," Jax said, "wasn't Warhol gay?"

"Yes, but Paul was gayer," Steve interjected. "Paul didn't even try to get mainstream interest. You know, he didn't paint soup cans. He painted penises."

"Penises are much gayer than soup cans," she agreed.

"It was more about how Rainbow West was a gayer version of The Factory," Paul said. Jax didn't know what factory he was talking about, but it sounded interesting, so she nodded. "Anyway, we wanted to be better," Paul continued. "We had plans to give visitors more of a living art experience. We were planning to build up the gallery infrastructure so it would become a work of art that would house our art, with sculpture built into the walls and one of a kind furniture we built ourselves."

"Planning," Steve said. He made quotation marks in the air.

"We were planning," Paul turned to him.

"You were planning to plan," Steve said, "but you didn't have a plan yet."

"Well, that's true," Paul said. "We were talking about it. We never got to the planning stage of the plan. Carl hadn't been feeling well for a while. He finally went to get tested and was diagnosed with AIDS and put in a hospice."

Jax gasped. AIDS!

"He died two weeks later. We were in shock. Total shock.

Everything came to a halt. We came to a halt. We were just a few weeks away from hitting our financial goal. Without Carl, we didn't know how we'd pay the mortgage. Then, after we got the news about Carl, Eddie had a meltdown. He told us he'd slept with Carl and got tested and he was HIV positive. He didn't have full-blown AIDS. The doctors told him he might live another few years if he followed their orders. He was a wreck, but he promised us he'd fight for his life. Then he vanished and we thought he went to give his parents the news in person. They lived in Long Island. He spent weekends out there sometimes. We didn't think much about it. A few days later, a cop came to the door and asked if someone could come to the morgue to identify his body. They found him floating in the Hudson River.

"No..." Jax wept. "Oh my God! Oh my God."

"Maybe we should stop," Steve said, touching Paul's arm. "This is too much for her to handle."

"No, please don't stop," she begged. "I want to know the whole story, please."

They told her about the panic that swept through the survivors. They didn't know how AIDS was transmitted back then. They had shared glasses and forks with their dead friends, kissed them on the lips, and sat on their furniture. Finally, Rolf said he was going home to Germany because he couldn't create art in a crypt.

"It wasn't just happening to us," Steve said. "Death stalked us all, everywhere we went. It was in the streets, the piers, the clubs. Everyone you met was either infected or knew someone who was. We were scared, we weren't sure we should even have sex with each other!"

Jax couldn't imagine that world. She was a child during those years, unaware of the war going on just a few miles south of her safe enclave. Occasionally, adults spoke about "the gay disease," but they made it sound like it was happening to a different species in a foreign land, not people in their own lives. Now she realized that while gay people were dying, hardly anyone, but other gay people, mourned.

"Paul really lost it. He totally abandoned me emotionally," Steve said.

"I got stinking drunk for two years. I didn't know who I was anymore, I just didn't want to be myself."

"You didn't want me to be myself either," Steve said. He faced Jax. "I became an AIDS activist because Paul became a drunk. I went to the gay center every night because I couldn't stand being around to watch him self-destruct. I decided to be as useful as I could be and to learn as much as I could about the disease, so I could protect us."

"You're a better man than me," Paul said.

"I'm not saying that, I'm just saying..."

"You are a better man than me," Paul said. "I fell apart."

"I still needed to socialize. I needed physical contact. Even if fucking had become lethal, I still needed affection to make life bearable. Paul is different," he said to Jax. "Art is his sex life."

Paul huffed. "I wouldn't go that far! But, yes, I withdraw into art, if that's what you mean."

"You withdrew into a bottle," Steve said. Paul humbly agreed. "So while Paul checked out on life, I checked in. If AIDS taught me anything it's that you have to seize the day, because the past is over, life is short, and you can die suddenly. That's what I learned from our friends dying so young."

"Is that when you had parties on the fire escape?" Jax asked. She'd been savoring the idea of sexy naked men lounging on her balcony.

"Yes, good guess."

"Is the bed the same?" Her voice had a catch in it. She needed to know if dozens of young gay men had fucked in her bed. She bookmarked that in her head for future masturbation fodder.

"No," Steve said. "There wasn't a bed in there then. It was mostly empty, like a bar back room."

Paul eventually hit rock bottom when Steve said he would leave if Paul didn't get help. By then their dream of fame and wealth had floundered. Galleries stopped calling and people stopped coming to their weekly opening.

"We were marked for death," Paul said. "No one wanted to come anywhere near us." Malicious rumors spread that the building was AIDS infested and the buyers stopped coming. "It was like people thought they'd catch HIV if they touched our canvases. It was unbelievable."

They concocted an emergency plan to recruit other gay and lesbian artists to move in, but that failed immediately. Then they considered turning it into co-ops, and making it an art co-op instead of an art commune. Again, no one was interested.

Paul started carrying his paintings into stores and cafes, slashing prices until he barely covered the cost of making them, and then he ran out of paintings he was willing to sell cheap. Steve's small but steady paycheck was their only security.

Finally, Steve said he had a financial plan. They could divide the unoccupied lofts into apartments and hang walls and doors on every floor, so it looked more like an apartment building. That would bring them other tax breaks and new loans to apply for to keep them afloat. Then they would rent them through an agency, knowing that whoever showed the listing would naturally not explain the building's recent history.

Em and Chaz hated the plan. Converting to apartments

meant the end of a shared community. Renting to strangers was the end of the whole communal foundation to their project. They would go from being queer anarchists to landlords for straight people. But they had no solution to the financial crisis.

Everyone cried together. What would they do? Only Steve knew. He found out they could secure a loan to get the additional renovations needed to bring the building up to code to become apartments. He said they would be able to live in their spaces for even less than before and earn back their losses over time.

"We don't share the same values anymore," the women said.

"This was an art project in community living," Em said. "We have to accept that it's failed. It's time for us to move on."

They told her how they emerged from the debacle. "Steve found the way," Paul said. They converted the building into apartments, they found tenants who were new to the West Village, they kept their old space on the top floor and neither of them got infected.

"Horrible times," Paul said. "We walked through hell together." He squeezed Steve's hand. "I couldn't have survived without Steve." Steve nodded and looked away, his eyes teary with emotion.

"I didn't blame Em and Chaz. The dream was over," Paul said.

"In a way, them leaving made you come back to life," Steve said.

"I had to," Paul said softly, "for you. For us. We were all we had left." He reached his hand over to Steve, and Steve kissed it and pressed it to his cheek.

It took them a few years, but they emerged from the fire together. They converted the building into apartments, they found tenants who were new to the West Village, they kept their old space on the top floor and life went on. Neither of them got infected.

Jax heard the tragedy of their beautiful dreams turning to shit, her creative genius of a grandfather who now probably had to plunge their tenants' shitty toilets and repair their leaks. It seemed sad and undignified that her artist grandpa had to literally clean up the shit of strangers. She sniffled.

"Are you still poor?" she cried.

They both rushed to reassure her, "We're okay, we're okay now."

"May I go to bed?" she asked. "I am exhausted."

She lay down with a guilt migraine, reliving their struggles in her mind. They had lived through so much. And they were so strong. Big, strong men who helped each other. How would she ever be strong enough to face life? She felt so weak inside, weak like her father. Inside, she wasn't the strong person she tried to be on the outside.

She woke up as tired as she felt when she went to bed. When Paul asked if the migraine kept her up all night, she said no. She'd already forgotten about the migraine. It was self-hatred that kept her tossing in her sleep.

As soon as she got to school that day, she went to the bulletin board to see if any jobs were posted. Maybe she could get a part-time job walking dogs. A pink flyer pinned to the board said the school was hiring two senior interns to welcome and mentor incoming freshmen and she decided it wouldn't hurt to try.

She timidly poked her head through the Dean's doorway. "There's an announcement outside for an internship. Could I apply?"

"Jax! Hello." He jumped to his feet and got a crisp form out of a file drawer. "I'm so happy you came by."

"Thank you! I'd love to get this job." She took the form and filled it out, signed it, and handed it back to him. "It would be my first job ever," she said.

"Good for you," he said kindly. "We have quite a few applicants, so don't be disappointed if you don't get picked. Selection is tomorrow, so we'll let you know when there's been a decision."

Waiting for their decision almost killed her. She could not eat, she could not poop, she could not sit still or stop herself from jumping when the phone rang, even though it never rang for her.

Finally, her homeroom teacher took her aside after class and handed her an envelope containing the words, "Congratulations, you have been selected..." and she whooped for joy.

"Congratulations, Jax!" Her teacher, Miss Sternberg, clapped her hands. "I couldn't wait to give you that envelope! You know, they only pick 2 mentors every school year."

Jax flew out of school on wings of happiness. She was delighted with herself. How did she pull it off? She wondered if some people voted for her because her father killed himself and they felt bad for her. If so, she didn't mind. She was doing her best. She was pushing ahead. Maybe orphans deserved pity votes! She began thinking about all the different groups that deserved to get pity votes to make up for the wrongs that society or their parents did to them.

She couldn't wait to tell her grandpas. Who else should she tell? Lucille. Of course. Dear old Mommy-monster. The time had come to touch base.

When she got back on her turf, she headed straight to McNulty's on Christopher for the best and cheapest espresso shot in the neighborhood. She needed the fortification. Then she walked back to Bleecker and turned left. At the end of the block, there was a bank of payphones outside a quiet old drugstore, away from the traffic.

She called the familiar number and heard the phone ring.

"Roaman residence. Who may I say is calling?"

"Hi, Honey. It's Jax. Is my mom there?"

"Why, yes, Miss. It's good to hear from you." Honey paused. "Are you ok, Miss?"

"I'm doing fine! Really good. Thank you."

"That's good, I'll get your mother for you."

It took Lucille so long, Jax had to put more coins in the phone. "So you finally decided to call me. Are you ready to crawl back yet? It's barely been a week, I thought you'd make it longer."

"It's been almost 3 weeks since you left, Mother," Jax said.

"Oh! I just flew in from the Coast, so jet lag..." Lucille's voice trailed. Jax had nothing to say to that, at least not out loud, so her mother continued, "So, are you ready to come home?"

"No," she said.

"Then why are you calling?"

Jax clutched the phone and squirmed. "I thought you might like to know I was alive."

"Don't be so dramatic," Lucille said. "So where are you staying? Are you at a hotel?"

"No," she said, "I'm staying with friends."

"What kind of friends?"

"Friends. You don't know them." She added more money to the phone.

"Are you shacking up with some old man?" Lucille cackled with amusement on the other end. Then she got really dark. "How do you know this isn't some kind of sex trafficking ring you're involved with?"

"Oh my fucking God, what's wrong with you?" Jax didn't realize how loud she was yelling until a passerby did a double take at her and crossed the street. "Look, I just wanted to let you know I'm safe and sound and that I got my first job. I wanted to give you the good news."

She waited for her mother to congratulate her, but Lucille was silent.

"You got a job?" Lucille finally said, as she'd never heard of such a thing.

"My first one," Jax said confidently. "Come fall, I'm getting a full-time one." She explored the street with her eyes. She planned to try five of the stores here, and another three on Christopher Street. She'd start with the pharmacy facing the phone booth and once she had sales experience, she'd apply to the antique store which would, one day, send her on glamorous shopping sprees to Europe.

"Then I'll pay my own way through college," Jax said.

Now, her mother laughed. "Sure you will. It will be so easy! You'll get a job waiting tables and then you'll be able to live on Park Avenue, right?"

Jax was so mad at herself. Why did she think it was a good idea to call Lucille? She knew better. It was never a good idea to call Mother. If only she acted like a normal mother for a change and pleaded with her to return, or tried to bribe her, or something, anything, that showed she wasn't ready to let her only daughter leave.

"Alright," Lucille said, "I'm not going to lose any sleep over it. You think you're a grown woman, so go right ahead and ruin your life. I won't stop you."

Jax ran home. She had to get away from the phone booth. Her feet flew over the concrete and she climbed the stairs to Paul's place so fast, she felt her heart would explode from her chest when she finally walked in. She would never make a call from that phone again. It felt cursed.

"You're a little late," Paul said. "Wow, you look like you saw a ghost? What happened?"

"I called Lucille," she said. "I'm sorry, I lost track of the time and ran back."

Steve leaned his head out of the kitchen. "You ok, sweetie?"

"I'm fine. It was fine." She stretched on the sofa.

"Did you tell her you're living with us?" Paul asked.

"No," she said.

"Oh dear," Paul said. "Why not? When do you plan to tell her?"

Steve walked in striking his newest thrift store toy, a musical triangle. "Dinnertime! If you got the appetite, I got the burgers!"

"Ooh, burgers," Paul and Jax said at the same time.

She hurriedly washed her hands at the kitchen sink.

Steve handed her a plate with a juicy burger smothered in cheese sitting on a toasted bun and a tall pile of fries that made her drool. "Here you go, princess."

Lucille was so far away now. Jax felt triumphant. She had escaped. She was never going back. The men were chatting and joking and touching each other's hands across the table.

"How about you, Jax? How was your day?" Paul asked.

"I got the mentoring job," she said quietly.

"You did?! That's wonderful, honey!"

"We're so excited for you!!!"

She blushed. "I got lucky. The Dean let me submit past the deadline. It worked out."

"Nice! Sometimes luck gets you further in life than hard work," Steve said. "Never look down on good luck. Celebrate it."

Paul was beaming at her. "Of course, we knew you'd get it. We just didn't know if they would recognize how magnificent you are, dear Jax."

Her young cheeks burned so hard and her smile froze so hard she could barely speak.

"Oh, Grandpa, no, really, it isn't a big thing."

"It's big enough for cake!" Paul said.

"Cake!" Steve said. "Huh. You know we have a cake!"

"I know we have cake," Paul said. "I found where you hid it."

"You know I wanted to save it for the weekend. This is for Jax, right? This isn't just your way of getting me to open the cake early, is it?"

"Well..." Paul ran his hand through his hair. "Can't it be both?"

Steve wiggled his eyebrows. "I knew it!"

They all giggled. They were relaxed. Their exchanges were warm and jovial. They kept grinning at each other and included her, too. They were so happy tonight. There they were, being a happy family together. They were her true family. They were her strength now.

They devoured the cake with their hands like wild animals, stuffing chunks in their mouths, their cheeks puffed out like chipmunks and crumbs falling from their lips.

"Caaaaake," Steve said, his words muffled by pastry crumbs,

"the staff of decadent life!"

"Caaaaake," Jax and Paul chanted, "caaaake, caaaake, caaaake!"

The final months of school passed quickly. The dependable routine of their daily lives was the best antidepressant she'd ever had. Her grandpas lived by a standard daily schedule. They got up at 7 am and shared breakfast. They did chores in the morning and Paul painted while Steve shopped and ran errands in the afternoon. Sometimes Paul went to meet with a gallery owner and fellow artists to drum up business, but he always tried to be home by 7 pm so they could all have dinner together. Sometimes they watched television together, sometimes they played Boggle. No matter what though, it was lights off at 11 pm. The grandpas retreated to their room while she went to hers to play computer games and smoke pot on the fire escape.

She had never realized how chaotic her parents' lives together had been, how random, how counter-intuitive. They fought the same stupid fights over and over again. They held grudges against each other. They could have easily talked about it, like civilized people, but they never did. She thought that was what marriage was: you get married and then spend the rest of your life fighting for dominance, each side wanting to be the only right side, each side wanting more control over the marriage and children and property. Everyone said marriage was hard work. That's what they meant by it.

Her grandpas lived more like best friends. They had a system of basic rules she found easy to adapt to. In fact, she loved their rules. They were practical.

For example, when Grandpa was in his art studio, no one, not even Steve, was allowed to disturb him when he was in "creative flow."

"Creative flow," he defined it for her, was "a state of altered consciousness in which you let go of all assumptions and explore with pure eyes, eyes don't expect, but which merely inform the spirit of what you see, a mystical state so rarified that it vanished when disturbed."

To fuck with the flow was perilous! Steve tiptoed around in his socks to dust furniture when Paul painted.

It was driven home to her one day when she got home, still singing to the music in her earphones. Paul snuck up behind her and pulled the plugs right out of her ears. She nearly jumped out of her skin. She twirled to see him behind her, his big feet splashed with paint, like a hobbit that had stepped into sticky rainbow puddles.

He brandished his brush at her, staring so fiercely that she cried, "Oops!" and fled to her bedroom, leaving the earphones still dangling in his hand.

There were other rules. The rooms on the north side of the apartment were off-limits unless it was an emergency or they invited her in. His studio was strictly forbidden, and they didn't want to find her alone in their bedroom or bathroom either.

She understood that some things in life needed to be compartmentalized, like her father's office was. Other things were more a matter of privacy. She didn't want to catch them naked in the shower, or God forbid, having sex in their bedroom.

By the end of a month, it felt like she'd been there a year. She could barely remember how she'd lived before. Her headaches and stomach-aches were diminishing, her appetite improved, her insomnia was going away. She felt more alive. She couldn't remember the days when she seemed to cry more than she laughed anymore or the nights she went to bed feeling sick instead of hopeful and still giggling over comments made earlier that day.

She wanted to be more like Steve. He acted happy-go-lucky but, underneath, he was sober and shrewd about how to deal with the shit-storms of life. She could tell he was at peace with himself, which fascinated her. She had read about the fabled "place of peace" but she never saw evidence that adults ever found it until she met Steve. She was convinced that, whether or not he knew he had it, he really did know the secret to life. She began spending every free hour she had running errands with him and helping him with chores, in hopes his wisdom would transfer to her.

At first, she thought he wouldn't want her trailing at his heels everywhere but, with his usual calm grace, he made her feel welcome and began planning extra adventures for them. He took her to thrift shops and church flea markets in the West Village, used clothing stores in the East Village and used furniture stores in Chelsea. They took buses and subways all over New York City, from the Cloisters to Coney Island. He taught her the importance of coupon clipping, and how to know if a melon is ripe, where to buy the best meat and the freshest fish, and how to bargain down prices. Once, he found a table in a junk store in Chelsea piled with vintage hats and called her over in excitement.

"Do we need hats?" he asked her.

"Maybe," she said, picking through the crazy pile of old church lady hats with feathers and veils. He tried on a pink bonnet while laughing uncontrollably.

"Oh, hey you. Nice to see you! Can I help you?" The clerk, a guy in his 40s with a nose piercing and a cobra tattoo on his neck, sashayed over to Steve like he knew him.

"Just browsing, just browsing." Steve dismissed him with a wave. The salesclerk looked hurt and returned to the lawn chair he set up by the front door to sulk. Steve made her try on a cone-shaped millinery concoction that sat at a comical angle on her head and covered her face and neck with a waterfall of dotted black lace. It sported bright red feathers on top that made it seem as if a bird had taken a nosedive into the pointed end, leaving its tail feathers behind.

She examined herself in the mirror. The hat was ridiculous but the veil made her look mysterious, even vaguely sinister. She checked the price tag. Paul pushed her hand away and said, "Never mind that, I'm buying."

"I can't let you," she weakly protested.

"Let your grandfather buy it for you!" The salesclerk must have heard him because he jumped off the chair and started walking back to them.

"Aw, is this your grandkid?" He smiled at Jax.

"Yes, John, this is my beautiful granddaughter and she really wants this hat, but I can't pay what's on the price tag. Can you do better?"

"I guess I can knock off 5%." The guy went to the cash register to ring them up.

Steve whispered, "I think I danced with him at last year's Pride."

"Aha!" she nodded wisely.

"Now observe the master at his work!" he said.

"Make it 15% and you have a sale."

"I can't," he said, "10% is my best offer."

Steve grabbed Jax's arm. "In that case, I guess we'll pass." He led Jax to the door. She was disappointed they were leaving the hat behind, but sucked it up.

"OK! Fine, 15%," John called after them. "Just rob me blind, everyone does." Steve took her back to the counter and paid.

"So, I'll see you at Pride?" he said to Steve.

"Wear those assless chaps again so you'll be easier to recognize," Steve said. "I barely recognized you with all those clothes on."

John turned bright red, and Steve led her out, flourishing the hat bag proudly.

"Did you see how I did that?" he asked her once they were on the street.

"Oh my God," Jax finally squealed. "I love you, Grandpa Steve. You are so... far out. Like really fucking far out." She worshipped him.

Steve chuckled and patted her shoulder. "I think you're pretty far out yourself. Hang on." He pulled the hat from the bag. "Let me put this on you." She stopped and he arranged it on her head, positioning the veil to cover her face. "Perfection! Wait until Paul sees you. He's going to love it." He hugged her.

She felt like another person in the hat -- more grown-up, more mysterious, more enticing. The hat and its veil drew a lot of looks from passersby. A couple of men even slowed their pace to stare at her. The hat was her super power! It made men react to her like she was a grown sexy woman. She felt the heat of their hunger in her blood.

"Holy shit, that hat!" Paul greeted them. "Very impressive."

"She looks like the Duchess of Windsor, doesn't she," Steve said.

"I'm thinking more of a 1930s femme fatale," Paul said. "I mean, look at her. Tall, slim, elegant and a veiled hat! Adorable!"

"Get ready for the man parade," Steve merrily warned Paul, "she's going to have suitors lined up in rows!"

Jax walked to the mirror hanging over the sofa and tried to see herself through their eyes. She did resemble a femme fatale from old movies. The veil added shadows and mysteries to her eyes and bone structure. Was this her? Could she grow up to be the femme fatale of her dreams? The thought cracked her up, but was it true? Did she have that potential?

That night, she kept tossing the hat around in her mind. One minute she was an invisible teenager on an outing with her grandpa and the next she was a grown-up seductress smiling from behind a veil. She never realized clothes had so much power. She always loved the sinister outfits she'd seen in fetish photos, from the bizarre thigh-high boots to the anonymizing latex hoods. If she could transform herself with just a hat and veil, imagine all the other illusions she could spin with clothes. If she could learn to be as self-assured and centered as Steve, as generous and free-spirited as Paul, and if she could afford the fetish outfits that turned her on, she could rule the world!!

Nothing was holding her back except her fears. But why was she still so afraid of her kinks? She didn't have to hide her true self anymore. She came out to her grandpas and they thought it was cute that she was kinky, maybe bi. She couldn't shock them. If she wore a leather skirt and vest, they'd probably tell her it was adorable. She could wear all the buckles she wanted now. Her grandpas wouldn't scream that she was mental, much less force her to take psychiatric drugs or stick her in a parochial school to punish her for being depraved.

Her grandfathers weren't anywhere near as crazy as the parents who banned him from her life and lied to her about him. Paul and Steve had seen her at her worst and still they welcomed her in and let her know every single day that she was loved. Her grandpas would always find a way to love her no matter who or what she grew up to be. Dr. Frank was right. She wasn't a problem child. Her parents were problem parents.

She jumped out of bed and got the hat, then got back under the covers and reached for the vibrator hidden between the mattress and the wall. She slipped the head of a bulbous wand into the sweet cavity between her thighs and turned it on. Her pussy became electrical, pulsing and throbbing in time to the vibes. She fantasized being a world-famous seductress, the kind of woman who catches everyone's eye when she steps into a room. The kind of woman that men could not resist and who women would want to emulate. She fantasized about sitting on a throne, with men crawling at her feet, begging for her attention, while she gaily laughed into a glass of pink champagne.

In seconds, she came so hard she bit the pillow to stifle her groans. She'd tangled the sheet with her writhing, and had to unpeel it from her drenched thighs. She slid out from under the bedding and lay naked on top of the bed to cool off. She idly played with her breasts as her erect nipples softened and shrank back to normal size. She felt completely emptied of anxiety, completely at peace.

She stared out the window from her bed, looking down on a world where lights glimmered and flickered all night, where people never stopped working and fighting and fucking, in a metropolis that was constantly awake, restless, alive. New York was constantly changing. She could change, too.

Chapter 3

IN AND OUT

Sometimes, you know the minute you see someone that they are different from all the others. There is some quality about them, some intrigue they possess that magnetizes you. You want to get close to them. You need to. That was how she felt when she showed up for her first day at her first job and saw that Booker was her teammate in the mentoring program.

He was tall and slim, with a mocha-colored complexion, a mop of tall hair, stylish outfits and a fine blue scarf. She'd never spoken with him before because they traveled in different circles: hers were mostly female classmates who formed their own sisterhood. He hung out mainly with the athletes and swim team. He was one of the best swimmers at the school and his lean body rippled with energy. But there was much more to him than that. He was deep. He talked about real things. There was an otherness about him that matched her otherness. All the things he wanted to pursue were things his rich father didn't want him to pursue -- from cooking to psychology, to art classes and stage design. This sense of displacement and powerlessness in his own life resonated with her. By the end of their first shift, they were friends and went out for a long cup of conversation at a local cafe. By the time she got home that night, she was in love with him.

Side by side, day after day, he opened up to her and told her about his dreams of becoming a Broadway actor or a psychologist or a famous chef or maybe all three. She talked about Barry and Lucille and how she ran away to live with gay grandfathers she didn't even know existed. He talked about how his father pressured him to take a job to teach him the value of money, but all he wanted to do was live. She told him that was all she wanted to do. They gave each other high fives and took an oath of silence. They vowed then they would never keep secrets from each other or betray each other.

Soon they weren't just friends but best friends and confidantes, who hurried to school each day and greeted each other effusively. They wandered Broadway, hand-in-hand, a tall, young, beautiful couple, who color-coordinated their clothes so they always looked like a couple. They drew wishful glances and admiring glances, and sometimes smiles from children, but also looks of disgust and disapproval.

They were above it all. They didn't need to be admired by anyone but each other and other people's feelings about them barely registered. She began skipping breakfast at home to meet Booker at "their" coffee shop for fresh bagels and lox. They returned for lunch to drink coffee and share a basket of french fries. They walked all over Central Park and visited the Museum of Natural History every week. They held hands and when they hugged they hugged like soldiers going off to war, not knowing if they'd hug each other again.

Booker became her boyfriend, her best friend, her social planner, and her sugar daddy. He phoned her every night, saying he missed her and wanted to hear her voice. He took her to museums and movies and shows, he showered her with gifts. He gave her his signature blue scarf to wear around her neck, and she never took it off except to bathe.

All her sex fantasies now revolved around him and the earth-shattering day he would take her virginity, when she would finally know bliss in the arms of a man. On that day, their bond would be cemented. He would bare his heart to her and tell her she was the woman of his dreams, that he wanted to marry her someday and raise the world's happiest children together because they would have learned from their own parents' mistakes and would raise them utterly differently.

Lust engorged her body and clouded her mind. Her breasts ached, her labia swelled. Words froze in her mouth. He seemed equally love-struck, but he was cool about it. He hugged her easily, kissed her cheeks and lips impulsively and told her how sexy she was. Any minute, she thought, he would take her someplace and ravish her! In her late-night fantasies, it happened in dark alleys or behind a tree in Central Park, but she would have settled for a cheap hotel.

She couldn't quite bring herself to fantasies about him doing kink with her. It was one thing to imagine anonymous submissives debasing themselves, but did she really want that from a boyfriend? Or a potential husband? It seemed disrespectful somehow. She didn't even know if he was into kink. And right now, fucking was a bigger priority for her. Just visualizing his hard penis and her dripping pussy naked together, made her gush. In a way she was relieved. That made her more normal.

When he invited her to a dinner at this father's house and introduced her to his family, she felt more secure about the relationship. This was the first step on the road to engagement. His family occupied a distinctive brownstone with tall gates on a tree-lined street on the Upper West Side. They were greeted at the door by a butler and ushered past a lavish wood staircase to an enormous dining room in back. She smelled the vague odor of lemon polish on the carved handrails as they passed. The floors were made of oak.

Mr. Dodson, a somber white-haired man in gold-framed glasses and a hand-tailored gray suit sat in an elaborate chair at the head of a long wooden dining table. The formal dining room was furnished with expensive antiques and family heirlooms. People of different ages filled the chairs on either side, except for two chairs closest to Mr. Dodson, on his right hand side. Mr. Dodson motioned Jax to sit next to him and she got shy, so Booker gently pushed her into the chair and pushed her chair in for her.

He leaned in and whispered, "Sorry if that was awkward. I think Dad just wants to get to know you. OK?"

"Oh, sure," she blushed. This was going to be a test! She wasn't prepared for a test. She thought she'd just vanish into the background. She glanced at the guests. She was the only white person in the room. So much for vanishing! Some of Booker's relatives gave her strange looks and shook their heads, so she focused on her plate and took small portions from platters, so they wouldn't think she was greedy.

Mr. Dodson asked her a few questions about herself and her dreams in life. She told him she was taking time off before college to get work experience and see how far she could go in a business career. She sounded confident, ambitious, optimistic. Soon he was smiling at her and urging her to put more food on her plate.

"So you like my son?" he asked in a low voice.

She whispered back, "I love your son."

"I do, too, girl," he said. "If you can make him happy, I'll be happy."

She put her hand over her heart and beamed at him.

A few minutes later, an elderly lady in a high-collared shirt noticed that Jax was only eating meat and potatoes, and began spooning veggies onto her plate. "Child, you gotta eat your greens," she commanded.

"Yes, ma'am," Jax said, wondering what manner of vegetables were in the wet pile of wilted dark leaves now on her plate. She didn't want to appear even dumber than she knew she had sounded earlier, so she ate it politely. It wasn't half bad. It was chockablock with savory ham that cut the bitterness of the greens.

She marveled that the woman had called her "child." It felt so motherly, as if the woman was accepting her into their family, and she was now one of their family's kids. After that everyone loosened up and Mr. Dodson gave her a hug when she left.

"Am I the first white girl you ever brought home?" she asked Booker over the phone when she got home that night. "Your relatives seemed weirded out at first."

"You're the first GIRL I have brought home," he said.

"Reaaaaaalllly?" Her heart jumped. She was the only. She was his only. The dinner felt like a huge turning point in their relationship, but was it? She was haunted by anxiety that one day he would vanish as suddenly as he'd appeared in her life. She wished he'd give her a ring, but that wouldn't prevent a violent attack, a robbery gone wrong, a car accident, a sudden catastrophic illness. She got headaches thinking about him. What would she do without him? How would she live? Her fear of losing him was so intense she was afraid to let anyone know just how weak she felt inside.

"You were perfect tonight. My dad was impressed. I love you," he said.

She hung up the phone kissing into it. Tonight she wouldn't

worry about losing him. She would only think positively. Not only did she have the smartest, handsomest and richest boyfriend, she had won affirmation from a sophisticated, powerful banker, a man who knew who's who and what's what. Plus, as she shrewdly observed from the antique heirlooms and fantastic china, it was old money. Very old money. The one thing that Lucille could never even pretend to be, could never become. When Jax married Booker she would become part of the old money world. Revenge was sweet.

From then on, he started calling her babe and hung on her words. Their relationship was perfect except for their sex life. Their sex life sucked. Even when they had a few precious minutes alone he would stop her from reaching into his pants, whispering, "Now's not the time," or, "Someone could walk in on us."

It was never the time for him. It baffled her. She thought boys always pushed for sex. She thought sex was all that men thought about. And here she was, offering it outright, at the legal age, at the right time in their lives, with the man she loved.

"Books, you know I never was with a boy, right?"

"Yeah. You seem a little hung up about it, babe."

"I'm not hung up. I'm just horny." She giggled.

"Who isn't?" he said.

"And you told me you've never been with a girl..."

"Yeah? So?"

She paused. Why wasn't he putting her two and two together and adding it up to "fuck me now?" If she was still a virgin and he was still a virgin, it was only logical that they'd devirginize each other and live happily ever after.

"We should have sex," she said. She took his chin in her hand to make him look her in the eyes. "I mean, it's only rational, right?"

"Ah, how romantic when you put it that way," he said. "Like we should do it because it makes sense, not because we want to."

"Don't you want to?"

"Of course I do, babe. We just haven't found the right moment yet."

She wanted to cry. How many more days or weeks of tormented desire would she have to endure? How long would she have to wait before he finally shared his dick with her? Was it possible he didn't have those kinds of feelings for her? Was he afraid of sex? Was it possible he didn't jerk off??? What if he had a genital deformity and didn't want to show it to her because he thought she would reject him.

"How do I get a guy to sleep with me when he's afraid?" she asked Paul and Steve during dinner one night.

They made a big show of pretend-choking on their food and she folded her arms grimly. They wouldn't joke their way out of this question. She was firm.

Finally Steve said, "Do you mean Booker?"

"Who else? I'm worried I have more feelings for him than he has for me."

"Is he worried it will hurt the friendship?" Paul asked.

"I'm not sure," she said.

"What do you think is holding him back?" Steve asked.

"I think he feels we're too young, like it is a really big deal and maybe we should wait."

"That's a legitimate reason," Paul said. "You are both so young. Maybe you should wait another year or two." He calmly sipped his drink. "Or ten."

Jax gave him a sour look.

"Invite him to stay over this Saturday night," Steve said.

"Steve, really?" Paul complained.

"Oh, please," said Steve, "we just celebrated her 19th birthday. Let her be 19." He turned back to Jax. "Paul and I are going out Saturday night, so you'll have the place all to yourselves for several hours. See if he accepts the invitation, and if he does, well, he's the fly and you're the spider." Seeing her confusion, he added, "I'm saying that maybe you just need to take the lead here."

Jax fanned herself excitedly. She had no idea she could invite a boy over for the night! Or that she could be the spider. It made perfect sense. She COULD be the spider. She had spidery fantasies of putting men in bondage and watching them suffer.

"Thank you, Grandpa Steve!"

"Oy vey," Paul said.

"I'll make chicken parmesan before we go out and all four of us can have dinner together." Steve started planning the menu. "My granddaughter's first lover! OMG."

"Please ignore him," Paul said to her. "We're definitely not telling you to have sex. In fact, I'd rather you waited. But I agree that you are old enough now to be alone with Booker. Whatever you decide is none of our business," he added, turning to Steve. "Right, Steve? We don't want the details of her sex life."

"Mmmm... speak for yourself, I want them. Let an old man have a few vicarious thrills, Paul!"

"Are you sure you're not my genetic grandfather?" Jax threw her arms around his neck and kissed his cheek with gratitude. He was so good to her and he didn't have to be.

She called Booker, half expecting him to make up another lame excuse about his study load at school. She couldn't handle another rejection from him right now. If he said no, it meant he really wasn't ready to have sex and if he wasn't ready, she didn't know if she could wait for him to get ready.

"Wow," he finally said. "Really? Paul is ok with that, babe?"

"He is now," she said brightly. "Steve suggested it. They're going out for the night, too, so we will have the place all to ourselves."

"I see," he mused. "Well, cool, that's great, babe, I'll pack a bag and be there by 5!"

Jax hung up the phone feeling triumphant. Then she trotted back to her bedroom and hit the vibrator. She was going to have sex with Booker four days from now. Four days till adios virginity, aloha sexy-ass womanhood.

Everything was going according to plan. She couldn't wait to feel his naked skin against hers. She needed to know how he tasted, how his sweat smelled, whether his cum would be bitter or sweet in her mouth. Booker filled the gap in her life. She needed to feel him all over, in the ultimate act of intimacy two humans could share.

She'd finally given herself permission to start adding BDSM toys to her fantasies about him. It wouldn't be anything like her biker gang fantasies. She couldn't imagine her handsome boyfriend dressed in heavy leather. She saw him in a leather harness on his chest and a leather G-string that showed off his round ass. Instead of thick clunky motorcycle boots, he'd wear soft, gleaming riding boots. Her vibrator's motor died and shot off a fiery spark that almost burned her in the middle of this gripping fantasy. She got dressed and went emergency shopping at the closest sex shop so she could come home and finish herself off. Desperation led her down Hudson Street, where crowds of men in black leather were standing outside of bars. She waded through the sea of leather, so turned on she could barely concentrate. Finally, she darted into the store, picked the cheapest vibrator in the glass case, and loped home to explode with built up tension within seconds of turning it on. Then she did it again. Then she did it more.

Booker arrived at Paul's house on Saturday dressed in a sexy black T-shirt and tight black jeans. When she saw him standing in her doorway, her pussy throbbed so hard her knees wobbled.

"Nice!" Booker walked in eagerly, admiring the penis art on the walls, the red rug and the all-white modern furniture that contrasted so wildly with the stuffed red couch. "Where do you sleep?"

"Oh, we have separate wings on either side, behind the painted walls," she said. "It's very private here." She looked at him meaningfully, but he didn't pick up on her clue.

Her grandpas had spoken to him by phone a few times, but this was their first face-to-face. Paul walked in and shook hands with Booker, inviting him to sit at the dining table. They exchanged a few niceties, talked about Booker's classes at Columbia and chatted casually until Steve joined them. Booker bonded almost immediately with Steve.

"I need to know what's in that sauce! It smells fantastic. Will you tell me your secret ingredient?"

It was all Steve needed to hear. "Come into my kitchen and I'll show you!" They left, chirping about red sauces.

"What do you think?" she asked Paul.

"He's very handsome," Paul said. "Very energetic and I can tell he's smart. He's well put together too, like a model. I wasn't expecting that. But most of all, he's in love with my granddaughter, so I know he has good taste."

"Good," she said.

She thought she'd feel excited about his approval, but she was too distracted by lust. During dinner, while the men expertly shoveled food in their mouths between laughter and conversation, she could barely eat and floated inside her own head. She could barely concentrate on what they were talking about, and they had to repeat her name to get her attention. All she could think about was Booker naked in her bed, what his cock and ass looked like naked, whether she could get him to cum and whether he could make her cum, and what it would feel like when he was inside her? Would it hurt? Or would it slide in like it was always meant to be inside her? She was quivering on the precipice of adulthood. She craved to fall into its abyss.

Finally, her grandfathers rose from the table and got their keys and phones.

"It was so nice to meet you." Paul shook the young man's hand. "I look forward to seeing you again, soon?"

"You will," Booker said. "You definitely will."

Steve opened his arms to Booker and Booker leaned in for a vigorous hug. She felt an odd twinge watching her grandpa hold her future husband in his arms. They were alike in some ways, but while Steve was frank about sex, Booker didn't like talking about it.

After they left Jax asked, "Wanna see my room?"

"Sure!" Booker followed her past the wall and down the hall, into her hidden paradise.

"What's in the locked rooms?" Booker asked.

"I wish I knew," she said.

"Ooooh, secret rooms with hidden treasure. I love it. Adds some spice, right babe?" He followed her into her room. He whistled when he saw the views. "You can see the whole city from here! It's beautiful, babe."

"Check out the balcony!" She raced to the window and beckoned to him.

"This is cool! Your very own window on the world," he said. "You could even grow some herbs out here in the summer."

"One sec." She ran inside and got a joint from the lamp's built-in box. Booker was now sitting on the iron steps, his legs sprawled out so she had to thread her way through him to sit down. She settled next to him and his arm wrapped around her. They shared a long deep kiss, then she fished the joint out of her shirt pocket and waved it under his nose.

"Oh, yeah, babe, great idea!" He lit it for her.

They passed it back and forth, huddling together. She wanted to live in every moment with him. She would always remember this night, their first night really alone together, really adults together, with the city at their feet and their bed just on the other side of the sliding glass door. In a few hours, she could officially call herself an adult, a full-grown woman. They finished the joint and went back inside. Booker walked to her desk and sat in the chair.

"Do you want to sit on the bed with me?" she asked timidly.

"Uhhh, sure, babe. Ok. I wasn't sure where you wanted me to sit."

"It's more comfortable."

"Ok." He sat on the bed next to her. She waited for him to grab her. Instead, he slipped down onto his back and closed his eyes. She lay down beside him, also on her back, and waited. Where was he taking them, she wondered? He had deep kissed her on the fire escape, but now when he was in the perfect position to ravish her, he looked like he was about to take a nap.

"I'm thinking of moving out of my aunt's place," he said, eyes still closed as if the lids needed to be down for him to articulate the situation. He wanted to be closer to campus, he said, and freer to socialize. He kept talking about missed social opportunities and extra-curricular activities he wanted to sign up for.

"Do you or don't you want to have sex?" she finally blurted out. Her question shut him down. She didn't care. She needed a definite answer. The ship of her desires was crashing on the cliffs of his monologue. "Yes or no?"

"OK," he finally said. "We should, right? I mean, we love each other, right babe?"

A wave of desire seized her. Did he just say he loved her? Yes, yes he did. He, too, believed they were meant to be! He was finally ready to take the next step in their commitment to each other and fuck their asses off.

"I love you so much, Booker!" she cried. "You're the love of my life."

He began kissing her and grinding against her just like in her fantasies. She started pulling off her clothes and tried to hurry him out of his.

"Let me help you." She grabbed his belt buckle and pulled his pants to his ankles. He was wearing white mesh underwear! Thank God. She was afraid he'd be in tidy whities. The mesh undies were a thousand times cuter.

"You are so hot!" she said. "I can't believe how fucking hot you are."

He pulled off the underwear. She had never seen a fully naked male in real life before. He had never seen a fully naked female. They played with each other's fingers and hands as young lovers do. They brought their mouths together softly. Their timid tongue-tips touched in kiss. His mouth tasted of cinnamon, dark cherry and marijuana. His tongue was slow and sweet in her mouth. Her arms circled him and pulled him into her core and there she clung, wrapping her legs around him, and letting herself go completely into the wonderment of sensuality. Finally, she pulled away and sucked air into her lungs. His penis wasn't standing straight up, the way penises did in porn.

"I'm sorry," he began to apologize.

"It's okay, you stay still." She put her hand over his mouth to hush him. "I'll do everything."

She surveyed him hungrily. His lean body was flawless and firm, like a young athlete's. The skin on his thighs was silky, but his legs had coarse hair and his feet were like a tiger's paws. She wanted to kiss them, but was afraid he'd think it was weird if she suddenly went for his feet.

His penis was long, with a narrow head that reminded her of Cupid's arrow. As she stroked and pulled, she stared at his balls. She had never seen a scrotal sac in motion. His balls were like sea corals, mysterious, eyeless, rippling to unseen waves.

She slid her palm over his cock and gripped the shaft softly, letting her hand dance up and down and then tightening her grip to stroke him more vigorously. Now his cock looked just like the ones in porn movies. A vein bulged and pulsed, the head turned almost purple.

He stopped her hand. "I won't be able to hold back if you do that," he said.

"Don't hold back," she told him. "I want to see you come. Let me see you come."

She continued to stroke, watching his face. He threw his head back and grimaced, the muscles in his face tensing, his eyelids squeezed shut. Then he grunted and wailed as milky juice rushed out of his member in a forceful stream that splashed his chest. She wiped it off with her t-shirt while he rested and caught his breath.

"OK, your turn," she told him. She got on her back beside him and waited. He was still recuperating. She took his hand and guided it to her breasts.

"Your skin is so soft," he said, his hand tentatively roaming. His touch was so light it felt irritating, so she moved it away.

"Do you like them?" she asked.

"Boobies," he said, "who doesn't like boobies?"

The way he said that made her uncomfortable. It sounded so immature coming from Booker. She wasn't sure why. "Are you sure you do?"

Without warning he rolled her onto her stomach. His sudden passion, the touch of roughness, the wildness of rear entry made her lust come roaring back. For one long moment, she thought he was going into the ass. As his cock poked and prodded her ass cheeks, his erection raged back to life. Suddenly, he was entering her pussy from behind, pushing and grinding until he penetrated the depths of her vagina, filling her up with feelings that made her head swim with ecstasy. They merged into one organism, thrusting and writhing. The walls melted and they were fucking in the sky, his strong hips rhythmically pumping over and over, her pussy on fire. She finally grabbed at her clit in front and buried her face into the pillow to muffle screams of pleasure and fall into a coma of bliss.

She was still half-dead when he pulled the pillow away. "Did you come?" he asked. He looked concerned. "You screamed so much. I didn't bust your leg or something?"

"I came. Oh God, I came. Did you?"

"No." He looked down at his cock. It was completely soft. "I don't think it's going to happen for me a second time tonight."

"Maybe it'll come back."

"I guess. I need to pee and get a glass of water. Would you like me to bring you water?"

"Alright." She closed her eyes.

"OK." He hurried out. "I'll be right back. Say, do you mind if I shower?"

"Sure, of course. Mi casa es su casa."

It seemed antiseptic to take a shower in the middle of sex, as if you were afraid of getting cooties or couldn't handle the smells. Or did he think they were done with the sex? She thought sex was a big deal that lasted for hours. That was the impression she got from the women's magazines she read. She checked the old digital clock. Fucking only took about five minutes. That couldn't be right. She was ready for at least one more orgasm.

Booker returned ten minutes later, freshly scrubbed and carrying two glasses of water.

"Let's sit on the fire escape and smoke," he said, walking past the bed and stepping outside.

She got out of bed with the blanket around her and joined him, passing the joint back and forth in the moonlight. She didn't know what to say and he didn't seem to have anything to say.

"Did something change between us? Are you sorry we did it?"

"Of course not, nothing has changed," he said. "I just didn't know what to expect. I told you it was my first time."

"OK," she said.

"It'll get better," he said.

"You're right."

This was probably how it was at first, before you really learn what you're doing. They'd get past it. After all, they had done everything on her bucket list for the night -- they both had orgasms, she got to play with his penis and he devirginized her.

By the time they curled up to sleep, they were themselves again. After that, Booker started staying over every Saturday. He began taking her on lavish dates to restaurants, Broadway shows, concerts at Lincoln Center, and dance clubs. When he realized she didn't have the wardrobe to keep up with their weekend social calendar, Booker surprised her with 2 shopping bags full of designer clothes in her size. She became a regular at Dodson family dinners and Booker's dad became like a second father to her, always insisting she sit beside him at the table.

Her sex life got better too. Booker showed more interest in her pussy and didn't mind going down on her as long as she kept her pubes closely trimmed. His favorite position was doggy-style, which helped him to fuck her for longer sessions without losing his erection. One night, they fucked for a solid hour and when he finally came, she came with him. Then he proposed to her and she accepted even before her heart stopped pounding from her orgasm. They didn't talk about that afterward, she knew it wasn't a real proposal yet, but she decided then she would give herself to him fully and forever, with all the passion in her heart. He was her forever man!

As winter drew close, their mutual energy for sex began to wither at the edges. Sometimes he would send her home by cab straight from a club, saying he had to study the next day. There were still wonderful Saturday nights together, but, more often than not, he left by midnight so he could get up early and work on a school project.

Having a boyfriend wasn't nearly as much fun as she had expected. She worried that her love of vibrators was hurting her ability to get turned on by him, so she stopped masturbating. This made her feel dependent on him for orgasms. Now, she never seemed to have enough orgasms or the right kind, the kind that left her breathless and satisfied to her core.

Their typical interaction was a "get the job done" sort of thing. He'd lean her against the glass doors so they could see out to the streets. As he slid between her butt cheeks to penetrate her pussy, he'd grab her lips in front the way she taught him, and a few minutes later, they were finished. He would immediately shower and come back fully dressed. She was so frustrated she wanted to scream.

"How's my favorite pumpkin?" Paul asked her one day.

"Getting moldy."

"Noooo," Paul said. "What's up, buttercup?"

"Oh, you know," she tried to sound nonchalant, "man problems."

"Man problems," Paul said. "Oh."

"Grandpa, what do you really think of Booker?"

"We love him. You two are so cute together. Why?"

"I don't know," she said, "he says he's serious about me, but he doesn't seem as interested in me as before."

"He's here every weekend!" Paul said.

"I mean... in the romance department." She paused. "Our sex life sucks."

"Oooooh. I see." He shifted uncomfortably. She could tell he didn't want to hear and wished she would stop talking.

Steve was eavesdropping from the kitchen and walked in. "Maybe it's stress," he said. "Does he have a lot of stress in his life?"

"Well, yeah." She thought of his intense school schedule and demanding father. "I guess it could be stress."

"That's probably it," the men assured her.

She decided they were right. Anxiety was eating her alive. She needed to stop worrying and get a job. While Booker worked on his future success in academia, she would work on hers in business. She picked out a uniform for herself: a black sweater and matching black skirt with cute flats. Booker's blue scarf was knotted around her neck for good luck. She had neatly listed every cool shop she wanted to hit from Sheridan Square to Hudson Avenue. That was her first-tier list. She picked up an old fashioned school notebook at the drugstore, titled it "My Career Journal" and copied the list onto the first page. The rest of the notebook would document her rise to success.

Armed and prepared for triumph, she headed out confident she'd land a job by the end of the day. Instead it took her a week to visit them all, one by one, waiting to see managers, sitting outside on sidewalks until they returned from lunch.

No one was interested in her. No one. They made her feel like a naïve, unqualified idiot who wasn't good enough to sweep their floors. She drowned her misery in coffee shops. She crossed the stores off her list, one by one, adding notes on why and how they had refused to give her a chance.

She made a list of second-tier places in the notebook, including some of the cafes and bars in the neighborhood. After that, she had to make a list of third-tier places, like the hardware stores and drugstores.

She tried 44 stores without luck and decided she had to look further afield. She reluctantly decided to cross Sixth Avenue and take her chances with the flashy trashy stores that lined W. 8th Street. She'd sell boots, she'd sell books, she'd serve sushi, she'd work at a juice bar, she didn't care. She just wanted a fucking job. When they asked why she wanted the job, she was truthful: "For a paycheck."

She stopped taking notes on her rejections. Her success journal read like a bitter epic on her shortcomings as a human being. She ended up throwing it in the hopper of a parked garbage truck and watched the truck eat it with grim relief.

She began scouring Help Wanted ads and felt vaguely optimistic when some employment agencies told her to come in and fill out an application. Only one place, with the weird name, "Gordon's Girls," actually let her speak with an agent.

"Go through that door to room 3. You'll be seeing Kay-Lee Kartin."

She tugged on her skirt and blouse and tied her hair back to look even primmer. This could be her only shot. She put Booker's scarf in her purse, in case it looked too flamboyant for business. "Gordon's Girls" sounded like a Las Vegas stage show, or some rich guy's harem. Those would be more interesting, actually, than a 9 to 5 in the suck-hole of human existence known as midtown.

Kay-Lee Kartin waved her in and told her to sit down. She was a middle-aged lady in a flowery red dress. Under her stiff helmet of black hair, she wore thick glasses that made her eyeballs disconcertingly huge. She had Jax's application on her desk and was reviewing it line by line.

"You're an interesting young lady. Private schools, good grades, a debating award, you even speak a little French," she said. "You aren't related to the rich hardware guy, Barry Roaman, are you?"

"What!" She didn't realize her father was famous. "Yes, I'm his daughter. I was. He passed last year."

"I know!" Kay-Lee said. "We heard he killed himself." She shook her head. "It's always the rich ones." She turned thoughtful and said, "You know, I don't see many girls like you. Which is why I have to tell you that you'll never be happy doing menial labor."

Jax agreed. "Thank you! I need something stimulating! Something creative! I was hoping maybe you could put me in marketing?"

"What I meant is, you don't have any office skills, so I'd have to send you out to be a file clerk. Then you'll get bored and quit in 2 weeks and we won't get our commission."

Kay-Lee thought she was a quitter! Jax stared at her resentfully.

"A girl like you should be in college! Or getting married. You don't have to work, do you, with a rich father?"

Jax was afraid she'd howl if she opened her mouth, so she looked at the floor and confined her defiance to her head.

"I'm just being honest. You don't have office skills or even any work experience. Again, I could place you as a file clerk, but you'll get bored and quit after 2 weeks."

"You don't know that," Jax slowly fought back. "You don't know me! You don't know I'd quit."

"You're what we call high risk. We can't have employers thinking we send out untrustworthy people." The eyeglasses pointed to the door. "I'm sorry, but your time is up."

Jax walked all the miles home from Gordon's Girls to Grandpa Paul's, brooding and stressing. Did she really want to end up like Kay-Lee, trapped in a windowless office for the rest of her life, sharpening pencils and getting coffee for the boss?

She went home defeated, got into bed in her black clothes, and only emerged to change into pajamas, sleep, and show up for dinners for the rest of the week.

Whenever one of her grandfathers tried to get her to tell them what was wrong, she denied that anything was wrong so vehemently, that they finally stopped trying.

When she got a job offer from Gray's Papaya on 8th Street on Friday, telling her to come in on Monday, she didn't know whether to celebrate or to kill herself. The pay was crap, the work was shit, and the polyester uniform shirt made her feel like a ton of trash stuffed into a 13-gallon bag. She took the job anyway. The agency experience taught her she didn't just need a job, she needed job experience to prove she wasn't a quitter. Her grand hopes were turning into putrid mush, one papaya at a time.

Her life became a constant cycle of mopping floors, wiping down counters, and carrying heavy boxes of fruit from the storage area to the front. She developed a habit of popping Tylenol all day to ease her back pain and struggling to find a comfortable position in bed. The back pain forced her to buy a pair of orthopedic shoes, so between the uniform, the shoes, and the cap she had to wear in the store, she felt miserably unattractive, even to herself. When she and Booker first met, they were equals. Now she was Cinderella to his Prince Charming. While he had moved on to a witty, rich college set, she was a lowly high school graduate working in a juice joint.

Where was this all going? For the first time, she regretted leaving home. If she'd followed Lucille's wishes, she'd be in college now, too, learning new things, making new friends, not worrying about money. She could be at Columbia, part of Booker's crowd. She still could have found Paul. She didn't have to run away.

A brutal anomie set in. Some days, she pretended she was a robot. She picked a path along streets without any shops or memories of rejection and walked it automatically, not looking left or right. She was the machine who served customers, silently enduring rashes where the cheap uniform pinched her skin.

After three months, she didn't feel like herself anymore. She slept fitfully, dreaming about getting trapped by endless piles of papaya.

One night, she fell asleep at the dinner table and her grandpas had to help her to bed. She felt so run down, she tried to get out of a dinner at Mr. Booker's house scheduled for the weekend, but Booker insisted she had to go with him. She rushed home after work and changed into an ice-blue dress he'd bought her and made it just on time. She made it through the cocktail reception, but began to drowse over her food during dinner. Booker saved her from nose-diving into the tiramisu and plied her with coffee.

As guests left, Mr. Dodson invited Booker and Jax to the library for their habitual after-dinner chat and nightcap. The last thing she remembered was sitting down in an armchair outside the dining room, too tired to walk the long carpeted hall, and telling Booker she would catch up with him in a few minutes. She checked her watch. She had passed out for almost two hours. Now the house was still, except distant voices.

She strained her ears. The voices were coming from the library. She removed her heels and crept along the carpet towards the door, then froze. They were having some kind of a fight. She'd never heard them fight before.

"Why would you do that?" Mr. Dodson was yelling. "I didn't raise a liar! You hear me, son? This is going to blow up on you."

"Everything's fine, Daddy," Booker said. "You're getting upset over nothing."

"Nothing?!" Mr. Booker bellowed. "If you thought it was

nothing, you would have told her by now."

Jax's ears perked. Which "her" were they talking about? HER her?

"Did you ever consider that this could be the answer, Dad?"

"Son, don't you know how much I've prayed on that very thing happening," he beseeched him. "But not by deceiving a girl."

Deceiving a girl? What girl?? Her heart raced.

Booker stepped out of the library, his eyes dark and flaming with rage. He was taken aback to find her standing in the hall in her stockinged feet.

"Come on, babe, we're leaving," he said. He hurried them out of the house and hailed a cab. They rode home in silence. She was still half asleep, but her confusion had turned to paralyzing anxiety. Was she the girl he'd deceived?

"What did you hear?" he asked her when they were a few blocks away.

"Just that your father was angry about something you're doing or did? What set him off? Why was he yelling?"

Booker stared stonily out of the window. "He never trusts me. That's the real issue. He just never trusts me to know what I am doing."

"But what was the fight about?" Booker had never looked so unhappy. He kept staring out of the window, avoiding her inquisitive gaze.

"I'm gay," Booker said.

"What do you mean?" she asked him. His words made no sense to her. "Is that a joke?"

The cab suddenly turned hard onto Bleecker St. and the driver's eyes briefly met Jax's in the mirror. She saw pity and contempt in his eyes.

"Driver, stop here, we'll walk the rest of the way," she said. She didn't want to spend another minute in that taxi.

Booker didn't question the sudden stop. He pushed some bills at the driver and they both climbed out at the curb. They walked apart, like strangers, Booker hugging the curb while she walked behind him down the middle of the sidewalk. The quaint streets were silent and icy winds blew up from the Hudson. The blast of cold finally woke her up. She sprinted and caught up with him, grabbing his arm.

"What do you mean you're gay? Is that a joke?"

"That's what we were fighting over."

"Why does he think you're gay?" she asked. Her voice came out funny, like someone else was speaking,

"I'm sorry, babe. I never knew how to tell you." Books faltered. "And, I, well, I didn't think it mattered. I thought maybe we could make this work, you know?"

"Never knew how to tell me what?" she said.

"That I'm gay."

"You're," she hesitated, "gay gay? Like you prefer boys to girls?"

"Well, mostly," he said, "but I always wondered if maybe I could be bisexual."

"So... You wanted to sleep with me to find out if you were bisexual?" Her brain felt like an elevator that went out of control, zooming up with breathtaking speed, then plunging down as if into a deathly abyss, then zooming up again.

"It's not like that, babe," he said. "I love you."

His declaration didn't move her. This wasn't happening. She wanted to go back to sleep and wake up and find out it was all a stupid dream, a very stupid, hurtful dream.

"All those times you had to rush home and hang out with school friends, were they gay friends who you had sex with?" She remembered calling him a couple of times and thinking there was someone in his bedroom with him, but he always denied it.

"No," he said. "Maybe once or twice," he admitted. "Look, it's not like it was a regular thing, babe. You're the one I love," he said. "They were, you know, just experiences."

"Is that why you always did it from behind? Were you pretending I was a man?" Her voice got shrill.

"Babe, calm down." He put his hand on her shoulders. She was beyond calm. She shrugged him off. She was dead.

"You said you were a virgin," she screamed.

"Well, I was! A virgin with a woman. You were my first, babe."

"Stop calling me babe," she ordered. He looked crushed.

No wonder nobody would hire her. She was literally the stupidest person in the world.

"We have to break up now." She burst into tears. "Everything is a lie. Everything."

"No we don't! We can get past this. Lots of gay guys marry women and have families," he said. "There are probably more of them than there are guys like Paul and Steve."

She didn't know this Booker. He was an alternate Booker, a selfish evil lying version of her boyfriend. She broke into a run for the door of Paul's house.

He ran after her and caught up with her at the front door, blocking her way in.

"Jax, think about it. You already live with gay men and you're happy, right? I fit in better with your family than with my own. We could make it work. You could take lovers if you want. I mean, anything is possible for people like us."

"Grandpa thought marrying Grandma would fix things. Look how well that turned out."

"Jesus, this is a totally different situation. We love each other for all the right reasons. You're not your grandmother and I'm not Paul."

"You can say that again," she sneered. "So do you wear condoms when you fuck men or do I have to get tested now?"

He gaped at her. "Oh my God, Jax, stop, please. You're tearing everything between us down."

"You already did exactly that."

She wanted to shake him and slap him and kick him. She wanted him to take her in his arms and tell her it was just a joke gone horribly wrong. She wanted to hold him and make them whole again. But she couldn't. It was all a lie.

"If you could be honest with yourself for one minute, you'd know you don't want me," she said. "I could tell you were already getting bored."

Booker stared at her, his eyes dark with pain, his lips gaping, one hand over his heart as if he was holding it to stop it from breaking apart.

"Jax, don't," he softly pleaded with her. "Don't break up with me because I'm gay," he said.

"You lied to me," she growled. "You made me love you based on a lie. You gaslighted me." She pulled herself up, pushed past him into the building and hurled her final insult. "And you were a lousy lay."

Her anger dissipated as she climbed up the stairs. She let herself into her grandpa's apartment and went to her chair. She stared at the couch as if she'd never noticed before that it was ornately embroidered red velvet, as if she had never noticed the intricate patterns of the gold threads, as if she hadn't even seen the thick fringe along the bottom, as if she was in a new house with new furniture she was seeing for the first time.

Paul sauntered in, still dressed. Apparently, he'd been waiting up for her to return.

"Oh no," he sighed when he saw her tear-stained cheeks and tensed lips. "What's wrong, Jax?"

"I broke up with Booker," she said.

"What?! Why?"

"He's gay," she said.

Steve appeared, wearing pajamas. The three of them looked at each other helplessly.

"I told Paul I got that vibe from him," Steve gasped. "But he seemed so in love with you."

"Not now, Steve," Paul said. "Jax, I'm so sorry. So terribly sorry."

"He's been cheating on me with his male college friends," she said. Her grandpas shook their heads sadly.

"Can we talk about this tomorrow? I'm dead."

They hugged her and kissed her, murmuring comforting words. She let them fuss over her, feeling empty inside as a stuffed toy, then pulled away and went to her room.

They couldn't understand. No one could. Even she didn't understand. It seemed impossible to understand how the love of your life could never love you the way you loved him. It was degrading that he could only get hard by fantasizing you were a man. It dawned on her that even if she could forgive him for lying, she couldn't stand being married to him knowing that, deep down, he wished she had a different body, a different gender, and a dick.

She lay in bed, staring at the ceiling, unable to stem the tide of tears washing down her face. There would be no miracle rescues, no exciting opportunities, no financial redemption. She would never be anything but a broken, lost, fatherless child. She'd failed at everything she wanted in love and in life. Shitty job, shitty salary, shitty boyfriend, shitty everything.

She wanted to die. It would be easy enough to jump off the fire escape or walk down to the Hudson and jump in. But she couldn't. She couldn't do that to her grandparents. They didn't deserve that. They were her sole bastion of unconditional love. She hugged herself tightly and controlled her trembling. As long as they were alive, they gave her reason to live.

೮ Chapter 4 ೮

AMAZON RISING

If you lived in New York, maybe you heard it on the news. Maybe you shook your head and felt sorry, or sighed and thought, "What a shame." Or maybe, like a true native, you said, "Just another day in the Big Apple," because you've run out of fucks to give about things that don't directly alter your life.

As far as New York tragedies go, it was an ordinary one. A car crashed into a bank near a hospital; one pedestrian was pronounced dead on arrival. Jax was busy serving juices when she heard it on the radio. After that story, there was news of a shooting in Queens, a drug bust in the Bronx, a sting operation on Staten Island, two stabbings in Brooklyn, and a traffic accident on the Major Deegan that claimed two lives. She shrugged and carried some garbage to the back. By the time she got back from the dumpster, a body was found on Staten Island and an unidentified man was stabbed on the Upper West Side. That was life in a metropolis. As long as it didn't happen to your family or on your street, it was swept away by the ineluctable tides of city life.

She was a different Jax from the one who broke up with Booker just a few months earlier. She was somber and philosophical. Frowns came to her more easily than smiles. As she numbly pumped cups of juice and cashed people out, she thought about the merciless ebb and flow of existence. She was impermanent. Relationships were impermanent. Life was impermanent.

The life and death of her relationship with Booker flowed contiguously with her recent obsession with mortality. Steve once told her, "For every death, there is a new birth. For every human tragedy, there's a human triumph."

She thought about that a lot. The death of her relationship with an abusive mother had led her to warm security with her grandpas. The death of her relationship with Booker meant she was free to explore her sexuality more freely. She dodged a bullet there. One day, she'd be 40, and the only man who'd want her then would be her husband. But if her husband didn't want her in the first place, how would he feel about her then? How would she feel about him? Would she turn into the eternally disappointed, dissatisfied Lucille, barking day and night about how he wasn't man enough for her?

A shiver went down her spine and she sighed heavily. In the end, she and Booker both got what they wanted. He wanted to find out if he could fuck a woman and she wanted her first fuck to be with someone she loved. But any future between them was doomed. She would spend her whole life waiting for a complete love he would never feel. And imagine if he found his Steve, and fell madly in love with him. How would she feel to see him enjoying a level of happiness and satisfaction she could never provide?

Was it even real love if it was based on a lie? Or was she just a girl with daddy issues who wanted emotional stability so badly she didn't see the red flags even when they flapped in her face? It didn't matter. It was over. She'd made new plans.

She shouldn't have yielded to her heart. A few weeks after the break-up, he called her and it took her days to return the call. Then he started texting her late at night. Then it was "good morning, beauty," and, "I love you," every day. Then he asked her out to lunch and she wasn't ready, and the texting dried up.

She thought they were done until a month later, when Booker just happened to volunteer to distribute flyers and petitions for the local LGBT center where Steve volunteered. The table was set up on the corner of Christopher and 7th Avenue, the stellar core of the West Village and in the direct line between the juice store and home.

She was walking home on a warm spring day in sloppy jeans and a t-shirt, old-lady shoes on her aching feet, when she spotted him. The unexpectedness of it, the ache of helpless loss hurt so much, she ran back towards Sixth Avenue, and took the long way home.

After a week of avoiding him, she began resenting him. It felt like a dirty trick. He knew she would pass by there sooner or later. It was an ambush. She was tired of walking an extra half mile to hide from him.

She decided to confront him. She changed into a slimming summer dress with a cardigan and low-heeled sandals at a bathroom in a bookstore across the street before walking home that evening. She dabbed pale melon lipstick on her mouth and added several new coats of mascara to her lashes. Booker was on HER turf. She swayed her hips emphatically as she walked. He was not going to see her looking like trash.

She wove through the chaos of traffic and approached the crowded table. A sexy gay guy was sitting next to him, while passersby pretended to be interested in the literature. Booker looked happier than ever at the center of the crowd. Booker had changed. He wasn't wearing scarves anymore. He looked a little leaner, less cherubic and a lot hairier. He'd grown a neat little beard on his chin and let his hair go natural.

When he spotted her crossing 7th Avenue, Booker ran out from behind the table and grabbed her up in a tight hug.

"It's so good to see you," he said. "I was hoping I'd bump into you some day."

He bent down for a kiss, but she turned her head.

"Come on. You gonna be like that?"

"Like what?" She asked him ingenuously, because she knew what.

"Cold to me, like we're strangers," he said. "Babe, you broke up with me, not the other way around."

When he called her babe a spike of sadness shot through her. As betrayed as she felt, she recognized that he, too, felt loss. He lost his dream of turning himself straight. He lost his dream of having a wife and children. Maybe he even lost his best friend. That was a grief they both shared.

"I'm sorry," she said. She grabbed his hands and squeezed them. "I know."

"Ok. Yeah. Come on, sit down and tell me what you've been up to. You look tired. Are you working hard at that place, what is it, Orange Julius?"

He let her whine to him about the indignities of her job, the stubborn stupidity of the customers and her slave-driving boss, Tony, who yelled whether he was angry or not. Booker listened intently, touching her arm, giving her tissues to wipe her tears. She left feeling empty and uncertain. Did this mean they were friends again?

A few days later, she returned. He greeted her enthusiastically and this time she returned his kiss. Whatever happened happened. He was still the only one she could cry to.

She became a regular visitor after her day job ended, sitting with him and handing out flyers. Being the token woman was a kind of uncomfortable she could handle because she'd experienced it so many times with her grandfathers. She pretended she didn't notice him flirting, or men writing down his phone number. It was strange to see him touch a man's face and hair the way he had touched hers. She had no rights to him now. She had not just given him permission to be gay, she had made it clear that it was wrong to lie about it. Well, he wasn't lying now. He was acting as gay as gay could be, from his impossibly tight pants to his effusive conversations with other men.

One night, she arrived to find him involved in a long conversation with a man she'd never seen before. He waved at her to sit down and gestured he'd be with her in a few. She sank into the seat and removed her clunky work shoes. She pulled off her sweaty white socks, rolled them up and pulled a pair of high-heeled sandals from her bag. She suddenly noticed a passerby had stopped to stare at her naked feet the way some men stare at boobs.

She idly wondered if he was one of those foot fetishists she'd read so much about. Apparently, they were as turned on by feet and shoes the way other men got turned on by breasts and vaginas. Impulsively, she fished the sock from her bag and gave them a quick sniff, making a nauseated face. Then she pushed them to the bottom of her bag, and wiggled her toes. She slowly slid her feet in the sandals, then raised them to let the shoes dangle from her toes, smiling as if she'd never seen a finer foot in a sexier shoe. She sneaked glimpses of him and, sure enough, he was frozen to a parking meter, leaning on it for support and watching her with fixed attention. He WAS a fetishist! Wow, she had finally encountered a real-life pervert.

She strapped the sandals on her feet as slowly as possible, ran her fingers over her feet as if making sure every little strap was adjusted perfectly. Then she suddenly stuck her feet under the table, where they were hidden by the tablecloth.

As she did, she shot him a knowing, scornful look that said, "I know exactly what you were thinking, you dirty boy."

The man blushed furiously and scampered away in shame. She watched him retreat with a cold grin. She felt victorious. Triumphant! That guy would be jerking off to her feet tonight, maybe for weeks or months to come. He was more excited by her than her ex-boyfriend ever was.

Booker was still talking to his mystery friend. The guy seemed about 20 years older than Booker, but his body was buff and his gray hair luxurious. He had broad shoulders and a small waist that she envied. She couldn't tell if there was sexual energy between them, but their conversation was intense. She yawned and stretched her arms on the table and passed out.

"Jax, I'm sorry. Jax?" Booker touched her shoulder gently. "I didn't mean for it to go so long, but he's one of my professors."

Her eyes popped wide. She stared blankly at Books. "I'm awake. I need coffee." She felt humiliated. The last time she passed out like that, it was at Booker's father's house and when she woke up, he was gay.

He fetched her a mug of lukewarm coffee. "Sorry it's from the thermos. Been sitting here all day. Tell me if it tastes bad."

She gulped it. It tasted like muddy shit. "It's fine."

"I'm worried about you, Jax," he said. "You look terrible."

"You always sucked at compliments." She drank another sip and spit it out in disgust, handing him the cup. "I can't." In the old days, he would offer to run to a nearby cafe and bring her a fresh cup. Now he remained motionless.

"I'm serious. I am worried about you."

"NOW you're worried?" She had to bite her tongue from completing the rest of her thought.

Booker's warm golden eyes were mournful. He was looking at her with pity, the way he looked at old ladies pushing shopping carts filled with junk. It's like he finally realized she was a working-class girl in a minimum wage job now.

"It's been an adjustment," she said as she pulled herself up. "But I'm in line for a promotion now. I'll be in management by the end of the year." It was a lie, but a lie that made her realize it was time she stopped cringing in anxiety and ask Tony for a raise or a promotion or, hopefully, both.

"Is that what you want to do with your life? To manage a juice stand? Is that you?"

"It's a job, Booker, it's not ME or my whole life."

But even as she said it, she doubted herself. She had applied for over 100 jobs and this was the only place that wanted her. Surely someone else would recognize her potential or take a chance on her. But the facts had shown that this actually was the best she could do, at least for now.

"You wouldn't understand," she said, standing up from the table. "You're too rich to understand how normal people even live."

"Jax, please, hang on a second." He dug into his pocket and pulled out a cool green Benjamin. "Buy yourself something," he said.

She stared at the money. It was free money. She could buy a new dress and eat at a restaurant and still have money left over.

"No," she said, "no thanks. I don't want your pity money."

From then on, she always took the long detour home. She was wasting her life by obsessing over Booker. She would find her path in her own way, without his help. Maybe she would devote herself to a career in business. She had a good head for numbers and learned fast. She got more praise from Tony in a day than the others got all week. She lost track of how many times he named her "most valuable employee of the week." It was a stupid award, but it still made her feel good to see her picture framed on the wall, with customers noticing it and smiling at her like she was special. In a few months, she would have one full year of work experience. She could leverage that into another, slightly better job. And then another better one, and then several promotions later, she would rock the world.

Tony would be proud of her. She would go back to Kay-Lee and show her that she was not a quitter, she was never a quitter. One day, she'd be rich and successful, and then she would have the last laugh. She'd have her own private office with a male secretary! And, who knew, she could open her own business some day after she saved up a nest egg. She had ideas for a deluxe line of cupcakes that looked like cats and dogs. No one could resist a cat or dog cupcake, could they? She would call it Cupcake Critters. She had it all planned out. By age 30, she'd be a millionaire from Cupcake Critters.

After a week of composing her speech in her head, and another week of practicing it, and more weeks of avoiding it entirely, she went straight to Tony's door one morning and knocked.

"May I speak to you? In your office?"

"I'm in my office right now and you are speaking," he grunted, looking over a ledger and checking inventory numbers. Tony was short and as wide as a delivery truck, with thick little arms that hung at 45 degree angles from his trunk. His thick brown hair was slicked back with a wide comb that left ridges so deep it looked like his head was crenellated.

She faltered. "I meant an appointment?"

"Oooh, you want an appointment! That doesn't sound good." He snapped the ledger shut.

"It's not bad!"

"You're gonna ask for a raise or promotion and hurt my feelings, I know it." He whipped through his day calendar. "Three pm good?"

"Today?"

"No, yesterday." He paused. "Yeah, today. Now get to work."

"Yes, Sir! Thank you!"

She was absurdly delighted. There was room for her to grow in this job. She went back to work, putting extra elbow grease into the counter wipe-downs for her internal boss. Nothing would stop her. She was getting a raise! She could tell by the fact that Tony didn't start yelling at her.

As the clock ticked, she rehearsed her pitch to Tony in her head. She reviewed her strong points. She was a hard worker. She got there early and often worked late. She was the first one Tony called when he needed someone to fill in and she never turned down a chance to make some overtime. She was really the employee of the year. That had to be worth something.

A few minutes before 3 pm, a ghost appeared before her eyes. Mr. Dodson was standing in line at her counter, waiting patiently for her to serve the two people ahead of him. She kept glancing at him. Why was he here? She spilled some juice and then she dropped a cup. She got a weird feeling in her stomach. Something bad had happened. What if Booker was the guy who got stabbed uptown? She panicked. But Mr. Dodson looked so calm. That couldn't be it.

"Hello, Jax," he said when he finally reached the counter. "Can I speak with you privately outside?"

What did he want? She looked at the clock on the wall. It was 2:53 pm.

"I can't leave my station," she said.

"Please, just five minutes."

Tony was in the back, talking to a delivery guy.

"I can't," she said. "The boss won't like it." Tony was a compulsive clock watcher and penny pincher. Anything could trigger drama. If you left work one minute before your shift ended, you were a thief, outright stealing from the company. Showing up late for a meeting that she had requested could send him into a rage and ruin any chance of a promotion.

She whispered, "Please order something." Then loudly and cheerfully said, "What would you like to order, Sir?"

"Juice!" He said crisply. Then he, too, whispered, "I promise it will be worth your while."

"I can't, Mr. Dodson," she whispered. "I just can't. Not now. Can I call you tonight?"

"Jax," he wouldn't give up, "we're practically family, aren't we?"

She sighed. How many times had he invited her home for dinner and treated her like a daughter? How many times had he taken her and his son to Broadway shows and restaurants? He'd never been anything but nice to her. Breaking up with his son didn't give her the right to be rude to him.

"Okay," she muttered. She followed him outside, jittering with anxiety.

"Is Booker ok?"

"This isn't about Booker," he said, "it's about you."

"Oh." She didn't know what he meant by that, but she didn't have time to analyze it. She had to get back inside. "So what's up?"

What if he was to try and engineer a reconciliation, to try and talk her into forgiving Booker and dating him again? She couldn't let him. She'd worked too hard for a promotion to let him suddenly insert himself at the worst possible moment to beg a case that was already lost. "I really have to go." She turned to walk away.

"Stop," he boomed. Suddenly she saw him the way his minions did, acting as if he ruled the world, and expecting automatic obedience. Her back went up. She owed him gratitude for his former generosity, but that didn't mean he could order her around.

He stepped closer and put his arm around her, giving her a tight sideways hug. "I miss you, Jax."

"I miss you too, Mr. Dodson." She let him hug her. "I'm sorry, it's just a really busy day here, I really need to get back."

"Book told me a little about your situation and asked if I could help you. I tried to think of a job at my company that would be right." He put his hand inside his suit pocket and pulled out an envelope. "But then I decided this would be a better way." He extended the envelope to her.

She opened the envelope. It contained a check for $30,000.

Suddenly, she realized there was a loud thumping coming from the store. Tony was banging on the window, ordering her back. She couldn't hear what he was saying, but his mouth was moving angrily and people inside were staring at him in shock. The clock on the wall behind him said 3:02.

"Are you sure?" she said to Mr. Dodson. "I mean, you're giving this to me?" She stared incomprehensibly at the beautiful numbers. "Why?" She'd never had so much money at one time. She could last a year on that, maybe even longer if she got a roommate. She could go to school!

"It's an old family tradition to give the new generation financial support to get started in life. I've done it for all my nieces and nephews and quite a few cousins over time. It seemed right to help a girl I thought would be my daughter-in-law."

She cut him off. "Please... don't."

"OK, I won't."

The awkwardness was unbearable. They looked at each other, unsure what to say next.

"Thank you, thank you," she burbled, "you have no idea what you've done for me, you saved my life."

"I know you'll use the money wisely." He patted her back. "You're very smart and much stronger than you think. You'll need to find that out for yourself, though."

She watched Mr. Dodson get into his waiting limo in wonderment. She didn't know what Booker told him. She didn't want to know. She could walk away from $100 pity money, but thirty thousand dollars was a miracle! She looked at the check again. It wasn't just money. It was freedom! She could quit and look for a better job. She could take classes at The New School in the fall. She folded the check and inserted it into the left cup of her brassiere close to her heart. Her entire future rested on her tit.

Tony was still banging. Feeling mad with joy, she twirled and bowed deeply, like an actress at curtain call, her smile stretching ear to ear. She removed her cap and threw it into the street. She merrily waved goodbye and flounced off. She couldn't wait to get home and tell Paul and Steve that she was rich!

She gloated for two blocks before slapping her side and realizing she'd left her purse at work. Now she galloped back, so embarrassed that she missed a step and tripped on a grate. She stood up painfully and limped as quickly as possible to get her purse. She patted her left breast to make sure the check was still there and was relieved to feel it.

"Oh, so you decided to come back." Tony stood by the front door, her purse in his hands. "I thought you'd want this." Servers stopped serving, customers swiveled their heads towards her. Before he could stop her, she snapped it out of his hands, squeezed the bag against her chest and sprinted away.

Tony came after her, shouting, "Aw, no, what the fuck?!" And then, more emotionally, "You shouldn't have thrown that hat away. It was a good hat!"

"I paid for it," she snapped back. "I'd throw away the uniform right now if I had clothes to change into."

"You know, I thought you were a classy girl. This isn't classy. And what about our meeting?"

"I quit."

"Good, that spares me from firing you." He turned his back on her and waddled back to the store, cursing and gesticulating.

She didn't care. Fuck her job. Fuck papaya. She'd never eat one again. Fuck it all. She was free! She bounced along the street exuberantly, swinging her purse, stopping to reward herself with a cappuccino, and savoring the complete happiness of fantasizing about all the ways she could use her windfall to advance her life.

She was going to get a new outfit and take herself out to a fancy dinner wearing it. After that, she would follow Grandpa Steve's advice and create a strict budget that would sustain her until she found another job or founded Cupcake Critters. Her back-up plan was to become a travel agent and get free trips around the world. She felt set and ready to start a new life and skipped the last block home.

She unlocked the door, shouting, "I have amazing news!

AMAZING!"

No one answered. She poured herself a glass of wine and sat by herself to drink it. Paul was probably stuck at a gallery. His work was having a sudden revival after a favorable review in a local bar rag described him as "eternally surprising, fiercely pro-gay," and a short but generous review in the Arts section of *The New York Times* which said he was "a pioneering spirit who shed light on the forbidden."

Now his days were a heady mix of long phone conversations with people he'd lost touch with, gallery owners who wanted to show his work and acquaintances who cut him off when the commune collapsed. Friends were inviting them to vacation with them in Spain, Greece and the Hamptons, and the gay community center was planning to give him an award. With the renewed attention, he put all bad memories aside. He generously forgave all the betrayals, the gossip, being ostracized. She'd never seen him so happy.

As for Steve, he had an appointment somewhere to get his cholesterol checked. He probably stopped on the way home to pick up groceries. Or maybe he found a bargain he couldn't resist.

She idly browsed apartment ads in *The Times*. Now that she had a big wad of money, she would find a small studio close to Paul's house and set up her own life. She would give her grandparents some money for the time she spent with them and she'd keep the rest in the bank. She hoped the next job would cover her rent, but if she needed to draw on the money, it would be there to help her through that first year.

The house was still quiet by the time she'd circled half a dozen places to call. She walked to Paul's studio to peek inside. Canvases were leaning against the walls and paints were stored away. She knocked lightly on the bedroom door. There was no response, so she knocked on it hard. Still nothing.

She took her wine to her bedroom and stretched on her bed. She woke up suddenly in the dark. The house was still silent. She walked into the living room and realized no one had turned on the lights yet. This was odd. She brewed a pot of coffee for them to share when they got back and filled a small thermos for herself.

It felt creepy in the house, so she went downstairs to wait for them. Steve might be carrying heavy bags, so she would help him bring them upstairs. She spotted the tattooed pierced neighbor and walked over to him. By now, they were street friends. His name was Alfred.

"Shouldn't you be helping your grandfather now?" he asked.

"Yeah!" she said. "I've been looking for him. Do you know where he is?"

"I think at Bellevue."

"What?" She laughed at the joke. "Are you saying my grandfather is in a mental ward?"

"At the morgue, honey." He cocked his head inquisitively at her. "Don't you know?"

"What do you mean? Know what?" Paul was dead? That was impossible. Paul couldn't be dead! She spoke to him that morning. No way was Paul dead, or in a mental ward, or even at a hospital. She felt angry at Alfred for making such a cruel joke.

He stuttered. "They didn't tell you?"

"Tell me what?"

"Oh my God," he said. "The whole block has been talking about it all day. Steve died in a car accident this morning. Such a tragedy." He hung his head. "I'm so sorry, Jax, and I'm even sorrier to be the person who had to give you the news."

She ran back to the house as if she was on fire, and up the four long flights. The dark silence of the house was terrifying. She quickly flipped all the light switches on and began walking back and forth, checking rooms and surfaces, looking for clues. Finally she spotted a piece of folded paper that had fallen off the sofa to the rug. She picked it up and read:

We're at Bellevue, 421 East 26th. Hurry!

It wasn't signed, but she knew Paul's handwriting, from the long lean letters to the perfectly even lines.

She breathed a sigh of relief and nervously tapped her shirt. The check was still there. Now she removed it and was alarmed to see that the date was slightly smudged by sweat. She lay it flat on top of her writing desk with a pencil holder on the fold, and ran out of the house.

She roved the streets until she saw an empty cab, then fidgeted the whole way to the hospital complex near the East River. She'd never been to this part of town. It looked deserted, even threatening. A sudden rain descended and traffic came to a halt.

"Can you get around this mess," she asked the cab, as the traffic got even worse on 3rd Avenue, with cars and trucks barely moving and impatient horns blaring.

"Sure," he said, "I'll just pull out the wings so we can fly."

"My grandpa is at the hospital!" she shouted.

"New York," he said skeptically, "land of a thousand stories."

She gave up and went back to obsessing over the scant information she had. Paul had written "we," which meant Steve was alive and they were together. There was hope! His injuries weren't fatal after all.

At last the driver pulled up in front of the Medical Examiner building.

"That's $14.30." He stopped the car and began scribbling in his log.

She looked at the plain brick building. "Are you sure this is the right entrance?"

"This is the address you gave me," he said.

She handed him a $20 without waiting for change and headed through the doors and into a reception area.

"I'm here to see a patient," Jax said. The nurse behind the counter searched the computer's patient records, but couldn't find a Steve Salzburg listed in any of the rooms. Jax told her he was in a serious car accident that morning. The woman studied her records again. "Oh," she said abruptly. "I found him."

"Oh, thank God," Jax said. "Is he going to be ok?"

The woman stared expressionlessly at her computer. "Just go through that door, walk to the end of the hallway, turn left, walk to the end of that hallway, and then take a seat in the waiting area. Someone will be with you shortly."

Jax walked in a surreal nightmare. The walls looked like paper and the floor muffled her footsteps. She felt like a ghost trapped in the basement of a haunted house. She wasn't ready to see him with tubes sticking out of him and machines keeping him alive.

She came to her last turn and saw a bank of orange chairs lined up by the wall. At the far end, she saw swinging double-doors with a big sign that read "DO NOT ENTER." She noticed a little old man sitting on one of the plastic chairs. He was bent over, his hands covering his face, his body shaking with sobs. Something about him looked really familiar.

He suddenly looked up. "Oh thank God you're here, thank God!" His eyes were red and sore from crying.

Paul was unrecognizable in his grief. His shoulders looked

narrower, his hair looked thinner, his hands trembled.

"It's all over, Jax," he said numbly. "My life is over. Steve is dead." She rushed to him and he clutched her like a dying man.

"No," she said. "He isn't. He isn't dead." She kept saying it as if her words meant it was true.

"He is," Paul said. "It's over." He sobbed. "I have nothing to live for now." He choked on the word, "NOTHING."

She wept. "Oh no, this isn't happening."

"Thank God I have you. Thank God you're here."

He told her what had happened as best he could. Steve was on his way back from a routine check-up to his long-time doctor somewhere near Bellevue. He called Paul around lunchtime to report that the doctor gave him a clean bill of health and said all his numbers were perfect. His sugar and cholesterol levels were the best they'd ever been. When Steve told the doctor he wished he had proof to show his partner, the doctor scribbled an A+ at the top of a printout of his blood work results and signed his name as a joke.

Steve left the office happy and crossed First Avenue. A speeding car sideswiped him, knocking him into another car, which threw him into the wall of a bank at the corner. The Medical Examiner was still trying to determine which of the impacts killed him.

"The EMTs found the paper with his blood work in his pocket, soaked with blood," Paul said.

"Oh, Grandpa," she said, crying with him. "Grandpa, no. Oh, Grandpa," she repeated, unable to find words. Now she remembered the little story that swam by with the morning news, that car accident in Kips Bay that killed someone. Steve was that someone. How could life be so cruel, so random?

"My life is over." Paul wept openly.

"No, it isn't, Grandpa," she said. "No, it isn't over. It isn't. You still have me. You said you have me. I'm here."

"Yes," he said, holding her hands between his own. "Thank God for you. But... I never got to say goodbye to him." He wailed. In the ghostly vector outside the silent morgue, it sounded like the agonized roar of a dying lion.

From that moment, everything was a blur. Time sped, time slowed to a stop, time whirled, time crawled, time felt endless. Neither of them could find their feet.

The following day they did what adults do when someone dies. They contacted authorities and banks and credit cards and filed papers and signed statements, arranged funeral services, authorized cremation according to Steve's wishes, ordered flowers and split a list of over 100 people to notify. They did everything they were supposed to do, everything relatives are expected to do, and then crawled off to their respective bedrooms to cry and grieve and do it all over again the next day.

The funeral service was held at a small Jewish temple on Charles Street. People stood up to speak to the urn holding Steve's ashes. Jax went to the bathroom to throw up. Paul collapsed as he walked to the front and was carried back to his seat. The rabbi asked her to deliver the eulogy. Jax had prepared a few words, but standing before the packed room, she suddenly opened her heart wide and proclaimed her love for him and how he and Paul were the best parents, the only parents, she had ever known and raved about her grandparents and their love for each other. When she finished, the crowded room full of mourners applauded.

She ran to Paul and flung herself into his arms. The applause grew louder behind her. He felt stronger now. He was more Paul now. He whispered into her ear that he was proud of her and that her eulogy was better than anything he could've said and that they would be ok, they would get through it together.

"Let us take care of him," one of the people who had helped Paul said. "I'm Em, by the way." She shook Jax's hand. Jax saw a second woman right behind her.

"Chaz?" she asked.

Chaz gave Em a smug smile, a look of, "I told you so."

"We weren't sure you knew about us, but we're glad you do!" Em said.

Chaz put her arm around Jax and kissed her cheek. "You're practically my niece."

"Chaz, let her breathe," Em said. "Jax, why don't you take a break outside, get a breath of fresh air?"

Jax was afraid to leave Paul's side. She was terrified he'd have a heart attack from the stress. Em caught her mood.

"We know how to take care of him. We've all been here before together. Let us help him, and let us help you by giving you a few minutes to yourself." She smoothed Jax's hair and Jax bowed her head. "Ask one of the people in a lawn chair for coffee and tell them you're Jax."

"Thank you," Jax murmured. Em and Chaz had a calm, healing energy about them, as if they'd survived hard times and found their own path to happiness. They brought a light of sanity back into the chaos.

Jax escaped the synagogue and turned the corner to step into brilliant sunshine. From this strategic vantage, she could see everyone in the crowd milling outside the temple's ancient doors. There were familiar faces from the LGBT Center, including a guy they all referred to as Steve's "office wife," because he joined every project Steve joined. He was with his partner and kept falling into his arms to cry. She saw John, Steve's old roommate, and Bob, a guy Steve knew from his Navy days.

Off to one side a group of suits and designer dresses were mingling and exchanging business cards. It was the money crowd who both wanted to show their respect and do some networking. She slowed her pace to eavesdrop. One guy was speculating about whether Paul's personal tragedy could translate into higher prices for his work.

Opposite the temple, a row of bright-colored beach chairs were planted on the sidewalk, most of them occupied by people passing cookies and thermoses up and down the line. An old fashioned school bus painted with rainbows was parked next to them.

She turned her face to the sun for one last beam and walked over to the lawn chairs. Before she had time to give them her name, a man cried, "Are you Jax?"

"Yes." She was startled.

He stood up from his chair. "I recognized you immediately. You have Paul's eyes and chin! Here, sit down, sit down, I'll get you your own thermos. I'm David, by the way."

She sat with them and drank the tepid bitter coffee without complaint. When Paul finally came out of the building, David hurried her into the bus, then returned to the chairs, folding them and loading them onto the bus with lightning speed while the others advanced towards Paul. She watched from a window as they surrounded her grandfather, joined arms to form a human wall, and walked him to the bus. They sat him next to her and the bus took off, next stop White Horse Tavern.

The day passed, the evening passed and by dinner time they were so drunk they couldn't walk. Friends carried them out to the bus and drove them home, then helped them climb up the stairs, fished keys from Paul's pocket to open the door and escorted each of them to their rooms. They were still there the next morning when she went to get a glass of water from the sink. They'd fallen asleep on chairs, couches and floors, and she had to tiptoe her way around sleeping bodies and random limbs hanging off furniture.

Jax didn't know what happened to them after that. She slept for almost 24 hours. She slept so long she overslept her hangover. When she finally woke up, she felt fine. The house was bright and sunny, the city was alive outside her window, everything was just as it should be, except that nothing would ever be as it should be ever again.

She found Paul sitting in his shorts in the living room, already part way into a bottle of gin.

"Did you just wake up too?" she asked.

"No, I got up yesterday afternoon, when they were getting ready to leave," he said. "They said we should move up there with them to heal."

"We?"

"Yes, they said they had room for us both."

"Do you want to?" she asked.

"No. Do you?"

"No." Her life was in New York! Her world was here. She couldn't leave. "Definitely not."

He poured himself a double.

"May I join you?" she asked, pointing at the bottle.

"There's vodka in the kitchen," he said. "I stocked up."

They drank until they were drunk, ordered dinner in and retired early. They drank the next day too, ordered dinner, but stayed up watching TV while they drank. By the end of the week, they drank vodka in the morning, in the afternoon and all night. They used alcohol to cure the hangover they got from drinking alcohol. Some days they forgot to order food and ended up sharing a block of cheese and stale bread. Sometimes they slept wherever they fell asleep, on sofas and even floors.

On one especially bad morning she had a nightmare about Steve calmly teaching her how to get a bargain in hell and she woke up believing she was dead. She threw on a robe and hurried to the living room for some booze to make her shakes go away. She found Paul staring intently at an empty bottle.

"I can't do this to you," he said.

At first, she thought he was talking to the bottle, but then she realized he was speaking to her. "I can't drag you down into the mud with me, Jax. I'm disgusted with myself. Steve would be disgusted. He'd be furious with me."

"We're still grieving," she said. "Booze is helping."

"No, it isn't. You think that it is, but you'll find out that it only causes more problems."

He stared past her. "It runs in the family, you know. My father was a drunk. I'm a drunk. Maybe that's why Barry killed himself. Maybe he was a drunk, too. The curse ends with you, Jax."

Barry was an alcoholic. It resonated so hard with her that she knew it had to be true. It explained so many things she'd noticed -- his stiff gait at times, his glazed eyes at the dinner table, the morning "headaches," that no one could explain. And those bottles she saw in his desk drawer. He never exactly slurred his speech, but sometimes he had marble mouth and flubbed his words. The way he withdrew from the family and locked himself alone in his office now started making sense.

Paul abruptly left for his bedroom and she sank into her seat and tried to reframe her personal history in her mind. Daddy was a drunk. The secrets, the hiding, the ill humor. Of course he was. It was so clear now.

Paul returned to the living room looking crisp and well-dressed for the first time since the funeral. His hair was brushed, his beard trimmed and her heart leapt to see him looking like himself again. He said he was going to see some gallery people uptown and would be back in time for dinner.

She looked through all the cabinets and found some leftover tequila with a dusty cap. It tided her over until 2 o'clock when she reluctantly dressed and walked to a bodega to get them ham and cheese sandwiches for dinner. On the way, she stopped to get a small bottle of vodka to hide in her room.

When Paul walked into the loft at 7 pm, he found her sleeping on the sofa. He could tell she'd been drinking, but he didn't say a word. They ate their sandwiches in silence and went to their rooms.

The next day, she woke up from another bad dream, but in this one, she was chasing after Paul while he kept evading her in the streets of the city. She was running after him, trying to catch up, but every time she thought she'd gotten close, she saw that he was really on the next block, or had turned the corner, and she ran until her lungs hurt. She woke up with the worst hangover of her life and had stomach cramps that kept her on the toilet for an hour.

She was failing Grandpa. She was a selfish bitch who couldn't help the most important person in her life through his darkest hours. Even if she didn't want to stop drinking, she had to, for his sake. She was done.

She took a shower and put on jeans and a white peasant blouse. In the mirror, she looked like Jax again. But she was Jax who still craved alcohol. She went out on the fire escape and smoked a joint. It gave her the energy to clean the house. When everything was dusted and vacuumed, she sank onto the sofa and ate a half box of cookies she'd found hiding next to the Tequila. They were Pecan Sandies, Steve's favorite cookie. She ate one in Steve's honor. Then she ate a cookie to honor everyone who hid their cookies.

After she finished off the entire honorable box, she got a tumbler of water. She did sit-ups with a belly full of cookies and felt so tired she had to sprawl on the red couch to recover. She flipped the TV on and surfed restlessly.

"Bullshit," she said to every show that came on, "big bullshit." The day dragged on. Whenever she craved a shot of alcohol, she did an exercise she hated to punish herself. She did push-ups. She did jumping jacks. She did upside down bicycles with her legs.

She was panting on the floor when a key rattled in the lock and her Grandpa staggered in. He had to use his whole body to push the door shut behind him. He swayed and pointed at her.

"What are you doin' here?" he slurred. "You don't belong here."

"Grandpa, it's me, Jax. I live here."

He stared at her blankly. His nose bloomed red, his lips pale and dry.

"Grandpa," she repeated, "it's Jax!"

"Fuck, I'm drunk." He stumbled to the couch and fell onto it head first. The neat crisp outfit he had put on that morning was sweaty and rumpled. His appointment that day to have lunch with an old friend in SoHo lasted until cocktail hour, then led to a drinking contest at another bar and ended at White Horse where he bumped into his crew.

She moved close to him and lay her head on his knee.

"It's okay, Grandpa," she said unsurely, "it's going to be okay. I have a plan to make it okay."

"A plan?" The old man sounded bitter. "Girl, I forgot you lived here! I'm losing my mind!" He folded his arms over his chest and hunched over in pain.

"No, you're just under terrible stress, Grandpa," she said softly. "It's the stress, nothing is wrong with you. You need to rest, Grandpa, that's all. You need to sleep and eat and cut back on alcohol and you'll be fine."

She helped him to his bedroom and left him there alone. He promptly fell asleep and she tiptoed out when he started to snore. She closed his door and went to his studio and powered up his computer. She was violating his privacy. He would scream bloody murder if he found out. But she had to do it for him.

She skimmed through hundreds of messages and email to see if there was anything she could latch onto to help him. She found an invitation from Em and Chaz to come up to Provincetown and stay with them for the summer. That was an idea, but then she thought of how he would end up reminiscing about Steve with them and reliving old memories. She kept looking. A gallery in San Francisco had expressed an interest in bringing him out for a show, but they weren't offering a place for him to stay. She kept looking. There was one with a strange return address. It was from Greece, where his friend Giorgos lived. She had met him once when he came to New York: a compact, sun-baked person with Mediterranean blue eyes and arms like a wrestler. She remembered Paul and he stayed up all night talking about a poem called "Why I Am Not A Painter."

She liked Giorgos. He was vigorous and optimistic. His letter said Paul could spend as long as he liked at a villa in Mykonos. Paul would have his own bedroom and all of nature as his studio. The crooked cobblestone streets, the dramatic views along the jagged coast would refresh his artistic palette, Giorgos said.

This was it. Paul had to go to Greece. She quickly printed out a copy, shut down the computer and went to her bedroom so she could read the rest of the letter.

Giorgos wrote that the only redemption was to drive all the grief and rage into art, not to wait until it was a dull ache or a cold memory, but to use the power of pain as fuel. He didn't want Paul to fear his grief. He wanted Paul to embrace it and transform it. He said true art wasn't about drawing pretty pictures, but taking shit and turning it into gold.

YES, she nodded excitedly. YES! She needed this advice, too. She needed to turn her own shit into gold. Yes.

She imagined Paul in Greece. Giorgos had sent some photos showing his villa, its pristine white walls framing azure waters, and a white urn overflowing with purple flowers beside a rough-hewn brown door. The brilliant blue sea dominated the view. Mykonos was the perfect place for Paul to heal.

She looked up Mykonos on her laptop. Beautiful men in bathing suits smiled from every picture. She imagined Paul painting while wearing a white shirt and white pants, working on art or heading to the beach at sunset with Giorgos, perhaps socializing with some of those beautiful men. That might cheer him up. It would cheer her up if there was a BDSM paradise where she could flee.

She went to an online travel agency and studied flights and prices. The $30,000 check had cleared, though she cringed to see she'd blown almost a grand already on booze and pot and some new clothes. Still, she had the money to do this for him. With Steve's death, her dream of moving out was on indefinite hold anyway. She couldn't leave Paul when he was grieving. But if he came back strong and happy, and he had new paintings to sell, then, maybe, at last, she could begin her life as an independent woman. Meanwhile, she'd save on rent for a month or two by staying put.

She clicked the BOOK NOW button and watch the charge go through. Seconds later, a confirmation email pinged in her mailbox.

She went to bed happy. The next day, she got up early and wove through side streets to an authentic French bakery on Bleecker. They had the butteriest croissants in all of New York. She felt magnanimous, and also hungry, so she ordered half a dozen.

She picked up a *NY Times* from a kiosk and spread out the Help Wanteds. Then she put the croissants on a plate and laid out napkins, butter knives, along with a crock of raspberry jam and a dish of butter and waited for Paul to wake up.

"I got us the best croissants!" she said when he came to the table.

"You're up early, Jax. Mmmmm!" he said when he saw her and the breakfast treats waiting. "Did you go to the French guy on 4th Street?" He stuffed the butt of a croissant in his mouth, then sliced the rest of it and smeared jam on it. Then he looked at her moodily. "I'm so sorry about last night, girl. It's been so hard to stay on the wagon with everyone constantly wanting to buy me a drink now." He shook his head. "They mean well and I haven't had the guts to say no."

"It's okay, Grandpa, really. I understand."

"No, no it's not. It's not okay." He took another croissant and punctiliously spread butter on it to ward off the tears welling in his eyes.

"You lost the love of your life," she said. "I understand. We lost Steve. I still can't believe he is gone." She put her soft white hand over his rough paw. "I have to talk to you, though."

"Then talk." His hand shook as he poured himself more

coffee.

"John Dodson came to see me at the papaya place," she said.

"That's surprising. Why?"

She told him the whole story, from start to finish, and for the first time since Steve's death, Paul paid close attention to what she said. She told him about how she'd planned to ask for a raise, but ended up throwing her work hat into the street, how she was so excited she forgot her purse, how she fell on the grate and her first thought was whether the check in her bra was safe, how she and Tony had a fuck-you standoff, and how amazed she was by Booker's dad's gift. The whole story -- with parts dramatized and re-enacted for effect -- streamed out of her while Paul laughed and gasped and hugged her. It was like old times between them. Old good times, when they were so happy they'd found each other, that they could let themselves laugh about everything, even the bad things that had happened.

Then she told him how she planned to use the money, how she would get a better job and maybe start taking some classes. She decided not to mention her decision to move out. She wanted him to be able to leave without worrying about the future.

"I saved the best news for last," she said proudly. "You're going to Greece!"

"Huh? What do you mean?"

"I booked your flights. You're going to Mykonos. To visit Giorgos."

The old man sat stunned. "How did you know about Giorgos? Jesus Christ, I never answered his email, that was weeks ago, I totally forgot, shit."

"He came here two summers ago," she said. "Remember,

you argued all night about this poem with oranges and sardines."

"Oh, my God, I remember." He chuckled. "Still, I can't go. It's too soon."

"Too soon to live?" She touched his fingers tenderly. "Grandpa, I already bought tickets."

"No! You bought them? With your money?"

"Yes. Consider it payback for my room and board this last year and a half."

"What, did you spend the Dodson money on me?" She shrugged. "Oh no! Oh no, no, no. I can't take that money from you, I won't," he insisted. "No, absolutely not. You need every penny if you want to go to college."

"Don't be so bourgeois about money, Grandpa!" This was his classic charge when he and Steve quibbled about money. "Money exists to be spent."

He screwed up his face. "Why, you little…" He didn't like having the tables turned. Her nostrils flared in delight. "No, Jax, just no."

"Well, one of us has to go to Mykonos because it's non-refundable."

He threw up his hands in frustration. "Are you sure you can't get a refund?"

"Nope, the tickets are non-refundable. You could change the date if you want, but you can't get a refund."

"I can't leave you here. How will you manage?"

"I'll be fine. I'll use the time to find work. Maybe find a new boyfriend."

Or maybe a slave or a submissive or a guy like Mr. Sweaty Socks who stared at her feet. She locked eyes with Paul. They'd wasted the whole spring together drinking and mourning. She couldn't let the summer pass without some kind of romance. She had a bundle of web images of Mykonos she printed out. She pushed them across the table to him. "Look at these, Grandpa. You know you want to paint that beach."

He glanced at the photos, all of them showcasing men flexing on cliffs and walking with their arms around each other on the beach. "There's a beach in these photos?"

"You have to look past all the muscles to see the waves," she said. "Come on, you have to admit, it looks fun, doesn't it?"

"Well... you know," he cleared his throat, "Giorgos has been inviting me for years. Whenever he sends pictures of his house, I've felt the pull. So beautiful in its simplicity. All those white cubic houses... And the windmills, did you see them? Giorgos sent me photos of them once. It makes me want to do landscapes, to go old style with a straw hat and an easel, working in natural light. What a dream." He stared wistfully beyond her. "W. H. Auden spent summers there."

She had her final argument lined up. "It's what Steve would've wanted for you. If he was here, he'd say it is time to live again."

He closed his eyes. "So when do I leave?"

"Yay!" she shrieked with joy. "You're going! Next week!"

"Yay," he echoed quietly.

One week later, they carried his bags down to the sidewalk and huddled together, waiting for his cab to the airport. A chilly breeze blew in from the Hudson. Grandpa turned up his collar and she leaned in for a hug as the cab pulled to the curb.

"Promise me," he said, "promise me you will stay safe for me."

"I promise. And you promise me you will get stronger

for me."

Their gray eyes met, their lips turned up, they smiled the same crooked smile at each other. They knew the promises were silly, yet it soothed them to pretend they knew the unknowable. Paul reminded her to shut the lights, Jax reminded him to take his vitamins, and Grandpa was gone.

The empty house was spooky yet divine. She strutted around the house in panties, headphones on her ears, joint in hand and spent the day looking at online BDSM porn and jerking off.

She was giving herself a 2-week staycation. She planned to do all the sightseeing she could cram into 14 days. The kinds of sights she wanted to see were all the places formerly forbidden to her.

She went to the porn district around 42nd Street and visited video stores to watch kinky movies in the tiny booths and skim through row after row of fetish magazines. She was a voyeur. She didn't know what she wanted from the experiences, she just knew she wanted to see everything, to break with taboos, to defy convention. She wanted to go to places her mother would never go, places that would scandalize every Upper East Side matron. She wasn't ready to meet people yet, not yet, but she had a hunger to see everything that was outrageous, forbidden, sexual.

She went to bars and dance clubs that served alcohol, and started going out alone at night to sit in sidewalk cafes and watch pedestrians. She'd sit and watch people, calmly absorbing their humanity like it was a Zen practice. She watched how they moved and how they flirted, she listened to the conversations they had, and she let it all flow through her.

One time, a drunk architect sat at her little table and told her he was going to marry her and if she didn't believe him, he would prove it. Then he left and she never saw him again. Another time, a couple sat down at her table and tried to convince her to go home with them. After that, she moved to a cafe where the seating made her feel more invisible.

What she sought from the passersby was some kind of signal that there were other people like them walking around. If she saw the sock guy now, she would try to talk to him. But how do you tell who's kinky and who isn't in a crowd where everyone looks kinky and not kinky at the same time? No wonder gay men wore handkerchiefs in their back pockets. It was a quick way to know what they were into.

All the experiences she couldn't have with Booker, he wanted them now, she hungered for them and she decided it would take a lot of different people to give her the variety of experiences she wanted.

But first, she needed the right clothes. She walked down the piss-stained steps to a punk clothing store in the East Village and walked to the back, where she once spotted outlandish shoes and boots. She grabbed a pair that laced up the front all the way to her thighs and walked around the cramped store, feeling like a conquistador. Then she browsed through their assortment of fetish-style dresses, at last finding a PVC mini-dress in her size. It zipped up the front and showed off the tops of her breasts. There were laces on the side and she pulled them tight. She looked like a goddess! She loved her new look so much she decided to wear her purchases home.

After all, she lived in Greenwich Village now, home to artists, writers, perverts and junkies. It was... it was INCUMBENT upon her to let her freak flag fly. With every step home she felt lighter, freer, fiercer, more herself than she'd ever felt. All the depression of death, all the anomie of walking alone vanished as she became hyper-focused on her own happiness. She was free, really free, the freest free any woman could ever be. She was herself without borders, without secrets. She had risen out of the pathetic wreck of clingy anxiety. She was a dominant woman!

She threw her shoulders back and walked the street like a cat on the prowl. She'd worried that people might mock her or stare cruelly, but instead, the passersby who noticed her looked intrigued, charmed, even excited to see her. One guy stared so hard at her that he tripped on a sidewalk crack and fell, while she hurried by, trying not to giggle. She stopped at a head-shop to pick up some rolling papers and the man behind the counter was beside himself with politeness, calling her "Ma'am" and trying to make the sale last longer by pulling out fancy scales and elaborate items he knew she wouldn't buy.

"If you were giving me one for free, that would be different," she finally said to end the conversation.

"Tell you what," he darted his eyes towards an unseen manager in back, "come back after 3 pm, when the manager isn't here, and we'll work out a deal."

When she left, Jax stood in front of a clothing store window to see if she could see what others were seeing. She saw a serene, self-possessed goddess decked out in seductively tight rubber and leather. The magic of the veiled hat now transferred to the boots, the dress, the laces at her waist and the wide, flashy zipper running up the front of her low-cut dress. The clothes brought out the woman she always wanted to be, the one she hid even from herself. She admired herself from the toes of her shiny boots to the frizzy curls that made her feel frumpy. Now, it looked like an ornamental crown, a glorious mane as untamable as herself.

She was in a glaze of adrenaline rushes. The world was in sharper focus, the buildings and sidewalks more defined, the people she passed more individualistic, more remarkable, the smell of the streets more pungent, the restaurants and bars more aromatic. She came to a full halt in front of a flower stand beside a grocery, overwhelmed by the sweetness and fresh perfumes.

Then it was dark. The night suddenly descended as a light rain pattered around her and droplets skimmed off her dress. She increased her pace until she reached Washington Street, a few short blocks from home. The rain hadn't reached her, and she walked the dry, deserted streets, her head still spinning with happiness and a certainty that she would find her path now, now that she knew who she was in mind and in body.

She spotted a group of people standing outside the doorway of a building she'd passed a hundred times. It seemed odd to find a crowd in the empty street, so she crossed over to get a better look at what was going on. Most of the people assembled were men wearing black leather jackets and black leather vests, holding cigars and mingling. A couple of women moved among them, too. Was this the notorious Leather Scene she'd read about? Would there be bondage equipment upstairs under the tent?

She knew the building. It had the mysterious black tent on its roof, the one she looked at every day and night. This was her chance to get inside! She shoved the bags with old clothes, shoes and rolling papers into her huge purse and made her way through the small crowd.

A heavy-set man with a gray beard that flowed down his chest was keeping guard. He looked more like a biker than a kinky person to her, but she took her chances.

"Are you here for the party?" he asked.

"Yes," she said. "I'm dressed for it, aren't I?" She looked at him coolly, the way she thought a dominatrix would.

He smiled kindly. "You look lovely, Mistress," he said. "Take the elevator to the top, then take the stairs to the roof."

She gulped. She was in! Was it really so easy to get into this secret club? Why had she wasted a year of her life on Booker when she could have been coming here all along and dating men who called her Mistress!

The elevator deposited her in an industrial hallway with dim light and linoleum floors. An EXIT sign blinked erratically at one end next to a handwritten sign that read, "Party on Roof." She walked up a narrow flight of steel steps and pushed open a heavy door.

The roof held a few stragglers sitting around, drinking beer and chatting. Everyone was in leather. She was so excited she could barely walk for running. The black tent was vibrating with music that got louder every time someone came in or out. Whatever they had wanted to hide from the outside world was exactly what she needed to see.

She stepped in. She never wanted to leave. It was like a living circus of her most secret and shameful sex fantasies. There were black leather swings suspended from wooden beams erected inside the tent. There were bamboo and steel cages, some with captives inside. There were things she couldn't quite identify and tops and bottoms acting out rituals she didn't quite understand.

She froze and her brain froze. She threw her hands up to her head as if it might explode off her shoulders. Everything she saw was new, yet it felt weirdly familiar. Everyone was a stranger, yet she felt a level of comfort with them she'd never felt in any group, as if they were all genetically or spiritually connected somehow. She knew that any rational person seeing implements associated with brutality and torture would probably flee. But what she saw were really infinite erotic opportunities to live out her most precious fantasies in a safe space where she would not be judged.

"First time?" A man wearing a red corset over a tailored shirt and loose, almost flowing pants stood at her elbow. A Zorro mask completed the look, making him look more like a raccoon than a rakish legend.

"Maybe," she said slyly. He amused her. His outfit was so bizarre and seemingly random. The corset was custom-made of red leather and cinched his waist so tight he looked like an hourglass. His pants billowed out below the girdle, like a harem girl's. On his feet were high red boots that matched the corset. He was part pirate, part harem girl, part fetish doll and, to her titillation, clearly a bona fide pervert.

"You should be wearing lipstick to match your outfit. I would never let my slave leave the house without lipstick that matched his corset." She dug through her purse and grabbed his face in one hand. He did not demur when she waved the lipstick at him and said, "Let me fix that for you." He obsequiously allowed her to apply it to his lips, then blushed and said thank you to her.

She couldn't believe this was happening! She wanted to squeal and jump up and down. Instead, she turned her head away from him to hide her facial expressions, hoping that he would read it as haughty disdain.

"May I please ask what your name is, Mistress?" he asked humbly.

She pretended to be looking for someone in the crowd. "You may call me Mistress... Amazon." She knew enough not to reveal her real name. She turned back to him. "Follow me," she snapped.

Zorro meekly followed a few steps behind, head bowed. Were all submissive men this easy, she wondered? Well, not the gay guys, of course, but still, how could Zorro know she was a real femdom? Did it even matter to him if she was real? She had no idea a woman could claim she was dominant, say a few bossy, bitchy things and a submissive would turn to mush.

With every step forward she felt a little more entitled to be there. By the time they were halfway across the tent towards the stage, where someone was performing, another man lined up behind Zorro. Then a third guy lined up, and now the crowd was starting to watch them. There were some whispers, some coughs of laughter rippling through the crowd. She stared straight ahead at the front of the room, striding with a tense grace, her reflection from the windows present in her mind. She was that woman, not the girl whispering in her brain that this was embarrassing and bizarre and she should run away.

She stopped. There was a large low platform set up as a stage in front, flanked by posters about AIDS and a table to the side that was collecting donations for a charity group. On the stage, a naked man, his body shaved from head to toe, was cuffed to a huge X-frame cross while two men in leather pants and vests were attaching metal devices to his genitals, working in concert as the naked man writhed.

She stepped close to the platform, mesmerized by the shiny steel gadgets and the quiet authority of the two men working in concert to push the bound man to his limits. One man held a small whip and randomly threw its lashes across his thighs and ass. The other one held something that looked like a pizza cutter. When he ran it on the naked guy's leg, the man twitched and groaned.

"It's a Wartenburg Wheel," Zorro whispered in her ear.

His words startled her from her trance. "What?"

"The little steel tool that looks like a spur? Those tiny little points, they feel like tiny needles."

She nodded in understanding. She imagined the wheel in

her hand. She wanted to run it all over a human body and see how much their body could take.

His voice got throaty and the eye holes in his mask got beady bright. "Would you do that to me?"

She ignored him. She was flying now. She was flying away.

She twirled. Her small submissive entourage looked at her expectantly. Were they expecting to do something dominant? She pointed at the ground.

"Kneel!" she ordered.

All three quickly got on their knees...

She walked to Zorro, grabbed him by the hair and stared into his eyes until he lowered his gaze.

"Now, thank me for giving you attention."

He murmured, "Thank you, Mistress Amazon, for the privilege of your attention."

She yanked his hair roughly, and saw the whites of his eyes.

"Louder," she commanded. "Say it louder so others can hear!"

"Thank you, Mistress," he shouted like a terrified military recruit to the officer training him at boot camp. "Thank you for paying attention to this humble slave." His voice was so loud, everyone turned to them for a second, laughing and whispering.

It was funny to her, but it was a turn-off. She turned to the second in line. This guy looked younger than her. He had ruddy cheeks and Beatles-style hair, with dark greasy bangs hanging to his thick eyebrows. Even she knew he was dressed all wrong for the event, in a neat white shirt and khaki pants. He looked smug, like he had snuck into a line for seats he couldn't afford. Her steely eyes inspected him mercilessly. She had an impulse to smack the smirk right off his face. Instead, she leaned her face so close to his she could see all the enlarged pores and tiny pimples on his young skin.

"You're new," she sneered, wondering if anyone would call her out on her own inexperience. No one did. Her tiny entourage would believe anything she told them. She felt it. They had recognized her as dominant. She was a sub magnet. The thought excited her. She wanted to collect men, to have a whole cadre of devoted men who would jump when she told them to jump and kneel at her command.

She continued, "Do you deserve the privilege of following me?" She didn't know if she meant it or not, but suddenly it FELT like she meant it. How dare this pimply grinning whelp, who dressed like a square and snickered like a coward, follow her around!

His smug look vanished. "Probably not," he admitted, "I mean, you're a dominatrix and I'm not sure." His Adam's apple bobbed up and down. "I don't know, maybe I'm not in your league."

"If you think I'm out of your league, then I am." She coldly dismissed him with a wave of her hand and turned her back to him.

Now she beckoned the third guy to approach. He was the oldest of the three and looked like he was made of tougher stuff. He had a huge head, with a wide nose and jutting jaw. He radiated calm and certainty, as if the rituals were familiar and comfortable to him. Both Zorro and the pimply Boy Scout looked shady by comparison, as if they had guilty secrets.

He looked humble, but not downtrodden and his big shaggy head was the kind of ugly that could, at certain angles, look handsome in a classical way. He wore close-fitting black clothes on his tall, trim body and his gray hair was thick and beautifully combed. She sensed he had experience and the way he looked at her pleased her. He looked humble and submissive, but also friendly and, if she had to put it in one word, sane. He looked strangely sane.

"What's your name?" she asked.

"Henry," he said.

"Thank me, Henry."

"Thank me for the privilege of following me, like the slave you are!"

He said it loud enough for people nearby to hear him, but not so loud as to stop the crowd. Then he lowered himself to his knees and asked, "May I please kiss your feet, Mistress?"

"Yes!" she cried. This was unbelievable. This was incredible. She was flying again. Not only did he want to kiss her boots, but he kissed them so affectionately, so genuinely, with such sincerity, the heat of his kisses rose to her head.

Zorro couldn't stand it anymore. "Can I kiss your feet?"

"No," she said coldly. "No, you may not."

He looked frustrated. "Can I get you a drink then?"

"Sure," she said, and he hurried towards the bar. It would be really mean of her if she left before he brought it back, she thought.

Henry watched Zorro retreat, shaking his head and chuckling. "When the blood goes to the penis, it leaves the head."

"What do you mean?"

"He didn't even ask you what you want to drink." Henry bent at the waist laughing.

"You're right!" She laughed. Was Zorro so scared of her, or maybe so horny for her, that he forgot to ask what she wanted?

"Would you consider going for a drink with me

somewhere?" Henry asked.

She looked at her watch. "Oh, it's late. I haven't even had dinner yet. I need to go."

"What a pity." He looked genuinely sad. "Would you consider seeing me another time? Do you have a private dungeon where I could visit you? I'd love to schedule a session with you."

"Oh," she fumbled, "well, I mean, not really, I'm not set up for that."

"Do you work at a club? I'd really love to see you professionally if you'd allow me."

"Professionally?"

"Yes, I think we'd have fun, don't you?" Henry took out his wallet and pressed 2 crisp one hundred dollar bills into her hands. "Let me pay you for an hour in advance," he said, scribbling on the back of a flyer he snatched off a table. "No strings. The money is yours. If you can't find time for me, so be it. But, really, I would love to get to know you and am happy to pay for the privilege." He handed her the flyer. "Email me if you can make time for me."

She stared at the money. She just got money for nothing. He didn't even know her real name. She folded the bills and the flyer and deposited them in her bag.

"You'll hear from me." She tried to sound as if this happened to her all the time. "I'll find room for you in my schedule."

He bowed. "May I kiss your hand goodbye, sweet Mistress?"

She shyly gave him her hand. He was perfect. Henry was sexy enough, and sane and holy shit, he wanted to pay her to do things she'd already dreamed of doing! Professional dominatrix! Holy shit! She knew women did that, but it had never occurred to her that she could become one!

She paced and smoked on the fire escape, then came inside to lie in bed and stare at the ceiling. From her toes to her brain, from her heart to her pussy, she was alive, more alive than she'd ever been. What had changed inside her? Was it in her hormones? She had never felt so horny in her life. She inquisitively reached her fingers into her pussy and smelled them. It smelled the same as always. She licked a finger. Her juices tasted slightly sweet and slightly salty as usual. If it wasn't hormones, what was it?

She closed her eyes and concentrated. What did she really feel right here and right now?

She felt aspirational. She felt capable. She wanted to live out her dreams. She wanted money and the luxuries it could buy. She wanted people to respect her. She wanted to play with a maximum of men. She wanted slaves to worship her. And, one day, she wanted to fall in love with someone who loved her for who she was.

She felt powerful. That was it. She had tasted power. Her body rippled like a shark in the ocean as the idea sank in. Power was her aphrodisiac.

∾ Chapter 5 ⍦
L'OUBLIETTE

If she couldn't have Booker, she would have all the other men. All the ones she wanted, which would be all the ones who turned her on, which meant all the kinky ones. That's just how it was going to be. It was her life and her body and she would give it all the pleasure it deserved.

That began with knowing what she liked and what she didn't like. She didn't like when men grabbed her up for kisses. It made her body tense up. She found them pathetic when they focused on their dicks and their own orgasms, never even asking her what turned her on. When they tried to force her head between their legs, she smacked their hands away. At the time, she thought it was sexy in a taboo way when Booker entered her from behind. In retrospect, she hated having her face squashed into a pillow, she hated not being able to see the look in his eyes when he penetrated her, it made her feel more like a meat bag than a woman.

She'd never date a non-kinky man again. Doing BDSM without sex was more arousing than sex without BDSM. She was on fire when she masturbated after a session, and the scattered memories of groans and squeals and the way a man's body dances in pain, occupied her waking thoughts. What was she thinking, planning to get married and settle down with a rich husband who would turn her into the same kind of angry old woman her mother was? No man was worth giving up her freedom for. Love affairs, oh yes... But marriage was a patriarchal rabbit hole. She wasn't a rabbit. She was a gazelle! She was fucking free!

She took out her newest diary. It was bound in black leather and had a small lock with a gold skeleton key. She kept it on a chain around her neck, where it glittered like a kinky cross, and matched the tiny handcuff earrings that dangled from her earlobes.

"I'm a free woman, I can fuck freely and freely fuck."

She smiled at her written words. They seemed more meaningful on the page. She studied it like a koan, saying it out loud again and again. She had new realities to incorporate and new images of herself to process. Repeating the words made them realer.

She flipped to the back pages of the diary to read a poem she'd been trying to write.

Closing the Book

I opened the book of my heart, he opened a book of lies.

I kissed him with my soul, he kissed me with his eyes.

I loved him forever, he used me like a toy.

She wasn't sure what more to say about him. She couldn't leak the goo trapped in her viscera onto the page. She didn't want to be a tragic figure. She didn't want anyone's pity. She wouldn't fall for a guy like Booker now, that's for sure. She was a hundred years older and a thousand times kinkier now. She tore the poem out of the book and ripped it into shreds. The destruction of the poem was the best poem of all.

She flipped through some notes she'd made about play dates. Since her night at the club, she'd hooked up with a few submissive men she met online, bringing them back to her apartment and experimenting with whips and light bondage. There was Bobby, a rope fanatic, who freaked out when she made him look at himself in the mirror, and Mercury, whose real name she never learned, who wanted to lick her feet, and Jin, a boy with waist-length hair who wanted to be treated like a girl.

She enjoyed them all, but the real story was not so much what she did with them, but how she experienced them. That's when all the epiphanies flowered. When they kneeled at her feet, a molecular change began inside her. By the time they stood naked and trembling in her candle lit room, shadows playing over their gooseflesh as they waited for the power of her imagination to unleash itself, she was Amazon. Amazon was an animal. Her arms were wings, flying through the air with precise beating strokes, her claws precise. She was sleek, beautiful and vicious, her cat-eyes staring coldly when she pounced upon her prey.

Tying men up kept them at her total mercy, unable to leave her, compelled to take all the sensations she wanted to give them, whether it was a slap on the cock or a tongue-kiss, made her happy. They gave themselves to her completely, naked and abject, and let her give them what SHE knew they needed. She knew, instinctually, how to draw that out of them. If she ever needed proof she was a dominatrix, she had it now, with four submissives already under her belt.

Having the freedom to control a man according to her whims clarified and calmed her soul. Every movement of her body, every footstep she took felt more emphatic. Kink was who she was. It wasn't just a sex fantasy, it was the material she was made of. She didn't have to struggle anymore. She could relax and let life take her where it would. She knew who she was now. She would always be safe. She would always get through.

She looked through her notebook and studied the growing list of toys, gear and fetish outfits she wanted to collect, adding a corset and a crop to the list. She wanted to learn about all the perversions, all the fetishes, all the rituals and mysteries of Mistress/slave relationships, even the things that horrified or mortified her. Maybe especially those things.

Henry claimed several pages in her notebook. She read through the section, smiling to herself and dialed his number.

"Where are you?"

"On my way now, I just grabbed the keys."

"Get your slutty ass over here," she said. "I want to do things to you."

"Be there in 20 minutes."

She went back to her room to be sure it looked perfect. She had prepped the bedroom for their session, shutting lamps, lighting candles, dimming the penis chandelier. She replaced the soft amber bulb with a bright red one. Now when she lit it, the penis hanging from her ceiling had a creepy, tortured look.

She spread out all her toys on a black velvet throw on the bed, some of them ones she bought, most of them presents from Henry -- or, more precisely, toys he wanted her to use on him. These included a leather collar and a matching leash, a whip with long thin lashes, a ping pong paddle, two types of nipple clamps, some cheap rope, basic handcuffs, a deer-skin flogger, a pair of bamboo canes and a vintage razor strop, made of thick leather. She was ready for more. She definitely needed a corset in case another crossdresser showed up, and the crop would be better than a whip to strike someone lying at her feet.

She went to her clothes rack. It was too hot to wear fetish clothes. Her small air conditioner could not compete with the torrid summer heat that pounded down on her roof all day.

She picked her old slinky red dress and pulled it over her naked body. It was tighter than she remembered, clinging tightly to every curve, leaving little to the viewer's imagination. She posed sideways. It made her tummy pouf out, but her ass looked amazing. It would do nicely.

She walked back and turned off the lights, then waited for Henry on the red couch. The air was cooler in the living room where an overhead fan churned the air and made the hem on her dress flutter pleasantly.

Twilight filtered in through the kitchen windows, casting amber-gray waves of diminishing light across the loft. It was a moment of perfect tranquility before the storms of drama, sweat and screams began. She stretched her muscles in every direction, filling her lungs with air. The dress tightened across her breasts. Her nipples were so hard. They were plump little grapes now.

The buzzer sounded and she let Henry into the building. She opened her door. As Henry climbed the last few steps, he caught sight of her standing in the doorway, back straight, arms folded and he tripped, falling up a step onto his knees.

"Good starting position," she said with a smirk.

"You look beautiful tonight, Mistress," he said, laughing in embarrassment. "Like a goddess!"

She grabbed him by the crotch of his pants and dragged him across the threshold.

"You're hard already." She mocked him, "Why am I not surprised?"

His cheeks turned red.

"Did I give you permission to get hard?"

"No, Ma'am."

"Barely inside the door and you already deserve to be punished."

"Yes, Ma'am."

"Kneel." She pointed to her feet and he got on his knees.

She unbuttoned his shirt and caressed his neck, sensuously, then more dangerously as her touch grew rougher and her grip tighter. She reached to the side table where she'd placed the collar and leash, and deftly buckled the stiff leather belt around his neck. Then she attached the leash. She worked slowly, deliberately, as if these simple tasks were complex.

This wasn't just bondage, it was a sacred ritual. She wanted him to feel his resistance melt as the collar was fastened around his neck. She wanted him to fear the padlock she attached to the back ring, to fear that she might never release him. She wanted him to know that she owned him now, that he had no choice but to obey. Then she attached the leash's clamp to the ring on his collar and yanked it upward, forcing him to his feet. All was silence now, broken only by the sound of his sighs and gasps.

She walked quickly towards her bedroom while he struggled to keep pace behind her. When they reached the bedroom, she dropped the leash.

"Take off your clothes and sit on the bed. When I get back, I expect to see you naked and waiting."

"Yes, Ma'am." He began undressing immediately.

"Thank me for not making you wait on your knees," she said. "I think it was exceptionally kind of me to let you sit on the bed."

"Yes, Ma'am," he nodded enthusiastically, "very kind, thank you, Mistress."

She went to the bathroom and checked her make-up and hair. Her neck was sweating so she brushed her hair up and pinned it into a tall bun, then applied another coat of lipstick and tugged the dress down so more of her breasts would show. When she got back to her bedroom, Henry sat with his head bowed, naked on her bed, beside the neatly displayed BDSM toys.

Henry had turned out to be a very pleasant and educational first partner. She emailed him after spending the two hundred on a blue latex outfit that she wore when he came to see her the following week. That was over two months ago. He showed her a few diabolical bondage positions, he bought her toys and fetish clothes and dinners at elegant restaurants, he taught her terms she didn't know, like calling a BDSM experience a "session" and he tried to explain the small, but important distinctions between a submissive and a slave, and a masochist and a bottom. He also told her about Mistress Katrina, a woman he had faithfully served for two decades, and how Katrina would invite him to parties where he had to serve all her friends wine in the nude.

If he wasn't 70 years old and married, with no intention of ever breaking up his family or letting his wife know about his sexual proclivities, Jax would have dated him for free, if only to hear more titillating stories about his decades of life as a sex pervert. Instead, she was his professional dominatrix, nothing more or less.

The nicest thing about Henry, she discovered, is that, as old as he was, he got hard at the slightest threat of punishment, even when the alleged infractions were chimerical. Once she punished him for calling her a "lady." She hated the word. She ordered him to write, "I am the lady in this relationship," one hundred times on a writing pad, while he squirmed in humiliation, his erection tapping against his gray belly.

It was the threat of, the fantasy of, the physical challenge of punishment that drove him crazy. She effortlessly transformed simple acts into grounds for punishment. Once, she told him to jump in the air, and when he landed, yelled at him, "I didn't give you permission to land! How dare you!!!"

On that particular occasion, he started laughing so hard at the threat, she ended up laughing with him, and then they hugged, and it was so affectionate, they stopped playing and went out to dinner until it was time for him to go to the airport and fly home to his Hallmark family in the Midwest.

She didn't begrudge him his double life. In the rest of his life, he was a successful businessman, an attentive husband, a devoted father, and a cheerful grandfather. But he also craved to be punished and later on to jerk off in secret, so that he could go home to his wife and say he was faithful to her. She understood more about double lives now. Her father had led one, after all. Paul led one until he finally came out. And, in a way, she too had lived two different lives. There was miserable, self-hating Jax who thought a conventional marriage would save her and then there was happy, proud Mistress Amazon, ruler of men.

Despite the age gap, she and Henry saw eye-to-eye on some things. Henry took kink seriously, but never so seriously they couldn't laugh about it together. He made her feel like the most important person in his life when he was with her. She didn't need more than that, she knew their relationship would end, she just wanted the endorphins his adoration gave her when they were together. Like her, he was scrupulously ethical. He told her the truth before their first session and told her he would understand if she sent him away. Instead, she pulled down his pants and spanked him. They both knew it was her way of rewarding him for being honest. There was a real trust between them.

"You can hit me harder, you know," he said to her at the end of their first month together. "I have a leathery old ass."

"Oh, if it's leather, then I guess you need a good tanning."

"Yes, Ma'am, I really do."

She ran her fingers over his chest and down to his balls, where she dug her nails in until he gasped.

"Let's see how much you can take," she hissed. "Your safeword is 'limp dick.'"

She used the whip on him that day, with no warm up. He was tied to hooks she had installed on her wall so he couldn't evade the blows. He flinched and jerked away at first, but no matter how many times she hit him with the whip, he never broke.

She increased the force of her impact. She increased it a little more. Then more. The old man was barely moving until she threw her whole arm into it, striking his ass over and over with all her strength. He began to writhe like an exposed worm, but he didn't use his safeword.

"Do you need to use your safeword?" She paused in case he was too far gone in ecstasy to realize he should stop.

"No, Mistress. I can take more."

She picked up a bamboo cane. She struck it lightly on her thigh and squeaked. She had no idea how intense a cane was until then. She thought it would feel like a twig because it was so light and thin. It felt like a fucking brand scorching her leg.

She turned to him and tapped him with it lightly, unsure how he'd react. His ass was impervious! He wasn't moving. She took a deep breath and with a flick of her wrist landed a sharp blow, and then another, and then, finally, he began moaning.

Under the circumstances, his pain was music to her ears, a music that prompted her to land a few brutal strokes to the tops of his thighs. He made a sound she'd never heard before. It was part high-pitched scream and part howl. She made a mental note to add a ball-gag to her toy wish list.

She pressed her body against his back. His body was so hot, she began to sweat through her silk. She pulled on his collar and his chin dropped to his chest.

"You need to go shopping for me," she said casually, "I want a good gag. I can't have your girly screams make someone call the cops on me."

"Yes, Ma'am," he whispered.

"Do you want to say something?" She pulled away and poked the tip of the cane between his buttocks, as if she was about to penetrate his anus.

"Limp dick!" he cried. "Limp dick."

She laughed loudly. "That's what did it? A little peeky-boo in your poopie-hole finally made you use your safeword?" She paused. "What's wrong with you?"

They laughed loudly and she quickly released him from the restraints. She would have hugged him, but his erection made it awkward.

"The truth is out." She pointed to it. "I've never seen it look so big."

"Now I'm doomed." He tried not to smile. "You know my secret."

"I should probably use that thing." She pointed at his swollen organ. It seemed a pity to waste so corpulent an appendage. She might never see one that big again.

"If you wish, Mistress, if that's what you really want." He consented, but he looked anxious about it.

"I don't know," she mused out loud, "it doesn't seem right. You have grandchildren my age."

"I agree, Ma'am, it wouldn't be right."

She heard his doubts. They made the decision for her.

"Obviously, the only solution is for me to keep on punishing you, because now you've insulted me by showing me your horse dick, knowing full well that, morally, I can't use it for my own pleasure."

He visibly relaxed. "You understand me so well, Ma'am."

She changed course, letting her imagination fly. "Of course I should punish you. Your member is useless to me. Totally useless!" She disdainfully flicked the head of his cock with her nails.

Henry winced, bending at the waist. "My dick is useless, Mistress. I deserve to be punished."

"Beg me for it! Beg me to punish you for your useless penis."

"Please, Mistress, please punish me for having a huge, useless cock."

She put the tip of her whip handle under his chin and forced his head up uncomfortably.

"Oh, so you think you have a huge cock?" She laughed. "Maybe I should shorten it."

A drop of sweat fell from his scalp to his nose. "Yes, Mistress," he whispered, gulping.

She looked around the room. "I know I have sharp scissors around here somewhere. An inch or two off the top and you won't be so conceited."

"No, Mistress, please," he begged. "Limp dick, limp dick," he said.

She couldn't stop laughing. "Alright, then tell me you love your big penis."

He wet his lips. "I love my big penis."

She slapped his cock lightly with the palm of her hand. He danced on his toes.

"But you won't be fucking me with that penis."

"No, Ma'am. I mean, yes, Ma'am, yes, I won't. You won't let me."

"Because you're my helpless depraved little slut, aren't you?" She shoved his head into her bosom until he struggled to breathe and then she let go of him so suddenly he lost his balance and fell on his ass.

She put her foot directly over his groin and slowly ground it into his still-stiff cock. Henry was both mortified and uncontrollably delighted, his eyes bright with submission, terror and devotion, his enlarged pupils glittering like black diamonds.

After he left, she felt a sense of disappointment. They had tried so many different scenes together over the months, but now she realized that the only things that he really wanted from her was a brutal beating on the ass and saving his penis for marriage.

If she had a few clients like Henry, she could make a decent living and never have to take a corporate job again. She could put herself through college and move on from there. She didn't have to limit herself anymore.

The Internet wasted a lot of time. You had to write to them and could spend a week texting and fantasizing about someone only to find you were incompatible in person. Like the guy, Bobby, who freaked out that she made him look at himself in the mirror in ropes after he pleaded with her for two weeks that she come to his place and truss him up like a turkey. She broke her own rule for him, about making men come to her, because he looked so cute in his profile. It ended with him rudely ordering her to leave, as if tying him up was fine, but making him see himself in bondage was a line no one could cross. It confused her, especially when he called a few days later to mumble some apologies and ask if she would see him again.

"N. O. NO!" She hung up on him. For putting up with that kind of bullshit, she thought, she SHOULD get paid.

That Saturday night, she donned a lace-up PVC skirt and a leather wristband she found at a punk clothing store, then hung a short new whip on her left, made of red leather and thin, bitey lashes. On top, she wore a short faux-leather vest that zipped up the front. She critiqued her outfit in the mirror. She wished she could afford better clothes, but she still looked good. It was all about attitude, she reminded herself. She threw her head back and practiced sneering and flaring her nostrils with disgust in the mirror. Her mission was to find at least one new client.

She returned to the building with the black tent, hoping to bump into another man like Henry, but maybe younger and more adventurous. The street outside the club was deserted, though she saw a man step through the door. The burley bouncer who seemed friendly to her last time, was smoking a cigar by himself and didn't seem to remember her.

"Sorry, doll," he said as he flicked an ash, "you can't come in tonight."

She panicked. Did she do something wrong? Did someone complain about her? "You let me in last time."

"That was a special fundraiser. It was open to anyone who wanted to come."

She flashed back to the AIDS posters that hung in one corner of the tent. "Ahhhh." Did this mean she'd have to wait a year to attend a BDSM club? Where would she find another one? "Well, that's disappointing," she sputtered, staring at the shiny heels she had planned to plant in a potential client's crotch.

"Try the Palace of Pain. It's a pro house, but they're having a slave auction tonight so the public can attend."

"Okay." She didn't know what she was getting into, but definitely wanted to get into it. "Palace of Pain" was a hilarious name, and she would finally get to meet real dominatrixes! She would study them and learn their ways and probably most of the men there would be submissives and even if she couldn't steal their paying clients, she could at least flirt with them. Or maybe she could steal just one. "Thank you! How do I get there from here?"

"I'll get you a cab." The bearded bouncer stepped to the curb, summoning a cab out of thin air, then gave the driver an address in the Meatpacking District. "Take a cab home, too," he told her. "Don't walk around the Meatpacking District by yourself. Promise."

"OK," she said, "I promise." It only made her curious to do just that.

Moments later, she stepped out of the cab into an atmosphere tainted by a stench of fresh meat, as if she had strayed into the world's largest abattoir. She walked a block north and south, peering down the side streets. She didn't know this neighborhood existed. She spotted a couple of transgender street workers plying their trade and furtive figures vanishing into alleys. Everything was dark, shuttered and shadowy, except for a busy donut shop where people were coming and going.

She saw a couple wearing leather walk into an open doorway with a dim lightbulb overhead and realized this must be her destination, too. Jax cautiously approached, and stopped 30 feet away to smoke a joint, her eyes scanning the streets in case a cop cruised by. There were no cops, just hookers and people with their chins tucked into their chests. She took a deep hit, then butted it out when a normal looking, hand-holding straight couple wearing matching khaki pants and white sneakers walked towards her. They made a small arch around her, avoided making eye contact, and hurried into the open door.

This baffled her. Were they regular straight people who came to the wrong place? Maybe they were khaki pants fetishists! Did that even exist? She giggled uncontrollably, which told her that she was high enough to go in now. If Midwestern tourists could enter a professional dungeon, she damn well could go in. The club didn't seem as intimidating.

She went inside and was surprised not to see a bouncer. She walked down a long, dimly lit hall and turned right at the end. A table was placed so that you couldn't go further without talking to the woman behind the desk who was taking money and had a coat rack behind her.

"Are you here for the auction?" the woman asked. "It's $15 to get in and I'll need to see ID saying you're 21 and $3 if you want to check something."

"I don't have anything to check," Jax said.

"Check your wallet," the woman, a stiff-faced brunette with heavily tweezed eyebrows, said sarcastically. "I need your ID and the entrance fee."

Jax paused. She wasn't sure about showing this woman her driver's license. They would know her real name. She felt safer just being the anonymous Mistress Amazon.

A man in leather pants, shirtless under an open leather vest, came over to them.

"You're new here, right?" he addressed Jax. "And a femdom?"

She nodded shyly.

"Then put your money away," he said, winking at her. "Femdoms get in free!"

"Really, Frank?" The woman looked annoyed. "I didn't even check her ID yet."

Jax held her driver's license out and Frank and the woman both glanced at it.

"Fine, go in," the woman waved.

"Welcome to Palace of Pain." Frank showed her the way in. He led her to a seat at the bar and called to the bartender. He lightly touched Jax on the shoulder. "I'm Frank. If anyone touches you or harasses you, you let me know. I'll be walking the floor all night. I'll take care of them."

The bartender brought her orange juice in a small cup and Jax explored the space with her eyes. It was unlike any she had seen before. The tent was set up more like a classroom, with all the large-scale equipment gathered on a podium up front. Here, equipment randomly lined the walls, a couple of cages near the bar, a suspension bondage station in the middle of the room, bondage crosses and bondage swings erected in every corner. Some people were dressed in leather, latex, corsets and rubber. Others walked around naked or nearly-naked. A guy wearing a diaper above black socks and black business shoes came to the bar and the bartender obligingly filled his plastic baby bottle with orange juice.

There were whips, chains, latex and handcuffs almost everywhere you turned. She couldn't believe it! It was like she left reality and wandered into a Hieronymus Bosch painting. She didn't even know what she was seeing. People were crouched in cages, standing for whippings, lying back in swings with all four limbs tied. She peered through the crowds to look for the khaki people. They were in a corner with a small group of friends, putting thick pewter fetters on each other's ankles and wrists.

She suddenly felt out of place. All the gay men made her feel more comfortable. Their space was neat and spotlessly clean. Here, there were layers of sawdust on the floor to absorb body fluids, the walls looked like they'd light up like Christmas trees under luminol. It was surprisingly heterosexual and cliquish. Pompous little men paraded female slaves with sycophants trailing behind them, holding their equipment bags. Couples and groups huddled at tables, while singles roamed chaotically from station to station to gawk at all the Masters and Mistresses and slaves playing.

"Hello, Mistress Amazon." A man sidled up to her elbow and ordered a drink. "Tina, make me a screwdriver."

Jax was startled. Who knew her here? She didn't recognize him!

"One virgin screwdriver coming up."

"They don't serve alcohol here," Felix said to Jax, who had already figured that out. He looked at his cup. "Tina! There's no juice in my juice, it's all ice."

She rolled her eyes at him and rearranged a nipple that had popped out of her bustier. "Here." She added half a shot of juice to his glass.

Felix took a gulp, then made a face.

"Tina, now it tastes like a nipple," he said.

"Fuck you," said Tina, busy with another customer.

He laughed and turned to Jax.

"Do we know each other?" There was something uncomfortably familiar about him.

"I'm Felix. I met you at the AIDS fundraiser in the Village. I was the one in the mask."

It was Zorro! He didn't look as slim and sleek without the corset. His belly was flabby, and gray hair popped out of his shirt. He wasn't as old as Henry. She guessed he was closer to 50.

"I remember you." What she remembered was that she left him hanging with a drink. Normally she'd feel a little guilty, but either he didn't remember or he accepted it as part of her femdom persona.

"Where do you work?" he asked casually. "Maybe I'll ask for you some time. I love trying out new Mistresses."

"I don't work anywhere," she said, "I only see clients privately." She inspected him. He was kind of appealing in a kinky way. He was meticulously groomed and seemed terribly experienced. His being at clubs also meant he might be able to introduce her to people or teach her about the new toys she was seeing.

"You don't work at a dungeon? Everyone has to work at a dungeon!" He began listing all the dungeons and dominatrices he had visited, like a walking BDSM encyclopedia of the joys to be had at Private Pleasures vs. Rubber Riot vs. Depraved Lotus, and how Mistress Alita did the best bondage, but Mistress Sienna had the best sissy collection. He pointed out a remarkably large Mistress in a vast latex cape. "That's Mistress Katrina. She works here and she is the bitchiest bitch in the bitchiverse." He glugged the last ice cubes in his cup. "Stay away from her," he said. "She doesn't respect safewords. I once saw her beat a guy until I thought he'd have to go to the hospital from what she did to his ass."

Jax gaped at her. Was this the same Mistress Katrina that Henry spoke of? Was that why he liked her, because she ignored limits? He spoke so highly of her, but he also left her when he met Jax. So maybe he preferred someone who treated him with respect, after all.

Katrina was a tower of a woman, wide and tall like a Henry Moore statue, with upper arms as big as Jax's thighs. Her latex cape was as big as a cave! She wondered if Henry ever fantasized about those arms destroying his ass. Maybe he compared her to Jax when he told her to hit him harder. Maybe that's why he withheld safewords from Jax. Maybe he was afraid that if he used it, she'd stop. Which she would.

And what if Henry was the very guy Zorro had seen?! That blew her mind. It was possible though. He wanted brutality. He wanted emotional suffering. He wanted to be told he wasn't good enough to fuck. That went beyond play. That was tapping into his negativity. She didn't want to see Henry again. She'd find someone else to pay her.

"The best place in the city is L'Oubliette, of course," Zorro rattled on. "You couldn't get in there, it's very private. This place is a pigsty compared to L'Oubliette."

"Then why are you here?"

Just then, a man popped out of the crowd and landed on his knees in front of her.

"Hello, Mistress, may I serve you?" he asked.

"Not now, John!" Felix looked annoyed. "Can't you see the Mistress is busy?"

"Felix!" Jax snarled. "That's not your decision. You may stay," she said to the kneeling man.

Felix looked taken aback. John sniggered.

"Of course, Mistress," Felix folded his arms, "but I thought we were having a great conversation."

"You have a low bar on greatness," she said, which further

delighted John.

"What are you laughing at?" she snarled at him and he crumpled like a wilting flower.

"I'm sorry, Mistress," he quivered.

She removed the crop from her keyring and lightly tapped his shoulders, as if she was knighting him.

"You may stay there, slave John," she said, "until I decide what to do with you."

"Thank you, Mistress." He bent down and gently kissed her boots.

Jax was starting to relax. With the two men hovering around her, it seemed like other people were noticing her presence. She couldn't tell yet if Felix was someone she wanted to enlist as a client. Clearly, he had plenty of cash to throw at femdoms so she felt confident she could get him to visit her, at least once. On the other hand, he seemed like a mansplaining control freak. Still, she could always gag him.

"Let's do an experiment!" she announced.

"What kind of experiment?" Both men were intrigued.

"You," she grabbed John fiercely by the scruff, and dragged him to his feet, "you follow me to that little stage." She pointed to a small, well-lit platform in an alcove, where people had intermittently been spanking or tying people. "You," she turned to Felix, "will assist me." She had her doubts about him, but she had to keep stringing him along if he was willing to pay for play.

John totally amused her. He wore a conservative haircut that looked incongruous with the shiny yellow Lycra jumpsuit that showed off his smallish penis and tight balls. From the neck up, he looked like he drove in from Long Island, where he worked a 9 to 5, maybe lived with his mother, maybe raised pigeons. From the neck down, he looked like Big Bird, but plucked.

"Why are you wearing yellow?" She couldn't contain her curiosity.

"It was on sale," he said. "It was 80% cheaper than the black one. Do you like it?"

She giggled. She was still high. Or maybe she was even higher, because she felt madly free and happy now. Everyone was so weird! They were even weirder than she was! It was wonderful!

"It's adorable," she said. "Especially," she wiggled her index finger at his penis, "your salute to masculinity." She gave him a thumbs up and he burst into laughter.

He had a beautiful smile and soft brown eyes. She felt a friendly flutter towards him. He probably couldn't afford a professional but, she reasoned, showing off her skills in public could draw other paying clients. This way, she could consider playing as a kind of PR! She amused herself imagining taking a tax deduction for pimping her SM skills.

"Do you want a safeword?"

"I trust you," he said.

"You really shouldn't," she smiled. "Not anyone, not until you know you can."

He looked touched. "I know. You're right." He looked up thoughtfully. "Sawdust!"

"You want sawdust as your safeword?"

"Yeah, because you should see how much of that shit on the floor sticks to lycra. I have to peel it off for half an hour when I get home. I wish I could safeword out of that."

Now she officially liked him. She pointed silently at the floor and he dropped to his knees immediately, assuming an even more servile position, his knees spread far apart, his ass so high you could see clear up to his nose.

She turned to Zorro. "Felix, can you find me a whip in this crowd? Is that possible?"

"I'll be right back!" Within moments, he held a whip with a braided leather handle and good heft. She'd never used a whip like this before, she'd only experimented a little with such substantial and expensive tools at The Leather Man. "It's called a flogger," Felix volunteered.

She swished it around experimentally, letting it graze her leg. The lashes were wide and soft. She swished it closer, letting it wrap around her leg. It was like dozens of soft little tentacles wrapping and unwrapping around her, like octopus hugs minus the slime.

A small crowd of voyeurs had gathered to watch so she turned back to John, excited to use this new toy on him. She gently moved some hair off his face. She stroked his cheek and said, "Are you sure you want this?" And he said, "Oh yes!" And she said, "Really sure?" And he said, "Yes, Mistress, yes, yes."

Without warning, she pulled him so close to her she could almost taste him. He fell into her gracefully, and she felt every curve, especially the penis curve, of his body through the stretched fabric. She reached down and pulled the Lycra away from his groin, bundling it fiercely in her hand so her knuckles pressed into his cock and balls, then twisting it roughly, giving him a wedgie in back and a knuckleball in front. He shrieked. The crowd moved closer.

"Get on all fours!" She released him cruelly.

"Yes, Mistress!" he whimpered, relieved to be free, but still trembling with fear.

She took the flogger Felix had held for her and began to stroke his back. It wasn't good enough to hit fabric. She wanted to see it fall on John's flesh.

"Pull that ridiculous Big Bird thing down to your waist, I

want you naked from the waist up."

Sweat poured down his face and his penis stood at full mast.

She half regretted mocking the jumpsuit he was so proud of. "Perfect," she cooed, "I didn't want to tear your lycra."

"Thank you, Mistress," he said.

She ran the flogger across his upper torso while he shivered and absorbed the experience as she described it to him. He was so lucky, she said, to have so many voyeurs crowding the stage to watch him, wishing they were him. And what about the humiliation of being on all fours, so exposed, so naked, with a beautiful woman standing over him giving him sensations he'd never felt before. Wasn't he lucky?

Slave John became mute with lust, unable to form words, communicating only through moans and high-pitched mewls. Did he hear her words or did they enter his consciousness through his skin? She'd never seen anyone in a trance like that. She continued stroking him sensuously, and finally finished with five hard strokes that made him moan.

Then she turned back to Felix and gave him the flogger.

She checked on John. He was still recovering, lying on the floor, but with his suit pulled back up, daydreaming.

"Are you okay?" she asked.

"I'm great," he said. "You were great. Can we do it again?"

She helped him back to his feet. "Would you like to see me professionally?"

"I wish, I can't afford it. My wife would find out. She doesn't know about any of this."

"Oh." Her panties were drenched and her imagination was on fire, but that was the end of John.

"In that case, no, you can't see me again," she said coldly, making a new rule in her head. People like him were precisely the ones who deserved to pay for domination. If they were lying and cheating to get their secret kicks, they should pay someone to keep their dirty secrets for them. She wasn't a BDSM charity.

She turned her back on him and looked for Felix. Apparently, he'd been keeping an eye on her because he immediately caught her glance and ran to her across the club.

"Are you done?" he asked. "You know you were very good," he said. "I was telling my friends about you, come on, I want you to introduce you."

She looked over at his friends, a couple in their 40s or 50s, she couldn't tell. They were obviously in a Mistress/slave relationship and looked as if they'd both just stepped out of a fancy fetish magazine's front cover, their leathers supple and soft. She was already jealous of the woman. She glanced around the room longingly. She so wanted to find just one paying client tonight.

Felix kept pushing, "No, really, you have to meet them, you should, they're like BDSM nobility," he whispered. "They're the owners of L'Oubliette. It's an honor they're here. You never know, maybe they can help you."

"You think so?" She looked at them again. She wanted to hear more about L'Oubliette. The idea that they could help her, whether true or not, hooked her.

"Meet Lady Lilith and her slave." He introduced her to a dignified woman with a tall, intricately braided coif. A calfskin dress hugged her full breasts and slim hips. Between them she wore a red silk corset with light sprays of glitter that twinkled when she moved. Her nameless slave looked like a crow. His nose was big and sharp as a beak, his eyes were black and nervous, and he hunched over his phone like a bird.

The older woman greeted her cordially, extending a dry hand. "I am known as Lady Lilith."

"Hello," Jax shook her hand, "I am known as Mistress Amazon."

The crow turned to Felix. "I already like her!"

Jax sat down with them, hoping to hear more about the high-class dungeon they ran. A few minutes into conversation, Lilith was instead telling her about a valuable collection of whips she just ordered from an artisan in England, while the crow was deep in conversation with Felix about setting up the lighting system to spotlight the standing X-frames. Lilith talked about whips the way Lucille talked about designer purses, extolling the quality of the leather and the attention to detail. The crow asked Felix, "Do you think if I use a filter I could get their sweat to glisten more in the light?"

They spoke so mundanely about things that were so weird. There was a strangeness to these people talking about BDSM like it was no big deal. It was stranger to her than Big Bird. They were really serious about their kinks. They were serious enough to spend fortunes on their sex lives, serious enough to live and breathe their kinkiness every hour of every day. She hadn't realized there were real life people who lived like this. She thought of BDSM more like a hobby, something you did for fun, not a way of life.

She looked at her watch. It was 10 pm. The slave auction still hadn't begun, but the evening had gone sideways on her. She wasn't in the mood now. "I should get going." she stood up.

"Aww," Lilith said, "so early?"

"You know, we should all be going," the crow said. He looked at Lilith inquisitively.

"Why don't you join us?" Lilith said to her. "I'd love to show you around L'Oubliette."

"Yeah," Felix urged her, "you gotta see it! L'Oubliette is like the Versailles of dungeons, no joke. You can't turn down the Versailles!"

"Can't I?" she whispered to him.

"If you don't like it, I will get you a cab home."

On the street, Lilith took her arm while the men walked a few steps behind them. "So, where have you trained, dear?"

"Trained?"

"Yes, where did you get your femdom training?"

She'd heard of slave-training but dom-training? You needed training to hit people and walk all over them? It had never occurred to her. Jax shook her head slowly. "I have not had training."

"What? You call yourself a dominatrix, but you never trained?" Lilith seemed offended. "It's an art! I train women to become the goddesses they always wanted to be."

The words got under her skin. How could she call herself a dominatrix if she didn't know the things that other dominatrices knew? Training sounded like an advanced degree in kink.

"My real name is Jax," she blurted.

The older woman smiled at her. "It's very nice to meet you, Jax."

They came to a factory building just two blocks away and the crow hurried ahead of them to unlock the front door and hold it open for them. The elevator was claustrophobic. On the top floor, the door slid open and she saw a bare foyer furnished only with a desk and chair. The place looked deserted.

Lilith walked ahead and opened a previously invisible door in one of the dark walls.

"Let me show you our rooms." Jax made her way to Lilith in the dark. Behind the door, there was a long hallway with spotless wood floors and closed doors. The wall was lined with framed photos of fetish goddesses. A thick runner rug ran almost end to end. It muffled their footsteps.

"This is the bondage and spanking room. It's our most popular private room."

She proudly waved her hand at the interior, which was furnished with a bondage cross, a large bondage table with steel rings bolted to the corners and sides, a saddle bench, a vintage low bench, and an armless chair perfect for an over-the-knee spanking. "We store the small toys here." She opened an armoire to reveal rows of small whips, canes, and glimmering nipple clamps, chains and ropes and locks and gadgets.

There was so much equipment, Jax wished she had her notebook with her so she could keep track of them all. "So, the dominatrixes who work here can use any of these things on men?"

"On men, on women, on transgendered people," Lilith said. "Look," she showed Jax the next room. "This is specifically for sissies and crossdressers," she said. It looked more like a whorehouse in an old Western than a kinky dungeon. The room had pink curtains, feather boas scattered on chairs and peacock feathers in a vase. Even the rug was pink.

Something soft and furry brushed Jax's leg. A tuxedo cat meowed and purred, arching her back in happiness. Jax bent down to scratch the furry baby. She missed her mother's cat, who sought her out whenever Lucille left the house, as if he knew their relationship had to be kept secret. She ached for a cat of her own.

"Buttons, shoo," Lilith yelled. "You know you can't come into the private rooms!" She looked apologetically at Jax. "Some people have allergies." She talked to the cat firmly, "You know the rules, Buttons, shoo! SHOO!" She chased it out of the room.

Jax peered behind a dressing screen and saw a rack of shoes on the floor and a standing rack with ladies gowns and cocktail dresses in bright colors.

"We prefer that clients bring their own, but we have clothes for them if they don't," Lilith explained. She showed Jax a closet that had been converted into a small make-up booth, with a vanity table crammed with product and a pillow-stool. Mirrors lined the walls. Lilith turned on a switch and the nook blazed.

The crow appeared in the doorway.

"We gotta speed this up," he said. "Lilith, you're needed out front." Lilith left and he took over, moving Jax swiftly through the remaining rooms.

"I think you'll like this." He opened the door to a small room with sconces on the walls. When he turned them on, their lightbulbs flickered like candles. A delicate crystal chandelier shimmered on the ceiling. The room faced an air shaft and cool air filtered in from the dark window. A scarlet runner rug led to a throne-like chair upholstered in gold jacquard. On the wall behind the chair was a golden mural of an Asian goddess with 8 arms holding a variety of whips, paddles and canes. There was no other furniture in the room, no menacing toys, no transformational costumes, no sign they were in a dungeon. If she didn't know it was part of a dungeon, she would have taken it for a spiritual space, like the inner chamber of a temple.

"This is our Goddess worship room," the crow said. "Did you know that men will pay you just to kiss your feet?"

She flashed back to the footie guy she teased at Booker's table. She could have charged him for the show! If men were willing to pay for that, it opened a whole new market to her.

"Next," the crow ran to another door, "this is the cage room."

Jax caught up with him and looked inside. "We try to only put one person in here at a time, but when it gets really busy, both cages may be occupied."

Jax eyed the cages. She'd never seen anything like them. One was for standing and one was for lying down. They were bolted to the floors so they couldn't fall over if captives got rowdy. The cages looked similar in dimension, but the standing cage had a front door you could walk through and the flat cage had a side door you had to crawl through. There wasn't anything you could do, but stand or lie down once inside. It was diabolical. She wondered how long most slaves lasted in there without safewording. This was some crazy fucking shit. You could put one person in the standing cage and one in the dog cage and see which one called out their safeword first. Ha! She imagined Henry and his crackly old bones climbing in. They'd have to saw him out.

"The only thing you can't do in L'Oubliette is have sex," the crow said, walking to the last room.

"Why not?"

"It's New York," the crow said. "It's the LAW. It would hurt our reputation."

"I see," she said, but she didn't. It seemed absurd that a place where naked people were being whipped would draw the line at orgasmic sex or that a house of ill-repute worried about its reputation.

"OK, one more room." The crow opened a door to an old fashioned, fully tiled bathroom, with a small sink, a toilet and a shower without doors or curtains. Instead, enema bags and tubes hung from the metal ring. "This is our wet room," he said. "Do you know what it's for?"

Jax tried to remember what she'd read online.

"Watersports?" she mumbled in embarrassment.

"That's right," he nodded.

They stood in silence.

"Um," Jax stumbled. "I'm not sure how I feel about those things."

"We don't judge people's fetishes here," the crow said.

It seemed like a very noble policy to avoid judging people because of what they needed, but instead, to help them safely fulfill those needs.

"OK, we gotta go back up front. Any questions?"

"Do you mind if I pee here?"

"I'll see you out front." He closed the door behind him.

Jax was beside herself. Her mind reeled with all the perversions that must have occurred in this room, the peeing and the enemas. It was so very strange, so comfortingly strange to know there were people even stranger than herself.

She finished up and found Lilith sitting at the desk, bent over paperwork.

"I love your dungeons," Jax said to her. "I can tell how hard you worked to build all this. I can't imagine how much planning and money it took."

"It was no picnic, let me tell you. I worked like a dog to build it!" Lilith held her pen mid-air. "I was a successful executive in the cosmetics industry. I retired early to build this business. Sometimes I regret it."

"Really?! Why?"

"You have no idea what people are really like until you run a fetish club," Lilith said with an air of fatigue. "The shoe fetishists really drove me crazy. They have such specific tastes! It's impossible. One wants open toe sandals, another wants high heels, then someone asks for sneakers. We're not a shoe store!"

Jax giggled and Lilith forced a smile. "Give me panty-sniffers any day of the year," she said. "They basically come in two flavors -- cotton like their mothers wore or the sexy bikini type."

"Wow," Jax mumurmed. This was the kind of problem she wished she had, trying to figure out how one could meet the needs of a howling chaos of horny fetishists. From what she'd read, there could be hundreds of fetishes, maybe thousands. She read a book which had explained that even within general categories of fetish there were specifics that made one fetish different from another one. Jax began adding up all the riches to be made if one could cater to them all.

She wondered how much a person could make doing this full-time instead of an hour or two a week. She wondered how much Lilith would charge for training and how long it would take for her to be a goddess who could work in a place like this or, better still, in this place. She didn't dare ask Lilith about it. The older woman would probably laugh at her naiveté for thinking it would be easy to become one of the elite goddesses who worked at L'Oubliette, the Versailles of the kinky realm.

"Come, I'll show you the main attraction." Lilith stood up.

"There's more?"

Crow scuttled past them, carrying a box to the front. Jax noticed that his legs were stiff and crooked with arthritis. She realized that he, and Lilith, were probably a lot older than they looked. She respected them even more. Felix was not wrong. They were like debauched nobility. There was a tantalizing world-weariness to them, as if they'd seen it all. They probably had. She wanted to be like them when she got old, a walking catacomb of weird wisdom and esoteric experience.

"Here is our pride and joy," Lilith said. "Fred, open the door!"

Jax watched the man rotate an enormous wheel on the wall

opposite the elevator. The wall slowly slid to the left, revealing an enormous room, several times the size of the back dungeons. She crossed the threshold and gazed up at the vast complex of track lighting rails and pulleys in perfect symmetries of chrome and steel. The massive structure made it look like a portal to another planet.

It was a cathedral of perversion. No sawdust covered the floors here. The oak boards were gleaming and immaculate. No random arrangement of big equipment. Everything was obsessively organized, perfectly aligned, craftily illuminated.

"I can control everything," Fred called out. "I can make spots dark." He turned down a group of lights and a corner of the room vanished into the dark. "I can focus on one station only." He played with some switches and the entire room vanished, leaving only a center bondage station lit like a torch in the darkness. "Me and Felix and some friends thought we could do it in a few months, but it took us almost a year. Lilith was ready to kill me over the delays." He turned the lights on high so Jax could get a good look around.

"Go on, go inside, check it out. People will be arriving soon, so walk fast. I need to dim them when they get here."

Whipping posts and large red-leather upholstered benches, curious benches and tables were lined up in perfect geometric symmetry, allowing for easy passage through the aisles. It reminded her of a fancy gym, except instead of stationary bicycles and weight machines, there were sawhorses, spanking benches and sturdy scaffolding that held bondage swings.

She walked in a daze to the back. A gigantic wooden wheel occupied half a wall, with heavily padded cuffs attached to the spokes in different places. Cages that could hold tigers lined part the far wall, alongside a mock jail cell with a narrow wood door and short bars for a window. There was also a cell that looked like a meat locker on the outside and a padded cell on the inside. A straight jacket was neatly arranged on the cushioned floor and an infrared camera was installed by the door. She shuddered and went to a human-size bird cage that was suspended from a ceiling rafter. She felt like she was in a movie. She gave the cage a push and it twirled slowly.

Lilith came bustling through, searching out any smidgeon of dirt or dust. Crow followed her with a rag in one hand and a bottle of disinfectant in the other as Lilith ordered him to wipe this and spray that. Then she screamed and summoned him to a corner.

"Fred, what the fuck is that?!" Crow man ran over on his stiff skinny legs, waving the bottle of disinfectant, prepared to do battle with whatever toxic mess needed cleansing.

"Oh, it's just a little cocky-roachy." He squatted down and caught the beetle in his hands, then opened a window and dropped it out to fly away.

"Did you just fucking rescue it? Tell me you didn't rescue a fucking cockroach!"

"It's a living thing," said Fred.

"Jesus Fucking Christ, Fred, you rescued a fucking cockroach. What's next, a rat?"

"It's a living thing," Fred repeated stubbornly. "It can't help that it's a cockroach."

Lilith and Jax locked eyes.

"Submissives," Lilith shrugged, "what are you going to do?" The women laughed together and moved on.

Jax quickly surveyed the club's sex shop. Behind large locked plexiglass doors, chrome tracks held hundreds of implements and kinky gear for sale or rent. She felt like an anthropologist who had studied ancient pottery for years and finally saw the precious relics in their native setting. Nipple clamps, leather hoods, harnesses, chastity devices, leather corsets, whips, cat o'nine tails, tawses, crops, cock rings, leather bras, dildos, gags, blindfolds, handcuffs, leg cuffs, toe cuffs, plus toys she could not identify.

Just then, a commotion broke out in the front hall. Jax thought it was the party guests, but instead it was Felix in his Zorro mask and corset.

"Here I come to save the day!" Felix sang out. "Got some fresh donuts for my favorite ladies." He placed the boxes on the desk as another secret door opened wide. Women poured out of it, clamoring for donuts. First 3, then 2 more, then 2 more after that, then another group of three and finally a woman with big hair, thick make-up and a long red latex dress. Apparently, they'd been waiting in a hidden lounge for customers to arrive.

Walls behind walls behind walls. That's how they survived. It resonated with her, just as the walls in Paul's apartment had. Walls behind walls behind walls. It was how underground people lived. It was how hedonists and anarchists lived. The outliers. The ones hiding in plain sight. The ones who had to keep their sex lives secret because prudes ruled the world.

The women were cooing over the donuts. Jax couldn't help staring at them. Their outfits were seductive and creative, playing up each woman's best features. A large round ass was encased in latex, two slim, small-bosomed women wore school-girl outfits, a thick-waisted woman with enormous breasts wore a heavy corset and low cut shirt to show them off. These women, Jax couldn't stop thinking, were the women who turned the power tables on men. Women who spanked men on their bare behinds and treated them like slaves and serfs, and got paid for it! Paid to put men through their paces on torture devices, and paid to sit back and allow men to worship their feet and confess their devotion. Paid for it! Yes. By men who wanted it. Yes! Paid to wear latex and leather and dress up in fantasy outfits. Her experience with Henry seemed so amateurish to her now. She could only imagine what these dominatrixes had done in the room with the cages.

Jax then took a chocolate donut. Her appetite died the second she picked it up. She held the donut as if she didn't know what it was for and stepped back from the crowd. She was overwhelmed in ways she'd never expected. She wished she had known about this place two years ago. She never would have worked at the papaya joint if she knew then what she knew now.

"Let me introduce you to the girls." Lilith took the donut out of her hand and put her arm around Jax's shoulder protectively. "Are you doing okay?"

Jax melted into the older woman's gentle hug. An intense sense of belonging vibrated into her core. She felt at home here. "Yeah, I'm fine. It's just... a lot to take in." Lilith seemed concerned. "But I love it. I love everything. It's like I found home." She blushed crimson.

"I'm so glad you feel that way," Lilith said. She took Jax to the group of women.

"Ladies, meet Mistress Amazon," Lilith said, "she's still new to our world, so be nice."

"Oh, Lil, you know we're not going to hurt her," the woman in the gown said. "Right, Miss Mary-Jane?" She stared at one of the women dressed in a school jumper and knee socks.

"That's right, Mama Donna!" The woman dropped into a curtsey. At first glance, she looked Jax's age, but now, up close, the schoolgirl was probably in her 30s. She was small, brunette and perky, with a pretty face and green eyes. "We only hurt the ones who pay!" she said like a brat. Next to her, another woman of uncertain age, but who wore the same school uniform, started giggling and threatening her with a spanking.

Mama Donna nodded, Mary-Jane beamed, a couple of women tittered, and the others looked bored. Jax smiled politely, unsure how to align with the mixed reactions.

"Welcome to L'Oubliette." Mama Donna walked up to her and gave her a hard hug. She was either the true alpha of the pack or she thought she was, and behaved accordingly. She was formidably solid, with wide hips and thick legs, a small mountain of a woman. Jax wondered if she was the femdom she once saw in a grainy old black and white SM movie Jax and Booker watched in a private booth at a dirty bookshop. When the woman in the movie lowered her enormous hips over his frightened face, her enormous thighs squeezed his face so hard, his lips and eyes bulged. Booker shouted, "Oh Sweet Lord Jesus, no! She's going to squash him! She's going to kill him with her vagina!" and then dragged Jax out of the shop while she screamed with laughter.

Now that she had Donna's approval, the rest of them introduced themselves. The schoolgirl duo were Mary-Jane and Suzie Q. The other names melted into a blur of fanciful titles and nicknames: Mistress Amber, Goddess Love, Sexy Queen Sadi, China Doll, Lady Fedora, who wore a fedora, Leather Lee, who was clad in black leather from boots to neck, a woman who went by "The Madame" and another called "Empress." Finally, the most exquisite among them introduced herself as Goddess Velvet.

The women were surprisingly friendly. They asked how she liked it and how she felt about L'Oubliette, and poured out advice as the partygoers started arriving. They told her to make sure to use safewords, to tell Fred if anyone crossed a line with her, and offered to let her stick close to them. She had never felt so protected before.

When they left to join the guests, Mistress Velvet pulled her aside. "I think we wear the same size," she said. "Would you like to borrow some fetish clothes for tonight? We have a closet of outfits to choose from."

Jax looked at Lilith. The older woman nodded.

Velvet led Jax through the lounge where the Mistresses had been waiting, a small comfortable room with couches, and a coffee station next to a bank of small televisions. At the back of the room, there was a door that opened neither into a closet nor a hall, but into a larger secret room.

This room held hundreds of dresses, pants, shoes and boots. There were twelve dressing tables with mirrors. Eleven of them held wigs and curling irons and make-up tools. One was empty.

Velvet showed her the inner bathroom. It was surprisingly spacious and had two glass-enclosed shower stalls, three toilet booths, three sinks and a long marble counter with a mirror.

They came back out and Velvet pointed to the empty vanity table. "If you do good tonight," she said, "that will be your table."

"What?" Jax's pulse raced. It was hard to conceal her excitement. "Do you think I could work here? Don't I need to take a training course first?"

Velvet said, "You'll learn as you go, sitting in on sessions and apprenticing to the Mistresses. When I showed up, my name is Shirley by the way, I didn't know a thing about BDSM. I was working as an escort, but when I heard you didn't have to fuck clients, I applied."

"I'm Jax!"

"Hi, Jax. Cool name. Anyway, they tried some fetish outfits on me and laid out the rules on consent and safety and keeping everything clean and hired me that day. It took me a couple of months to get up to speed. I bet it'll go even quicker for you."

"But you're so beautiful!" Jax said. "Anyone would hire you. I would hire you!!"

Velvet giggled and threw her strong arms around Jax. It was the second time a woman had hugged her in the last hour and the only time women had hugged her for no reason. She hugged her back with enthusiasm.

"Honey, I can already tell you're a natural. We watched you checking out the public dungeon. You looked like a little girl in a candy shop, the way you were running around and checking out each and every toy!"

"How did you see me... ?"

"Oh, we have a security system." She took Jax back out to the lounge and pointed to the small bank of TVs. "We can watch all the rooms. Let's get you dressed!"

Shirley took her back to the wardrobe and selected a sleeveless black PVC jumpsuit with a built-in corset, a plunging neckline and laces down the legs from thigh to ankle.

Jax slipped out of her clothes and Shirley handed her the garment. Jax couldn't figure out where to begin, it had so many laces and buckles and ties.

"Stand still, I'll deal with it," Shirley said. The jumpsuit was suddenly in motion around Jax, climbing up her legs, squeezing her waist tight, forcing her breasts so high and firm she could carry her purse on them. She giggled.

"How long have you worked here?" she asked her new friend.

"Sometimes I think too long," Shirley said. "Now turn around and look in the mirror." She put her hands on Jax's shoulder and swiveled her around. An honest-to-god fetish queen stared back from the mirror.

"It was made for you! Look how great you look! What size shoes do you wear?"

"I'm an 8."

Jax was transfixed by her reflection. The jumpsuit made her reedy body look more voluptuous on top, with a small waist that accentuated her hips. Her hair and make-up felt wrong, but from the side, she looked absolutely flawless.

"Me too!!" Shirley ran to a bin and came back with red ankle boots that laced up the front. They looked intimidating, but once Jax put them on, she was surprised at how easy they were to walk in. She jumped in the air, then twirled on her toes.

"Those were custom made for my feet," Shirley said. "It's like we're sisters."

Jax beamed at her.

"OK." Shirley grabbed her hand and pulled her to the empty 12th table. "I'm 11," she said. She grabbed a bunch of her supplies and went to work on Jax. She quickly brushed and sprayed Jax's hair to give it more volume. Jax was spellbound by Shirley's make-up skills. Shirley dusted her hair with gold glitter, applied fake eyelashes, painted her lips until they turned into a large red bow of color on her pale face and finished off with a powder that made her skin glow.

"We don't get a lot of girls like you," Shirley murmured.

"What do you mean?" Jax stood up and went to the full length mirror. She had never looked so perfect. She had never felt so perfect. She practiced poses, trying to look domineering and fierce.

"Hahaha," Shirley came up behind her. "You're going to make a fortune."

"What do you mean by girls like me?"

"High-class. You seem like you come from money."

"I do??" Until now, Jax didn't realize that anyone saw her that way.

"Just how you act and talk. You don't even have a New York accent. I bet you went to a private school, right?"

"It was a long time ago," Jax said.

"Yeah, maybe," Shirley said, "but it still shows." The older woman looked at her thoughtfully. "You have rich people manners and you use big words."

Jax laughed. "Well fuck me," she said, winking at Shirley. "I didn't realize." No one here needed to know about her former life as a rash-covered working-class girl. Maybe coming from money could be a unique selling point for her. "My parents are wealthy, but I went to live with my grandparents and money's been tight."

"We all have our own reasons for working here." Shirley nodded sympathetically.

Buttons casually trotted by, as if he thought he was invisible. He resisted Jax when she grabbed him by the scruff, but when he realized petting was involved, he went limp and gave her his belly.

"I love this cat!" Jax said.

"I'm glad someone does," said Shirley. "Lilith calls him the moocher. He wandered in from the street one day and never left. He's supposed to catch mice, but the one time he found one, he wouldn't kill it." She burst into a shrill giggle.

"How adorable!" Jax released him and he trotted off.

"We don't need another moocher around here. Right, Buttons?" Shirley called as the cat ran out the door. "Run away, coward!"

"Who's the first moocher?"

Shirley leaned in close, looking warily around even though they were alone, and whispered, "Felix, the guy with the donuts. You saw him?" Jax nodded her head. "He never books private sessions. Don't tell anyone I told you, but he was Lilith's former sub, who just stuck around after she dismissed him. I guess she didn't have the heart to make him go away. She pretends he's part-time help, and lets him get the donuts and help Fred with things."

Jax listened thoughtfully. It surprised her that a slave wouldn't go away when his Mistress dismissed him. It meant he didn't take her power to dismiss him seriously. So who had the real power in their relationship?

"Avoid Felix," Shirley said, as if reading her thoughts. "I mean, he's okay, he's just a mooch. Focus on paying customers." She put her arm around Jax. "Come on, you're ready for your debut."

She loved Shirley then. She loved her so much she wanted them to turn around and have sex in the wardrobe room, hot, furtive, forbidden sex. She leaned in hard against her and Shirley received her love warmly and walked her back to the party.

The foyer was packed now, as people lined up at the desk where Lilith and Fred were busily checking invitation lists and collecting money. Felix was in charge of crowd control and moving guests smoothly from the elevator to the registration desk to the opulent dungeon.

"Let's go inside." Shirley was as revved up as an ambitious actor before a big scene. "It's going to be a great night!"

Shirley explained that people were back from summer vacation. Now all the married men, the boyfriends, the fathers who lived double lives like Henry were on home turf again and restless. The club would be full. Jax noticed that a few men brought their own femdoms, a few had slaves, some had girlfriends and wives, but the majority of men were alone.

Shirley whispered, "Do as much or as little as you want. I'll stay with you."

The two goddesses walked inside arm in arm, their heads high, leaving a cool breeze in their wake. Jax could feel heads turning, but kept her eyes straight ahead. Shirley led her to a big table with a wide hole carved into it about two thirds of the way down and small black dials on either side. Within seconds, people began to gather around them, and within minutes, there was a small crowd.

Shirley called out, "One hole, two balls. Who's ready for a stretch?" She bared her teeth and extended her arm, slowly pointing at the people assembled. "Don't be shy. Raise your hand!"

Three men shyly raised their hands slightly. Shirley picked the shortest among them.

The man Shirley selected went to the table and, at her command, undressed until he was stark naked.

"Nice to see you, Larry," Shirley said to him, then whispered into Jax's ear, "He's one of my regulars. I don't mind sharing." Jax tried to look cool and in charge even though inside she was on a sweltering hormonal high.

"Thank you, Velvet," she said.

"Mistress Velvet, who is your lovely assistant?"

"Folks, please meet Mistress Amazon," she spoke loudly to the crowd. "She's been working privately uptown... for a billionaire, very closeted, so that's why you've never heard of her."

Jax cackled to herself as Shirley invented the backstory, making her sound intriguingly glamorous and exclusive. A few men in the crowd now stared hungrily at Jax, who pretended she didn't even notice they were lusting after her.

"Will she be working here?" Larry asked. He turned to Jax and said, "You are very beautiful, Mistress. It would be an honor if you let me see you privately."

"We are considering her, yes," Velvet said, "and she is considering us."

She lowered her voice so only Larry and Jax could hear her. "Be extra good, this is her audition," she said to Larry, tapping him on the nose like a dog. "If she does good tonight, I'll make sure you get her first booking."

"You take such good care of me, Shirley," he murmured back. He tried to take her hand, but Shirley slapped it away and mouthed, "Not now," to him.

Jax preened. Did Shirley just book her first appointment at the club?! How was this even happening? How did people who'd never even see her do anything have so much faith in her? Well, Felix saw. Had he told them about her escapades downtown? Perhaps they saw her better than she'd seen herself. No one questioned her right to be there, her suitability for the work, her right to call herself a dominatrix. No, they embraced her as if they recognized her as one of their own.

Larry hopped on the table and stretched out comfortably. Shirley clipped heavy weights to his scrotum. Jax moved in close to watch his balls slide down into the hole. Shirley carefully turned the dials and tiny metal doors with a hole drilled in the center closed around the top of the scrotum and his balls vanished under the table. Jax gaped, palm on cheek. He looked oddly relaxed for a man who was 100% helpless.

"Help me, hon," Shirley signaled, "you tie his feet." Jax quickly bound them to the rings attached to the bottom of the table, while Shirley tied his hands to the rings on top.

"May I touch him?" she asked Shirley.

"Yes, go ahead."

Jax ran her fingertips up his thigh so sensuously that he squirmed and strained against his ropes.

"Are you trying to escape?" she teased him, conscious of the onlookers at her back. She leaned over his face and whispered loud enough for everyone to hear, "The table will cut off your balls if you try." He moaned.

"Do you want that to happen? Do you want to castrate yourself?"

"No, Mistress, no, please, I'll do anything..."

Ten minutes later, Larry was on his feet, chatting happily. "That was something else," he said. "Wow, I'm still flying."

Velvet kissed him on the lips. "You're welcome. Now, thank Amazon."

"Yes, Mistress." He pulled out his wallet. "This is for you," he handed Jax 300 dollars. "A little extra because I got to be your first." She took the money and stuck it under her breast.

"Good boy," Velvet said. "Amazon, would you mind being on your own for a while. I need to talk to Larry."

"Oh, no, not at all." Jax was so grateful to her, and the 300 bucks in her boobs made her even happier. She danced away.

She didn't get far. It seemed dozens of men had noticed her. They stopped her to ask if they could serve her. She said yes to them all. She found herself going from scene to scene, most lasting only 10 or 20 minutes. The night passed in a blur of excess and ecstasy. Men paid to worship her feet, they paid her to tie and whip them on crosses and tables, they paid her to spank them with their own paddles. As the money pile grew in her brassiere, her imagination and ambition soared. Midnight became 1 am, then 2 am.

At 4 am Lilith found her, sitting in the lounge with the other women, trying to recover from exhaustion.

"Let's talk," she said to Jax. The other women looked at each other knowingly. Shirley shot her a smile.

Lilith walked her to the far side of the main dungeon and opened the emergency doors. There was a door on the right marked "Office" and an unmarked door on the left. Lilith opened the office first. "This is the company office, where we do all the bookings and paperwork." Then she unlocked the facing door. "This is the loft. Wait. Did I tell you about the loft? I'm so tired, I can't remember if I told you."

"No. What about the loft?" Jax looked in. The open space had a brand new galley kitchen and the same wood flooring as the main dungeon. Light poured through the avenue-facing industrial windows. It was a little gem in a factory building.

"I don't want to rent it to a stranger," Lilith said. "I'd rather lose money on it than rent it to someone who'll rat us out."

Jax nodded. She could see herself living here, next door to glorious dungeons, friends who already felt like family coming and going all day, then evenings blissfully alone with only Buttons for company. She wished she could live there.

"I can't afford that," she said mournfully.

"Sure you can. You'll earn the rent in a week's time if you work here!" Lilith said. "You'll never find a space this nice in Manhattan for this price. You don't have to move in tomorrow. You can sign the lease on the first of next month. That gives you three weeks to think about it."

Jax could not process this! What the hell was happening?! Did Lilith just answer all her prayers? This was such crazy shit! It was amazing. It was wonderful. It was Lilith telling her, "Yes, this is my kink paradise, now please make yourself at home and move right in." Jax stared at the older woman with love.

"Oh my God," she whispered. "Oh my God."

She wanted to live here. So much. But Paul wasn't even back yet. She couldn't move out before he got back from Greece. Despite his cheery postcards assuring her that everything was great, she knew there was something he wasn't telling her. If he wasn't telling her, it couldn't be good news, either. She had to wait for him to come back before deciding. Yet the loft called to her. It was made for her.

Lilith sat her across from the desk, then took out employment forms.

"Just fill this information in," she pointed to several boxes, "and you can start working on Monday."

"You're hiring me?" Jax whispered.

"You exceeded my expectations tonight. Of course I'm hiring you. We'll train you as you go, but you have what it takes, that's obvious."

Jax was speechless with emotion. She had never felt so wanted! She had never felt like she even fit in anywhere. She was going to get Table 12 to herself, as Shirley predicted, and work alongside these amazing women! She started to cry. Lilith was empathetic and said, "I know. It's a lot and it's been a long night."

"Yes," Jax sobbed, fraught with emotions in all directions, "so much to process."

"You know what will dry the tears?" Lilith said. Jax shook her head.

"Count the money you made tonight," Lilith said.

Jax removed the stacks she had stuffed all the way down her bodice. "Nine 50s," she counted, "six 100s, that adds up to $1050." Her tears dried. She counted all the tens and twenties.

"Oh my God!" she squealed. "I'm rich!"

"I knew that would cheer you up," Lilith said, staring at her fondly. "And this is just the beginning. You're going to be my million dollar race horse."

Chapter 6

THE EDUCATION OF A DOMINATRIX

Every time Jax collected her paycheck for a week of spanking and humiliating men at L'Oubliette, she pressed it against her heart and raised her eyes to the heavens. Prosperity was her new religion.

Getting paid to wear expensive fetish clothes and play sex games she loved felt as if she was getting away with a crime. Maybe it was a crime, in a deeply socially unjust way, but that made it even more satisfying. Her father sold hardware. She sold human ecstasy and self-actualization. Which was really the more meaningful business? Filling the hunger of the human soul or hawking specialty door handles? She rejected the idea that one was somehow more moral than the other.

She had barely slept since her debut night at L'Oubliette. There was always something to do at L'Oubliette, whether apprenticing or helping with clean-ups or making runs for coffee and donuts to keep the lounge stocked. Each night, she brought a carton of take-out food home with her and sat up in bed reading notes, making lists, updating her log of expenses, and manically catching up on the Internet 10 tabs at a time. Her mind raced. She had to save. She had to plan. She had to think. How did she get here? Where would she go? Her expectations had been raised to an all-new level. No more did she think that a comfortable corporate job would make her happy. She wanted to be rich. She wanted to be famous. Who didn't? But as a high-class New York dominatrix, maybe those things were not outside the realm of possibility for her anymore. Maybe she'd never be as wealthy as Lucille, but she'd feel like a rich bitch if she was living in Lilith's 1200-square-foot loft. Even if she couldn't be famous, she could be notorious.

The spectacular debut of Mistress Amazon had impressed enough partygoers for her to book 6 paid hours in her first week, plus Lilith gave her a couple of last-minute appointments. At $150 an hour, she made as much in her first week at L'Oubliette as she made in 2 months at the juice bar. The next week, bookings doubled, and the week after that Lilith handed her another contract to sign that guaranteed her a minimum of 3 hours a day or 15 hours a week. In four weeks, she had earned back all the cash she dropped on booze and the trip to Greece for Paul.

It wasn't just money. She had learned more real world skills in the last week than she'd learned in high school. She learned more about herself than she thought possible. She learned she wasn't as weird as she thought. There were far weirder people. It was liberating to know that. She learned that she was one of a whole underground movement of sexually enlightened people who weren't just talking about a better world, but building and inhabiting it, heart and soul. And now she was training to be a Mistress, a healer, therapist, educator, liberator, and Goddess of eroticism in this world.

BDSM sharpened her focus. Playing forced her to live in the moment, to be as quiet and as observant as possible, aware of how the client breathed, how he moved, what narratives drew him out and which words shut him down, and always vigilant to potential risks. She didn't wistfully daydream about the future. She planned for it.

She was examining her face in the mirror over Table 12 one day. On her way to work, she had picked up a wildly bright lipstick called "Crimson Seduction" at the drugstore. She painted it on her pink lips and inspected her mouth. It smelled nice and made her lips as shiny as red PVC. It also made her nose look bigger and her eyes smaller. She sighed sadly. She wished God had planned for her to have a smaller nose.

"Let me give you a few make-up tips." Lilith leaned over her affectionately and they gazed in the mirror together. "Can't you see how beautiful you are?"

"Noooo. I'm really not." Jax shook her head. "My eyes are nice."

"Young women are their own worst critics," Lilith scolded. "Why do you think so many clients are lining up for you? You're hot, you're sharp as a tack and you've got class. You got the perfect trifecta!"

She looked in the mirror again. Maybe her nose didn't look big, but strong. Distinctive.

Lilith turned her chair, grabbed a brown pencil and added definition to her pale brows, then smudged them with Q-tips. She brightened her lids with a white pencil and created cat-eyes with a brown one. She handed Jax a tissue. "Blot your lips with this to help it set." She applied color to her cheeks and then applied a light gloss to her lips. "Blot," she said. "Put these on." She handed her fake eyelashes, then stopped her hand. "Let me show you a trick." She showed Jax how to glue the lashes on with mascara and applied extra coats to make them look natural. "Ok, look at yourself now." She swiveled Jax back to the mirror.

Her eyes looked huge and her nose seemed smaller. The lipstick was perfectly muted and her cheekbones stood out. She turned her left to right. "I look like a model."

"Lift your chin a little. Like that. Good. Now, some hair tips. She gathered the girl's curly blonde mane and pulled it back and up. "When you want to look severe, go with an up-do. It can be as simple as a high ponytail. If you're doing a spanking or governess scene, go with a bun. You know, something demure and old fashioned. If you want to look like a wild woman, bend your head forward and brush your hair from the neckline up. When you stand up, you can tame it back down or keep it fluffed out. With enough hairspray, it'll stay that way for hours." She released Jax's hair. "Natural is okay if you really want that to be your signature style."

Jax picked up the elastic Lilith dropped on the table and drew her hair back up in a high ponytail. She gazed at her flaming lips, pale gray eyes with spidery black lashes and dark brows. "I think I just found my signature style."

"It suits you." Lilith smiled approvingly. "A woman looks more confident when she sweeps the hair off her face."

It was yet another of the thousands of teaching moments she'd experienced at L'Oubliette. Lilith wasn't the only one accelerating her passage to adult womanhood. A month of apprenticing to the army of powerful, pragmatic femdoms at L'Oubliette made Jax feel differently about her own presence in the world. She felt taller and visibly dominant. She felt seen when she walked into stores and heard when she voiced a complaint.

What few inhibitions she had about sex had melted away. It was electrifying to see women push men's buttons, to make them do things she never thought anyone outside of a porn movie would do, whether it was enduring grueling genital torture or acting like a little girl. She had learned three different ways to tie a man's balls and a dozen ways to keep him begging for more. She had learned whole worlds about male nipples.

She felt like an anthropologist, seeking out unfamiliar rituals and customs. Her first observation was that kink could be purely psychological, or purely physical for masochists, or could combine both aspects. She could be the sadistic whip-mistress, the cock teasing sensualist, the unmerciful authority figure, the mother figure or the resplendent goddess, depending on the client's desires. All of these roles felt natural, as if they'd been hiding inside her all along. She didn't need to push herself. She learned to let go of her inhibitions and let her other selves come out.

"I don't need this whip to make you grovel before me," she said to a client one day. He was holding onto a cross to steady himself as she delivered a shower of light whip flicks across his back and buttocks.

"No, you don't, Mistress," he moaned. "You are a powerful woman inside, I can tell."

"I would be doing this to men even if I wasn't getting paid for it," she said.

"I can tell you really like it." He shied away from her blows, yelping, and she stopped, enjoying the livid marks on his behind.

"I will whip you twice as hard if you don't grovel immediately and worship my feet," she said.

He eagerly dropped down on his belly and began lavishing

kisses on her shiny boots. She leaned down and caressed his hair, sweetly murmuring, "You're my good boy. What a good boy you are."

"Thank you, Ma'am," he repeated over and over in a trance of sublime gratitude.

She loved those moments, she loved the intimacy of holding them after hurting them, and telling them that she was proud of them, that they were good boys, that they had pleased her.

The only thing wrong with her life was that home was lonely without Paul. She'd never felt lonely like this before, not even when she broke up with Booker, because Grandpa and Steve were there. Grandpa had extended his stay twice without fully explaining why. She noticed he kept saying "we" in his emails -- "We attended a party," "We're going to a gallery," and the highly suspicious, "We just woke up." Was he having an affair with Giorgos? Was he thinking of staying permanently? He kept signing off, "See you very soon," but he wouldn't commit to a date. If he was happy, she was happy, she told herself. But she wasn't happy. Her room at Paul's was narrow, the bathroom was tiny and the kitchen was filled with the memory of Steve, which was good and bad at the same time. Without Paul there, she was stuck living with Steve's ghost.

L'Oubliette soon became her second home. Lilith offered her free rent until the first of the month, so Jax brought her pillow and began crashing there. The business was open from 11 am when Lilith arrived in her office, until midnight when Fred finished cleaning up and shut down for the night, so she was never lonely. She only went home now on errands to check the mail, see if anyone had left messages on the phone machine, and to do laundry.

The rest of her time was devoted to becoming the best

Mistress she could. She knew the best way to learn her craft was to study her elders. It seemed as if there was no dark corner of kink they hadn't penetrated, no fetish culture they hadn't explored, no bizarre ritual they hadn't witnessed.

Shirley was a storehouse of knowledge on cock and ball torture, explaining butterfly boards and cock cages and all the contrivances a person could use to confine, restrict, and terrorize testicles without leaving any damage.

Shirley would say things like, "Make very, very sure his ball isn't in the way, then insert the needle through the loose skin and pin him to the board," or, "Your typical male sub can't shoot in a chastity cage, but they usually drip, so keep Kleenex handy in case you get slimed on. Well, unless you want him to eat it, of course."

"Of course." Jax nodded, scribbling as fast as she could in her notebook. She was sitting in a session that day. Shirley's client wore a hood over his head and was chained to a St. Andrews cross. His genitals were hidden by pounds of metal hardware locked around his penis and balls. Jax didn't see any drips.

"Do they all like eating their own cum?" she asked.

The man clanked loudly. He was wagging his head side to side.

"Is that a no, slave?" Jax asked him.

He nodded his head up and down as emphatically as he could, given that his hood was chained to the cross.

"Well, some of them hate it," Shirley said. "Then you have to figure out who hates it in a good way that turns him on and who just hates it. See, the first kind of guy will get off on something he hates if a femdom forces him to do it, and the second type just wants to throw up, which is usually the opposite of the reaction you're looking for."

"Which type is he?" Jax hooked her thumb at the hooded man.

"The type who gets off on being forced into it," said Shirley.

The anonymous man clanked and went limp, defeated by his Mistress' words which exposed him as a cum eater. An unctuous drop splashed from the penis cage to the floor.

"See what I mean?" Shirley got a paper towel and a bottle of disinfectant from her toy bag to clean it up. "Just mentioning what a pervy boy he is got him hot and bothered."

The women laughed in silky tones.

Making a man eat his own cum seemed so weirdly delightful. Jax didn't like the gritty goo of semen, though she'd dutifully swallowed for Books. Giving men a taste of their own medicine was a great payback.

Leather Lee showed her how to care for leather and all the different ways one could use striking implements. Lee's salt-and-pepper hair was cropped short and her skin was pale and smooth. She didn't wear any make-up, but she wore so much leather you couldn't see the shape of her body. She wore the same black motorcycle boots every day. She had a ring in her nose and a massive ear piercing that intimidated Jax at first. Lee was the kindest teacher of all. She spent hours patiently showing Jax how to use crops and paddles and whips, from soft deerskin floggers that thudded sensuously to single-tail whips that stung, soft leather paddles that spread a warm sensation to wooden ones with holes drilled through them that landed with ferocious thumps. She made Jax experience how all the different implements felt on her own body, striking her experimentally with each one then stopping to explain that she wouldn't experience the sensation the way a masochist would.

"If you were a masochist," Lee lectured after lightly stinging her with a riding crop, "you might need two or three times as much force to feel what you, as a non-masochist, feel from a light blow. To a masochist, it might not even register as pain," Lee said. "More like pleasant intensity."

Jax wrote down, "Masochists feel pain differently. Are masochists wired for pain??"

It was a staggering concept to her, yet it made sense. It explained why Henry got aroused by an intense ass-whipping. She wouldn't have been able to sit for a week if someone hit her like that. He, on the other hand, was sprightly when he left, giddy and looking forward to a long jerk-off session in the hotel room.

Jax didn't think she'd use the more extreme whips, but she asked Lee to teach her how to balance a single-tail properly and hit her target expertly, in case a client asked for that. The ubiquitous Felix agreed to be her whipping practice post. At first, she was nervous, but once she achieved perfect contact with his saggy ass, Lee gave her a rough sideways hug, to let her know she'd done good.

"You through with me?" Felix asked peevishly. "My ass is killing me, I gotta sit down."

"We're done with you. You can put your clothes back on." She turned back to Jax. "Never use a toy without first learning how to use it safely and don't rush. You'd be surprised how many people say they want a whipping or a caning, but can't handle it in reality. So go slow and build up the sensation, checking on them to be sure they are ready for the next level of pain."

"I will," Jax vowed, writing down, "Lead them to pain slowly and monitor their reactions."

"Also, don't wait for them to use their safewords," Felix interjected. "You can't get lazy and expect them to tell you when it's too much. If you think it's time to stop, then stop. If you see them look upset, stop!" Jax was startled by his vehemence. Had this happened to him? Had Lilith pushed him too far?

"Listen to Felix," Leather Lee said, "some subs won't use their damn safewords, out of pride or stubbornness or wanting to prove they're macho."

"And some don't use them," said Fred, "because they're so far gone in lala land that they don't realize it's too much for them to handle."

"Don't trust subs in subspace," Jax scribbled in her book. Apparently, femdoms had to be mind readers, too. This shit was really hard, but mostly it felt like a lot of responsibility. She wasn't afraid of the responsibility, but she felt its burden.

The schoolgirls had tricks to teach her, too, but their lessons were more basic. From them, she learned volumes about roleplay and Tease and Deny scenes, where you made a helpless guy crazy with lust.

"You're so handsome and strong," they'd say and would rub their clients' biceps with open-eyed admiration. "I wish we could have sex."

"Why can't we?!" they grunted hungrily while the girls sat in their laps and teased them with light touches and flirty smiles.

"Because you're a grown man and I'm a schoolgirl," Suzie Q shouted in mock outrage, sliding her hand over their groins.

"Look at us, so young and soft and cute," they both cooed, slithering their hands over the men's thighs and unbuttoning their blouses. "Look at how young and firm our breasts are."

"Oh, yes, yes, oh, yes, so young, so firm," the men salivated.

"You can't have that!" the girls would gaily admonish them, as the men struggled against the ropes the girls used to tie them to their chairs, making sure their hands could not rove.

"We're just playing with you until the teacher calls us back to class."

No matter that these schoolgirls were really middle-aged women under their make-up and clothes, the men bought into the fantasy from the minute the nymphets flounced in wearing jumpers and knee socks. Jax was fascinated by their dynamic. The men wanted to believe they were young girls. Knowing they were actually legal age allowed them to enact the fantasy safely. But once the games began, the fantasy became their reality, and reality was suspended for the duration.

Sometimes, clients paid for more baroque scenes. Once, to Jax's surprise, Lilith burst into the room, crying, "What is going on in here!!!" She looked so shocked and disgusted, at first Jax feared they had broken some house rules. Then she saw that Lilith was wearing a bright floor-length skirt and a stiff white button-up blouse. Her hair was pinned in a bun and she wore round granny glasses. Lilith was in roleplay as a school mistress! Jax slid her hand over her mouth to hide a smile.

Lilith scolded and fussed at the girls, admonishing them and then giving each one an over the knee spanking while the bound man leered from the chair.

"A grown man like you," she scolded him after sending the "girls" back to their "studies."

"Why would a respectable man like you allow a couple of schoolgirls to tie him up? Didn't you realize they were up to no good?"

The blush on the man's face and the tent in his pants thrilled Jax. He was loving it. He loved everything about it, from the two charming vixens teasing them to the governess catching them at it, to watching the girls get spanked.

"Maybe you should be spanked for letting them do that to you?" Lilith growled. "You're not too big for a spanking!"

"Uh... how much?" he asked.

"An extra hundred," Lilith said calmly. Then she barked, "You deserve one, don't you?"

"Yes, Ma'am, I do. OK."

It was inspirational to Jax when she realized how easy it was to pry cash from a horny man. She stayed to see their scene together. Lilith was very good, knowing just how to elicit a few screams and promises that he would be good from now on, and then sweetly easing him back to reality.

Although school uniforms were not her style, they helped Jax understand that clothing, toys, but most of all attitude was the way for a woman to win at the kink game, whatever the kink. She knew that from the hat Steve had bought her, but these clothes were purposeful, not just amusing fashion accessories. These clothes enhanced a woman's aura and mystique by targeting the erotic iconography of kink -- the uncommon fabrics, the modest yet outrageously revealing dresses that could be worn anywhere, but would also attract attention anywhere one went.

Fedora, their resident fetish queen, advanced her understanding of the role of clothing and footwear in the fetish realm. She seldom removed her signature hat, though she sometimes wore fanciful hats with feathers. Fedora had a thick, full body, from her full bosom and generously wide hips down to her heavy thighs and curvaceous calves. Jax always found a certain beauty in large women. The thought of being crushed by a big woman gave her a little thrill, and dominating a tower of a woman was even hotter. So much soft flesh, so much femininity to play with.

"For a typical shoe slave, the type of shoe matters," she told Jax as they rested between sessions in the lounge one day. "You can't assume they're going to like your shoes or even your feet until you know what really turns them on."

"Oooh, yeah, Lilith mentioned that once. Can you tell me more?"

"Only if you get me a cruller." She sat on a couch and kicked off her shoes. "I'm starved."

There were two in the donut box. Jax brought them both back, along with a Boston Cream for herself, and sat down beside Fedora.

"OK, good, so, like, if a guy likes an open-toed sandal, then a boot might turn him off, well, unless he's versatile and has fetishes for a few different styles. Like, he could have a sneaker fetish, right? That's totally different from a stiletto freak. Right? So, imagine this, a loafer-lover could hate high heels and a heel-lover could hate loafers, but some loafer-lovers love high heels and vice versa, so I guess you could say they are versatile, but it still doesn't mean they like Mary Janes for example or ballet boots, so you still have to ask."

Jax stopped chewing her donut to listen closer.

"You ever hear the expression 'knowledge is power?'" Fedora didn't wait for her to answer. "So, some guys want bare feet only, some want shoes only, others want stockings or pantyhose or socks, right? Some want little feet, some like big feet, sometimes they want them smelly, sometimes they want them fresh. You never know with fetishists," she said. She lowered her voice confidentially and said, "One of my clients asked me for male feet."

"What did you do?"

"That's where Felix comes in handy," Fedora smirked.

"Really!" Jax could imagine Felix peeling off his socks and obligingly grinding the sole of his foot into a customer's face, treating it as just another day on the job.

"Anyways, like I was saying, once you figure out his exact fetish, once you have that knowledge, you have power over him. He'll keep coming back for more."

Jax thought about Henry. "Could a whipping be a fetish?" she asked her mentor.

"I guess so," Fedora said. "Good question."

She munched the second cruller thoughtfully. "You could see any kink as a fetish because some people only want a spanking and others only want to dress up like girls, so I guess it is like fetishism because people can get very specific about what they want." Fedora stared into the distance for a long minute. "I remember doing a guy once who wanted to be spanked with a hairbrush, it had to be a wood one, no plastic, only wood, with a long handle, and he said I had to call his ass a "fanny" and that if I used any other word, it would turn him off, can you believe that? Was that a fetish? A quirk? A fantasy he had his whole life that he had to try once? What do I know? Anyways, your average sub might like some rubber, but a real rubber fetishist is going to be devoted to rubber. I mean, one person's diving suit is another person's fetish. I've had a few customers who fetishized rubber bondage sacks, which are hard to find."

Fedora stood and stretched out her lioness form, then beckoned Jax to follow her to the wardrobe room. She showed Jax two rubber sacks L'Oubliette had in their collection, one white and one red. They looked like enormous and sturdy garbage bags.

"Get inside, I'll show you. Take off your shoes."

Jax removed her shoes and stepped in. Fedora raised it to her shoulders and buckled belts around her feet, torso, and upper arms. The bag constrained her from shoulder to ankles. Jax wiggled around. It was warm and soft and cozy, but she was afraid she'd fall over if she tried to walk, like people in potato sack races.

"People find this erotic?" She didn't understand the attraction. She fingered the bag. It was so pliable. It was, she realized, like a womb. A big soft sac of thin rubber flesh. It was a return to the safe zone, a zone-out-zone within a confined zone. She understood that. It was so primal and innocent and strange and fucking hot to imagine entombing a man in an artificial womb.

"Some men cum in them, just from being forced to wear them," Fedora said. "Nice, right? I learned to put them in diapers first in case they mess."

"Men in diapers inside rubber bags!" Her hands flew to her cheeks. "And they pay for that?!"

"What do you think, that I'd do that for free?"

Jax bit her lip. She would do it for free!

"Washing semen off equipment after a scene is... well, it's fucking disgusting, I can't lie, but it's part of the job. You'll get used to it."

Fedora unstrapped her and helped her out of the bag.

The more she learned, the harder she played. Jax had expanded on Shirley's cover story that she was the former owner of a secretly submissive billionaire. He put her up in a penthouse and she traveled with him in private jets to exotic lands. He anticipated her every whim. He wore her mark, a small tattoo under his balls with the letters "As," for "Amazon's slave."

She was not at liberty to reveal the billionaire's name, of course. His lawyer made her sign an NDA (Non-Disclosure Agreement), she said. But she could talk about being on the billionaire's yacht for a tour of the Greek Islands, stealing details from Paul's letters about a sailing trip he took with Giorgos. Her clients hung on her words, transfixed by her stories. They wanted to prostrate themselves at the boots a billionaire had once kissed. They wanted to believe she was the most desirable dominatrix money could buy. She didn't know if they were really worshipping her or the billionaire. She didn't care. The more they believed her fairytale, the more cash they tipped her.

"That's exactly how the billionaire kissed my feet!" she'd tell her slaves, raking her fingernails through their scalps. "Don't forget to lick the sweet spots between my toes. He loved performing that service for me." They sighed with pleasure, praising her strictness as much as her beauty, worshipping her spirit as they sucked her toes.

The day of Grandpa Steve's funeral she swore to herself that she would do exactly as he had, and live on a budget, putting money aside for emergencies. It was Steve's careful savings that saved him and Paul when the art commune collapsed. His funeral insurance paid for his service and cremation, and a small life insurance policy allowed Paul to close out their mortgage loan. She swore she would follow Steve's method and make sure that, when the day came, she could provide for Paul, too.

As her femdom legend grew, so did her bank account. Her once basic budget now included a lot of fun clothes, purses and shoes, and a weekly appointment at a full-service beauty salon, where her hair got snipped and her finger and toenails got shaped and painted. The hole in her life was Paul. When he promised he'd be home in a week, she moved back in to clean up and await his arrival. A few days later, they had an awkward phone call. He apologized and explained he'd been delayed again, but would definitely be home the following week.

By Thursday of the following week, she gave up hope. It would be another solitary week without him. She couldn't keep

Lilith waiting. If Paul didn't return by Sunday, she would sign the lease on the loft and move in until he returned. Even if she couldn't occupy the loft full-time, she could at least spend a few nights there every week.

As she headed home from L'Oubliette that night, she spotted a small crowd outside Da Silvano. It was a celebrity hotspot and served the best pounded veal shoulder chop in the city. She ate there once with Paul as the guest of a gallery owner. Now she could pay for her own meal. She stopped on the sidewalk and called them to ask how long a wait it would be to get a table for one. Surprisingly, they said they had a table for one ready if she came right now. Seconds later, she pushed through the heavy front door and into the packed restaurant. The Maître D' greeted her as if they were old friends and air-kissed her cheeks. He made a show of her wiping her chair seat with a white dish towel he carried on his shoulder, then held her chair for her. He briskly summoned a waiter, who rushed over and subserviently bowed to take her order as if she was a VIP. All around her she could feel men darting hungry, sexy looks at her.

Of course, it was the clothes, she thought. She was wearing a tight, low-cut black bodysuit with a black leather miniskirt and thigh-high black leather boots. Or maybe it was the high ponytail and dramatic eye make-up. She held her head high, conscious of the stares and enjoying them.

Since bringing Amazon to life, a piece of Jax was slowly evaporating. The low self-esteem side. Her shyness left. Her fear of being noticed went with it. She soaked up attention now. She purred to herself, knowing that flaunting her dominance in public was causing whispers. A dominatrix in their midst! How unusual. For them. How beautiful. For her.

As she sliced into the sumptuous chop, she slid her eyes around the room, taking notes on how many men were watching her, some so discreetly only she realized it, and some so clumsily their girlfriends and wives got annoyed. If only there was a way to tell them all where she worked!

As she casually swiveled her head around the room, pretending to look for a waiter, she froze when she locked eyes with a famous pair of deep blue eyes. It was James Allendorf, the star of such big screen silliness as "The Tyrant of Terror Creek" and "The Bigger the Gun," B- cowboy movies she and Booker had laughed at together.

It took her a minute to regain her composure. She cut the veal in small bites. The way Allendorf looked at her made her wonder what secrets lay hidden under his on-screen macho shtick. He acted all tough in his movies, the kind of hairy-chested brute women couldn't resist. In person, there was a softness about him, a hint of erotic otherness that made her wonder if he had a fetish for women's lingerie. Was he a submissive? A masochist?

His movies were sexist and dumb, but he was drop-dead gorgeous. He looked bored with the company at his table, and kept trying to make eye contact with her as if he didn't care who knew. It was so rude. He really did deserve a whipping.

She suddenly scribbled her name on the back of a L'Oubliette business card she carried in her purse. She would dip past his table on the way to the bathroom and slip it to him. But when she looked up again, he was standing up and saying goodbye to the table. She watched him walk out the front door. What a disappointment. It would have been fun to add a famous name to her list of conquests. It would have been even more fun if she could land her own rich client and keep him loyal to her for a while, especially a guy like Allendorf. She sipped her wine thoughtfully. Actually, the best of all would be if he introduced her to other rich closeted Hollywood types. She bet she could make a fortune off that crowd. She consoled herself with a slice of tiramisu and a cappuccino, regretting the opportunity that could have been.

She took the long way back to Paul's. It was a beautiful night. The Village had never looked so warm, so lovely, so bright. She walked slowly, inhaling the heavy stench of tobacco and booze drifting out of clubs and bars she passed, catching bits of conversation as people rubbed past her on the congested sidewalks. When she crossed Hudson, her mood began to turn as dark and shadowy as the streets she now navigated. Her emotional energy calibrated to the moribund sorrows of abandoned buildings and garbage strewn alleys.

She was happy right now, right in this minute, but what would tomorrow bring? If Paul wanted to stay in Greece, what would she do? She wasn't ready to live without him. And, despite her soaring income, there were whispers in the lounge that L'Oubliette would close down. How did she get so dependent in only a few months' time? How would she find fifteen clients a week on her own? She could end up working at a place like Palace of Pain, with sawdust on the floors. She'd never find enough of the rich men that L'Oubliette drew in droves, the ones who didn't mind paying outrageous fees and handing over generous tips to visit an exclusive club and have access to magnificent equipment and a dozen beautiful goddesses.

"You need to have money to make money," her father once told her. "Money loves money. You gotta go where they go and look like they look and write big checks."

Barry made it sound so easy. In reality, who would ever invite a professional dominatrix to a swanky charity ball? She had no network to exploit, no favors to call in. Every year, her high school alumni newsletter solicited her for stories about her successes since she'd graduated. What could she say about herself? What had she accomplished? "Jax Roaman is proud to announce she knows how to make grown men cry."

She turned around and headed east on Charles until she reached 7th Avenue. She went to the Riviera Cafe at the corner of 10th and claimed her favorite table.

"Hey, Jax," a slim brunette came up and kissed her cheek. "Same same?"

"Hey, Patti! You're looking good." She hesitated. "Sure, why not?"

"One Samuel Adams, coming right up."

Jax settled in and sat back to watch the street show. Throngs of people walked along 7th Avenue, stopping at the health food store, some heading to restaurants and clubs, and some adventuring to a nearby sex shop that sold BDSM toys. She stared glumly at the couples walking hand-in-hand, the women who had boyfriends who loved them.

Suddenly she felt self-conscious about her fetish clothes, almost bitterly aware of her almost non-existent chances of finding a man who would accept her as a dominatrix, a man who would be more than a submissive, but a true slave for life. As a dominatrix, she was doomed to be the eternal side-chick, the one who gives the man peak experiences and spends weekends and holidays alone.

She drank beer and forced back feelings she hadn't felt in a long time. She was unloveable in the first place. Now, as a sex working dominatrix, who would ever love her, except maybe Paul? She didn't want to end up a lonely old woman who had never been truly loved.

She flashed back to the movie star who stared at her so hard she knew he was undressing her with his eyes. He seemed almost to recognize her. He definitely recognized she was a domme. Or did he? She wondered what kind of opportunity she had really missed with him. She fucking hated herself. Why didn't she follow him out to give him her card? Why had she been so passive? Who knows how many doors he could've opened for her? She'd never know. She was an idiot. He vanished with the wind like Barry, like Paul, like Booker. She ordered another beer.

The rumors at work bothered her more than she would admit. Whispers said they were on the NYPD's radar as part of a city-wide crackdown on so-called vice. When two clients canceled their appointments in two days, the women started to panic. If they got arrested, it would be the end of their lives. Their families, children and neighbors would find out what they did for a living. What would happen if the newspapers got their shit-stained hands on the fascinatingly intimate things she did with clients? No doubt they'd snigger and label her a whore. Fucking prudish unevolved mollusks would treat her like some kind of a criminal!

Jax took a deep swig of the icy brew. Fuck them! She always knew life sucked. She was overthinking it. She went back to staring at the crowds when something caught her attention just outside a glaringly illuminated front door. A couple of men were passionately kissing against the wall just outside, and for a moment, it was as beautiful as a painting. When they finally separated to walk in different directions, the older man going north and the younger one dashing to the subway, it sprung into real-life focus. It was Booker and an older man.

Booker! She followed him with her eyes as he dashed to the 7th Avenue station and vanished, then turned to watch the man he left behind, as he hurried north on 7th. It was the silver fox Booker was so interested in that time she fell asleep at the LGBT table. Apparently, they were dating now. The way they kissed, maybe they were in love. Booker had never kissed her with that much passion. Jax ordered another beer.

She knew in her heart that, by now, Booker would be dating

men, sleeping with men, maybe even immersing himself in men the way she was immersing herself in kink. But she wasn't sure, because he never seemed that sexual to her in the first place. That kiss, though. It looked like Booker had immersed himself in one man. She didn't know why she felt so shocked and hurt. It was exactly what she had predicted. He had a boyfriend he loved in ways he never loved her. It was the reason she left him, for fuck's sake.

She hadn't felt this bad since Steve's death. Everything was good but at the same time everything was terrible. It was good Paul went to Greece, but she realized now, it was a mistake. What if he had taken ill and was hiding it from her? He might never return! Maybe if he hadn't gone, she would never have gone to work for L'Oubliette in the first place. Maybe it was a mistake not to follow her dream of going back to college this fall. Without Paul to center her, she was lost. She had been floating in a fantasy world without him. Her image of herself as a fierce rebel was just a cloak over the truth, that she was weak and lonely and now, possibly in danger of ruining the rest of her life. She was a child who still needed an adult in her life.

And Allendorf! She was so busy thinking about him as a financial opportunity at the restaurant, she hadn't realized how much he'd turned her on physically. An unfamiliar lust was devouring her. Maybe it was the beer, but just thinking about him made her pussy throb and ache and spasm with desire. His face, his body, his ass, his legs, even his thick dark hair turned her on. She wanted to fuck him. She actually wanted to fuck him. After she dominated him, of course, but when was the last time she was dying to fuck someone? She'd pushed fucking out of her erotic vocabulary after Booker. But she wanted to CLIMB that movie star. She wanted to sit on his cock, grab his tits and ride him.

Patti tapped her shoulder. "Last call, honey. Want anything

else? Maybe coffee?"

"Nah, no." Jax waved at her. "Nah, I'm good." She stood up and had to lean on the table to get her feet. "Here," she said and pulled out three twenties and stuffed them in Patti's hand.

"It's too much," the waitress called after her, as Jax walked away unsteadily, but determined.

"Too much," Jax shouted back. She didn't know what her words even meant, but she didn't care. Fuck it. She didn't want to go home to an apartment full of memories of Steve and without the presence of Paul. But she had to. She didn't want to sleep in a 9 by 12 room and wake up in the same state of uncertainty. But she had to. She didn't want to fight off the old demon that swallowed her courage to live. But she had to before she crumbled.

A wave of dizziness overcame her. She unsteadily veered to a brownstone and dropped down to the steps, where she hastily unzipped her dress part way to give her more breathing room. If a passerby caught sight of a nipple, she decided, it was their lucky day. Fuck it. She took deep breaths and waited for her mind to clear. She had to forget Booker, to forget the movie star, to focus on what she had to do: earn as much as possible in case L'Oubliette closed.

Her bladder was bursting. There was a small alleyway between two of the brownstones on 10th Street. She scuttled to the entry and hid herself behind the wall when she heard footsteps approaching. She crouched low to the ground so the stream wouldn't be loud. She was afraid to look up. She saw legs quickly pass her without stopping and waited till the footsteps died before emerging again. She instantly felt a little better, a little more clear headed.

Time stopped on the walk home. The cloudy skies, the still streets, the eerie lights from orange lanterns and the spontaneous weirdness of the last few hours made her see her life with emotionless clarity. First, she had to see a maximum of clients and save every penny as long as the club was open. She would move into the loft immediately, so she was available 24/7 for random clients who asked for odd hours. Those last-minute clients were usually desperate enough to pay extra. If she couldn't have Booker or Paul or the movie actor, she would have money. Lots of it.

She finally reached her door. She'd gone from depressed to coldly grim. When she got the door open a light brown man with a small white towel around his waist was eating something out of a bowl.

"Doddy!" he cried out in heavily accented English. "There's a big scary dominatrix in the living room!"

"Who are you?" The hair on her neck stood up.

"Who are YOU?" He put the bowl down on the coffee table.

They scowled at each other.

"Who are you!" they shouted at the same time.

Suddenly, Grandpa stormed in, a metal can of solvent raised high in his fist, ready to smash the intruder.

"OMG!" he said. "It's you! You're finally home! Darling girl!"

She was dumbfounded. Paul was home. He looked healthier than she'd ever seen him. He had a deep tan that made his teeth whiter and his gray eyes fiercer.

He opened his arms wide and she ran to them for the bear hug she had missed for so long. "Grandpa," she mewled, "OMG, Grandpa, I'm so happy to see you, thank God."

"Who is this woman?" The towel-clad stranger stood at Paul's side, still eating. "Why is she dressed like a dominatrix?"

Paul was home at last and, apparently, had brought home a

souvenir. Who was this guy roughly her own age and why was he calling her grandfather Doddy? Or was it Daddy! Oh no, it was Daddy. What?

"Raf, this is my granddaughter. Jax, this is Rafael. Raf, put some pants on."

Raf didn't move. "You never told me Jox is a dominatrix!" He laughed. "I don't know why I'm surprised the Picasso of Penises has a dominatrix for a granddaughter."

"Jax, what's with the get-up?" Paul was bewildered.

"I always told you I was kinky."

"Well, kinky," he nodded his head, "but I didn't know what it really meant. I mean, wow." He pointed at her. "Look at you! I mean, I'm not criticizing." He looked her up and down. "You gained a little weight. It looks good on you. Very va-va-voom." He twirled her around. "You look so womanly now. But what's that mean, being a dominatrix?"

"I found a job working at a private BDSM club."

"What kind of a private club is it? Is it a disco?"

"DISCO?" Raf guffawed. "Doddy, no, it's where Mosters and Mistresses go to whip slaves."

Raf was a smooth-skinned man, with liquid chocolate-brown eyes, a rock-hard belly, bulging biceps, and a tight, V-shaped ass. He didn't look like he belonged in New York, the land of gray faces and concrete sidewalks. He looked like the native son of white sands and azure waves, created to be admired from a distance as he ran barefoot as a carefree god.

She stared from young man to old. Apparently everyone in her life had a boyfriend, except her, even her white-haired old grandpa. She knew that probably, one day, many years in the future, Paul would find Steve 2. In her mind, new Steve would be another old guy, maybe a platonic friend who turned into a caring companion. She never considered that her grandpa would be captivated by a muscle-bound macho boy-toy.

"So, how long is Raf staying?" she asked Paul.

"I just moved in," Raf said.

Paul walked to Raf and put his arm around his shoulder.

"Moved in?" She couldn't believe it. Was he a grifter? A wave of paranoia and jealousy swept over her. "Where are you from?"

"Jockson Heights."

"Where?"

"Jockson Heights, Queens? Oh, you mean my occent. We came here from Olgeria when I was 11. I am Pieds-Noirs. You know what that is?"

Paul cut him off. "Jax, I know this is sudden to you. I'm sorry. From the minute I got to Greece, Giorgos was pushing me to work harder, and live harder, and travel harder than I've ever done before. It was good for me. New situations, new people, new places every day. Getting high on paint fumes and working side-by-side with him in fields, both of us dripping sweat and shouting as we worked. And then," he gestured to Raf, "I met him and time stood still." He paused and gazed romantically at Raf. "I've told him everything about you, and about us, Jax."

"Except for the dominatrix part," Raf said. "I had no idea she was this interesting." He winked kindly at Jax, as if they already had a bond. She realized that he had accepted her as a package deal. She didn't know if she accepted him.

"Raf is an artist too," Paul said.

"Oh," she mused.

"Pah," the younger man said. "Paul is the true artist. He is a genius! I just do stupid portraits for tourists."

"But you're so good at it," Paul said. "I see your potential!"

"Oh. I see." She was seeing it now. Paul had fallen for a sweet, struggling young painter who worshipped his talent and looked up to him, who called him Daddy and made him feel like a sexy gay man again. Maybe it wouldn't last, but it made sense.

"I know the two of you will really get along," Paul continued. "You're the two people I love the most."

"I have to pee or I'll explode," she blurted. She galloped off and sat down on her toilet. The beer flowed.

She heard Paul's footsteps coming down the hall and nudged the door shut.

"Jax, are you ok?" he called to her.

"Yes, fine. Privacy?"

"I can't believe you're working as a professional dominatrix," he said in a hushed voice.

She washed her hands and opened the door. "It pays really well. I like it. People respect me there." She walked past him into her room and he followed her in.

"It sounds dangerous to me. Who knows what kind of people go there!"

"I'm the people who go there, Grandpa."

"I'm the people who go there too, Doddy." Raf suddenly appeared in the doorway. He had put on white pants and a sheer white shirt, with leather thongs on his feet, as if he was ready to hit the beach. He walked over to Jax in solidarity.

"We are the people who go there," Raf said.

Paul raised his eyebrows.

"An artist should be free to go anywhere and live any life," the younger man said. "You told me that the night we stayed in Santorini."

"A person should be true to themselves because that is the only life worth leading," Jax said. "You told me that the first time we met."

"Ok, Jesus Fucking Christ, quoting me back to myself is so unfair." Paul threw his hands in the air. "I should've come back sooner. I should have been here for you. We could have at least talked about it."

"No, I don't think so." Jax shook her head.

The old man looked hurt. "Why not?"

"Because..." She didn't want to escalate things by mentioning his long-held taboo against hearing details of her sex life. "Because this was my personal journey," she said. "I needed to take it alone. I had to grow up, and I did."

"That's terrible," Paul said.

"Growing up?" she laughed.

"No, no, that's good. What's bad is that I wasn't here to help you, to see it happen," he said. "I feel like I missed your first baby steps all over again."

"Oh, Grandpa, you didn't miss anything, you were always in my heart." She flew to his side. He hugged her tight just like old times and stroked her hair just like old times. The weight of fear washed away. She felt a certainty in her stomach that things would work out okay. "You're here now! That's all that matters to me, Grandpa."

She took his rough old paws and held them in her silky pale hands like a precious vase.

"Grandpa," she said softly, "this works out better than I hoped, it really does. The fact is, I found a beautiful loft I can afford. It's right next to work. It's perfect. I had to sign the lease to be sure someone else didn't get it first. I was just waiting for you to get back, so I could tell you in person."

Paul got dramatic. Outrage drew his shoulders so high he looked a foot taller. "No, why? You don't need to go. I thought you were happy here!" Then, with sadness, he said, "If I was here, you never would have signed that lease, it was because you were alone, you felt alone. I completely fucked up, Jax. Accept it."

His words stung because they were true. She could have been happy coming home every night to their cozy meals and seeing what he had worked on that day. Sitting out on the balcony after dinner, drinking hot chocolate while he spun fantastic stories and shared his philosophies, his feelings and his many happy memories of Steve. She received his words as those of a wise elder handing down all his stories to his only heir. She experienced it as a sacred and ancient human ritual, a sense of connectedness to the past she never imagined she could forge until she found Paul.

"This is not because of me, is it? I won't stay if it's because of me. Doddy, tell her."

"It's not because of you," she assured Raf. "Not at all, I swear. If anything, you being here makes me feel better about going." The men exchanged doubtful looks and shook their heads.

"Jax, I never imagined this would happen. Please stay. I don't want you to move out. I just got home. Don't be so stubborn."

"Grandpa," she took a deep breath, "please be proud of who you helped me become. I could never have been this stubborn without you."

"Aw, shit," he said under his breath. "Why are you like this?"

"Please, Grandpa," she cajoled, "I love you to the moon, you know that."

"Aw, shit." Paul drummed his hands on his thighs. "You know that love is my Achilles Heel."

"I don't want to hurt you," she said.

Raf chirped, "I'll take care of your wound, Doddy."

"Not now, Raf!" Paul snapped at him, exasperated.

Jax guffawed. Maybe Paul found Steve 2 after all.

Chapter 7

AMAZON HAMMER

"Time to get up!" Buttons was stoically curled tight in her armpit, refusing to move. She caressed the sleeping fur ball. He rolled onto his back, his little legs up in the air. She buried her nose in his belly. "What a sweet baby Buttons," she cooed. "Are you hungry, good boy?"

She stretched out beside him, belly up, exulting in her life. She was exactly where she wanted to be. She was in the blossom of her life, her leaves just beginning to open, her bloom in no hurry to show forth. She was flowering into herself, as a woman of power and means. She felt it within.

Her work at L'Oubliette flowed like a tranquil stream of timeless perversions where every day made her richer, wiser and kinkier. The rumors died and so did the paranoia. The cops never came, the clients returned, and the club was more successful than ever. The staff entered a new period of prosperity and optimism. When Lilith publicly vowed she would not close the club down until she was too old to work, they celebrated.

Her new loft, whose lease she had signed and keys she now owned, had a full bank of windows, high ceilings, all new appliances and a luxurious bathroom with heat lights overhead and a walk-in shower with pebbled glass doors. She loved making coffee in her brand new espresso machine and poured it into her new black mug with "She Who Must Be Obeyed" printed in white letters across the front, which she found on sale at a gag-gift store. She splurged on a king-size bed and a leather couch and bought linens and towels. She didn't need more. The loft came with a marble kitchen counter with high stools, a walk-in closet with lots of hangers and a huge, custom-built wood armoire with drawers and shelves that partitioned off a dressing area, with a small vanity table and stool.

The only furniture she brought with her was Paul's penis lamp and the ceramic lamp Steve was so proud of. She put the big lamp on the kitchen counter and hung the lamp like a piñata from a long hook on the wall in her dressing area. The lamps looked ridiculous in the cool minimalist decor, but in a happy way that reminded her of her grandfathers. Paul also dug a small television out of one of the locked rooms and gave it to her. It was small enough to keep on a side table by her bed, so she could fall asleep to old movies.

After feeding Buttons and drinking her first cup of coffee, she walked across the front dungeon in a towel wrap, her hair still damp from her morning shower. She went to Table 12 to use the hairdryer and mousse there to style her hair and apply her make-up. Then, she picked up her outfit for the day from Fred, geared up, and went off to her appointments. After her last client of the day left, she stripped off the fetish gear and walked back to her loft in her towel to shower away the workday.

It was good to have an organized life. Weekends with

Grandpa and Raf drifted and flowed with new routines. Raf would never be her grandfather, or replace Steve in any way, but she was glad he was in Paul's life. They were a family now. They created their own rituals. Raf made Middle Eastern dinners, with delicious stews and rice pilafs, which she always looked forward to. Every Sunday at 11 am, Paul led them to the brunch spot of his choice, sometimes hidden gems, sometimes new restaurants. Jax always brought dessert. She and Raf built the kind of bond that two people who love the same person often form. She saw he made Paul happy, and that made her happy. Raf saw how much Paul loved Jax and he approved. The pang of jealousy she felt had vanished. Each of them had completely different roles in Paul's life, and each of them was essential to his happiness.

She adapted Paul's philosophies about an organized life and built rituals into her days. She went to bed and woke up at the same time each day. She prepared simple dinners of brown rice and steamed vegetables on Sunday, Monday and Wednesday, and treated herself to steak or sushi on Tuesdays and Thursdays. She swept the floors before bed and dusted in the morning, when sunlight illuminated the dust that drifted in from city streets. After that, the night was hers to watch old movies, read new books, surf the Net and play with her sweet feline stepchild, Buttons. When she shut the lights, Button ran away to do cat scouting in the dark and she eagerly reached for an expensive vibrator she bought at The Pleasure Chest. She'd revisit her adventures of the day while she worked its head between her legs and guided it into her vagina. She could moan and groan to her heart's content in her loft, which made her happy. She imagined the men going further in her fantasies than she could ever ask them to go in real life, suffering the most grueling and grungy degradations to prove their utter devotion to her. She gasped and humped the vibrator in ecstasy. A few minutes later, she decided she needed one more orgasm to sleep. The daily BDSM play had supercharged her libido. Her capacities for experiencing pleasure were expanding just as her mind and spirit were expanding.

Sunday nights were reserved for paperwork. She paid her bills, balanced her checkbook, checked her bank account and a small investment she made in a utility company and looked at her budget to make sure she hadn't overspent that week. She felt like her father, sitting behind her little table in the wardrobe, writing checks and shuffling papers, then putting everything away in a small locked safe she kept hidden behind a collection of tall boots.

Her last task of the week was to review Lilith's email containing her client schedule. Lilith required them to plan their preferred outfits in advance each week, so Fred could start cleaning and prepping them at L'Oubliette's fetish wardrobe. Jax looked through the clients and their requested scenes, then picked out three all-purpose fetish outfits, plus a governess outfit for a Victorian-style spanking scene and a rubber suit with matching rubber hood for a fetishist.

The clothing calendar was vital to maintaining the wardrobe and keeping client traffic moving smoothly. Lilith blew a fuse every time someone submitted their calendar after 10 pm on Sundays.

As Jax had learned from experience, there was nothing worse than two women needing the same white latex nurse's uniform in the same size at the same time.

"How long?" She remembered pacing back and forth in her towel as a harried Fred hurried through spraying down a latex dress Shirley stripped off mid-way through her own scene to lend it to Jax for long enough to remove an enema tube from a client's waiting butt.

Shirley had committed the ultimate sin by neglecting to turn in her calendar, putting Fred in a state of near hysteria. "His ass can wait," Fred said. "Just tell him he was really bad and deserved it."

"He can't wait much longer. The tube has already been in his ass too long," Jax whined. "He'll explode."

"Here, take it, take it," Fred threw the dress at her.

She ran back to her client, pulling it on as she went, then walked in calmly, pulled the tube out carefully, and ordered him to the toilet sternly. As soon as he sat down, she walked out, then ran back to the wardrobe room undressing again.

Shirley snatched the dress from Jax's hands, not letting Fred clean it while he protested, and darted off to finish her scene. She returned fifteen minutes later, and Fred quickly sprayed it and wiped it, then Jax pulled it back on and went to the toilet where her client was still sitting.

"Go on, take your time," she said. "You obviously had a lot to get off your... bowels."

"Yes, Ma'am." He bowed his head and farted.

After all the "patients" had finished, and the nurse uniform was handed back to Fred for the last time, Jax dropped onto a couch. "I'm exhausted."

"Those quick costume changes will kill you," Shirley sympathized. "Latex is hard."

"It's all your fault," Fred yelled at Shirley.

"I know," she said apologetically. "I'm really sorry."

"If I had advance warning, I would have told Lilith to reschedule or I would have had time to check out our home inventory," he said. "Shirley, I swear, I'll fucking kill you if you forget again."

"What if I let you kiss my feet?" she asked him.

"Really? Well, in that case," he bowed at the waist, "I grant you eternal life."

L'Oubliette made Jax laugh every day. She found herself smiling and humming instead of frowning and fretting over the past. She felt so good, she decided to reach out to her old Montessori friends and accepted a few invitations to dinner parties and charitable events she had evaded for years.

She was ashamed when she was a counter-girl, but she wasn't ashamed of her success or her luxurious loft. Just as Shirley created a thrilling backstory for Mistress Amazon, now Mistress Amazon created a new backstory for why Jax had ghosted her high school friends. She used this to great success at the next alumni party.

To the first woman who asked where she'd been, she explained that after her father died, she took a year off to find herself, having exotic adventures, renting a place in Greenwich Village, even getting to meet some homosexuals. This bohemian trajectory caused a small buzz. She got involved with the art world and assisted a gay artist with his shows in SoHo. Now women started openly eavesdropping. She completed an expensive private training program, Jax said, and now she was part therapist, part life-coach at an experimental therapy collective that offered roleplay and psychodrama.

All of it was true in a way. Running away to Paul made her find herself. She often carted canvasses for him in a cab and helped him hang the paintings. An "Experimental Therapy Collective" sounded like one of the kooky cults that rich people joined in droves. It was the perfect cover story and it was also the truth in its own way, so she felt comfortable repeating it around. Now instead of labeling her a whore, they thought of her as someone doing important work.

"Your practice must be very successful if you can afford Gucci," her old friend Felicia said enviously. Felicia had married well, but apparently high fashion clashed with her mother-of-four lifestyle and she now wore flowery dresses that disguised the stains that went with motherhood and hid her maternal weight gain as well.

"I'm at the top of my field," Jax said the way an asshole would, knowing it would cow Felicia.

"That's wonderful, Jax." Her face fell. Apparently Felicia expected Jax to end up in a flop house. "Good for you, Jax! I used to worry about you because you were so... you know, different from us. I thought you'd end up joining a feminist cult or something."

"Hahaha," Jax burst into gales of laughter. The funny part was that it was true: the all-femdom staff was indeed a kind of feminist cult.

She had a deeper understanding now about power dynamics and power games. For vanilla women, power came by comparing clothes, fertility, jobs, expensive vacations, and husbands. That was their validation. Now Felicia, who used to snub her, felt insecure next to her. Why? Money and status and status and money.

She felt a million years more evolved, more relaxed in herself. She didn't feel competitive or jealous of any of them. They had all married for money and were as dependent on their husbands as they'd once been on their fathers. She earned as much as their husbands. She owned herself, her body and was the sole Mistress of her home. That was HER validation.

Zelda, a sweet girl who sometimes ate lunch with her at school approached her eagerly. Zelda had matured from a shy skinny brunette with a big nose and crooked teeth into a curvy platinum-blond extrovert with a button nose and perfect teeth.

Zelda was a standout among the women in more conservative clothing. She looked very posh in a Prada dress and Miu Miu heels, with bold gold Tiffany jewelry draped around her neck and wrist. Nothing was bolder than the wide wedding ring and flashy diamond on her left hand.

"You got married!" Jax hugged her. "Congratulations."

"Jax!" Zelda hugged her back. "You look fantastic. You have such a glow around you! I heard you're working with some kind of experiential therapy group?"

"Experimental Therapy Collective," Jax corrected her. She was delighted that her new backstory was already becoming a legend in this gathering. Of course, she still couldn't submit an update to their newsletter, but she was having a great time pretending to be the kind of person these snobs would look up to.

"It sounds very progressive. Tell me!"

"It is," Jax invented as she went. "We have standard treatments, but clients are encouraged to choose from a smorgasbord of custom experiences."

"Really! So you tailor the experience to their needs?!" Zelda rubbed her thick gold necklace as if it was a talisman. "I got rebirthed once, but honestly, I was a breech baby and I felt like it would've been better if they did it differently for me. I mean, I didn't come out head first. Could I get that experience with you?"

Jax imagined Zelda in her dungeon, her expensive clothes and flashy jewelry neatly arranged on a chair, bound naked to a cross. She could give Zelda some experiences, alright. But she couldn't afford to mingle her work life with her alumni circle.

"I'm sorry. We focus on male mental health." She decided not to mention that, now and again, a woman showed up for a session, usually a lesbian or bisexual woman, but sometimes a straight woman who just needed to be spanked and couldn't find anyone she trusted with her secrets. Jax had worked with three or four women, and wished more would come in. The time she had with women felt different, often more special than with men, who tended to be selfish and brusque, afraid to really cede control. Women were more open, not so afraid of vulnerability. She wondered how a rebirthing scene with Zelda would go. Did she have the talent to do it for Zelda? Maybe. But she also had the common sense not to offer it, lest Zelda report back that Jax wasn't just a sex worker, but a lesbian and a pervert too.

Zelda was disappointed. "So what kind of roleplaying do you do with guys? I bet men have some really weird traumas to work out!"

A small smile crossed Jax's lips. "We do our own kind of re-birthing for them," she confided in a low voice.

"OH! How?" Zelda was titillated. "Do you form a circle around them?"

"Oh no, we put a man in a huge rubber body bag, so he really feels like he's in a womb."

"Oh! My! That sounds so powerful"

"It is very powerful," Jax said.

"It's like sensory deprivation." Zelda pondered. "I did a sensory deprivation tank last year, but it felt more like a short holiday from noise pollution than a meaningful experience, if you know I mean."

"I do understand." She touched Zelda's arm. "I'm very sorry you didn't get the experience you wanted. We push our clients towards transformation."

"Really? You must have the skill to penetrate all the dark places that conventional therapy never reaches."

Jax recalled the pegging scene she did, the week before, with a man who kept asking for bigger and bigger dildos. His asshole was capacious beyond all human understanding.

"We go deeper than most people could imagine," the dominatrix said earnestly, staring deep into Zelda's eyes. To her surprise, Zelda blushed and lowered her gaze.

"I bet," she whispered again. Jax recognized the signs of Zelda getting a little too fascinated, the kind of fascination that could draw more details out of her. She excused herself and walked to a different group of friends.

As they were leaving, Zelda pressed her business card into Jax's hands. "We have to get together. I want you to meet my husband. I think he needs something like that rubber bag." She laughed nervously. "He has mother issues up the wazoo!"

"We go right up their wazoo," Jax said as seriously as she could.

Zelda looked puzzled, then giggled. "You're so funny, Jax! You go up their wazoo. You make it sound almost obscene! Hahahaha."

They walked downstairs promising to stay in touch and hugged again on the sidewalk. Zelda hung on a little too long, so Jax cried, "I have a client waiting," disengaged and quickly walked away. As soon as she turned the corner, she collapsed against a building wall and laughed. It was the most fun she'd ever had with her high school friends. She quickly tore up the card and dropped it in a wastebasket.

Finally, tentatively, she reached out to Lucille. She wasn't expecting a miracle, but after all this time surely Lucille would be happy to hear from her only child. It was late on a Monday afternoon and the club was empty except for Lilith in her office and Fred cleaning up and closing rooms down for the night.

Jax closed her front door and called her mom.

"So. It's you. After all this time," Lucille greeted her.

"Hello, Mother. I wanted to let you know I'm okay. I'm doing good. I think you'd be proud of me." This was the introduction she had rehearsed all day. She waited to hear Lucille's response.

"OK, so what do you need?" her mother said wearily.

"What do you mean?"

"If you're calling me, you need something from me," Lucille said. "Money, right?"

"No, I don't." This was the last reaction she expected.

"Then why are you calling now?"

"Because... you're my mother. I wanted to talk to you. I was hoping we could..."

Lucille cut her off. "I was your mother for all these years and you didn't give a shit, why now?"

"I just wanted to talk to you." Her blood turned cold. Her mother hadn't changed, except perhaps for the worse. Or perhaps she was just hearing it more clearly now, from a more rational place.

"Are you getting married? Because if you are, I'm not paying for it," Lucille said. "In fact, I was considering disinheriting you."

This wasn't the first time Lucille had made this threat. Disinheritance was always in her armory. She couldn't hurt Jax with it now.

"I'm not getting married."

"What? I thought for sure you'd be married by now." Lucille switched to a different knife. "Why, can't you meet a guy who'll put up with you?"

Lucille said goodbye first. Jax curled up on the bed with the cat. He let her hold him, and as he listened, blinking, she told him things that she'd never say out loud to a person. She told him her mother was a heartless bitch. There was no point trying to resurrect their relationship. What relationship? Her mother had never helped her or comforted her. Her mother never did anything but order her around and ruin her life and kill her turtles. She could win the Nobel Prize and her mother would still make her feel like a loser. That was Lucille. She had to accept it.

She shook it off like a bad dream, but the conversation left one deep bruise. She had no marriage prospects, no man she loved, no man who loved her. She was all too aware that she had not found a man to replace Booker, that she hadn't felt even the ghost of an attraction to a man since their break-up. She was paid to touch men, but none of them touched her. Most of her clients were just like Henry: they wanted what they wanted and once she honed in on their biggest turn-on, they never wanted anything different again. It grew boring and annoying and it made her feel cheap inside.

Deep down she knew that she was as much of a sex toy to them as her whips were to her. One day, she'd be replaced in their affections by someone newer and shinier. She had an invisible expiration date stamped on her face that began to emerge in her 30s and would be unmistakable by the time she hit 50. After all, she was booking three or four times as many customers as Donna, who usually only got clueless noobs who didn't know they could ask for someone specific.

She longed to find a single version of Larry, the man she tied up with Shirley on her fateful first night at a club party. Larry was kind and courteous and a sponge of perversion, willing to try every new fantasy and follow every femdom's lead when they played. But he was married to a woman who knew nothing about his double life and had kept Shirley on a string for years.

Larry met Shirley the first year she worked at the club, and they had a whirlwind clandestine romance. Legend had it that he spent $50 grand on her because he was so obsessed. By the end of the second year, he had to cut back for financial reasons, but proposed to her and promised to marry her when his 14-year-old twins reached college age. Soon after the twins turned 17, he showed up with a long face and weepy eyes to tell Shirley that his wife was pregnant. He cried and claimed it was by accident. Shirley quickly blamed his wife, saying she tricked him into having another baby because she knew he was leaving her.

"Are you going to wait for this one to grow up too?" Jax tried not to sound judgmental, although she was.

"I don't know," Shirley said wistfully. "I'm not sure what he'll decide."

"But you're staying anyway."

"I don't know," Shirley repeated. "I love him. And he loves me. You know he loves me, right?" She searched Jax's face in a way that made Jax feel even sorrier for her.

"Of course he does." She'd heard Larry say it often enough around L'Oubliette. She was tempted to add, "He just doesn't love you enough to give up his straight life," but she held her tongue.

Maybe she was wrong about that, maybe some people can lead peaceful double lives. In any case, it was Shirley's choice. Jax's choice would be different. She wouldn't get involved with a married man. She was afraid she'd just get hurt again, and in the same way, by loving someone she could never really call her own.

"I've already invested four years of my life in him," Shirley said. "It could take years to find someone like him again. By then, I'll be too old for children. I mean, he could leave her, even with a baby, right?"

Jax squeezed her hand. "Anything could happen," she said.

Jax wanted someone who was hers and hers alone. No wife, no alimony payments, no kids, just a single kinky man ready to put down some roots and have a family with her one day. The logistics of finding a man like that, though, were daunting.

Her dungeon clients wouldn't publicly acknowledge they knew her if someone put a gun to their heads. She once saw a frequent flyer at L'Oubliette strolling towards her down 5th Avenue with a petite blonde woman in a fur jacket at his side. When he spotted Jax, he grabbed the woman's hand and towed her to the other side like a small doll.

How was Jax going to find a serious relationship when the only men she met treated her like a dirty secret? She was losing faith in men in general. She'd heard them scream, she'd seen them cry, she saw them kneel and plead and degrade themselves. She had seen every permutation of male behavior. Men didn't seem so special or exciting to her. She hungered for one special man to love. To him, she would give everything she had, all the love and passion bottled inside her.

And yet, and yet. A lifetime of masturbation was no substitute for the surprises of intimacy, the thrill of touches, the heat of kisses, the musk of men's bodies, much less the security of having a full-time, committed relationship and knowing the long search for a special person was finally over.

Her stomach ached when she thought of Booker and what they had together before she realized they didn't have it. The sex wasn't really so bad. The cuddling was fun. Their social life was glamorous. He was a perfect man in so many ways, the kindest and most generous one she'd ever met, besides Paul. Maybe she could have sustained it, maybe she could have accommodated Booker's gay needs, maybe her life would have leaned more towards women, and they would have built the world's weirdest functional life together. Maybe he thought because she lived with Paul and Steve, she would make a wonderful wife. Maybe she still could be. Nothing was impossible as long as it was true and based on love. Maybe it wasn't too late for them. Maybe while he did gay sex she could do BDSM.

She remembered how he kissed his older friend on the sidewalk. It didn't matter, she rationalized, because her relationship with Booker would always be different from his relationships with men. Maybe marrying a gay man was as close to a happy ending as she would ever know.

She picked up the phone again, ready to dial Booker's number, when God knocked on her door in the form of Lilith yelling, "Jax! Jax! You are not going to believe this!"

"What? What?" Jax dropped the phone and grabbed Buttons in her arms, running to the door in alarm. Lilith never knocked on her door.

"Do you know about James Allendorf, the movie star?" Lilith said, waving her glasses in her right hand like a fairy wand. "You know, the smirking cowboy guy in bad movies?"

"No, I mean yes, I know who Allendorf is. What about him??"

"Did you ever see him?"

"I never met him. I did see him once, though."

"You did? Where??"

"At a restaurant. He sat across from me. He stared at me a lot during dinner. But we never talked."

"You must have made a big impression," Lilith said with smug pride. "He just called us and he requested you. By name. Mistress Amazon, he said specifically. It has to be Mistress Amazon!"

Jax dropped the cat. "OMG, he booked me? James Allendorf?! Holy shit!"

"He didn't just book you, he booked you for three hours tomorrow," Lilith said, "from

3 pm to 6 pm. It's wonderful! A big movie star here. Word will spread."

"Tomorrow? How can I do it? I've got a two-hour bondage session in the cage room at lunchtime, a session with Larry and Shirley at 2, and then Mr. Rhumba Pants in the sissy space at 5."

"Don't worry about Rhumba Pants, I'll make him dance," Lilith said. "Shirley can do Larry on her own, it's probably better to leave them alone right now, anyway. The bondage session is more of a problem."

"Well, if Allendorf is 3-6, I can still do the bondage session," Jax said. "It's from noon to 2 pm, so I'll have an hour to prep."

"Wonderful, that's wonderful," Lilith said. "You're on your way!"

"I can't believe he asked for me by name. How?" Jax was mystified. The waiters didn't know her name, she paid in cash, how did he find her? There was simply no way he could have tracked her down yet clearly he had.

"Allendorf could bring us a whole new crowd," Lilith was chattering, her hands still agitated. "We don't get a lot of West Coast people here. He could change that for us. So be extra nice to him. Get him to want to come back. Maybe throw in a freebie."

"A freebie? What would you consider a freebie?"

Freebies were seldom given and never openly discussed. They were treated as magic relics that Lilith summoned from a sacred well and then privately entrusted to a chosen mistress.

"Whatever suits your mood. A little more time in the

dungeon, more aftercare, maybe, a kiss, a handjob. Whatever you think is right."

Until that moment, Jax had no idea that masturbating a client was even allowed at the club. Because of local ordinances, the BDSM was supposed to be asexual, more about keeping men endlessly aroused and not allowing them orgasms. She interpreted the law literally and never touched a man's genitals unless she was putting bondage devices on him or using a whip on him. From Lilith's casual tone Jax suddenly realized that other femdoms were more sexual when they were alone with their clients. Jax half-regretted all the lost opportunities to do lewd things.

This meant she had carte blanche to do all kinds of things with him, that she could kiss him and touch him all over, even make him cum and cum herself. Her lust spiked, her pussy throbbed and she felt a sharp ache so deep in her vagina it seemed to come from her womb. James Fucking Allendorf was going to be her slave and Lilith had just lifted the restraints on the degree of eroticism she could merge into her BDSM.

It would be a first for her, a new kind of devirginizing. She'd had regular sex with Booker, and BDSM with a lot of other men, but she never had regular sex as part of an elaborate BDSM scene. What would it feel like? How wild would she feel? Could she even emotionally handle it? What if she fell in love with him? What if he didn't fall in love with her? She alternated from rejecting every fantasy to feeling certain that he and she were fated to be together.

For the rest of the evening and all the next morning, she couldn't stop ping-ponging between the two mysteries. First, how the hell did James, as she thought of him now, find her? And second, would this be the love she always hungered for? She couldn't even snap out of it during her lunchtime session with her bondage client, a man who called himself *slave tom* and had a fetish for chains and fetters and other metal toys.

Tom was a police captain in the Bronx. He was handsome and vain and kept his pencil-thin mustache meticulously groomed. Mirrored sunglasses hid the wrinkles around his eyes and his three-piece suit hid the trunk of his body. He looked fit and youthful on the outside, but once the clothes came off, gravity took a near-supernatural hold of him. His tits sagged, his ass sagged, his thighs sagged, and his belly resembled deflated bagpipes. She couldn't tell if he was a very old man or a man who had lost a huge amount of weight. His duality amazed her. He was powerful outside and fragile inside, like a living caricature of the male ego.

He put on two toys he brought with him -- a bulky steel chastity device he locked over his genitals, and a locking steel belt that compressed his soft waistline by several inches. He waited obediently, head bowed.

"Thank you for seeing me, Mistress Amazon."

"You're welcome, slave tom. I always enjoy our time together."

"You do?"

Most of the femdoms didn't want to see him anymore because they said he was too much work but she didn't mind attaching all the appliances and locking all the locks.

"Yes, you're fun," she said.

"I am?!" He seemed touched.

"I think so." She tapped his calves lightly with a cane. "You're unique. I love that in a man." She knew the man inside was a lot more insecure than the man he showed the world. Boosting his ego was a quick way to get him to relax.

What relaxed her was seeing a man at his rawest and most real, she told slave tom as she circled him with her cane. She loved playing with him, she said. He went to the bottom of his submission. She inched closer to him, giving him light pinches and little slaps in random spots to see him jump around for a few minutes.

"Perfect." She came back to her original position in front of him and grabbed him roughly by the scalp. "I know what you need. You need to be chained up like the naked animal you are."

He whimpered.

"You need to be cruelly restrained and thrown into a cage without mercy. Like a dangerous ape!"

"Oh, yessss."

"I have no mercy. I know you want to suffer for me. You crave to suffer for me, don't you, slave?"

"I do, Mistress," he sighed.

"I should put you in an ape suit, you ape," she said, "so you can barely breathe."

"Oh, Mistress." He hung his head.

"And then take pictures of you and send them to your precinct. Who's that ape, everyone would ask."

The chastity cage moved as his cock strained against it. Jax deftly wrapped a small towel around the cage.

"Don't you dare drip on my floor, slave," she said.

"No, Ma'am."

"Put this on." She handed him a leather gag. He bit down hard and she buckled the strap around his head. She handed him toe cuffs, then gave him shackles for his ankles which he fastened to his waist belt with a heavy chain, then he deftly locked on some wrist shackles. Now she gave him long sections of thinner chain and watched him truss himself tightly. He worked dexterously until he seemed to vanish inside a metal cocoon.

"Enough!" she finally said, adding several strategically placed master locks to keep his crazy chain art together. "You look like the chain department at a hardware store." He struggled to move. "Can you move your hands to safe signal me? Wiggle your hand to say stop and wiggle your fingers to say ok."

He wiggled his fingers.

"Good, that's too ridiculous looking for me to miss."

He was nearly invisible behind the bars and chains and shackles, transformed from a shapeless man of flesh into an abstract sculpture of metal.

"Mphwoo Mphhhhoooo. Hooooooo?" he called through his gag.

"No, I'm not putting you in a hood." She opened a drawer built into the bench and found a pair of new earplugs. "You can wear earplugs if you want."

He waved his fingers up and down in agreement. She tore the plastic open and placed them carefully in his ears.

She helped him painstakingly get down on his hands and knees. He waited patiently on all fours until she chained his wrists to the metal belt and put his personal blindfold on. He had retrofitted old fashioned flight goggles to ensure no light could escape through the lenses. She guided him as he wiggled into the cage and shut the door with a loud clank.

"Are you okay?"

He waved his fingers up and down again.

She set a timer and sat on the bench adjacent to the cage to monitor him with her eyes.

She took a deep breath and let her mind race. She had an hour of nothingness before the timer went off, and then another half hour helping him out of his chains. She usually brought a book to read but today, she used the time to obsess about James.

What would she call him? Slave? James? Or maybe Jim or Jimmy. How did he find her? She hadn't given her name to anyone at the restaurant, she hadn't paid with a credit card. Was it magic? Was it God? She had felt a twinge of recognition, a 6th sense, an intense rush of attraction as soon as she saw him. Was it love at first sight? Was it on both sides?

The timer rang. Tom's time was up. She let him out of the cage.

"You were so quiet," he said. "It really felt like you abandoned me."

"Oh, I'm sorry, I was sitting right here the whole time."

"No way!" He laughed. "I never knew. I hate when doms poke me through the bars or start talking on the phone. It destroys the experience for me. This was great. I can't believe how relaxed I feel. Can I see you again in two weeks?" he asked.

"Absolutely," she chirped, "just stop at the desk on the way out to book it before my dance card gets full."

"Can we do it exactly the same way as today?"

"Sure, of course," she said politely.

She hoped to God that Jim didn't turn out to a one-trick pony. She knew actors were trained to be spontaneous and creative, free of body shame, unafraid of taboos. That meant they were free spirits who could play any role. Was it all meant to be, destined by God, or was she just really horny?

A sudden clap of thunder shook the building. Jax almost flew off the ground. Was that her answer? If so, what the fuck was the answer?

"Oh, wasn't expecting rain," Tom said. He was back in his clothes, looking 20 years younger again. "Mistress Amazon, you know, you can leave the room next time if you want."

"I never leave the room, Tom." She regained her composure. "House rules."

"I guess that's a good thing."

"It's for your own safety," she said.

"Yeah, I guess, but some danger is sexier." He winked at her.

She wasn't going to lecture Tom on the risks of being left alone in extreme bondage and end their session on a downer. People amazed her when they exposed their inner madness. Was it her job to fix them all? No, it was her job to make them feel wanted, not judged, to guide them, and protect them when their fantasies were self-destructive.

"Would it help if I said I emotionally abandoned you instead?"

He guffawed. "Ok, ok, that works, sure!"

"It comes naturally to me," she joked.

"Of course it does, Mistress." He smiled.

Once he was gone, she dutifully cleaned up his drool and drops, sprayed and wiped down the equipment, ran a vacuum over the rugs. She gathered the chains and cuffs and shackles and put them back into a rolling footlocker Fred left in the room, then took the gag, earplugs, disinfectant and cleaning rags and put them in a plastic bag, and wheeled everything back to the wardrobe area.

"I'm done with the bondage room," she said as she greeted Fred, who was taking a coffee break on his knees and swirling his tongue over Amber's toes. "Can you help me?"

He acted like he couldn't hear her and sucked Amber's toes more passionately.

"Hey!" Amber languidly bopped him on the head. "Don't be greedy, go help her."

Fred rose to his feet stiffly and mumbled under his breath as he walked to Jax.

"I never get to do my fetish enough," he whined. The women rolled their eyes at each other. Fred's foot fetish was unsurpassable. He'd glue his mouth to any consenting female feet he could find and stay there all day if you let him. It was almost scary how much foot sucking he could sustain without jaw injury.

Jax removed the leather pants and corset blouse she wore for Tom's fantasy and put them in the plastic bag with the gag, waiting patiently until Fred handed her the dress she had reserved: a simple, low-cut black latex number with a large pink latex bow in the back that accentuated her taut ass. She exchanged the biker boots she wore for Tom with a pair of matching black spike heels with pink bows.

She had originally planned to wear the fetish ensemble for Mr. Rhumba Pants. She had thought up a game she named "who can wiggle their ass faster," so could pretend it was a reason to punish him with a hard spanking whether he lost ("bad wiggler!") or won ("how dare you deny your Mistress a victory!"). Rhumba was another one-trick pony: put him in panties, get him hard, then spank him until he came in his panties, and goodbye. He was very nice though and brought his own panties to soil, which was considerate.

She grabbed a quick shower to smell fresh for Jim and put on the dress, admiring how it flattered her body type. It showed off her more feminine side, which was the side she wanted Jim to see. Her breasts spilled gently from the scoop neck and the soft latex felt like a second skin. She dabbed Opium perfume behind her ears and on her wrists and trotted back to her make-up station to reapply lipstick and eyelashes. Finally, she went to the lounge to drink coffee. Sadie and Amber were there, waiting for their clients.

"So we heard you got a movie star!" Sadie said. "I can't wait to hear the gossip."

"Is he single?" Amber asked.

"I don't know, I think so." Jax walked to the donut table so they couldn't see her face. She knew damn well he was single. She had been stalking him on the Internet all day, reading every fan site and gossip page to build a case study of his likes and dislikes, his habits, and especially his love life.

"Try to marry him," Amber advised. "Can you imagine? You could quit and live a life of luxury and travel all over the world with him!"

Sadie agreed, "You won't get a chance like this again. How often do you see a movie star here? NEVER."

Jax blushed. Had they read her mind? "What? I don't even know him!" she weakly protested, feigning interest in the donuts.

"Once," Amber nudged Sadie.

"What?" Sadie said.

"Donnie Dickface, remember him? He was a famous actor."

"Oh, yeah, that guy, I remember. But he wasn't a star star, more like a second banana."

Amber looked insulted but before they had a chance to quibble over it, Lilith poked her head through the lounge door, craning her neck like a giant bird.

"Jax, Jax! He's here! I put him in the party dungeon. He said he can't wait to see you."

Jax was overjoyed. Clients were restricted to the fetish rooms on weekdays unless they were willing to pay a considerable extra fee. Either money was no object to Jim or it was more proof that he was madly in love with her. Jax walked through the lobby in a daze of lust, her legs vibrating with excitement. He was here. It was happening. Her mind couldn't process it, but her legs moved her swiftly towards him.

"He's such a gentleman." Lilith went on, "Go in, he's waiting for you. Such nice manners. He's going to love you!"

Jax strode into the main dungeon in a tsunami of body-drenching adrenalin. Jim was ensconced in a throne chair, chatting on the phone, one leg rakishly slung over the side. He had a California tan, almost bronze, and wore a starched pale blue shirt, unbuttoned just enough so you could see the glittering gold chain he wore around his neck. His jeans were stone washed and his signature black cowboy boots gleamed. He was thinner than she remembered. Except for the cowboy hat on his head, he was everything she wanted.

"Ok, Chuckie, I'll ring you up when I'm back on the West Coast," he said, hurriedly shutting his cellphone, his eyes appreciatively scanning her latex dress and spiked heels. He removed his hat and dropped it to the chair with his phone, raked his thick brown fingers through his dark hair to fluff it up, and smoothed his moustache with thumb and forefinger. So he was a peacock, she blinked. Of course he was. He was a movie actor. He lived to stick his face in front of a camera and get attention.

"You look great," he said, as he walked up to her extending both arms. "Even better than I remembered." He crushed her in a full body hug. The speed of this familiarity overwhelmed her senses. She could feel the muscles of his chest through his shirt, his taut thighs, and the lump in his groin. She'd never been hugged like this in her life. This was the hug of a man in his sexual prime, violent and invasive yet tender and emotional all at the same time.

She fled his embrace. Her body trembled with feelings and needs she didn't know she had. It was happening too fast. She masturbated to fantasies of him last night. Now he was here, a stranger to her, not the figure of her fantasies, but a human being she would have to learn.

"Follow me," she ordered him. When he didn't move, she took his hand and pulled him to a sofa. He followed her lead, grinning boyishly.

"Yes, Ma'am," he said cheerfully when she pushed him down onto a sofa, then seemed disappointed that she didn't sit next to him.

She had to push her feelings away. She had to maintain dominant space. She sat on a throne chair that was in easy crawling distance from the sofa. She didn't want to play with him right away or let him think he could push her around. Goddess Love taught her that establishing clear cut physical boundaries was intrinsic to maintaining your dominant space. You couldn't let slaves touch you without permission because it blurred the power lines.

A Mistress occupied a singular place in her slave's life. She wasn't his girlfriend or his wife. She was his owner. To be ethical, she should be a caring and compassionate owner. She provided the space for him to escape from everything else, including all the cultural assumptions that weighed him down. He didn't have to be strong with a femdom, because she was his strength. Her mere existence was living proof that there were women more powerful than men, women who were consumed by the desire to control men, to tie them and tease them to torment, who found their pleasure in seeing men suffer for them.

"I wanted you the minute I saw you," he said. "You're so fucking sexy."

She felt like her resolve was melting and drew herself up straight, inspecting him coolly.

"That's no way to address a dominatrix," she said. "It's disrespectful."

He looked bemused. "I guess you're right."

"Try it again, with respect."

"Mistress, you are the sexiest woman I've ever seen. There's this quality about you." He released a heavy sigh. "I don't know, but you are like pure sex."

Pure sex? She hadn't fucked anyone in almost 2 years. If only he knew she was more like pure masturbation. "How did you find me? How did you even know my name to find me?"

"It was Kismet," he said. He leaned towards her seductively. "Do you believe in Kismet?"

Kismet had been her favorite theory: stars had aligned, gods had intervened, and mystic spheres had spun in the heavens, all to bring them together.

"No," she said, "I believe in reality. How did you really find me?"

"Awww," he said. "I was skimming an issue of the Dominatrix Directory and you were in it," he said. "Right away, I knew you were the girl I saw at the Italian joint. So I told myself, next time I get to NY, I'm going to see her!"

"Oh. I see." She remembered posing for a profile in the directory. Lilith got all of her workers into the Directory to advertise the club and draw business. She wished it had been a more magical connection but she was satisfied to have a rational explanation.

"Shall we begin?" She tried to fight back her attraction to him. His jeans now hugged his crotch so tight she could see the outline of a plump penis. Her brain went blank. He was too good looking, too friendly, too nice, too famous. Something had to be wrong with him because she found him perfect and no one was perfect.

"I want to see your obedience." She sounded as stern as she could, which wasn't as stern as she wanted to sound. "Remove all your clothes." She heard the word "clothes" come out of her mouth like a squeak but he didn't seem to notice.

He stripped instantly and stood before her, comfortable in his nakedness. He looked more beautiful naked than in clothes. His large nipples looked juicy and his rose-colored cock was thick and meaty. Dark brown fur spread from his chest down to his ankles. He turned sideways, posing like a bodybuilder, then faced front, clasping his hands behind his neck, his chest pushed forward. She suddenly recalled that a gossip site mentioned he'd done male modeling before landing an acting job. He certainly had the moves.

She had some moves too. She led him to a standing cage.

"So you like being naked and wild," she said crisply. "This is where I put wild animals."

He darted inside and began jumping around like a gorilla and pounding his chest. He looked awfully happy for a man in his predicament. She put her hand through the bars and he maneuvered his head under her palm like a big puppy who wants pets.

He was so playful. So hot. He was a rich and famous actor who thought she was the sexiest woman on earth and now he was in her cage.

She pushed her palm down so hard that he dropped to his

knees. "Ow," he mewled, "that hurt."

"Isn't that why you came here, slave? To be hurt and debased and owned?"

She reached through the bars and grabbed one of his nipples, twisting it until he moaned.

"Debase me!" he cried. "Hurt me! Own me, Mistress, I want to be owned by you."

She motioned for him to follow her to the large X-frame cross and he jumped out of the cage to follow her obediently. She tied his hands overhead and began teasing him with her fingernails, running them from his lips to his thighs and back again, while he writhed and groaned with ecstasy.

"Oh my God," he whispered. "Oh my God, I love you!"

Her heart stopped. Time stopped. Everything stopped. He didn't say that, did he? Even if he did, he couldn't have really meant it. It was just an actor getting into a role or something. It wouldn't be real unless he asked her out on a date. She untied his wrists and rubbed them gently to ease any soreness.

"How dare you speak of love to your Mistress," she said. "You should be spanked!"

"I should," he agreed.

She led him to a spanking bench, a sturdy wood one with padding across the top. With her hand on his neck, she guided him into position, then turned a side-crank and elevated his bottom until his cheeks were raised high.

"Oh, your ass is too pale," she said. "So pale. You need some color in your cheeks!"

He snorted.

"Are you laughing, slaveboy?" Jax asked, leaning so close to him she knew he would smell the rose water she put in her hair and the Opium she dabbed on her body. A wave of heat rose between them as if their bloodstreams were trying to connect.

"Oh no, Mistress Amazon, never! Especially not in this position!"

"Don't you think your cheeks are too pale? They're like two bright moons."

"Yes, Ma'am, please fix them, Ma'am."

She smiled and began warming his ass with her palms, building slowly to sharp slaps, then paddles and hard whacks, while he body-danced on the bench in abandon, his calves twitching, his back arching, his shoulder muscles rippling, his anus winking, and his hard belly bouncing him back up like a rubber doll after every hard blow.

"Oh my God, oh my God, oh my God," he chanted like a crazy priest.

"There!" she announced triumphantly. "Now your ass has some color. A bright red color. It's a good look for you." She cranked him back down and helped him stand up.

"Thank you, Mistress. It feels... very hot."

"As hot as me?"

"Nothing could be as hot as you." The head of his penis was reaching for the ceiling.

She inched closer to him. She wanted to touch him all over. She lightly, oh so lightly, encircled his penis with her hand. He gasped and stared hungrily into her eyes.

"You work with so many beautiful actresses," she squeezed his member, tightening her fist until he grimaced, then releasing him.

"I do," he said, relieved. "I've worked with gorgeous ladies, and maybe some of them are prettier than you, technically. But

I never met anyone who was sexier than you." He wasn't smiling now. He was humbly searching her face for confirmation that she believed him. She squeezed his cock again, even tighter, as if to squeeze the truth out of his soul. He winced and squirmed. "You are the sexiest woman I have ever met in my life."

No one had ever said that to her before, not in those words, and certainly never with carnal passion. She could barely control her feelings for him. They were coming at her in every direction: her hunger for true love, her mother's stinging question, Amber and Sadie's advice to marry him, a future with children, her brain, her heart, her pussy, her soul, all of them screaming to rush into a relationship and run away with him.

Now she took him up to a St. Andrew's cross and showed off her rope skills. She tied up his balls, his penis, wrapped him in ropes that held his trunk in place, and wove skilled knots at the end of all four limbs.

"Can you move?"

"Barely!" He fought the ropes and lost. "You're amazing."

She picked up a soft brush from another station and used it to tease him over every uncovered inch of his body. He became so wild with excitement when she brushed it along the head of his cock that the whole frame shook and she worried for a second he would break the floor bolts and come tumbling down. But the cross endured and he finally calmed down when she moved to his arms.

The time had passed effortlessly. She had never felt so completely engaged with a man. She carefully untied him. He was unsteady on his feet so she gently helped him to sit on the floor and draped herself over him to let him rest his head on her breasts until he had recovered.

"You were so good," she murmured, cradling his head in her arms. "Such a good boy."

"I think I'm in love," he said in a whisper.

They hugged like that until he said he was ready to stand up.

"Can you show me around the toy store?" he asked. "Is that okay with you?"

"Yes! That's a wonderful idea!" She pointed to his clothes. "Do you want to get dressed?"

He shrugged. "Not really."

"Alright, then. Follow me, naked boy!"

They went to the large glassed in emporium in the dungeon. Jax pressed a concealed button and a glass door slid silently open.

"I fucking love this place," James said. "You guys have the classiest dungeon I've ever seen."

"It's where everyone's dreams come true," she said.

He paced back and forth, picking like an expert. He chose a stiff high leather collar, exquisitely made leather cuffs, a two-sided paddle -- leather in front and fur in back -- and a pair of lace-up bondage mittens. "This is a start on our private collection," he said to her, "just for you and me. I'll pay for them now if you can store them for us until I get back. Can you?"

"Yes." Her heart was pounding. "I'll store them in my loft so no one touches them but us."

"Cool. Where's your loft?"

"It's here, at the back of the club."

"What? You live here? You actually live here?"

She couldn't believe she broke her own rule about never telling clients where she lived. It was too late to take it back.

"Oh my god, that's just perfect, perfect. So you're here all the time?"

"I do occasionally leave the building." She arched an eyebrow at him.

"Yeah, of course, shopping and stuff but, you know, actors have crazy schedules. If you live here, I could come by during off hours!"

She was dubious. Lilith wouldn't let her keep the dungeons open on her own. If he wanted to see her, they'd have to play in her apartment. Would Lilith allow that or would she consider that client-poaching? And how would she charge him if it was in her loft? Would she still have to split the fee 50/50 with Lilith?

"Maybe I could spend a night sometime?" he asked. "But only if you wish, Mistress."

"Maybe." She stopped herself. The conversation was breaking all kinds of dungeon rules. On the other hand, if this was going to be a love relationship, maybe the rules didn't apply.

"I need to think about it. I need to talk to my boss."

"I understand." He went back to the rack of dresses and removed a sleeveless number that laced up the front from navel to neck. "May I buy this for you?"

"Oh!" She was touched. "Yes, you may."

"One more question, really a humble plea from a slave." He got down on his knees and implored her. "Please, Mistress, will you wear this for me the next time I see you?"

"That depends," she said. "When will you see me?"

"Is tomorrow too soon?"

She wasn't expecting that. "No, it's not too soon."

"And can we go out to dinner afterwards?"

"I guess." She turned away so he couldn't see the shock on her face or her lips silently saying, "Omg, omg, omg."

They walked back silently to where he left his clothes, but before he could get into them, she unzipped her dress so her breasts tumbled free, slid down her panties, then pulled him onto a couch.

"You're doing this now? When I have to leave?" He joked. "Why did you wait?" He began kissing her neck.

"Shut up. We're off the clock. You're on my dime now."

She held him down and kissed him on the lips until they were breathless. She raised her body off his, and softly slapped his face.

"You're going to please me now," she said.

She wound her legs around him and ground her pussy against him. She arched her back. She bit him on the neck. He lay still in a narcotic trance of surrender. His eyes turned dark and glimmering. She wanted to consume him and to be consumed by him into a fire of ecstasy. She wanted everything. She pushed him back roughly. He melted in submission. She straddled him and slid slowly down until his cock was deep inside her. It felt like a velvet torpedo had shot into her hungry body, aimed directly at her orgasm. She groaned, blinded by ecstasy, and dragged herself off him. He was hard and unsatisfied as she sat beside him and swept her damp curls off her face.

"You're not going to leave me like this!" he protested weakly. "I'm dying to cum."

She pulled on her panties and zipped the dress up.

"Good," she said.

He gave her sad puppy eyes.

"Get dressed. It's time to go. And pay Lilith for the toys and dress on the way out."

"Oh God, you're amazing." He sat up. "You're merciless!"

"Why, thank you."

He slipped back into his clothes and removed a bulging wallet from his back pocket. "You're getting a big tip, baby, a really big tip."

"I already did." She smirked at him.

"I'm glad you liked it." He preened.

"I'd like more of it."

He came back the next week. Then the week after that. He booked her for 3, 4, 5 hours at a time. They wore themselves out in the dungeon, went out to dinner, and came home to fuck to the point of exhaustion.

She pulled down his pants and he pulled up her dress, and they lay down together, the commotion of their limbs frightening Buttons off the bed. He entered her with that violent tenderness that rocked her the first time he hugged her. His fingers and hands were soft and gentle, until they weren't and gripped her tight, leaving pale bruises on her skin. When she allowed him on top, he plunged into her like a man on fire jumping into a river. He held her tight, kissing her, coaxing her to orgasm with sweet words and confessions of adoration. They often came simultaneously, clenching their muscles and timing their ecstasy so they could scream in chorus.

They grew drunk on lust together, addicted to the smell of each other's bodies, hungry to squeeze every pleasure out of every moment they spent together. She had never felt so alive, never so intensely aware of herself as a sexual being.

"I never want to leave you," he said when it was time to leave for the West Coast.

"I hate coming home," he said on the phone, "it's so lonely without you."

"I'm not happy unless I'm with you," he told her when they

finally reunited.

"I feel the same," she said every time. "I wish we didn't live on different coasts."

"What am I going to do?" he sobbed, half drunk, alone in his mansion on the beach. "I love you so much."

"You'll love me and I'll love you until the ends of our lives," she comforted him.

And then, a few weeks later, he asked, "Would you consider moving here?"

Jax had been waiting for the question. Living together was their next step.

"I have a big old house all to myself, you can have your own office space, lots of closets, you can even have your own bathroom if you want."

"Are you sure?"

"Haven't you been listening? I need you in my life. I need you in my bed. I can't live this way anymore. I want to know that you are really with me now, not just a woman I date when I'm in New York, but someone permanent."

She didn't need more incentive than the word "permanent." She was decided. He was her man. He was the only one who understood her -- her wild moods, her unique personality, her independence. He gave her room to be herself completely. She was ready to give herself to him permanently.

She talked to Lilith the next morning.

"Are you sure about this?" the older woman asked with concern. "You've only known him a few months."

"I know it's fast, I know," Jax said. "But it was love at first sight for us both. That means something, doesn't it?"

"I've heard people say that." Lilith looked dubious.

"It's more than BDSM." Jax wanted to convince her. "He takes me places and we sit up all night talking sometimes."

"That's sweet. But he's an actor," Lilith said.

"Are you saying he was just acting with me?" Her back went up at this. Was Lilith trying to ruin her chances for romantic happiness so she'd keep working?

"I just want you to be careful." Lilith gave her a hug. "I won't stand in the way of your happiness. Come into my office and let's figure out a plan."

Appeased, Jax sat with her and came up with a compromise. Jax would come back for a week every month. Meanwhile, Lilith would run new ads and rebrand her to clients as, "The most exclusive dominatrix in New York, with a growing business in California." As they plotted how to spin her move, Donna and China Doll walked in. They hooted and jumped up and down about her news. They had watched the relationship grow, they'd seen Jax acting like a woman in love, they saw him fawning over her, and treating her like a queen. At heart, these femdoms were romantics who believed in true love. Many of them wanted exactly what she wanted: the dream slave, that sexy, sweet, devoted and financially stable person who found joy in being owned. So they all got it. Or, as Shirley succinctly said, "Rich, famous and kinky! What else could a girl want?"

China Doll insisted they change the wording to make it even more tantalizing. "Say she's a jetsetter, traveling around the globe to visit wealthy clients. A jetsetter sounds hot."

Shirley jumped in. "Make it jet setting around the world for those fortunate enough to afford her priceless charms. That's good isn't it? Use those words. Then you can raise her prices too."

Lilith was amused but took their advice. She read the revision aloud to them. Jax sounded like the Empress of the

Universe, her rate was doubled, and they cheerfully speculated on how the ad would draw interest and bring in more clients for everyone, including people who felt better just going to a pro dungeon which featured an "internationally renowned Mistress."

"As long as you eventually come back to us full-time," Lilith looked at her.

Jax blushed. She wasn't planning on ever coming back. She was planning on living with him, and marrying him, and then letting their relationship lead them where it would. She would travel with him to movie locations and keep up with his busy schedule of parties and social engagements. But she simply said, "You are my family," and everyone got tears in their eyes, and they said no more.

Jax wanted to hug them all in gratitude. She half-expected anger and recriminations from Lilith and resentment from her co-workers. Instead, they made it easier for her to leave them while giving her even more incentive to return every month for a week. A one-week stop in New York couldn't last forever, but it would ease the transition from New York to LA, and give her guaranteed quality time with her two chosen families, Paul and Raf and the crew at L'Oubliette.

It was a good plan. It was the right choice. From the day he picked her up at the airport, looking like a suitor should, she knew everything would work out. She saw him first across the airport. He peered over the crowd, and seemed a little nervous as if she might have missed her flight. The second he spotted her he smiled and waved a bouquet of red roses. He wore a suit. The hats and boots were conspicuously missing.

"I didn't expect a suit," she said as she ran into his arms and he lifted her, twirling and twirling around, kissing her face all over. She was sure of it: he was the one. The only one.

"I thought I should clean up for you." He grinned happily. "Besides, I'm getting used to wearing a suit so I can marry you in style."

"Oh," she swallowed hard. A sweetness filled her. Her happiness was completed now.

She was a little disappointed when they reached his house. It was not how she expected a rich movie star to live. The location and property must have cost him a pretty penny but the interior needed a facelift. Her loft looked futuristic compared to the basic 1960s kitchen and baths in his home. Some pieces looked like his grandma bought them, including two overstuffed burgundy recliners that clashed with the rest of his 1970s California decor.

"We're home, baby!" He carried her bags in proudly. "See how much room you can have here? Wait until you see the beach."

"Nothing a good decorator couldn't fix," she consoled herself, following him out to the patio and swimming pool, and then taking a private path down to the beach. She spread her arms wide at the ocean's edge, letting her hair fly in the wind, in a state of perfect bliss. James hugged her from behind, his arms around her waist. She relaxed and leaned back against him, resting against his heart.

They clung to each other every night after sex, confessions of love and endearments falling from their lips. Three weeks passed in a blur of late mornings, later dinners, and solo trips to the beach while James went to meetings and auditions around town.

Sure, there were slight cognitive dissonances, minor incompatibilities. He once referred to her grandfathers as "fags."

"That's a horrible word," she said.

"What? Some of my best friends are fags. My make-up artist

is a fag! I got no problem with them."

"Please call them gay. It's much more respectful."

"They call each other fag all the time," he said. "It's always fag this and fag that."

"That doesn't make it less horrible. Do it for me, ok?"

"Sure, baby, if that's what you want, that's what I'll call fags from now on."

The conversation pissed her off. He lived in the sandcastles of celebrity life and she lived in the realities of the world. He didn't know or care about gay rights or how AIDS destroyed communities or what words had become obscene because of the history of hate behind them. All he cared about what acting, and meeting other famous actors, and trying out for roles, and envying everyone who got the roles he wanted to have.

"I think you should forgive him," Paul said. "His work must be all-consuming. He probably doesn't have time to keep up with politics or social trends. You can educate him."

"Yeah, but it makes me wonder how uptight he really is. I mean, he's amazing with me but he doesn't seem to have much of a social life. I never knew you could be so famous and still be so alone when you got home."

"It's a different life," Paul said. "But it makes sense you'd think differently about people and priorities. Maybe you need to give him more room to be himself before you try to make him over."

"I'm not trying to make him over," she said.

"Darling," Paul said, "you are."

She reflected on it. Paul was right. She needed to let him do his thing and not pick on his mistakes. She could guide him but she couldn't force him to be enlightened. Little by little, they would begin to merge in spirit and he would begin seeing things from her perspective without her having to demand it from him. She didn't want to think about what would happen if she didn't succeed.

There were other cringey moments she couldn't tell Paul about.

One night, Jim returned drunk from a dinner that ended up lasting half the night. She was asleep when he got into the bedroom. He clambered onto the bed and crawled on top of her back. She smelled his breath and cringed before she heard the words, "Open wide, bitch, I want to deep fuck you."

She didn't know how to react. The word "bitch" hit her badly and commanding her to do it made her want to smack him and call him a rude, selfish pig. She rolled away from him to a corner of the bed, complaining that she was too tired and if he wanted to have sex, he should have gotten home earlier. At the same time, he was still her sweet, beautiful James, her future husband, and he just wanted to get laid after a long night of missing her. Who was she to judge another person's boozing? Maybe she was the selfish one.

She tried to brush it off as a one-time event. The next morning, he claimed he didn't remember that happening and apologized if he did anything that upset her. She quickly forgave him. The only thing that mattered was their commitment to each other.

She lived for their mornings waking up naked with him, his cock already hard, his arms reaching for her. Some evenings he came home early so they could watch old movies together in bed. They lay on the beach at night and talked romantically about their future. Everything was in motion, waiting to happen. There would be a wedding on the beach, a honeymoon in Rome, and later there would be babies, at least two or three, and a brand new house to start their brand new family.

She hadn't considered the complexities of living with a movie star until he laid out some rules a few months in. She could never ever publicly reveal that she was a prodom or that they had a kinky relationship. She could never answer the phone or doorbell because it might generate gossip which could lead to a tabloid story which could lead to reporters finding out where she worked which would lead to him being unemployable in Hollywood. If the story that macho man's live-in girlfriend was a dominatrix ever spread, he'd be industry poison, he said. All her fantasies about parties and opportunities to hob-nob with Hollywood royalty and discreetly network for new clients were squashed. If he brought a woman to parties, the gossips would make it their business to learn everything they could about her, he said. They were vipers, he said. He almost shed a tear over how mean and vicious they were. He wanted to protect her from them.

She uneasily agreed to share his kink closet. To her, it felt more like a cocoon of lust and happiness. Fuck the outside world. She had her happiness in bed with him every morning and night. She settled into living invisibly and anonymously, the clandestine companion of a closeted star who left early in the morning each day and often didn't return until 9 or 10 pm at night.

But then came days when she woke up to an empty house and tripped over the half-packed suitcases and boxes of memorabilia cluttering the bedroom, and the rows of Hefty bags stuffed with fan letters he kept in the living room. Opened letters were spread on the coffee table, on chairs, on half the surfaces in the room. On the outside, it was a handsome Spanish villa but the inside had a funny smell and a sagging ceiling in the den.

It was as if the house had given up on itself. Surfaces wouldn't shine, stains wouldn't bleach out, and no matter how much she vacuumed, sand constantly drifted under their doors and filtered into the rust-colored shag carpeting. She hated the carpeting. She hated the color and she hated the sandy grit when she walked barefoot. She had a nightmare that she fell asleep for a week and that when she finally woke up, James was gone and she was trapped under two feet of sand.

At first, giving up a week to fulfill her obligation to L'Oubliette was tiresome. Now, she looked forward to seeing her friends, catching up on gossip, going to parties and having delightful adventures with clients who paid and praised her generously. L'Oubliette became an oasis once again, the way it was when she lived at Paul's. She loved to sleep in her own, bigger and more comfortable bed and to drink coffee from her own funny mug and play with Buttons. She felt stronger and more confident than ever in her goddess persona and, as predicted, she could make almost as much money in one week now as she used to make in two weeks. That was enough to keep paying rent on the loft, with a little left over to save.

As long as they woke up together, and he told her all the things she needed to hear, she could put up with it. As long as she knew that one day they would have their own home, she could deal with living in a dilapidated mansion in a prime location. Shitty carpeting and old appliances could be replaced. She should be grateful for what they did have. When he called her beautiful, when he told her he loved her, when he told her exactly what she craved to hear, it seemed worth it. He would never leave her. She felt that in her heart.

It should have been perfect. It should have been enough. She started calling Paul three or four times a day, feeling guilty that she was taking so much of his time but so happy that he gave it to her freely and with love. He shared her concern that something fundamental was missing from her life without trying to define it for her. She was lonely, they decided. She needed to build her own life there, apart from James.

She began attending self-improvement classes, where other lonely women gathered in sacred sisterhood to beat pillows and scream. After three sessions, she did not want to scream any more. She took a class in origami but she never got past making birds. She took a jewelry course with a brief fantasy that she would make custom jewelry for kinky people, studded collars and jeweled nipple clamps, but the teacher insisted she had to learn to bead first and by the time she had strung her 2nd necklace, she was done.

She saw a flyer outside the jewelry class advertising Hatha Yoga. "Find inner peace!" There were daily classes in a gym just half a mile away. She walked in as class was beginning and found a mat to sit on. The room was hushed, the teacher sat up front smiling serenely at the students. After the teacher chanted in a singsong voice, there was nothing to do but follow her instructions and move your body into strange positions that required concentration and effort to hold. Jax was surprised at how hard it was to maintain even simple poses. Months of lying around and feeling sorry for herself had made her soft.

Yoga became her new obsession. She hadn't felt so focused since working someone over at L'Oubliette. Yoga wasn't about doing but being. She bought books and audio tapes for home study and practiced constantly, no longer noticing when James came home late, no longer fretting about keeping dinner warm for him. She had her own schedule. When she achieved a perfect pose and breathed into it, unexplored spaces opened in her core. She worked on her breathing techniques until she could breathe herself to calm, breathe herself to sleep and, finally, breathe herself to emptiness. Blankness. Removal from the world. Self-control. Pure energy.

Yoga helped compensate for the growing loss of power she felt over James. Although he swore to be her slave, lately it was almost impossible to put him in the mood for anything but a blowjob. The one time she wanted him to lick the cum off her lips, he had a meltdown.

"Aren't I enough for you?" he asked.

"What? Of course you are!" she said. "I love you."

"Then why do you always want the kinky stuff?"

"What do you mean? You found me in a kinky magazine and came to see me at a dungeon, for Christ's sake. What are you talking about?"

"I feel like you love the kinky stuff more than you love me."

"That's not true!" she shouted. "I gave up everything I love to move here and be with you!" She got defensive. There was a kind of truth to it that pained her. She never would have fallen in love with him if he hadn't acted kinky. So, in a way, if he no longer felt kinky, if the whole thing was just an act on his part, didn't that negate her reason for being with him in the first place? If she had to choose between a man and her sexual identity... she couldn't bear to complete the thought. Her brain froze. "I gave up everything," she repeated.

"Oh, come on, what did you give up, being the whipping queen of New York?" She heard the venom in his voice. She was not really his queen, his Mistress, his goddess. She was a whore to him, and not in a good way, but in a demeaning way. She never would have moved in with him if he hadn't sworn to be her slave. Now he was tearing down the pedestal he built for her.

She didn't speak to him for a week after that. Every time they passed in the house, she wanted to scream that they never would have met if she wasn't a sex worker, that everyone was a whore and he was the worst whore because he whored himself relentlessly and was still broke.

"I can't be submissive to you right now." He finally broke the standoff by falling to his knees in front of her. "It takes the energy out of my art." He turned his tear-stained face to her. "Please try to understand, baby. I need to preserve all my energy, all the drama, for the art! It's so hard to get work these days."

She had heard this before. He blamed his work for all his problems. But he looked so pitiful that she sank down and took him in her arms. She remembered Lilith warning her about actors. One slow-burning insight she'd had was that no matter how famous they were, movie actors' lives were fraught with change and uncertainty. From the way James described it, he was running out of money fast and planning to take out another mortgage on the villa. He refused to tell how much he already owed on credit cards, and claimed he didn't care if they sued him. His recklessness upset her. He borrowed a grand from her last month because none of his cards had room to pay for a fancy dinner he hosted to discuss a new movie project -- a project that crashed and burned days later, when the main backers pulled out. It was another pile of money he'd wasted, only this time it was her money.

"I just need you to love me." He clutched her like a frightened child. "Just love me, baby, that's all I want."

"Of course I love you," she kissed his hair, "of course I love you, baby, you know I love you."

The next day, he was awake before her, sitting casually at the kitchen counter, reading *Variety* and eating a bowl of cereal. Two years earlier, just the sight of him barefoot in jeans, his shirt opened to his belly, and a two-day old stubble on his cheeks would have sent her into romantic overdrive. Now he just looked like a slob. Who was this person who had gone from macho hedonist to Victorian puritan who had to reserve all his sperm for his art?

She went back to the bedroom and he soon followed. He began filling one of his half-packed suitcases.

"Going somewhere?" she asked.

"I'll be back Sunday," he said, pecking her on the cheek and running out the door.

She sat on the bed and cried. She hated everything -- the house, her life, her boyfriend. She was right to take her chance at love. Paul taught her that. But she didn't know if it was love or if it was just two broken people so desperate to be in love they kept acting like they were. He stayed because he needed a housekeeper to stock the fridge, a maid to vacuum the sand, and a full-time babysitter. She stayed because he would never abandon her. He would never kill himself. It was a sick codependency.

He didn't call or text while he was gone. She waited patiently for him to return on Sunday. Then she waited impatiently as Sunday came and went, and left him texts all day Monday asking where he was. Tuesday morning, he texted, "See you tonight, baby, miss you."

She stayed out of the house all day, and took herself out to dinner to a Japanese place whose vegetarian menu was nearly identical to her favorite take-out restaurant around the corner from L'Oubliette. She came home to find a naked James sitting on the couch, his gut sticking out of her pink bathrobe, working his way through a six pack and reading fan letters from the shopping bags.

"You're home awfully late," he said to her. "It's almost 10 pm."

"You're home." She walked past him to the bedroom and locked the door.

"Jax, don't be this way. What's wrong? Come on, let me in." He knocked repeatedly. She turned over and buried her head under a pillow. "Please, Jax, at least let me explain." His voice broke. "Baby, I can explain."

When she woke up, she found him asleep outside her bedroom door, an empty bottle under his neck. When she stepped over him, he woke up.

"Ow, my neck!" He rubbed it and sighed pitifully.

She ignored him and went about her busy daily routine of making the bed, cleaning up the kitchen, wiping down the bathroom, vacuuming sand, doing yoga, practicing breathing, meditating and reading until it was time to shop or make dinner or both.

James stayed home all day, watching TV and drinking. Then he stayed home the next day, and the day after that. When she came back from errands, he was always fuming about the bills and overdue notices he kept getting in the mail. He started messing with thermostats and bellyached about electric bills.

"Maybe I could afford a new shirt if you weren't eating steak every night," James said, dourly examining the refrigerator's contents.

"I don't eat meat. I switched to vegetarian when I started yoga last year," Jax said. "You're the one who wants steak every night. Besides, I pay for all our groceries, so what the fuck."

"Yoga? You're doing yoga? I noticed you were looking leaner. Why didn't you tell me?" He acted as if had never seen her practicing the Sun Salutation every morning, as if she hadn't talked to him about yoga dozens of times. Was he just acting like he didn't know? Or was he acting before, when he seemed to be listening to her?

"So do you want me to stop buying you steaks because they're so expensive?" she said sarcastically. "Would you prefer if I spent the money on a new shirt for you?" He looked like she slapped him.

"No, that wasn't what I meant, you misunderstood." He tried to wiggle away.

"Yeah," she thought to herself, "yeah, fucker, you want Mommy to keep buying your goodies as long as you don't have to pay for them."

He shut up and went into another room. She was relieved. She didn't want to fight with him. Not now, not ever again. She was done trying to fix him, to hold his hand through life and enable his narcissism. She wasn't going to defend herself against the unfounded, even ludicrous, charges that he made. Fuck him.

She was just letting the relationship be what it was. Dutiful. Tedious. Claustrophobic. Sexually dead. The less love she felt for him, the harder he dug his claws into her, and vice versa. When she went to the kitchen, he trotted in to ask her to make something to eat. When she went to the bathroom, he sat on edge of the tub to talk to her. He interrupted her yoga practices to ask stupid questions. Sometimes she could barely get through a few paragraphs in a book before he was yammering at her again.

She was sitting alone and relaxing in a lounge chair on the pool patio, while James watched soap operas and drank more beer inside. She tried to empty her mind but couldn't stop thinking about when and if and how she would leave him. Admitting to all her friends and her Grandpa that she'd made a horrible mistake felt worse than leaving James. The shame of her failure would haunt her the rest of her life.

"You need to stay visible in Hollywood." James suddenly plopped down in the adjacent lounge chair. "I can't get hired because of you. That's the reality I'm dealing with now. I'm losing work because of you."

"How the hell am I responsible? You've blocked me out of

your professional life. I am a non-entity in your Hollywood life, I don't even exist."

"You don't understand the pressure. I'm supposed to be a sexy macho man, right? I had to turn down an invitation to a Playboy party!"

"Thank God for small favors."

He looked tragic. "I'm trying to be faithful, here! So I can't be a player -- which is what everyone expects of me -- because I have a girlfriend, but I can't tell people I have a girlfriend because then they'll find out she is a dominatrix who does weird shit with me."

She snorted. "If only."

"I need a drink." He stood up huffily and marched back to the house.

He could drink all he wanted but what she wanted was a fat juicy half-pound charbroiled cheeseburger in her mouth, vegetarianism be damned. She dialed a restaurant and ordered cheeseburgers and fries for them both.

He came back with a bottle of gin. He switched targets and began raging about Hollywood actresses, how they were all opportunists and bitches. He said Hollywood directors were all con artists and all producers were thieves. His publicists and agents trapped him into B-movies when they knew he was a better actor than that. Now they were saying he was too old for some roles. That was bullshit. Lots of old fucks got to play opposite young starlets as romantic leads. His contempt for writers was vicious.

"They're all hacks," he said. "How could they expect me to show my true talent when they give me stupid fucking lines a ten-year-old could've written?"

Jax listened with her eyes closed. Did James really believe

that time stood still, that beauty was forever, and that everyone but him was to blame for his sinking career? Had he never read his own reviews? Critics called him a ham, and described his performances as gimmicky and self-conscious. If he was trapped in B-movies it's because he was a B-quality actor.

"I can do Shakespeare!" he shouted. "I DID Shakespeare! I reinvented Shakespeare!" He pointed his finger in the air. "When I was in drama school," he added. "But everyone said I was good enough for the professional stage! They told me that, my teacher and the director."

She didn't need a college degree to know that anyone who claimed they had reinvented Shakespeare was talking out of their ass. Did sober James believe what drunk James was saying or was he just talking trash now?

He staggered to his feet and rose to full height, holding his nose imperiously high and flourishing an arm. "This shoe is my father. No, this left shoe is my father; no, no, this left shoe is my mother. Nay, that cannot be so neither. Yes, it is so, it is so; it hath the worser sole. This shoe with the hole in it is my mother; and this my father." He looked proud of himself. "Two Gentlemen of Verona," he said, sitting back down and swigging a shot from the bottle.

The doorbell rang.

"Fuck them!" James yelled. "Whoever it is, fuck them."

"I ordered food for us." Jax stood up.

"Oh. I guess I could eat."

She returned with two plastic shopping bags and a blanket, and went down to the beach just as the sun was setting. She arranged their picnic for two. He walked to her slowly, hugging his bottle. They ate in silence. She chewed slowly, savoring each mouthful as if it were the last taste of cheeseburger she'd ever have. Or maybe it would be the last meal they would ever share.

Melancholy washed in on a wave and swept over her.

She wished they could live forever in this moment of silence and peace, watching the splendor of the ocean and the wide open skies, the bright streaks of reds and yellows turning to orange and brown and purple. She wished she could stretch this moment out, until, somehow, some mystical spiritual conversion reunited their hearts.

James had too much gin in him for that fantasy to come true. He started with a mournful monologue about the vast armies of sharks and vipers in his business who wanted to take him down. He recounted dubious stories about all the favors he'd done for people and how, now when he needed them to help him, they all let him down. The best they could do was offer him a movie in Romania, and he walked out on that meeting because it was such an insult to his pride. He told her that he never would have lowered himself to call in favors or beg for jobs but he did it for Jax, so they could get married someday soon.

She didn't know what to believe about him anymore, so believed in the beauty of the night. She turned her face to the stars that were filtering into the sky and stared until she was immersed in the cosmos, far above the shore. She listened to the heartbeat of the ocean as its waves kissed the shores. She listened to the pulsing waters with her core. The sea drowned out his words and her mind moved to the deep spaces inside. She was alone, completely within herself, bodiless, elevated above reality. When she looked down at the beach she saw an angry man gesticulating at a ghost of the woman who once loved him.

Chapter 8

DE SADE IS SMILING

Who was that woman grasping onto the culturally manufactured dream that perfection was a husband who came home for dinner and would never divorce her? Why did she EVER wait for a man who vanished for days at a time and strolled back in when he felt like it? She thought she picked someone like Grandpa Steve, but instead she ended up with Barry, an unhappy, self-obsessed man-baby.

She took a cab to Paul's when she landed, and ran up the stairs despite her heavy suitcases. They hugged as if they hadn't seen each other only a few weeks early. This was a special hug, a reunion hug. She was going to move back in with him for a while.

She didn't feel connected to the woman she was even yesterday afternoon, the one who catered to a narcissist, trying to leave planet Earth in her mind. Maybe she had a nervous breakdown. It felt like a seismic wave had vibrated through every crack in her personality and shattered her inside out. The night on the beach was the Karmic shock that sealed all the cracks back up.

"I'm so happy you're home for good," Paul said. He wore a red silk smoking jacket and brought out his prized Japanese-style tea set that a ceramics artist friend made for his 60th birthday. She settled next to him on the big blue couch Raf bought during his last phase of redecorating. She told Paul about her last night in California in a long rush of words. He listened thoughtfully, pouring tea each time a cup was emptied.

"I realized there was no rainbow at the end of that road. I mean, what was the real end-game? Ending up trapped in a marriage with a guy with huge debts, who couldn't even deal with keeping a clean house and kept me as his dirty secret? At first, I thought, ok, I'll be the strong one, I'll be the wife who does it all and the Mistress who fixes him. It was still better than being all alone. And then I thought, well, I love him, I made a commitment in my heart to stay with him, and relationships are all about loyalty, and I'd hate myself for failing at love again. But then he stopped being a slave and turned into a self-pitying tyrant who blamed everyone else for his problems. I was suffocating! I felt dead inside, Grandpa, dead. The only thing holding me together was talking to you. You were my life raft." She couldn't hold back her tears, which flowed in a mix of grief and gratitude.

Paul stared into his teacup.

"I was scared," she admitted.

Paul's whole body got stiff with rage. "Did that bastard threaten you?!"

"Oh no, not like that. I was never afraid of him, I was afraid of myself! Afraid I was losing my mind. I've meditated before but nothing like what I felt on the beach. That was an out-of-body experience, but not in an enlightened kind of way. It felt like I had dissociated so completely, that I could watch myself being angry and unhappy and yet passive and weak, and that scared me most of all. I was afraid if I stayed another day, I'd just float off into an alternate reality and never return. But then, I had a sudden epiphany. I knew that no failure could be worse than staying with him. Leaving him was mandatory. It was over. I was terrified to face it, that I'd made such a massive mistake again. I had to stop denying it, and pack my bags and come back to New York."

He nodded and refilled her empty teacup. Exhaustion overwhelmed her and she melted into the cushions.

Paul finally spoke. "I always thought he looked like a lizard. Those bright beady eyes and the way he licked his lips. He's handsome but, I don't know, he was a little clownish to me, you know, unnaturally smooth like a sanded pineapple."

"I should have listened to you when you said there was something off about him. You know, Lilith warned me too. I was an idiot."

"Anyone would be tempted to shack up with a famous movie star."

"B movies," she said. "Ridiculous ones."

"Still famous, though."

She lit a joint and closed her eyes. "It was lust. Pure unmitigated pussy madness. Demonic pussy. Brain-eating pussy. It turned me into a sex zombie!"

"Oh my, sweetie darling! You followed your heart." She sucked her cheeks in protest. "OK, or maybe your genitals. What's the difference? They're connected."

"I will never make that mistake again."

"Of course you will. It's called being human. And, in your case, being young. You saw him, wanted him, and for a time, he made you happy."

"I need to be able to tell the difference between what my pussy wants and what's real."

"Everything that happens is real. Your feelings for him were real. Discovering you made a mistake was real too, but it still doesn't cancel the experience of love you had."

"Meaning?"

"Meaning you loved him with all your heart at the time. Now the time is past. It's time to find someone else to love."

"Not ready."

"Yet," he said. "Sometimes you have to take a leap of faith. I'll never forget Raf."

Rafael moved to Palm Springs a year earlier to take up with a richer, younger iteration of Paul, claiming he had finally found true love, even though he had said the very same words about Paul. Paul firmly maintained that it was worth every penny he spent because Raf brought him back to life after Steve. Raf was his grief rehabilitation and the most fun he could imagine," he told her.

"I never understood what you saw in him. He was wonderful," she added, "I just didn't know how long you could tolerate someone calling you Doddy."

Paul laughed. "I thought it was endearing. It was fun at first. We went everywhere and did everything together. If I liked it, he liked it. If I wanted to do it, he wanted to try it."

"I assume you're talking about food," Jax said, suddenly hungry.

"Of course," Paul said. "Are you hungry? You look hungry." He got her a pack of Carr's water biscuits and a jar of Bonne Maman's raspberry preserves.

"Nom nom!" She tore the box open.

"Raf was the right person at the right moment in the right place. He was a complete distraction from my old life."

"Especially when he redecorated the house. I remember how distracted you were during that phase."

It started small, with Raf occasionally removing a small piece of furniture, putting it in one of the locked storage rooms, and replacing it with something nicer. Despite her teenage fantasies that the locked rooms were filled with gay sex toys and gay sex art and everything gay, they actually held Steve's astonishing hoard of bargains and finds from 30 years of scavenging flea markets and thrift shops.

After Raf replaced most of the furniture, he announced that the whole place needed a re-do because nothing matched anymore. At that point, Paul started to panic. Raf expected him to fund the renovations, which seemed fair to Jax but aggravating to Grandpa, who constantly complained that he was going broke.

"You up?" Paul would call in the middle of the night. "I don't know where I live anymore. And I'm running out of money. I could be homeless next week."

"You will never be homeless," Jax said, "and these renovations mean you'll get a much better price if you ever want to sell it. Stay calm, Grandpa. The future is here."

"I liked my gurgling toilet," Paul said. "It sounded like a little creek in the house when I worked."

"He's doing you a favor, Grandpa. You need to be modernized."

"Well, if my granddaughter thinks I need to be modernized, I guess I need to be modernized."

"Come on, Grandpa, you'll love it."

Raf had hired an architect to tear down a lot of walls and

open spaces up. He insisted on an all new kitchen and dining area, with custom cabinetry throughout. He called the old bathroom fixtures primitive and turned a closet into a sauna room. All the vintage furniture smelled funny to him, as did the carpeting so everything, including Steve's hoard, was sold or donated.

As much as Paul hated to part with Steve's treasures, the profits from the sales ended up paying him back as much as he'd spent on the renovations. It was as if Steve was still taking care of him, and she and Paul both wept over it together. They agreed, through their tears, that Steve and Raf had just given Paul a better, more comfortable life.

What neither of them had realized then was that Raf would move out just weeks after he finalized all the renovation details. It was, apparently, his last epic show of love for Paul before flying to be with his new lover.

"He made this place a showpiece, didn't he?"

"Yeah."

"I was relieved when he left. The relationship had run its course. When we were in Greece, we were on the beach and going to clubs and parties. But winters in New York, trapped indoors together, that only showed me that we had nothing to talk about, no common interests, nothing that really held us together. He really never wanted to do more than paint pictures he could sell to tourists. You know? I thought he was my younger doppelganger. But he was just a sweet young man trying to live the best life he could."

She nodded, jamming biscuits in her mouth.

"But we parted on a friendly basis. He sent me a postcard from his latest romantic vacation with Brad." Paul directed her eyes to a photo of a beach with tall palm trees sitting on the coffee table.

"Sucks," she agreed, picking the card up. Raf had signed it, "Love you forever, Daddy."

"I think what hurts the most is that he left me for a BRAD. How could I compete with a Brad??"

"Men suck," she said.

"I should hope so."

"GRANDPA!" She spat crumbs.

They spent the rest of the day talking about the future. She wanted to go to college. He wanted to do a triptych for a new gallery. She wanted to travel, he wanted to spend more time sitting on a Hudson pier and using natural light.

The next day, they decided to get breakfast at a local dive, and he showed her all the old stores that had closed and were replaced with flashier shops. On one quiet corner, customers formed a long line outside a specialty cupcake shop.

"I wanted to open a cupcake shop once," she said as they passed.

"Ha! You? It's a big thing in New York right now," he said. "You could have been a millionaire!"

"Maybe." She wondered how long a cupcake craze would last. Whatever was hip and trendy today was gone when the next overnight sensation landed. What kind of margin could you charge on cupcakes, anyway, she wondered? Enough to pay exorbitant rent for ten years? That seemed like a risky investment. "You know," she said casually, "there's probably more money in professional domination."

Paul's steps froze. "I never thought of that. I mean, I guess I know you probably made a decent living, but..."

"I make an obscene living," she said casually, "and I plan to keep on doing it until I'm 35."

"And then what?"

"And then I'll retire and take care of you, Grandpa. You'll never have to worry about money again. In fact, you might as well stop worrying right now."

He snorted, so she leaned up and whispered into his ear and a loud exhalation blew from his mouth.

"No way."

"Way."

"Goddamn, you're rich."

"Not compared to Booker or even my dad."

"Still. I need a quadruple espresso now."

They changed direction and went to their favorite place, Cafe Vivaldi, tucked into a side street. They sat at a table out front and watched a stooped old man limp slowly past a young mother with a baby carriage.

"L'Chaim," Paul raised his cup to them. "One day you're a baby and the next you're at death's door."

"Jeez, Gramps, that's fucking dark."

"Is it?" he mused. "Or is it life?" They smirked and toasted each other. "So... I've been meaning to tell you this for years..." He looked anxious. "I wasn't trying to keep it a secret from you, you understand."

"What?!" It didn't sound good. Did he have a disease? Did Raf give him HIV? She couldn't handle more stress. She dug in her purse for a cigarette.

"Not again! I thought you said you quit!"

"You try living with James for 2 years." She blew smoke. "Now what horrible secret were you going to tell me?"

"Nothing horrible!" he said. "I'm Jewish. I don't know why I never mentioned it, it's just never been a big factor in my life."

He waved at a waiter. "Can you bring my granddaughter a chocolate croissant?" He turned back to her. "You still love those, right?"

"Yes. Thank you. But what do you mean you're Jewish? Did it have something to do with Steve being Jewish? Did you convert for him?"

"No, no, no, nothing like that." He removed a worn social security card from his wallet. "See?"

She stared blankly at the card with a stranger's name on it. "Who is Max Schwartz?"

"Me," he said. "It doesn't really change anything for you."

"Wait. Does this mean I'm Jewish?!"

"No. The mother has to be Jewish for the child to be considered Jewish. Lucille and Barry's mothers were Protestants, so even Barry who was half Jewish wasn't technically Jewish according to rabbis. You are 1/8th Jewish, which is barely Jewish at all."

"Oh. I'm sad now, I wanted to be all Jewish." She bit into the croissant and the dark chocolate melted in her mouth. "I know we're two peas in a genetic pod."

"I don't know why it never came up. I got reminded when I went to renew my cab license. It's registered to Max Schwartz. I drove as Max when times were bad, but you know all about that."

"I'd like to drive as Max," she said idly. "Driving a cab sounds relaxing and entertaining."

"RELAXING? Did they put LSD in that croissant? I think you're better off doing what you're doing."

"So you're finally good with me being a professional dominatrix?" Paul never openly criticized her but he had peppered her with so many questions and concerns that she knew he would never feel really resolved about it.

"I'm proud of how you've built yourself up, and now I'm amazed at how well you've done financially. I wish Grandpa Steve was here to see it. He would be so proud of you. He cried when you took the papaya job. He thought no one would ever give you a chance to shine."

"Me too, Grandpa, me too! I just had to find people like me. I probably never would have had the nerve to do it without you. You were my role model for living my truth."

"That's terrifying," he said, but she could tell he was happy.

They looped arms for the walk home and talked more about the past and the future together. "You're the only woman I've ever really loved," he finally said.

"Oh, Grandpa! Oh, Grandpa, that's so sweet!" She felt so embarrassed and thrilled it made her feel like a young girl again. "Oh, Grandpa."

It was time to give up the loft and save the rent in the bank. She was going to pile-drive her way through the next few years of professional domination so that Paul would never want for anything. That's what Steve would have wanted. The next day, she returned to full-time work at L'Oubliette. Everyone was happy to see her but there was sadness too. They all wanted to believe in the fairytale of sex worker hits the big time, redeems herself and gains social status with a glamorous marriage.

"I'm so sorry it didn't work out," murmured some. "Men are such a disappointment," Donna said. "Don't worry, you'll find someone better," Shirley and China Doll reassured her.

Only Lilith was unmoved. "I warned you about actors." She hugged Jax hard, lowering her voice to a whisper. "They're never who you think they are."

"I should have listened to you," Jax said.

"You had to find out for yourself. That's how we learn."

"I learned." Jax hugged her back.

Jax needed a new look, more befitting her maturity. She changed her lipstick to a dark blood red, penciled her eyebrows charcoal black, and put aside the false eyelashes. That night she took scissors to her mane and cut it brutally short, then dyed her hair platinum blonde. The haircut laid bare the wrinkles sprouting around her eyes and lips. Good. She had earned every one of those lines. She ran to the living room.

"Look what I did!" She shimmied like a disco queen.

"Well!" Paul said, circling her to appreciate the full effect. "Well, huh. Severe! Really shows off the angles of your face."

"Do you like it?"

"Yeah, I do. Kind of Laurie Anderson meets Elvira. I like it."

"Stay tuned, there's more to come! We're getting modified."

Paul was mystified. "Modified?"

"Ink and needles, Gramps."

"Oh my God."

A few days later, she got a black heart tattooed on her left shoulder, with "discipline" inked in blue. She got a small tattoo of a whip on her ankle. Paul insisted on accompanying her to make sure the place used sterile equipment, and ended up getting a heart with "Steve" tattooed on his left wrist.

The final step was getting some new ear piercings. She went to a shop on Seventh Avenue which advertised "piercing with or without pain."

"I'll take the pain," she told them. She wanted to feel it in full, as part of her journey. She gave into the pain like a submissive, breathing her way into the journey to enter a transcendent state for the minutes it took to secure 3 small steel rings.

In a few weeks, the curly sweetie who pined after a movie star was gone. Now she was a grown woman, a little worn by life, a little mannish, and a lot meaner looking. Her new ad in the Dominatrix Directory made her look like a Teutonic Ice Queen. She showed it to Paul.

"Maybe you should change your nom de spank to Ilsa the She-Wolf," he said.

"I hope James sees it and strokes out from the big hard-on he gets."

Grandpa couldn't stop laughing, but the new look had the desired effect at work. Men feared her more. Their fear fueled her sadism, which resulted in more bookings and bigger tips. It amused her in a bittersweet way that she'd gone from the sweet girl next door who teases you to the Savage Bitch Goddess. Rebranding herself for her 30s was the right move: she would never be this young or pretty again. She had to exploit it for all it was worth, and it was worth quite a lot, particularly with Lilith's shrewd marketing, which firmly positioned Jax as the world's cruelest and most expensive dominatrix.

Men became her career, not her passion. She liked dominating them without lust, working with toys like a scientist instead of a hedonist. She took all the clients others didn't want. She didn't care. It was all the same to her as long as they paid her fee. She liked being a romantic. It was healing. She was happy to go home at the same time every night, have dinner with grandpa, watch a movie or two, and wake up feeling safe and serene. Raf had torn out the wall between her closet and two adjacent rooms, giving her a 3-room suite and a renovated bathroom three times as big as it was before. It was perfect. She'd never live anywhere else again.

Then Cece happened. Cece was that rarest of all birds, a

female client. Jax was intrigued when the curvy, brown-eyed brunette walked in. She wore a gray suit with a tight skirt that showed off her bounteous curves.

"Am I late?" Cece asked nervously as Jax looked her over, head to toe.

"No, you're perfect."

"Well, I..." Cece fumbled and blushed. "What? You really think so."

"Yes. Strip naked for me."

Cece tore off her clothes and kneeled at Jax's feet, breathless with excitement. Jax cupped her chin gently. Cece's brown eyes sparkled with golden light. Her skin glowed with health. A dark blush spread from her honey-colored cheeks to her round, heavy breasts and she wore a tiny gold cross around her neck. Jax stroked her cheek and Cece buried her face in it, making love to her Mistress' hand with plump, hungry lips.

Cece returned faithfully every week. She was enthusiastic and affectionate, with pain limits that defied explanation. She quickly became Jax's favorite client. During one especially intense session, a play-piercing to Cece's nipples and pussy lips, she screamed so loud Jax reached for the panic snaps before realizing Cece was having an orgasm. She caught Cece in her arms, and held her as she groaned and called her name over and over in a transcendent fog of submission. "Oh Mistress... Thank you, Mistress, I love you, oh God."

One night after a session, Cecilia asked if she'd like to get some dinner. Jax was leery. She liked Cece but she'd made a rule about not dating clients.

"Please accept," Cece implored. "I just want to pamper you."

She decided to break her rule for Cece. She didn't want to lose her as a customer. Besides, she wanted to learn a little more about her and what made her such a spectacular sub. They went to a quiet Spanish restaurant in Chelsea and took a booth.

Over dinner, she learned that Cece's life was complicated. At work, she ruled over 40 thousand employees. At home, she had three children, a nanny from Utah, four affectionate giant poodles, and two housekeepers to clean up and prepare meals for everyone. Jax admired her ability to juggle so many responsibilities and still make time to read to the kids every night.

After a few glasses of strong red wine, Cece told her about her battle to divorce her controlling husband. Their custody battle was vicious. He would do anything to prove she was an unfit mother, which is why she had to stay closeted. If she could leave her life behind, she would, Cece said, but she couldn't because of the children. She showed Jax pictures of her children over dessert. This was exactly the trap she feared falling into with James. Jax cringed to think of all the times she recklessly fucked James without birth control.

Jax's heart broke for her. "It's an impossible situation when you have kids." She wanted to hug Cece, who looked so lost, so uncertain, nothing like the happy woman she'd dominated just an hour earlier.

Cece said that until she met Jax, she had never realized how profoundly she craved to be a slave. Now she didn't want to live any other way.

"I'll still pay for sessions, of course, it's better to do it at the club for me because it's so private. But could I also take you out to dinners or shows, or maybe take you shopping?"

"Oh, I don't know..." Jax shook her head but her brain was already adding up the numbers. It would be fun and relaxing and there would be bonuses. Jax really liked her. It wasn't great love, but the friendship and kink compatibility were solid.

They began to date and, true to her word, Cece pampered her at fine restaurants all around the city. After six months, Cece ordered champagne for them both and handed Jax a small box. Jax eagerly popped it open. Cece loved to surprise her with earrings and other baubles.

A diamond solitaire glittered at her. Her smile faded. It was an engagement ring. "Are you proposing?"

"Yes and no," Cece said. "I'm proposing that you move in with us. Would you? The kids love you. The dogs love you."

"And you?"

Cece gasped. "I love you so much," she whispered over the table. "Oh, Mistress, I love you SO much."

Jax removed the ring from the box and slipped it on her wedding ring finger. It fit perfectly. "I'm inclined to say yes," Jax said. She hadn't meant to say yes. It popped out naturally.

"I'm going to faint," Cece said. "I'm so happy."

Paul wasn't quite as happy when Jax came home that night to give him the news.

"Who is this strange woman and what does she want from my granddaughter?"

"We're in a Mistress/slave relationship."

"And you're the Mistress?"

She couldn't tell if he was joking. "Um, yes."

"Well, if that will make you happier..."

"I don't know yet," she said. "I just figured I'd try it. If that's okay with you."

"It's fine. I'll be fine. Just be here for Friday dinner."

"And don't forget Saturday night sleepover so we can do

brunch on Sundays."

They locked eyes, nodded, and it was settled. When she packed, she decided to keep it simple. She would leave most of her things at Paul's, and just pick up anything she needed when she visited him.

She thought it would be hard to adjust, but life at Cece's moved so fast that by the end of the week, eating pancakes with the kids and spooning with her sexy girlfriend became her norm. She easily adapted to the tsunami that was Cece's family life. The kids began to call her Mamita and crawled into her lap whenever she sat down. When she held their warm, sticky little bodies close, she felt complete. She loved them. She even loved the poodles. After a long day at L'Oubliette, having children and dogs climb on top of her made her strangely, inarticulately happy.

The relationship moved along so smoothly, Jax started to relax. Their temperaments aligned well and they never fought. It felt like it could go on like this until the ends of their lives, when they'd be little old ladies together, rocking on a porch someplace pretty. Cece didn't mind that she spent weekends with her grandfather. She admired Jax's devotion to him. It all felt so right. It wasn't mad love but it was a love-filled security Jax had never known anywhere but at Grandpa's home.

On their first anniversary celebration, they toasted their future together. They began talking about going to Hawaii to get legally married. Cece held a small dinner party at Café des Artistes and they invited Shirley, Larry, Donna and China Doll and announced their official engagement to their friends' loud congratulations. Jax flashed an even bigger diamond ring at them. "She treats me like a queen," she said proudly.

Midway through the meal Cece turned pale. She had spotted someone at the bar. "Fuck," she muttered to Jax, squeezing her knee under the table.

"What's the matter?" Jax followed her eyes to the bar, where a menacing bald man was chortling into a wine glass.

"Fuck, fuck, that's my husband's lawyer, fuck."

They returned home in silence. When they got in, there were multiple voice messages from Cecilia's ex-husband. His lawyer had proof she was living a lesbian lifestyle. If she didn't end the relationship, he was going to file for sole custody of their children on grounds that she was a lesbian pervert who was exposing minors to depravity. If she didn't take him back, he would destroy her career, her relationship with the kids, and her family. She would end up with nothing.

"By pervert, does he mean he knows we're Mistress/slave?" Jax asked.

"No, God no, nobody knows about that!" Cece cried. "What am I going to do, what am I going to DO? Oh my God, if they start investigating you, they'll find out about the BDSM! Oh My GOD." She was disconsolate.

Cece frantically opened a locked cabinet she installed at the back of her closet to keep her curious kids from finding them. She dumped the toys, the lubes, the dildos in used Amazon boxes, tearing off her address from each. Then she covered the boxes with duct tape and placed them in trash bags. Jax looked out the window to spy on Cece lugging the bags out of view and reappearing empty handed a couple of minutes later.

"Bye-bye Amazon boxes," Jax murmured. The irony of the words made her wistful.

When Cece got back, Jax was already packing her things. Cece exploded in tears. It was all her fault, she said. She was a hypocrite and a bad mother and a disloyal slave. But she just couldn't let the children live alone with their father. He would destroy them. If Cece's Cuban mother and aunties found out, they'd ostracize her. If her company found out, she would be blacklisted. If her priest knew... she broke down at the mere thought. She had to sacrifice not just for the children, her job, and her relatives, but for her church too, she said.

"You're a wonderful mom," Jax comforted her. "You've been a wonderful sub, too."

"You really think so?" Cece asked.

"We'll get through this. We'll just take a break until this blows over." She knew she was lying.

"You're right, it's just a break," Cece echoed. She also knew she was lying.

"Just a break," they lied to each other.

"Maybe don't come to L'Oubliette for a while either," Jax said, calling for a cab. "You know, they might have a tail on you."

And that was the end of Cece.

Paul was surprised when she got home and carried her bags straight to her room, then returned to collapse on the soft blue sofa.

"You're home?"

"It's over with Cece."

"I thought you just got engaged."

"Not engaged enough," she said. She flashed the ring at him. "It's a memento mori now."

"Oh dear. I'm sorry. Another lesson learned, I gather?"

"Another lesson learned, I guess." On some level, she felt relieved. She'd miss the kids and the dogs, but she wouldn't miss the straight life she was forced to live with Cece. It registered clearly that, like James, Cece was just another unresolved kinky person who couldn't decide what was more important: being true to yourself or pleasing others. Cece was gorgeous and smart and fun in bed, but their karma didn't line up.

"You don't seem too broken up about it."

"That's because I have you to come home to. Otherwise I would have had to murder her ex."

Then the dam broke and tears flowed down her face uncontrollably. "I hate straight people," she whimpered.

Paul dropped his book and took Jax in his big teddy bear arms. "Awwww, sweetie, nawwww." He held her until her tears dried.

She was three for three in the love department now. What would it take for her to accept that romance was not in her destiny? She was wasting her life chasing fantasies. Her life goals had fallen by the wayside. She wanted to see Paris and London and all the great cities of Europe and Asia too. She wanted to be more intellectual and less emotional, more productive in her life. Even the best full-time job wasn't enough to complete her. No man would complete her. The only thing that would complete her life was if she tried to live it to the fullest.

Jax talked to Lilith. "What if I travel to see clients?"

"You want to do that?" Lilith asked. She began doing the math. "Then we can charge by the day or week. What do you think about $1,500 for a day and $10,000 for seven days of availability?"

"Travel expenses included?"

"Yes, of course." Lilith made a note. "Anything else?"

"Would you come down on your share, since I won't be using equipment or wardrobe here? Also, I'll split any clients I find on my own," Jax said. "I'm going to run ads and look for people online. I promise I'll never screw you on customers, ever."

Lilith smiled. "I trust you." She agreed to take only 25% of her earnings, half of her usual 50%, and to continue to publicize and promote Jax while she was away. In exchange, Jax would make sure her clients knew the name L'Oubliette.

Jax's first adventure was in Denver, to see a high-rolling lawyer from Oklahoma named Delroy -- "Call me Del." She found him on a fetish site. When they met, he looked much older, much heavier, and less hairy than his photo. Seeing that he'd lied about his looks and age, she made him pay in advance.

Del turned out to be alright. He installed her in her own suite of rooms in a mansion his company had rented for him. He had a good sense of humor and treated her like a queen from start to finish, giving her a credit card to pay for all her food purchases, and offering to pay for her tuition so she could attend a couple of classes at a local college. Del only needed her at night, when he got back from his nightly dinner with his team. She would greet him at the door in fetish gear. Some nights they did BDSM, some nights he just wanted to talk. When they went to bed, she chained his collar to the bed and lay down beside him, dozing in her clothes. When his morning alarm rang, she unchained and unlocked him, and went to her own bed to get solid sleep.

He brought a range of unique custom bondage gear with him for them to enjoy. Her favorite were tight leather pants studded with small sprays of spikes in the groin. She couldn't stop running her hands over his crotch, squeezing gently to hear him moan when the strategically placed spikes bit into his balls.

"So many screams," she teased him.

"So much terror!" he said. "You're insane."

"Am I?"

"I mean insane in a good way, insanely wonderful, insanely hot. Insanely cruel. I wish you never had to leave."

But she had to leave. Three months was too long to be in any one place but New York. She shouldn't have tied herself down to one client. If she wanted to get to Europe and Asia and yet more exotic destinations, she had to see more clients for shorter periods of time. She wanted to see the famed cities of Europe and Asia, and meet foreigners with different ways of living and different attitudes.

When a German pony fetishist named Horst sent her an overly polite email inviting her to the "little horse farm" he owned outside of Munich for a week-long stay, all expenses included, she was gleeful. A silent chauffeur dressed in all black met her at the airport in a black Mercedes and drove them out of town and deep into the countryside. The further they went, the faster he sped through the regal mountainous landscape. After almost two hours, he drove onto a private road. Sheep grazed on a hilly lawn. Horses wandered a distant field. Straight ahead, the tall towers of a Bauernhaus style castle rose above the pastoral land. They drove up to a formal courtyard.

"We are at our destination," the driver said. He opened her door and got her bags from the trunk. A man in a dark green suit walked out of the castle. His hair was pomaded and his face was powdered. He looked like a self-conscious Maître D' trying to look younger than his age. Was this a private resort of some kind? Was she meeting the mysterious Horst at a hotel? She looked up at the towers. Was this some kind of secret Nazi hideaway?

"I am Horst." He clicked his heels and bowed to kiss her hand. "You are Amazon." There was no question about that. She was exactly as she'd described, wearing a navy cashmere coat over a pale blue dress. He, on the other hand, had stepped out of a bad historical romance, from his dyed black hair to his waxed moustache and ornately engraved cufflinks.

He led her inside the castle and into an enormous hallway and offered a short tour of the main areas, including a stark formal dining room with a vast wood dining table, a smoking room with burgundy leather on couches, chairs and walls, and an art gallery of portraits of Bavarian nobles, some in military uniforms.

"Your ancestors?" she asked.

"Only those who did not bring us shame," he said with a vague smile on his lips.

He walked her to her sleeping quarters, where her suitcases were already waiting. He quickly explained that she was free to explore the grounds but to remain in this wing of the house, where his wife never came. His wife knew she was there and for what purpose, but out of respect, Amazon's meals would be served in her chamber. Staff would provide for her needs. She was also free to visit the horses and gardens and the butterfly house. If she needed anything from town, the chauffeur would drive her.

Horst expected to see her nightly from 10 pm to 11 pm. During their hour together, she would deliver a sound whipping on his buttocks for exactly 30 minutes, followed by 30 minutes of chasing him around like a pony in the hallway outside her bedroom while using dressage whips to control him. He would provide her with a stopwatch, plus the whips and crops he wanted her to use on him. He wanted her to call him "schlechtes Pferd" during the chase. "Pferd" was easy but it took hours of practicing "schlechtes" to get the pronunciation right.

Horst's ritualistic and specific desires were easy to fulfill. The surreal nature of the situation delighted her. On her last night with him, she went outside to smoke the emergency joint she brought with her. After two weeks, it hit hard. She threw herself so completely into his fantasy that night, she scared him. He suddenly sat down on the floor and hugged himself.

"Are you okay?"

"I'm broken now," he said.

"What do you mean?" He looked calm but it sounded bad.

"You could ride me now. You tamed me. I'm not a bad horse anymore." He crawled back to her bedroom and finally stood up and put on his clothes. "Thank you, Miss Amazon," he said in the doorway, bowing his head.

From Germany, she flew to England, where Lilith booked her for a week with a magistrate who wanted to live out a chastity fantasy. He was a jolly, plump man named Lloyd who wanted to be told he was a naughty boy and spanked. The steel chastity cage he loaned her would prevent him from being naughty. He entrusted her with the key to its lock after she promised to release him at their last meeting.

He put her up at a first class hotel in Cambridge and visited her four times that week. It amused her to think of it as four times she had subverted British justice. On their third date, she threatened to keep him locked up. She spanked him harder than before and told him that she planned to force him to remain chaste until the next time she returned to England, which could be months, even years, from now.

He showed up trembling and clumsy with lust, clutching a gift of expensive perfume to win her mercy. He fell all over himself to be submissive and sweet. Again, she gave him a thorough thrashing, replete with threats of never releasing him. When she finally ended the long evening and unlocked his device, returning the key to him, he dropped to her feet, worshipping her as a goddess.

"I will never forget you," he mumbled, "never."

"Be a good boy, or I'll be back to carry through on that threat."

"I can only dream that you will one day."

From England, she traveled to Edinburgh for a week of foot fetishism with an elderly bachelor named Ian. They met at a luxury spa hotel where he'd rented them a three-room suite. She was his vacation, he told her. He didn't ask for much. He wanted her to wear the white toeless sandals and old fashioned dark stockings he brought and let him worship her legs for hours. The legwear made her look like a 1960s UK tabloid model, but it made old Ian happy.

She was back home for a few days when Lilith called her to pack again, she was going to Paris. A husband and wife couple wanted her to treat them as servants and force them have to sex. They were waiting for her when she landed at Roissy Airport and walked ahead of her, quarreling all the way to their Bugatti, and then all the way home. Jax didn't understand a word of it and stared placidly out the window. They resided in a spacious flat in Montparnasse, with a secret chamber they had set up as a dungeon. She spent the weekend ordering them to dress her and fetch her coffee and polish her boots, then forcing them to have sex together at her whim. She guessed they really needed someone to force them to have it at this point. They'd been married 35 years. By the time she left, the arguing had stopped.

She flew home, giggling to herself about Paul's reactions when she'd recount her latest adventure. He loved every story she brought home and she loved the wild variety of her experiences and the excitement of seeing new cities and unfamiliar streets.

The paradoxes of BDSM never failed to fascinate her, along

with the way pleasures, and taboos, and personal boundaries were so different for different people. To a man she visited in Istanbul, it was all about enduring the most difficult challenges she could set, whether it was an extreme whipping or mummification. For a transgender woman in Warsaw, it was all about dressing and learning to walk perfectly in 4-inch heels. For a client in Vienna, it was all rubber all the time. Rubber pants for breakfast, rubber dresses for lunch, rubber hoods and gloves at night. Then there was the Spanish doctor who hired her to do complex, degrading enema scenes but scoffed at bondage. "That's too kinky for me."

She began traveling to Europe once or twice a month. Between her recruitment and Lilith's contacts, she managed to pick up some regular clients, including a smitten submissive in Rotterdam who booked her for two weeks at a time, and ultimately asked for her hand in marriage. After that, she wouldn't see him anymore.

She finally got to Asia when a businessman named Yuto politely invited her to stay in one of the hotels he owned in Tokyo. He lived in the same hotel, so it would be convenient. He asked her to stay for three weeks. Tokyo was overwhelming so she gave herself the mission of visiting every noodle shop she could find, becoming a noodle maven as she went. Yuto treated her more like a girlfriend than a Mistress, and saw her every night she was there, always beginning with a formal meal and ending with him naked at her feet.

He asked her to verbally abuse him and tell him how worthless he was while he groveled. He wanted her to hit him with a *muchi*. The Japanese horse whip didn't handle as well as the ones she'd used before, but he seemed delighted by her skill with it.

At some point, inevitably, he would become silent. At first it alarmed her, and she thought he was angry, but apparently it was his part of his kink. He would spend two or more hours in silence, naked and prostate at her feet, as if it was an endurance test to see how long it took before his penis and balls started to ache on the wooden floor. When he couldn't take the stiffness, or perhaps the pain, he would timidly ask to be allowed to stand, and she would have to help him get to his feet. Then he'd hurry back into his clothes and vanished until 7 pm the next night.

From Oslo to Singapore, Moscow to Dubai, she spun around the world only to be drawn back home like an intercontinental yoyo. It was exhilarating, numbing, funny. Then it was irritating, exasperating, exhausting. She spent her 37th birthday sleeping on a flight from Brussels to New York. The trip was a disaster. The client ghosted her. She walked the lobby for an hour, looking for him. The hotel clerk looked up the name he'd given her. They didn't have a reservation in his name or in hers. He looked at her with sympathy. "You can't stay in the lobby," he said. "I'm sorry. It's for guests only."

She left the hotel, shaken. She was all alone in Budapest on her birthday, with no client, no hotel room, nothing. She felt sick to her stomach. Was it a misunderstanding or a confusion in the time zones? Should she wait for him? Or did she need to use her ticket home right away before he canceled it? She got into a cab waiting at the curb and returned to Budapest Airport where she argued and pleaded with ticket agents until they finally approved her to fly back on the original ticket.

"Wow!" Paul said when she walked in midday looking haggard. "Did you make it to Budapest?"

"Don't ask." She walked past him to her bedroom and slept for 14 hours.

She woke up in a gray, migraine aura mood. She was tired of sex work. There was no future. She was already two years past her planned retirement.

She decided to drop into The New School and see if she could sign up for some classes. She would finally fulfill a promise she'd made to herself almost two decades earlier. When she walked down the steps into the lobby, and crossed a glassed area to the registration tables, the lines stretched to the back of the room. It seemed like everyone in the room was half her age and had twice her energy. She waited self-consciously for an hour to get up to the front. She said she wanted to transfer credits and enroll.

"You are in the WRONG place." They waved her away and told her to go to Room 232.

The elevator was packed and she began to sweat uncomfortably. It seemed like everyone was going to the same room. The line was so long, it wrapped around a corner and continued the length of the next corridor. She saw a few guys napping on the floor, using their school bags as pillows.

Jax got back on the elevator. She wandered aimlessly down Sixth Avenue, stopping at Bagel Chateau to brood over a poppy seed bagel. She looked out the store window. A bright orange sunset cast its beams across the Village. She would rather spend her evenings watching sunsets than sitting in a class.

Did she need a college degree? No. Did she enjoy the classes she took long ago in Denver? Not really. What would she do with that degree? Nothing. She wasn't in the wrong place so much as the wrong time. She was trying to fulfill a promise she made to herself almost two decades earlier, however it wasn't relevant to her life anymore. She was a wise crone now, a sophisticated world traveler, a student of life.

She wiped the crumbs off her lip and reapplied her blood-red lipstick. She walked home slowly, weaving in and out of shops, and went to the cupcake shop where lines had become shorter with every passing month, and bought two for dessert with Paul that night. On a whim, she retraced her steps on Christopher and went to the LGBT Center where Steve once worked. She was amazed that some of his old friends were still around. They welcomed her like a long-lost child, and were tickled by her radical look. Steve's friend Judy took her to a wall of photos. A framed photo of Grandpa Steve beamed at her. He was surrounded by friends, dressing in pink and black, like the first time she saw him. Underneath, a copy of the eulogy she delivered at his funeral was preserved. She had a dim memory of someone saying they'd taped her eulogy and planned to type it up. Now she read her own words and re-lived that mournful day.

"You're part of his legacy," Judy comforted her. "Everyone who comes through here stops to read it and learn about Steve. I've seen people crying when they read it."

"Oh no."

"Naw, it's good tears. You know? The way you talked about Steve, your love for him shone through all the way. It gives them hope. They need to hear stories like yours."

"I hope I've helped someone." Jax felt humbled and awed.

"Hundreds."

The women stood silently, each lost in their memories of days gone by.

She returned home cold and sober. The writing was on the wall. This was the day she said no to college and yes to the LGBT Center, where she found out that, without ever realizing it, she had helped people who were hurting.

It was time to quit L'Oubliette. Every time she came back from a trip over the last couple of years, there was a new problem. Once it was the plumbing, then it was the wiring, which forced them to close the club for a week. The furnishings in the big dungeon were deteriorating -- upholstery that needed mending, leather padding that cracked, and a couple of crosses that needed repairs.

Jax quietly accepted that L'Oubliette was no longer the glittering palace of hedonism it once was. Clients were fleeing to new shores of perversion. There was a new generation of femdoms on the rise and new clubs catering to younger crowds.

Only six women sat at the 12 tables in back now, and their sessions were reduced from a weekly guarantee of 15 hours to 5. At vanity tables where her best friends once sat, much younger women now powdered their faces and preened. A prodom's career, she reflected, was short like a ballerina's or a boxer's. You're only in demand when you're in your professional prime and your professional prime only lasts as long as you are young.

Mama Donna moved to Las Vegas to live with her adult children. Leather Lee moved to San Francisco to be with her Leather Family. Shirley left Larry, quit L'Oubliette, and was never heard from again. Fedora married her long-time girlfriend and they moved to Vermont. The schoolgirls married twin brothers and moved to the same town in South Jersey. Furry old Buttons was no more, having crossed the Rainbow Bridge peacefully the year before.

China Doll was the last close friend she had left, and she was planning to quit too.

"I could work for my sister-in-law Jennie in her real estate business, a block from my house. I could eat all my meals at home and play with my dog at lunchtime and still make almost as much as I do here."

"It could be time for a change." Jax said it to herself as much as to China.

"It could be," China sighed. "But not today."

They were chatting in the wardrobe area. China was finished dressing, but Jax didn't have an appointment for another hour, so Fred was taking his time getting her outfit assembled. Jax was still waiting for her boots when she got a text from China.

"Stay where you are," it said. "Don't move. Trouble up front."

A moment later, Fred got a message on his phone and ran out of the room carrying a baseball bat.

"What's happening?" she texted to China, pacing back and forth. Was this the big bust they had all feared? Were cops going to lead her away in handcuffs and smear her all over the tabloid press? How much of her savings would she have to spend on lawyers and court expenses? They could bankrupt her if they wanted, freeze her assets, or worse.

"Client freak-out," China finally answered. "Stay there. Don't come out until I say so!"

Jax eyed the emergency exit but didn't want to trigger an alarm that drew cops to the back rooms. She went to the back of the wardrobe and crawled under a clothes rack and hid by the wall, feeling trapped like a rat.

She hugged herself tight and closed her eyes. Her phone vibrated.

"He's trying to throw a couch out the window. I can't fucking believe this."

"Who??"

"He's pushing it like a rhino, using his head to bang it through! He's a BEAST! Holy shit!"

"Who is?"

After another 20 minutes, her phone buzzed.

"The cops are here. Don't move!!"

Jax pulled a couple of fetish dresses off the rack and

covered herself up until he looked like a laundry pile. She panicked when she heard the door open and footsteps hurried in.

"Jax?" China Doll called to her. "Jax? Are you here? Where did you go?"

Jax shook off all the heavy fetish wear and crawled back out.

"Oh Jesus." China Doll was incredulous. "Good disguise, though."

"What the hell happened?" Jax got to her feet, still shaking.

"Some moron came here and tried to make one of the new girls dominate him."

"Which girl?"

"DG."

"Oh, her." Jax rolled her eyes. "On some level, I'm not surprised."

DG, also known as Dominant Goddess, was neither dominant nor a goddess. She was just a college kid, doing her best to navigate BDSM to pay her bills. It was sad to Jax but it was the BDSM world now, filled with people who were just around for the money and nothing else. Besides, wasn't she doing just that, losing her passion but sticking around for the money? She wasn't in a position to judge. Still, the young woman was a magnet to unstable, pushy men who saw all her weak spots and took advantage of her.

Recently, she was having problems with an obsessive client they called The Fart Monster, because he expelled noxious fumes throughout his sessions. The first time, DG tolerated it because she thought maybe he had some bad food. But it turned out he was on a liquid protein diet and had turned into a farting machine of deplorable odors. Lilith offered him his choice of other Mistresses, but he insisted it had to be DG. Lilith finally informed him that DG couldn't deal with his "digestive issues," as she politely described it.

"She won't see me because I fart, is that what you're saying?" He pleaded, saying it was a medical condition, then began cursing her out, telling her she had the shittiest club in town, and threatening to destroy DG, Lilith, and the dungeon.

They thought they'd never hear from him again. But today he came in, high on some drug and demanded to see DG. She was in session in the bondage room, keeping an eye on two clients, and refused to come out. That made the client even angrier. He ran into the big dungeon and kicked the toy store's glass door until it shattered, then went inside and grabbed an armful of toys. He ran with them to the window, and hurled a few outside before lifting the sofa and attempting to push it out after the toys.

"Oh my God. Was anyone hurt on the street?"

"No, the toys all fell into the parking lot, nobody got hurt but you know New York, a crowd of people stood by the gate taking pictures!"

"Good God almighty! Are you okay?"

"If you call shitting your pants and being fucking terrified okay, then I'm fine," China said.

"Fuck."

"The cops got here in time to save the couch, though he broke two of the legs trying to push it through the window."

"What about Fred and Lilith, are they okay?"

"They went to file a report at the police station and take out a restraining order against him. Did you see Fred had a bat?"

"I did! Did he use it?"

"Of course not. He waved it around a lot and cussed up a

storm, but he didn't go anywhere near the guy. He kept shouting, 'I'm gonna get you,' but he never even tried to get him."

"What did the cops say? Are they going to bust the club?"

"I don't think so. All they said was, 'It takes all kinds,' and then they dragged him out of here, letting Lilith and Fred take their own car to the station. They had to take DG to the hospital. She's an emotional wreck. She thought he was going to kill her."

Jax pulled off her latex dress and got back into her street clothes.

"I'm taking this as an omen," she said to China. "Things are going downhill here."

"I don't need this shit in my life, I really don't."

They left the club together, telling each other all the good reasons why they needed to quit. When they stepped out onto the sidewalk, the crowd of onlookers were still lingering.

"I guess this is goodbye," China said, suddenly tearful. "I'll miss you, Jax." She hugged Jax and walked away fast without looking back.

It wasn't the ending she wanted, Jax decided, but it was the ending she got and she would live with it.

Over dinner with Paul that night, Jax announced her official retirement from professional domination.

"You don't want to do BDSM anymore?" he asked. "What happened?"

Jax judiciously limited the details of the drama at L'Oubliette to the humorous tale of the client they called the Fart Monster and how he went crazy and threw dildos and butt plugs out the window before the cops finally arrived and carried him away.

"Are you saying he was hoist on his own petard?" Grandpa

said, looking proud of himself.

"Oh my God, Grandpa, that stinks!" They cackled at each other.

He looked proud of himself in that dad way.

"So no one got hurt, right?" he asked.

"Nope, they took the guy away and the girl had to get sedated at the hospital, but I bet you that when the *Post* gets its hands on the story, they'll claim pedestrians were injured by hundreds of toys, and then they'll blame the dominatrix and the club for what happened, not the ex-cop -- did I mention the Fart Monster was a cop?"

"You picked a good time to quit," Paul said. "Will you keep doing BDSM?"

She gave him a long look. He still didn't understand that being kinky to her was like being gay was to him. It was who she was. It would never go away. She would never get off fantasizing about fucking. There would always be hunky bondage boys in her sex dreams.

"Of course I will, but from now on only for love and pleasure, not money."

"Oh! I like the sound of that. Good for you, sweetheart. You don't really need the money anymore."

"I dropped by the gay center," she said.

"Did you see how they framed your eulogy under Steve's picture?" Grandpa got excited.

"Judy showed me. She said I've inspired people."

"I'm sure you have. It was the most loving, beautiful speech."

"I feel like it's an accomplishment, like my legacy is right there, next to his."

"It is! Absolutely. All my friends remember the speech you gave that day."

They beamed at each other.

"I also decided not to go to college."

"What? When did that happen?"

"Last week. I realized that I was trying to live according to what my 20-year-old self wanted. I want to live according to what I want now."

"Makes sense. So what do you want now?"

"I want a cat. In fact, I want a lot of cats."

"What the actual hell?"

"I love cats."

"I love them too," he said. "Steve was the one who was allergic."

"And I want to drive the cab."

"Really? Why?"

"I feel like I need a year or two to clear my head. Too much drama, too many people, just too much everything the last 15 years," she said. "I want a regular job where I can write my own schedule and be my own boss and come home for dinner with you at the end of the day. Cab driving fits the bill."

Paul didn't pretend he was any less worried about the hazards of driving a cab than he was about his granddaughter whipping strangers, but he helped her detail the old cab to sheer perfection and made sure her paperwork was in order.

She loved the cab. She liked the fares no one else wanted. Making long trips out to the boroughs and driving back empty was like sitting on her balcony at home: she could think and dream and nosh in her cab cocoon. She loved long trips up to the Bronx, a land of steep, confusing streets and great taco stands, and out to the flat lands of Sheepshead Bay in Brooklyn, where clam bars were open at all hours, and late night runs out to Queens, often stopping in Astoria to bring baklava home to Paul.

They lived in harmony, her and her old gramps. Their life together expanded to include his old friends, some new ones, and a few people from her prodom days. She regularly emailed with Lilith, Donna, and Leather Lee. Then Shirley rejoined their fold, apologizing and explaining she had to get away from the "Larry situation," and had resettled in New Mexico and was doing phone domination.

Jax had never known so much stability or harmony in her life. A huge burden was gone. Now she could eat whatever and whenever she wanted, no longer fretting over whether she'd fit into a tight leather dress. She could spend every holiday celebrating with Paul. She had cats to play with, and money in the bank, and lived in a gorgeous condo that Grandpa had already willed to her, along with his art collection.

It seemed like life would never change until it did. Booker's call came out of the blue, dredging up feelings she didn't want to feel anymore. Apparently, he was still keeping tabs on her, sniffing around the gay center and people who knew Paul. He knew all about L'Oubliette and that she was now driving Paul's cab. It pissed her off at first. Did he hire a PI to follow her? How did he know so much? But the more he talked, the more he explained, the more he apologized for lying to her so very long ago, the more she remembered his good qualities. He was never bad to her, not like James. He never abandoned her the way Cece did. Booker's boyfriend looked young and cute and sub to her. It was tempting. Too tempting.

But now that she was home, sharing eggs and contentment with Paul and the kitties, Booker's proposition seemed laughable. He had no idea who she was or what she had seen and done in her life. Booker was living in the past, when everything seemed possible for them. Nothing was possible for them now. She had seen too much. She knew too much about people, about their weaknesses and betrayals. She didn't even know if men turned her on anymore. Or women, for that matter. Paul was the only human she really cared about. Melancholy filled her chest. She felt old.

"Why don't we get out of town this weekend? We could go back to the B&B in Mattituck again and eat dinner on the beach," Paul said after she washed her dishes and sat down at the table with him to share a joint. The sun was rising in the east, washing the apartment with white lights.

"I have a better idea. Let's go to Provincetown for a whole week. Maybe two. A real American vacation!"

"Provincetown! Oh!" There was a catch in his voice.

"You can catch up with Em and Chaz."

"Em and Chaz! I haven't seen them in decades." Yet he seemed unsure.

"Let's do it. I'll do the craft shops and hit the beaches all day while you hang out with your artist friends and then I'll join you for dinners."

She slept in the next morning while Paul made arrangements with Jinn, their downstairs neighbor and friend, to pet sit and pick up their mail while they were away. Then he called a few friends who didn't have email to let them know he'd be away. She called Em, who was overjoyed, and told her to get there in time for breakfast the next day. "We all can't wait," she kept repeating.

Jax and Paul took off for New England after dinner, and dropped a set of keys off at Jinn's. They took turns driving and napping in the passenger seat, stopping to stretch their legs and fill up on coffee. They sang together and played word games to keep themselves awake as they sailed under black skies.

She woke up with a start as the first signs of light appeared in the sky. She'd been dreaming that Booker and James and Cece were all in the backseat of the car, controlling the steering wheel. She gasped in relief to see Grandpa at the wheel, calmly driving, while the backseat was empty. She grabbed her thermos and drained the last cold slug of coffee.

"Where are we?"

"Almost there. Another hour, tops," he said. "Do you need more coffee?"

"Yes, please!"

He stopped at the next rest area and told her to wait in the car. He didn't want to leave it unattended when it was full of their stuff.

She watched him go inside then got out her hairbrush. She'd been growing her hair back. The curls came back full force, thicker than ever, and she struggled to get the brush through her tangles.

She remembered how much Booker liked her hair when they met. "You have a BloFro," he once exclaimed, patting the curls affectionately. "A blonde fro! I love it."

As Paul sped past Hyannis, she concluded that there would never be a happy ending to that story. At least not for her. She didn't want to fall for somebody else's boyfriend, especially not Booker's. It would be the same thing all over again: one day she'd realize that she was just there to fill a gap in their lives, not to become an organic part of their lives. She rolled her window down to breathe in the salty air, the landscape opening wider with every mile.

"I don't ever want to talk to Booker again," she announced.

Paul raised his eyebrows. "OK."

They reached Provincetown and Paul pulled over to a food truck in a small parking lot that held a couple of cars next to a paved patio and a long strip of deserted beach. Green waves lapped the shores like plates of glass that foamed at the edges. It was more beautiful than she expected.

"We're about 10 minutes away but it's still a little early to show up. Let's toss the crappy coffee and get something more palatable from the truck. Paul looked at his wristwatch. "We have time, let's stare at the ocean for a few minutes."

Jax got two cappuccinos and carried them back to Paul, who had removed his shoes and was sitting on a wooden bench, staring out at the water. The beach was white and calm, the waves mesmerizing. Jax wiggled her toes and inhaled the salt deep into her lungs. It was a perfect day in mid-May. The sun above warmed the top of her head while ocean breezes chilled her naked toes. She could live here, she thought.

"Paul! Paul!" A voice resounded across the beach. In the distance a man stood up from a blanket and started hurrying to them. "Paul, why are you here?"

"David! Wow, what are you doing here!!" Paul jumped to his feet and walked across the warm sands towards him. They met and yelled at each other in glee, then they hugged and then they exchanged a deeply intimate kiss. Jax was disconcerted by how long it lasted. They huddled together. Paul pointed at her. David pointed at his young companion, who trailed after him with the beach blanket and a basket. She wondered how David's friend felt about his partner passionately kissing a stranger on the beach.

He didn't seem perturbed, in fact he looked practically starry-eyed. He hung on every word the old men were saying, as if they were gods.

She put her shoes back on and crumpled her coffee cup in one fist, squeezing it down to the size of a ball, glancing back at the car, anxious to leave.

"Jax, meet David. He's one of my oldest friends. We haven't seen each other since Steve's funeral!" The trio came to her bench.

"You probably don't remember me, but we met briefly at the temple." David shook her hand. "I've heard so much about you from Em and Chaz! This is my son, Cory," he said, introducing her to the young man at his side. "He's a sculptor. He's having his first gallery show next month. You have to be here for the opening!"

"Hello, Jax," Cory said, "please don't mind my dad, he's decided he's my PR agent."

"Oh, he's your dad?" She felt a little relieved. Cory was about her age, with bright blue eyes, thick eyelashes, and a sharp chin, like his father. She noticed that his jeans fit like a second skin over his flat belly and round butt.

"I could get you into a gallery in town," David said to Paul. "I could probably line up at least one other show on the Cape this summer, more if we take you to Boston."

"David and I met at art school," Paul said to Jax.

"We dated for three years," David added.

"And then, I don't know what happened, we drifted apart."

"You moved to New York."

"I did." Paul turned to Jax. "I hated winters up here."

"I never forgot you," David said.

"I never forgot you either," said Paul.

There was something going on between them that they weren't saying.

"This is great," she said, "but Em and Chaz are expecting us."

"Oh, right," Paul said. "David, I hope to see you again?"

"You'll see me in about 5 minutes," David said, "with everyone else at the party."

"What party?"

"Your welcome back breakfast party!!"

"Oh no! What?" Paul combed his fingers through his hair.

"Oh no. Didn't you know? That's why I was confused to see you sitting on the beach. Oh honey. I'm sorry. I ruined it!"

"No, actually." Paul lowered his voice to an affectionate murmur and said, "I'm kind of glad we met here and not there."

The men looked at each other for a long moment. Jax shifted uneasily. Their body language said it all. If they weren't lovers in the past, they were going to be lovers in the near future. She could feel it.

"I'll wait for you in the car."

"Hey, wait up." Cory caught up with her and they walked side-by-side while the old men walked slowly behind them. She side-eyed Cory. His hair was dark and curly and his profile looked cut from a Roman coin. A shiny triskelion medallion hung from a black leather cord around his powerful neck. His right ear was pierced. She felt a murmur of lust. Was he kinky?

"So you're a sculptor?" she asked.

"Working on it," he said. He had a mellow deep voice. "I was a defense lawyer in Boston until I was 36. Then I realized, no, all I wanted to do was sculpt and make things. So I moved up here to learn whatever Dad was willing to teach me. That was 3 years ago."

"That's really sweet."

"I'm a sweet guy. You should get to know me."

"Married?"

"Nope. One relationship that lasted 4 years, another that lasted 3, and a lot of friends with benefits," he said. "How about you?"

"I prefer benefits without friends," she drawled.

He burst into laughter. "Wow. Really?"

"I had three partners and lots of friends," she said. "Never married. Almost. Once. But it wasn't real." Then she let it slip. "I also left my career."

"Really? What kind of work did you do?"

She wasn't going to tell him her past. Not yet. Even if he was kinky, she wasn't ready to open up. That was just inviting complications. Maybe if they hit it off but now wasn't the time or place. She looked into his baby blues. "I was a professional dominatrix for 18 years."

He came to a full halt. "No way," he whispered.

"Shit, shit," she cursed herself, speeding her pace. Goddammit. Why did she do that? Well, whatever. If he was going to reject her for being herself, she wasn't interested in him anyway.

"Wait, wait." He jogged after her. "Listen." He jogged in front of her and stopped her. "I swear I've never done anything like this before, but would you have dinner with me?"

"Why?"

"You know why!"

He fingered his medallion. "I'm in the lifestyle," Cory said. "I'm sub."

He searched her eyes and she searched his soul.

"Then ask me the right way." She knew the minute she saw him that he was kinky. But why was her heart pounding so fast.

"Please, Ma'am, may I have the pleasure of taking you out to dinner?"

The old men suddenly showed up, side-hugging and chatting like best friends.

"OK, let's hit the road!" Paul called out to her.

"Please say yes," Cory begged in a whisper.

"Ok," she said, "yes."

"Yay!" Cory whispered. "We'll talk more at the brunch, we'll set it up. I knew at first sight."

"Knew what?"

"That I'm going to marry you someday," he said. "You'll see."

Jax folded her arms. Her heart pounded so fast she felt dizzy. She hadn't felt half as turned on by any of the people she'd played with at kink clubs. Her brain fired up with fantasies about what she could do with that body and how she wanted to kiss his beautiful lips. Everything about him was sweet and desirable.

"De Sade is smiling in his grave," Jax announced abruptly when she and Paul got back in the car. She felt Cory staring at her from the other car and waved to him. He waved back and bowed his head. A throb of lust shot through her.

"What? What does that mean?" Paul was amused.

"De Sade believed that women should pursue whatever kind of sex they wanted for their own pleasure," she said, applying lipstick in the car mirror. "In the end, they'd be happier than the obedient girls who played by the patriarchal rules."

Cory cruised past them on the highway, beeping and waving like a teenager. She and Paul laughed at his antics.

"Is this about Cory?" Paul asked. "I noticed some chemistry there."

"Maybe," she said. "I don't know," she said, though she did know. "But right here and right now, I am the happiest woman in the world."

❧ About the Author ☙

Legendary author, sex therapist, and long-time lifestyle dominatrix, Dr. Gloria G. Brame has been a pioneer of BDSM/fetish study, education, research, and advocacy for over 30 years. She founded the first online peer support forum for kinky people on Compuserve in 1987 and published her first bestseller, *Different Loving* (co-authors, William Brame and Jon Jacobs), in 1993. Since then, Gloria's maintained a passionate commitment to helping sexually non-conventional people overcome obstacles and find their joy. She is the author of nine books that take radically different approaches (non-fiction, autobiography, and fiction) to spread her gospel that sex and gender diversity are the true norms. *Amazon Hammer* is the sequel to Gloria's novel *Champions of Pleasure*.

Gloria Brame may be contacted through her website **gloriabrame.com**, and you can follow her on Facebook, Twitter, Amazon, GoodReads, LinkedIn, Alignable, and other social platforms.

Julian Murphy – Cover Artist Bio

Born in England in 1959, award-winning and critically acclaimed artist Julian Murphy brings a unique and fresh approach to the subject of eroticism in art. His works hang in more than a dozen museums worldwide, and he even has a piece hanging in the famous Moulin Rouge, Paris. Murphy leads the way as one of the "new masters" of erotic imagery. This was endorsed by his inclusion in the book *Ars Erotica: An Arousing History of Erotic Art* by Edward Lucie-Smith. His artworks have been published in over 500 international magazines, including *GQ*, *FHM*, and *Design Week*. Julian was Art Director of the "World Erotic Art Museum" on Miami Beach, considered by many as the world's greatest collection of erotic art.

Julian Murphy on Facebook:

https://www.facebook.com/julianmurphyart